A Foreign Shore:
Rain of Fire, Rain of Blood

by

Forrest Johnson

Illustrations by

Liz Clarke

Cover by

Tania Kerins

ACKNOWLEDGMENTS

Thanks to the Wordos group for their criticism, and especially to Liz Clarke and Tania Kerins, the best artists in the business. And of course, to Dawa Fruitman for his beautiful maps.

First Edition, September 2016

ISBN-13: 978-0692784280 (Forrest Johnson)

ISBN-10: 0692784284

"What is the use of a book, without pictures or conversations?" - Lewis Carroll, *Alice in Wonderland*

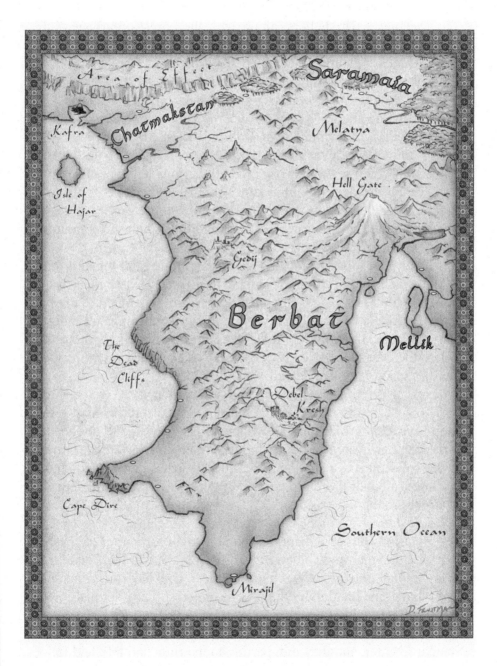

1 : Krion

Everyone loves a parade.

The makeshift shelters, along with the corpses, garbage and other detritus from the siege, had been cleared from the streets of Kafra. Gaudy Akaddian and allied flags fluttered from the buildings. Music from his drum and bugle corps filled the city, not quite drowning out the *clop clop clop* of horseshoes on cobblestones.

For the parade, he'd chosen the army's most impressive-looking units: First came the Royal Household Guard, their polished, brass-trimmed armor making a dazzling display in the sun. Next, representing the Free States, were the Illustrious Knights of Tremmark, each rider decked with quaint heraldry in the style of his ancestors. Bandeluks and Chatmaks whispered to each other as they pointed out the griffins, unicorns, lions and other fantastic creatures decorating their shields and helms.

Lastly, on foot and picking their way around the manure left by the cavalry, with the skill gained from much experience, was the Covenant Heavy Assault Group: big, grim-faced men, fiercely equipped in spiked armor and carrying heavy, smashing weapons. Those citizens of Kafra who'd ventured into the streets for a closer look at the riders tended to duck back into their doorways when the Heavy Assault Group appeared.

Just be grateful they never had to attack your city.

To ride up the main avenue with an armed force behind him brought a feeling of exultation. Banners fluttered above his head. Girls stationed at second-floor windows threw flowers into the street as the band played a stirring march. He reached into a saddlebag and threw a handful of gold coins into the crowd, provoking a mad scramble among the spectators.

Life doesn't get much better than this!

Entering Heroes Square, he found a small formation of spearmen blocking the way. They were equipped in the familiar Bandeluk style, but had blue plumes on their helmets. One bore the crimson-silver flag of the Bandeluk Empire. The crowd shifted nervously, not sure what was going to happen.

"MAKE WAY FOR PRINCE KRION!" yelled Bardhof, his Standard-bearer, and they did, parting to the right and left, and falling to one knee in submission. They left their flag, as planned, on the ground, so the iron-shod hooves of his horse could grind it into the cobblestones.

He threw another handful of gold into the crowd as his planted agents began the cry: "HOORAH! HOORAH! HOORAH!" The crowd took it up in anticipation of more gold coins, and another shower rewarded them.

On the other side of the square Davoud, his newly appointed mayor, an amiable if somewhat bewildered-looking man in an oversized turban, waited to give him the keys to the palace. Beside him stood Hisaf, the new commander of the city watch, a hard-bitten young tough in a fine blue uniform. Krion had no great responsibilities in mind for either man, but it was important they be there, nominally in charge of the city and able to take the blame if things went wrong.

And it's also important I hold the head of their clan hostage.

As he slowly rode across the square, the formations behind him spread out to fill it. He was almost in place for the surrender ceremony, when a small stone bounced off his shoulder. It did no damage except to his composure, which was shaken.

What fool threw that?

Looking around, he saw a shower of stones was pattering in the square, some striking the riders, and some the crowd. They seemed to be falling like hail from the blue sky. A strange, foul smell engulfed him as the stones hissed and gave off smoke, then burst into flame. In seconds, the whole square was a chaos of fleeing spectators and panicky horses. The martial music came to an abrupt end, replaced by screams and curses.

His horse bucked furiously in its haste to escape the stinging flames and choking fumes. Dropping the reins, he held on to the saddle for dear life as his mount lurched to the right and left, and finally reared up, causing him to fall backward from the saddle and onto the paving stones. As he lay stunned on the ground, all he could think was:

Not again!

Humiliating as it was to fall, it was more so to be rescued by his aides, who took his arms over their shoulders and dragged him up the steps toward the palace. Here, they met another obstacle: a group of men in chains desperately shuffling around in an effort to avoid the burning stones. They were blocking the entrance to the palace.

He vaguely remembered ordering the former prisoners of the Amir to be chained up again, so he could unchain them for the ceremony. Now, they were just getting in the way. It was intolerable. He pulled himself to his feet and, brushing off the worried aides, yelled, "OPEN THE DOORS!"

Davoud rushed forward with his keys, and soon everyone was trying to push through the palace doors: a mob of people, invaders and natives together, all coughing and hurrying to get away from the fiery stones, which now seemed to be everywhere.

Inside the palace was a dark hallway leading to a central atrium, where burning stones, falling through the skylight, had set the shrubbery on fire. The room was filling with smoke. The crowd surged toward the fire, stamping on the flames to put them out.

Krion, who'd been pushed along with the mob, now made his way back to the entrance, where he had a good view of the city. The rain of burning stones had let up as suddenly as it started though some were still hissing and fizzing on the ground.

Heroes Square was empty except for a few horses, running around riderless in no particular direction, and the bodies of three people who'd been trampled.

Smoke curled up from a few, small fires in the city though there seemed no danger of a greater blaze: The masonry of Kafra wasn't vulnerable to arson. He could see several clouds of smoke that rose from burning ships in the harbor. His personal standard lay forgotten in the middle of the square.

From behind him came the quavering voice of his aide, Mopsus. "What was that, my Prince?"

"That was an attack. Go find Gen. Singer. Tell him I want to see him at once. And tell him to bring his Witch."

Next to the atrium was a conference room lined with mirrors. Portraits of the palace's former owner, Amir Qilij, had been removed or painted over. Krion sat alone in Qilij's great, gilded chair, away from the smoke and the whiny crowd, and contemplated the situation. The mirrors on the walls reflected his scowling face, staring back at him from every angle.

This seat is much too comfortable.

It had been much too comfortable for the former owner, who had sat there inactive through weeks of siege, despite the hunger and misery that prevailed in his capital. In the end, he was killed one night in the adjacent bedroom, amid all his wealth and comforts, and despite the armed guards that surrounded him.

Davoud and Hisaf had merely shrugged when asked who killed Qilij. They promised an investigation, but Krion didn't expect any quick results. Even if they did find the mysterious assassin, what of it? There were always more assassins.

A fixed target is so easy to hit!

He'd been in Kafra less than a week, and already the Emperor had found a way to strike at him. It was, he assumed, only the first in a series of such diversions . . .

There was a timid knocking at the door. Mopsus brought in Gen. Singer, followed by a tall woman dressed in black. Singer, careless of protocol, was wearing his golden lion helmet. The magical ruby eyes seemed to glare ferociously at Krion. Hardly less predatory were the Witch's sparkling green eyes, which matched the large gem hanging from the chain around her neck. This woman, Krion knew, had broken the enchantment that had shackled him for weeks while the late Gen. Basilius usurped control of the army. He'd never learned her name.

He'd had sorcerers on his staff, but they were either subverted or incompetent. Only this woman was able to free him. It seemed contrary to nature a woman should have such power. And her self-assured comportment suggested she could do great mischief if she were so inclined.

I'd hoped never to see you again, dark lady, but my enemies have decided otherwise.

Krion rose and greeted the two as if they were old and dear friends, seating Singer to his right and the Witch to his left. She was carrying a small glass jar, he noticed, which she set on the table. Mopsus, who spoke excellent Bandeluki, sat next to the Witch.

I wish I had one of the Ragmen here to keep an eye on her.

The Ragmen, unfortunately, were still back in his camp on the other side of the lagoon. Lately, they'd been behaving oddly, almost insolently. He didn't want them to mix with the populace and could only pray they'd escaped the flames.

The visitors sat patiently and waited for him to speak. "What do you know about this attack, Gen. Singer?" he began.

"I can't explain it, sir. I was trying to find quarters for some of my men, when I heard screams and looked out the window. There was fire falling from the sky. It continued for about a minute. Most of it seems to have landed in the lagoon. Perhaps Lamya can tell us more."

So that's her name!

Krion smiled vacantly while Singer said something in the strange language of the Bandeluks and listened to the reply.

I really must study this language!

Lamya offered him her jar, which contained water and a small, smooth stone, pale yellow in appearance.

"She managed to get a sample," Singer said. "It's called *alfes-fewer.* It bursts into flame on contact with air. She says it's not native to this world."

"Then where did it come from?"

After another translation, Singer said, "She doesn't know. *Al-fesfewer* is common on the plane of the fire demons and some other places. It could only have been brought here by magic."

"Who brought it here and how? More importantly, how do we

stop them?"

These questions set off a long conversation in Bandeluki between Singer and the Witch. Mopsus seemed to follow the back-and-forth with great interest though he offered no translation.

Singer is getting too friendly with this Witch. A dangerous pair!

Finally, Singer turned to Krion. "It's a complicated business. She knows of no spell that would have this effect, but she believes it's the work of a sorcerer, who must be located somewhere nearby. She will need to research the matter. If the attack is repeated, she can trace the source."

There was obviously more to the conversation, but without any knowledge of the language, he'd have to trust the summary. Mopsus was silent, so there was probably no attempt at deception. He stared for a minute at the small, yellowish stone that had caused so much pain and woe.

"If" it's repeated? "When" is surely the correct word. I must take action!

"Mopsus, tell the W—, tell Lamya I'm appointing you to assist her. See she gets everything she needs. I don't care about the cost. Tell her to start work immediately.

"Gen. Singer, stay here for a moment. We need to discuss strategy."

"I don't see how such an offensive would be possible," said Singer, after Krion laid out the plan for attack. "This region has never been conquered." He was staring at a map, spread out on the table, of Berbat, the desert country to the southeast of Kafra.

"You don't have to conquer the place," replied Krion. "Just give the local tribes a few sharp kicks to show them who their master is and hang all the pirates you can catch."

"Chasing pirates would be a lot easier if I had a navy."

"You will have to do without. The navy is occupied with the transport of supplies and reinforcements to our position here. The Emperor is assembling a huge army in Saramaia. I estimate at least 100,000 troops. We can expect another battle when the passes open in spring. You'll have to complete your mission by then."

Singer shook his head doubtfully. "It's a tall order, sir. Berbat is twice the size of Chatmakstan. That desert has swallowed up armies much larger than mine."

"Precisely because they tried to conquer a region that's unconquerable. That's not your mission. There's only one objective that absolutely must be taken, the port of Mirajil."

On the map, Berbat formed a roughly triangular peninsula with Mirajil on the southern tip. The royal cartographers had been unable to survey anything far from the shore. Travelers spoke of caravan tracks, oases and numerous dry river beds. There was also said to be a chain of mountains.

"Mirajil?" Singer leaned forward to examine the map more closely. "We cleaned that place out years ago."

"Your Free States sent an expedition against piracy, which burned the town. But you failed to destroy the walls. The town has been rebuilt."

"We didn't destroy the walls because they're over a hundred feet thick, huge blocks of stone. We surprised the pirates with a sudden assault from the seaward side. From landward, they say Mirajil is impregnable."

"I'm betting you can prove them wrong. Since the beginning of the war, both sides have been forced to suspend anti-piracy patrols. The scum of every nation is gathering there in hope of easy booty. There have already been raids on my transports. Several vessels have disappeared. We need to eliminate this pirate base before it becomes a threat."

Singer leaned over to study the map more closely. "There seems to be no road except on the coast, and look how it snakes around! The defenders of Mirajil will see us coming at least a week before we get there."

"Which I hope will be a week when they're too busy to attack my shipping. But they really can't do anything to stop your army. They're just pirates. All they can do is run away or hide behind their walls."

"About those walls, sir. According to the stories I heard, the city is built on an island connected to the shore by a narrow causeway, and the entrance is completely blocked by two giant walls, one behind the other. We can't get in without siege equipment."

"You didn't have any trouble with Barbosa."

"It was just a lucky stroke. That old castle was practically undefended."

"Luck is also an asset. But in case you run short, I'll lend you six onagers."

"Onagers throw 30-pound stones. They won't make a dent in those walls."

"Then you'll have to try something else. Six onagers is all I can spare."

"I'll need a supply train as well."

"I can assign you a hundred wagons."

"With horses and drivers?"

"Of course. And supplies, and one of my quartermasters."

"We can't carry enough water for five thousand men and their horses."

"It shouldn't be a problem, so long as you stick to the road. There are fishing villages on the coast. Presumably, they have water."

Singer stared silently at the map. Krion could easily imagine what he was thinking: The siege of Mirajil would take months, even assuming naval support, and there wasn't any. On the face of it, the mission was impossible.

Which is why it's your mission and not mine, dear Singer. If you fail, it's on your head. But win or lose, the pirates won't be bothering me for awhile.

"What is Gedij?" asked Singer, pointing to a spot near the shore less than a hundred miles from Kafra.

"A Bandeluk fort and trading post near the border. It's built on top of a small mesa or bit of tableland. I don't expect the garrison amounts to much."

"It looks like that will be my first objective. It's blocking the road south."

"Gedij should be no great problem. Bypass it if you must."

"What about this place Debel Kresh? Is there really a city there?" He pointed to the symbol of a walled city in the otherwise blank center of the map.

"Debel Kresh is a religious center governed by a mysterious person called the Hierophant. The location is approximate. Outsiders are unwelcome, and we've not been able to talk to anyone who's actually been there. I believe there's nothing to be accomplished in

Debel Kresh. The native superstitions need not concern us."

"And the Hell Gate?" Singer pointed to a mountain on the east side of the map, near the Bandeluk border.

"I assume you've heard of that. It's a massive volcano that has been belching fire for hundreds of years. Said to be the gate to hell. Just avoid it. No need to go sightseeing."

Singer sighed heavily. The difficulty of the mission was becoming obvious to him.

He looks so tired and uncertain! Is this the hero of Barbosa? The one they call Demonslayer? The man the Ragmen are afraid of? Is he sick?

By some accident, the mirrors around the room were reflecting Singer's golden helmet. Its magical ruby eyes seemed to be staring at Krion from every direction, even following his movement when he stepped to one side. (The enchanted mirror that showed Krion whatever the ruby eyes were looking at had disappeared at the time of Basilius' coup and was thought to be at the bottom of a well somewhere.)

I should never have given him that thing! Diomedos enchanted it! It was supposed to bind him to me, but now it binds me to him!

At last, Singer turned from the map. "I will attack Mirajil, sir. But victory cannot be guaranteed."

"Victory is never guaranteed. I can appoint a different commander if you prefer."

"If my men are in Berbat, then that's where I must be."

"Well said. I have great confidence in you."

And more so when you're somewhere far away!

2: Raeesha

"Mother, I'm pregnant."

Mother didn't look up from her sewing. She was covering a piece of pink satin with embroidered flowers. The fountain in the center of the small courtyard made a faint tinkling sound. Distant noises from the street could be heard, where the wheels of a passing cart ground against the paving stones. After a short pause, she said, "Now that you're grown up, I think you should call me by my proper name."

Raeesha could only grit her teeth. No matter how difficult things were, Mother always seemed to make them worse.

"Kismet, I'm pregnant."

Mother continued with her sewing.

Say nothing. Let her chew on it as long as she likes.

Her mother finished off the last bit of green stem on the tulip, then carefully folded up her needlework and put it away in the sewing box, before turning to give Raeesha a disapproving look. "Who is the father?"

"Gen. Singer."

Mother sighed and rubbed her forehead as she had years before, when Raeesha, as a young girl, had clumsily burned all the cakes on the day of the Paralayan festival.

"Does he know?"

"I'm afraid to tell him."

"You know what happens if you don't?"

"My brothers will try to kill me."

"They killed Amir Qilij in his own palace, in spite of all the armed guards. And Hisaf is now commander of the city watch. Do you think they'd have any trouble killing you?"

"No."

"Then what's so terrible about this General?"

How can I explain to my mother what a disaster this will be for Singer?

"The General will be angry."

Mother looked at her closely, as if her hair weren't quite in order.

"Would he not be even angrier if you were killed?"

"He's a foreigner. I don't know what he'd do."

"But you do know he'll be angry?"

She keeps twisting around everything I say!

"I assume so."

"Is he an angry man?"

"No, but he has many responsibilities."

"He takes these responsibilities seriously?"

"Yes, very."

"Then he will take this responsibility seriously."

What an orderly world my mother lives in.

"Some men see these things differently."

"And Gen. Singer is such a man?"

"I don't know."

"Then you should find out."

This was the answer she'd expected, which didn't make it any more agreeable.

"Perhaps I should ask Uncle Davoud."

"You've already asked one person more than necessary. The next you ask may be your executioner. Go talk to your General. He's the only one who can help you now."

She took the pink satin from the sewing box and continued with her embroidery.

Everyone is staring at me!

She tried to ignore them, but it was unsettling that every single person she passed on the street stopped what he or she was doing and stared at her.

Yesterday, no one noticed.

Yesterday, she was dressed like a proper Bandeluk girl, and no one paid her any attention. But now, wearing her armor and carrying a sword, everyone could see she was the woman who'd read the proclamation in Heroes Square, announcing the occupation.

They called her "Raeesha Qilij" because "qilij" meant "sword". By an unfortunate coincidence, the late Amir also bore the name Qilij, so people assumed there must be some connection between them. Thus, the story spread that Raeesha had swum across the lagoon, broken into the Amir's walled palace and killed the tyrant with her sword, a heroic deed. Since no one seemed to know who killed Amir Qilij, it was hard to disprove. In Kafra, it was now an established fact: "Raeesha the Sword" had become "Raeesha the Qilij-Slayer".

The stories they told about her! Raeesha, the anonymous Bandeluk girl, heard how mighty Raeesha Qilij had killed demons, scaled the walls of Barbosa and rescued Prince Krion from the rebel Gen. Basilius. It wasn't true. Other people had done those things. She herself had killed no one, accomplished no legendary feats, hardly even drawn her sword. But still, the stories sprang up, wilder ones every day.

On Dock Street, she ran into a gang of ragged little girls, who stopped their game of skipping-squares to look up at her with wide brown eyes. "Raeesha Qilij!" said one, pointing.

"Don't call me that," she muttered as she brushed past them.

I must look ten feet tall to them. What if they knew I were going to beg for my life from a foreign officer because I'm pregnant?

It wouldn't matter. They'd just weave it into the fantasy of the fierce amazon warrior. Compared to her legend, she felt small and helpless.

Next, they will say I made it rain fire. When can I just be Raeesha?

Turning onto Draper Street, she saw the mansion Singer had commandeered for his headquarters: a three-story, blue-tiled structure with four small ornamental towers. In the back was a dock where a boat was tied. Until recently, the mansion had belonged to an important judge.

Lt. Ogleby sat at a table in front of the building, surrounded by a mob of urchins who carried bottles, jars and bowls. Singer had announced a reward of one copper coin for each piece of *alfesfewer* they fished out of the lagoon, a sanitary measure. As she watched, Ogleby dumped the contents of a small bowl into a barrel and doled out three copper coins to one of the boys, who promptly ran off to get more *alfesfewer.*

I hope none of these children drown because the foreigners are so particular about sanitation.

Raeesha saluted Ogleby, who merely glanced up and waved

her past. Inside, the mansion was bustling with soldiers. They were stuffing things in bags and boxes and carrying them to the boat.

It looks like Singer is about to leave. I came just in time.

Because of the confusion, it took awhile to find Singer. He sat in an office on the top floor, writing something on a piece of paper. He looked up, distracted, as she came to attention before him, and then his face broke into a grin.

"Raeesha! Where have you been? We almost left without you."

"I was with my family."

"Well, I can understand that, but next time, don't wander off without telling me. I need to talk to you." He got up and closed the door. "The army is leaving tomorrow for Berbat, and I'm short a Standard-bearer."

He still wants me with him, after everything that has happened.

Singer mistook her silence for modesty. "You're the best soldier I have. The virtues of a soldier are courage, loyalty and perseverance in adversity. You're brave, loyal and stubborn to a fault. You pick up military skills with ease and seem to learn new languages in your sleep. And you're a born leader. I can't imagine anyone I'd rather have beside me."

Suddenly, she could feel his hands touching her again, the muscular warmth of his body, the furious passion of that night, which went on and on like it would never end. She would gladly go with this man to Berbat or anywhere.

She said, "I don't think that would be possible, in the circumstances."

Singer's face flushed with embarrassment. "I know how you feel, but I promise it will never happen again. You will have your own quarters. I made a mistake, a serious breach of discipline, but you have to let me make it right."

A serious breach of discipline? Is that what they call it?

"Your real mistake was to send me away afterward."

"I was trying to protect you. We were both in danger. When you followed me, I understood how wrong that was. Whatever happens, we must face it together."

With these words came a black hopelessness.

This isn't love. He just wants me on his team with the crazy engineer and the orphan bugle boy. Another homeless misfit to admire him.

She opened her mouth to tell him she was pregnant, but . . .

Then what?

Everyone would know about the "serious breach of discipline". There were important men among the foreigners who envied Singer and would gladly bring him down. Would he still be the General tomorrow? Would he be an officer? Would he even be a soldier?

A soldier's life is all he knows. He needs a comrade, not a pregnant teenager who'd be like chains on his feet.

"I'm sorry," she said.

Singer looked so crestfallen, she thought he must be sick. "I guess some things really can't be forgiven," he said.

But they can!

"Perhaps I can help you in a different way," he continued, not looking at her. "Prince Krion wants to form a company of Bandeluks. I think you'd be the best person for the job."

Insanity!

"General, the Blue Bandeluks joined your army because they had no choice. Now, they just want to go home."

"So do I. So does every man in the army. But we're all in for the duration. No one's going home until the war's over. Not them, not me and not you. No one."

"That may be so, but still, they'll never accept me as leader. You may have noticed, I'm a woman."

"They followed you before."

"Because they thought I was a man. A puny little man, but still a man. You still don't understand my people. They won't follow a woman anywhere unless it's into a brothel."

Singer waved his arm as if shooing away a fly. "Then recruit some women. I don't care. All we need is a few horse archers. We already have lots of pikemen."

Has he gone mad?

"General, women can't do these things!"

Now, he turned and grinned slyly at her. She'd fallen into his trap. "There you stand, in armor, with a helmet on your head and a sword in your belt, and you say women can't do these things."

"I'm special. Normally, women just want to marry someone and raise a lot of brats."

"Then hire the abnormal ones. We just need a few hundred. This city is full of young widows and overworked servant girls, women with pasts and women without futures. I see big, healthy women carrying heavy water jars on the street every day."

He makes it sound perfectly reasonable: Recruit a company of women!

Before she could think of another objection, he added an incentive: "The job comes with a promotion. That would make you the first female officer in this army or, so far as I know, in any."

Her mouth hung open, but no words came out.

I don't want to be an officer! I just want you!

Unable to stop herself, she burst into tears. Then, she ran down the stairs and into the street. Singer didn't follow her.

Lt. Ogleby was still busy with his urchins and his *alfesfewer.* He paid no attention as she hurried down the street and around a corner.

She stood there for a minute, not sure what to do next. Could she still go home? No, Uncle Davoud's house wasn't her home anymore. It was the most dangerous place in the world, a nest of enemies.

Why didn't I tell him I'm pregnant?

Singer, she realized, carried his own little world around with him. When she was in his world, everything seemed possible. For a moment, she really thought she could be an officer and raise a company of Bandeluk girls to fight for the King of Akaddia.

But a pregnant Raeesha had no place in Singer's little world. A pregnant Raeesha could destroy that world and possibly Singer himself.

Don't blame Singer. He'd have done anything I wanted. If I'd said, let's buy a farm somewhere or go back to Halland and open a shop, he'd have done it.

With Singer, everything was possible. He could talk her into anything, and he'd easily have talked himself into a hasty marriage even if it ruined him. And then they'd have lived together in a rubble of recriminations, miserably ever after.

She felt sick, almost nauseous. Brushing away her tears, she saw the street was empty. The little girls were gone, but they'd left behind their game: a series of overlapping squares chalked on the paving stones.

How do you play this game anyway?

It had been a long time since she'd played, and she hardly remembered the rules. You put your right foot there, and then the left one in the opposite square, and then reversed them . . .

While she was studying the game, a red drop of moisture fell on the street in front of her. It looked like blood.

Am I bleeding?

She wiped her nose, which was clean. While she examined her fingers for cuts, another drop fell next to the first. Then a third and a fourth. When she looked around, she saw that drops of blood were falling everywhere, from a clear sky.

She heard frightened screams from down the street and the pounding of feet as people sought shelter from the rain of blood. She stepped under the arch of a doorway and watched it fall, a red downpour.

First fire, then blood!

She reached down and touched it, then rubbed it between her fingers and sniffed at it. It looked like blood, felt like blood, smelled like blood. The rain of blood lasted about a minute, then ended as quickly as it had started. It left puddles all over the street and, she assumed, the city.

The streets are running red! How did this happen?

She was pregnant, she'd lost Singer, her brothers were going to kill her, and now it was raining blood!

My life can't get any worse!

She was still standing in the street, staring at all the blood, when the strangers came and before she could even turn around, threw a sack over her head. Tying her hands and feet, they stifled her frantic screams and carried her away.

3: Singer

The old woman couldn't stop coughing. One racking cough after another shook her frail body. There was a pile of handkerchiefs on the nightstand, all soaked in orange mucus, which had a strong odor. The makeshift infirmary, an attic in the headquarters, was full of it.

"So far as I can tell, her lungs are coated with turmeric," said old Dr. Murdoch.

"How the hell did that happen?" asked Singer.

"Damned if I know. When she stops coughing, I'll ask her."

"When will that be?"

"I'll tell you when I find out. I've never had a case like this before. I'm treating with licorice, cherry bark and lungwort, but so far without much success."

Gwyneth gasped in air and tried to say something, but it only set off another round of coughing. Having used up all her handkerchiefs, she grabbed the edge of the sheet and began soaking it with orange mucus. The young private in the next bed, who was recovering from purulent cock lesions, looked thoroughly disgusted.

"Can't you do something for the pain?" asked Singer.

"Can, but won't. You have to be careful with someone this old. I've got to drain her lungs pretty soon, and it's a tricky procedure. Very uncomfortable. I'll save the laudanum until then."

"Will she live?"

"Probably. But I bet she'll wish she were dead."

"Could this be connected to the rain of blood?"

"I doubt it. Look at the spots on her clothing. She was caught in the shower, probably when she returned from the *fui* demons' camp. But she inhaled the turmeric sometime before. There are traces of it on her face."

"Is there anything I can do?"

"Pray to Narina. I'm out of answers."

Narina, can you help me with this?

Nothing. Singer sighed.

Maybe praying to the gods would work better if I had some faith in them.

The gods were not to blame for this, Singer felt sure. Somehow, he was. He'd been treading water in a sea of despair since Raeesha left, and now this happened.

It was not that he'd wished anyone harm. It was just that Gwyneth, an old woman long exiled to the plane of *fui* demons by her sorcerer husband, was destitute and couldn't go home. Singer had helpfully decided to hire her as a liaison to the small group of *fui* demons which were assigned to him as commander of the Free State Contingent. She was the only one who understood their weird, buzzing language.

So far as Singer was aware, no one had ever asked the demons what they wanted. Everyone had just assumed they reveled in chaos and destruction, and feasted on the flesh of the innocents. When Gwyneth brought back their first request, Singer felt somewhat re-lieved. Instead of the usual army rations, they wanted fresh fish, more vegetables and plenty of turmeric. Apparently, the *fui* demons were crazy about turmeric, and Singer was happy to give them all they wanted.

But now the request no longer seemed so innocent. Had the demons turned on Gwyneth? Were they becoming rebellious? The fifty *fui* demons were like a small army.

Maybe I should surround their camp.

Suppressing the *fui* demons would cost a lot of lives. And so far, they hadn't done anything except, apparently, harass an old woman.

I'm responsible for these demons. Nobody else will do this for me. I'll have to take care of it myself.

"No sir, the camp appears to be quiet," said leathery-faced Capt. Stewart.

Singer had assigned the *fui* demons a field some distance from the lagoon and from the nearest road, and he'd stationed Stewart's Thunder Slingers on a rise nearby, where they could keep an eye on the demons and shoo away any curious visitors. Stewart had found a grove of bamboo somewhere and turned it into a fence and a watch-tower for his camp. The fence looked rickety, Singer thought, but it gave the Thunder Slingers a lot of freedom to use their weap-ons against any attacker. The watchtower was also rickety, and it couldn't hold more than two people at a time, but it afforded a good view of the demons' camp.

From there, Singer could see the *fui* demons had surrounded it with a ditch and a massive earthwork rampart as if it were a fortress. The peaks of their tents were just visible over the top. Two of the seven-foot green creatures were sitting or, more accurately, sprawling near the gate. The rest weren't visible.

I hope I never have to attack that place!

"Has anyone been there today?"

"There was a delivery of supplies this morning," said Stewart, "and the old lady came by shortly after that. Since then, no one."

"What exactly was in the delivery?"

"A cartload of fish and another of fruit and vegetables."

"And spices?"

"A couple sacks of turmeric."

So!

"Any disturbances?"

"None that we noticed. Those two at the gate have been sitting there like a pair of stone idols for hours." Stewart paused and looked sharply at Singer. "Is something wrong down there, General?"

Besides the fact the place is full of unruly demons?

"I hope not. But it looks like I'll have to go and find out."

"You're going in there alone?"

"You volunteering to come with me?

Stewart looked him up and down, from his golden helmet to his polished riding boots. "General, you're the Demonslayer."

"Don't call me that."

Despite his expensively-earned nickname, Singer felt quite lonely as he trudged down the path to the demons' camp. There was, he knew, no reason to blame Stewart. No armed guards could protect him from the *fui* demons, and the presence of soldiers might even provoke them.

And if I bring guards, the demons will know I'm scared of them. That's something I can't afford.

On the other hand, how could the demons *not* know he was scared of them? Everyone was scared of the *fui* demons with good reason. On the day of the invasion, he'd seen these fifty fight off a thousand enemy lancers, killing at least a hundred, without any losses of their own.

Of course, they know we're scared. That's why they wear those silver masks to hide their repulsive faces.

The soft tread of his boots seemed impossibly loud as he approached the silent camp. He waited expectantly for the two demons at the gate to get up, but they paid him no attention. One was leaning back, asleep or staring at the sky through the eyeholes of its ornate silver mask, a mask that always reminded Singer of the goddess Narina. The other had fallen on its side, and the silver mask had slipped off. Singer had never seen the face of a *fui* demon before. Out of curiosity, he stepped closer for a look.

Oh gods, that's not a face, it's just a lot of . . .

He turned away and retched on the ground, then fell to his knees and vomited again until his breakfast was entirely gone. About a minute later, the shock of what he'd seen was receding. He still felt weak, but no longer had the urge to vomit.

What was that anyway?

Already, the memory was fading, as if he were waking from a bad dream. Some kind of protective amnesia had set in. There remained only a vague impression of a writhing mass of . . . Tendrils? Tentacles? Teeth? None of that would have knocked him over. Whatever, it was an abomination he didn't care to see again. Not daring to look at the *fui* demon a second time, he fumbled around blindly with one hand until he found the fallen mask and put it back on the thing's head.

And Gwyneth lived for years among these creatures?

Neither of the *fui* demons had moved.

Are they dead?

Studying the nearer demon, he thought he saw some signs of breathing under the heavy green scales that covered its chest. He wasn't sure how the creature breathed, but the regular motion seemed proof enough that it did.

Not dead, but unconscious, or in some kind of stupor.

There was orange powder on the clawed fingers. Singer recognized the odor of turmeric.

It must be a drug for them! Poor Gwyneth saw them having fun and decided to try it, or was forced to, but all it did was make her cough.

Inside the camp, *fui* demons were sitting or lying around everywhere. Apparently, none were able to resist the lure of turmeric. One nodded and beat time to some music only it could hear. Another kept wiping something invisible from its arms and legs as if they were crawling with vermin.

They must be hallucinating!

He remembered the incident a few weeks ago when he was in the Madlands. His childhood choirmaster, a dried up old man named Thorndike, had suddenly come at him out of nowhere and demanded to know why he was so late for practice. Singer was dumbfounded. The Witch had taken his hand and told him there was nothing there. But still, Thorndike was in his face, threatening him with a whipping if he didn't report at once to the temple. It was one of the most disturbing things that had ever happened to him.

And they do this just for fun!

The camp was a mess. There were piles of garbage, besides weapons and entrenching tools scattered on the ground. Singer would have issued a stern reprimand to their commanding officer if he himself were not in charge.

Somewhere in this mob of demented demons was Twenty Three, the only one who admitted to speaking any human language. The *fui* demons all looked the same to Singer, but he thought he could recognize Twenty Three from the scar on its left arm where it had been wounded in battle, and also by the burn marks on the palm of its right hand.

Looking closely at the demons, he saw they were all scarred. This one had apparently taken an arrow in the thigh at some point. That one had lost the tip of its tail, which had grown back in a slightly darker color. Another had the signs of a deep axe wound to the neck, something no human could possibly have survived.

How did they get so beat up? It wasn't just fighting for me! Those sorcerers in Westenhausen must have hired them out as mercenaries for decades, maybe even centuries!

Picking his way carefully over and around the recumbent demons, he found at last one that had a slash mark on the left arm, where a Bandeluk scimitar had left its trail. Twenty Three had collapsed in a seated position, its head falling forward between its legs, and its tail curled on the ground beside it.

Singer cleared his throat, but the demon didn't even twitch.

"Twenty Three!" he said loudly, leaning forward. There was

still no response.

This demon is really whacked! Yes, "whacked" is the word, as if something hit it on the head. But how do you un-whack a demon?

Lying on the ground nearby was one of the pole weapons the demons used. It had three nasty-looking blades on one end, and a heavy iron knob on the other, for balance. Singer picked it up and brought the knobbed end down sharply on Twenty Three's tail.

"BZZT!"

In the blink of an eye, the *fui* demon was on its feet and looking around for enemies. Singer took a step back and dropped the weapon.

This monster doesn't even need a weapon to kill me.

"This is incorrect!" he said loudly in Akaddian. "Correct" and "incorrect", he knew, were words of huge importance to the *fui* demons.

The silver mask looked down on him inscrutably. "I will *bzzz* tell you some *bzzz* thing, Demonslayer," said Twenty Three with its weird, tongueless voice. "We are all *bzzz* incorrect. All of us *bzzz* are here because we *bzzz* are incorrect."

These demons are criminals sent here as punishment! They truly are the damned!

Several of the *fui* demons were looking at him now. He swallowed nervously. This revelation, that they were all criminals, was unsettling, but he knew it would be dangerous to show any sign of fear before the *fui* demons.

"Don't call me that," he said sternly. "My name is Singer!"

"If you are *bzzz* Singer, you *bzzz* should sing!" said Twenty Three, taking a step in his direction. Reflexively, Singer raised his hand, and Twenty Three suddenly stopped, as if the empty hand held a dangerous weapon.

Is this thing afraid of me? It called me Demonslayer!

To his right and left, and very likely behind him as well, the demons were getting up, even the ones he thought were unconscious. He was surrounded by an implacable circle of silver masks, a circle that was growing smaller. He could feel a thin trickle of sweat crawling down the left side of his face, under the cheek plate of the helmet.

"SING!" yelled Twenty Three, and, revealing a fluency they had thus far concealed, the other *fui* demons repeated it, "SING!

SING! SING!"

Fearing the demons would turn violent, Singer did the only thing he could think of. He sang:

> When freezing winds blow
>   across a wintry land,
> Where no tree dares to stand,
> When friend turns from
>   friend, and hope turns
>   to despair,
> When no one seems to care,
> In hunger and in pain, in the
>   cold, in the rain,
> You will hear us sing Nari-
>   na's song.

It was the first thing that popped into his head, the childish song they'd taught him in the choir many years ago. He still didn't know what it meant. It was completely simpleminded, but by some chance, his voice cracked and he sang it as if he were a child again.

Was that me?

The demons had stopped moving. This wasn't the kind of song they'd expected to hear. They seemed to hesitate as if waiting for the next verse.

"More *bzzz*," Twenty Three said softly.

"Not now. I have something important to say." Boldly, he stepped forward until he could see himself reflected in Twenty Three's silver mask. The ruby

Liz Clarke 2014

eyes of his golden helmet stared back at him.

"I have no more use for you. This will be your last war. I'm sending you home."

All around him, he could hear the *bzzz-bzzz-bzzz* of the demons talking excitedly to each other in their own language.

Twenty Three raised its clawed hands in protest. "The Arbiters *bzzz* will not allow us *bzzz* to return!"

Who are the Arbiters? On second thought, who cares!

"The Arbiters are not in charge here, I am. Your services are no longer required. At the end of this war, you're going home!"

"The Arbiters *bzzz* will nail our hides *bzzz* to the Tree of Penance!"

So they're afraid to go home! I meant it as a promise, but they take it as a threat!

"Then listen carefully: You have behaved as if 'correct' and 'incorrect' had no meaning! That is over! There will be no more turmeric! You will do what you're told promptly and without question!

"We will leave this place tomorrow morning. Be ready to march! If you anger me, I will send you somewhere you won't like! Do you understand what I'm saying?"

"Yes *bzzz*," said Twenty Three, and the other demons repeated the word. All of a sudden, the camp exploded into activity: Some demons began cleaning up the garbage. A few picked up the weapons and stacked them neatly. Others grabbed entrenching tools and began demolishing the rampart that surrounded the camp, using it to fill the ditch. It was as if they'd never taken any narcotic.

They destroy their fort, so it can't be used by enemies. They really are what Gwyneth calls them, the Clever Ones!

Outside the camp, Capt. Stewart was waiting with a nervous-looking group of Thunder Slingers. This assistance was too little and too late, but Singer nonetheless found the gesture reassuring.

Stewart watched in astonishment as the massive earthworks disappeared before his eyes. An avalanche of rocks and dirt was pouring down the face of the rampart. "What did you do to them, General?" he said.

"I gave them a motivational speech."

"Maybe you could sometime give my men a speech like that?"

"Let's just hope they never need it."

A short way along the shore was the warehouse where the new quartermaster, an earnest young Akaddian named Lt. Gallites, was checking the inventory of supplies as they were loaded into the wagons. He snapped to attention and saluted when Singer appeared.

"As you were. How's it going?" he said in Akaddian.

"Well enough, sir," said Gallites in Hallandish. "There wasn't much timber available. The Prince seems to have felled every tree he could find to build his forts, but I was able to beg three wagon loads from my uncle, who's a vice admiral . . ."

"It will have to do. What about the extra wagons?"

"I pried four out of the Chief Quartermaster. But I have no manifests for any of them."

"Don't worry about it. Sgt. Littleton will take charge of that. Is there any turmeric on your list?"

Gallites flipped through a ledger until he found the item, and raised one eyebrow. "Right you are, sir. They put it down at two hundred pounds, which seems like an extraordinary amount."

"Yes, that's far more than we need."

"How much do you want then, General?"

"None at all. I don't want a single grain of turmeric in any of the supply wagons."

Gallites thoughtfully took a pen and crossed the item from his inventory. "May I ask why, sir?"

"You may not."

Under Dr. Murdoch's care, Gwyneth was no longer coughing, but she still seemed short of breath, besides looking nearly as pale as her nightgown. She glanced up in embarrassment and confusion as Singer entered.

"General! I'm so sorry . . . I didn't know the Clever Ones were so *bzzz* . . . I mean . . ."

"I know what happened."

I sent an old woman alone to deal with the demons. What was I thinking!

"I reminded them of the Strictures, but . . ."

"But you were expecting a better class of demons. Don't worry about it. In the future, I will handle them directly."

Gwyneth's pale blue eyes grew wide. "But then . . . what am I to do with myself?"

"Whatever you please. I'm adding you to the pension roll."

"A pension? You're giving me a pension? But why?"

"On grounds of disability. You were injured in the service of the state."

4: Erika

From her window, she could see the long column of Free State soldiers moving east across the plain. Somewhere out of sight, at the head of the column, was Singer.

Does he still have that Bandeluk girl with him? Or is it someone else now?

Whoever it was, it wasn't her.

She'd known this would happen, known it from the moment he'd greeted her outside Jasmine House two weeks ago. The engagement was off. Singer did not love her. And now, he'd left without even a word.

It was not entirely undeserved. She'd crossed the ocean and risked everything to be reunited with Singer, but then she'd allowed herself to be tempted by Clenas, with his princely title, and by the prospect of great wealth. Now, that wedding was off too. Prince Krion had banished her. Her bags were already packed. The ship was leaving in an hour. An armed escort was at the gate to make sure she boarded.

There was a knock at the door. Hikmet had arrived to take her luggage. He smiled at her in a fatherly way. "What's wrong?" he asked. "The samples are already on board. They look fine. Everything is in order."

"I'm sure the samples are excellent. They'll bring in plenty of sales. It's my personal life that's a total mess."

"Perhaps not so much as you think."

"What does that mean?"

"Prince Clenas is waiting downstairs."

He was standing at the foot of the stairs, wearing one of his stunning uniforms, this one a brilliant white and decked with gold braid. He smiled at her with that mischievous look that always made her lips part and her heart beat faster.

Oh, Clenas, you overgrown schoolboy! You came at me again and again until I was ready to forget about Gen. Singer and our engagement. And now, I'm losing you as well!

She offered him her hand, but he ignored it, instead taking her by the waist and pulling her close to him. His lips pressed against hers. She tried feebly to push him away, meanwhile turning her head and protesting: "Really! We can't. You know I have to go . . ."

Clenas laughed. "May I not kiss my bride on our wedding day?"

"WEDDING?"

As Erika stared at him with her mouth hanging open, Clenas planted a kiss on it. Then, taking her by the arm, he led her down the hallway. Hikmet followed at a discreet distance.

"It will have to be a private affair," Clenas said, as if he were telling her about his plans for dinner. "I thought it best to keep things to myself until the last moment. My brother wouldn't be pleased if he knew."

"But . . . but . . ." was all Erika could find to say. Her head was spinning.

"No buts! It's all arranged." Clenas opened the door to the chapel.

Inside, she could see that someone had removed the old Bandeluk idols and replaced them with a statue of Theros, who scowled down at her, sword in hand. Standing in front of the altar in a dress uniform was a thin, grey-haired man she vaguely recognized as the chaplain of the Royal Light Cavalry. Next to him, wearing a fine silk dress and beaming amiably at her, was Hikmet's plump wife, Leyla. She carried a basket of rose petals, which she began scattering around the room, replacing the stale smell of incense with a cloying sweetness.

They must have planned this for days!

Clenas dragged her, stumbling, toward the altar. It didn't take much force. Erika was stunned and only slowly recovering her wits. Behind her, she heard a soft *click* as Hikmet closed the door.

"I never agreed to this!" she protested.

Clenas, who had a firm grip on her elbow, leaned intimately close as he whispered, "You said you'd answer my proposal soon. That was weeks ago. This is it, now or never. No more delays. Is this not what you wanted?"

"I wanted to be married, yes, but not like this!"

"You can have a big, gaudy wedding later. For now, we must be stealthy and swift. It will be a secret marriage, but all quite official. It has already been entered in the regimental archives. And look, I have the ring!"

Reaching into a pocket, he produced a gold ring.

"One ring? Where is yours?"

"That will have to wait. A ring would give us away. I got you this one for the ceremony, but you will have to keep it in your purse until we're ready to announce our marriage."

"But when will that be?"

"When I get free. At the moment, I'm under my brother's thumb, but that could change."

"Really? How?" asked Erika in confusion as she was hustled before the chaplain. He smiled benevolently at her, his mild blue eyes and swept-back grey hair balancing a prominent hawk nose.

"You never know," said Clenas. "Things happen. We must seize the day. Let's not keep the padre waiting. You may begin, Captain."

The chaplain cleared his throat apologetically. "I've abbreviated the ceremony somewhat due to the time constraints . . ."

"Just do it!"

"As you wish. Do you, Clenas, Prince Royal of Akaddia, take this woman to be your lawfully wedded wife, to have and to hold in sickness and in health from this day forth until death do you part?"

"I do."

"And who gives this woman in holy matrimony?"

"Skip over that part."

"Very well. And do you, Lady Erika, take Prince Clenas as your lawfully wedded husband, to love and obey in sickness and in health from this day forth until death do you part?"

"I . . . I . . ." There was an awkward pause, as she stammered.

"She said 'I do'," said Clenas, slipping the ring on her finger.

"Then I pronounce you man and wife. You may kiss the bride." Clenas took his time about it.

An hour later, she was sitting in her cabin, which rocked slowly back and forth as the ship left port. From her window, she could see the city of Kafra, its spires alight in the sun, growing smaller in the distance. Her bags were piled next to the bunk, on which lay three items Clenas had given her: the gold ring, a copy of her wedding certificate and a letter of introduction to his sister, Duchess Thea.

Her head was still spinning. She could hardly believe what had happened.

Am I really married? Am I a princess?

It didn't seem real. Bemused, she picked up the gold ring and studied it. It was perfectly simple, round and smooth, without inscription. You could get one like it in any pawnshop.

This doesn't mean a thing!

Alarmed, she tore open the envelope to read the certificate: "We hereby certify that on this date _____, _____ and _____ were united in matrimony . . ."

It's just a blank form!

She remembered signing the marriage certificate. Clenas must have swapped it for a blank one!

Reaching to tear open the other envelope, she thought twice and took a minute to heat her sewing knife with a candle, then deftly removed the wax seal. The letter inside was quite short:

Dearest Thea!

I must once again rely on you to assist me in an affair of the heart. This young woman, Erika by name, is a cloth merchant from Tidewater. She has some fabric she wishes to sell and also some entertaining stories that may enliven your soirees, but is not really a person of great importance. I would be most grateful if you would consider her your guest until I am able to return and relieve you of the inconvenience.

Your loving brother,

Clenas

She read it twice before the implications became clear: Clenas was introducing her as a casual lover! Her marriage was a fraud, or worse . . .

In Akaddia, a woman's property belonged to her husband. If Erika's plans for the sale of *pamuk* went well, she'd earn a fortune, which Clenas could claim whenever he liked by producing the marriage certificate and the witnesses. If, on the other hand, the scheme failed, he could just deny the whole thing.

Her curses were loud enough to alarm the cabin boy, who tapped on the door until he was told to go do something implausible to himself.

5: Lamya

Sitting in her library on the second floor of the house that the army had assigned her, Lamya studied the report she'd just written according to the instructions from Mopsus:

FROM: Mistress Lamya, Staff Sorceress
TO: Prince Krion, Commander-in-Chief of the Allied Forces
SUBJECT: Rain of Fire, Rain of Blood

Examination of a blood sample reveals unusually large corpuscles, suggesting an origin in one of the *ingenti* planes, inhabited by beings of immense size. It is possible the source creature did not even notice the loss of blood, which amounted to thousands of gallons.

Both dimensional anomalies are traceable to the same person: Sgt. Raeesha, formerly Standard-bearer of the Free State Contingent, presently unassigned. The subject does not practice sorcery, as originally assumed, but is infected with a demon embryo of the Extinctor type, most likely contracted during a recent expedition to the Madlands. She is ignorant of the infection and erroneously believes she is pregnant.

Demons of this species generate a dimensional flux that can render other demons uncontrollable. It can also attract inert material and even living beings from distant planes through a process of dimensional funneling. Because the demon is not yet fully formed, the process is undirected and of low intensity. As it develops, the dislocations will become larger and more violent.

At present, the subject is in stasis and therefore presents no danger. Any attempt to remove the parasite at this point would require exploratory surgery with severe trauma to the patient. Alternatively, if the demon is simply allowed to develop, it will in a week, or two at the most, implant itself in the form of a cyst that can easily be removed.

Lamya noticed her neatly-polished fingernails were tapping sharply on the table, a bad sign.

There is something wrong with this.

She'd read it three times and found some small errors of punctuation, but not the reason for her persistent feeling of unease. Her fingers were tapping harder now.

They're trying to tell me something!

What could it be? She'd done what she was told, completed the tests and analysis, identified the problem and proposed a solution. There were no errors that she could see. It was all in order. Her teacher, the Old Woman of Barbosa, would be proud of her.

But still her fingernails kept tapping, tapping.

Well, I can't sit on this much longer.

She rang the bell to summon Mopsus. The young man came promptly. His lieutenant's uniform was immaculate, but he hadn't bothered to comb his hair, and there was something insolent about the smile on his face.

"The report is done," she said. "The Prince will want to see this right away."

"Yes, *Mistress*," said Mopsus, picking it up.

"Don't call me that."

"Yes, *Mistress*," he repeated, studying the report.

Lamya gritted her teeth. Mopsus had subtle ways of annoying her. He insisted everyone in the army must have a title, and *Mistress* was the correct title for her. There was some double-entendre nesting in the Akaddian word, she suspected, but she had no way of proving it.

"This seems to be in order," Mopsus said finally. "I'll get to work on the translation right away. Shouldn't take long. Will there be anything else?"

"No. Just give it to him."

Lamya's fingers had become quite frantic. As Mopsus turned to go, she said, "Wait! What do you think about this?"

Mopsus stared blankly at her. "That's one question I seldom hear. I've only made it this far because no one cares what I think."

"But you know the Prince as well as anyone. How do you think he will deal with this?"

Mopsus laughed, a girlish kind of giggle. "No mystery there." He drew a finger across his throat. "Good night, *Mistress*."

They're going to kill her!

She should have thought of that. The Prince only cared about his army. Whether one week or two, it was too long for him. Anything that endangered the army had to be sacrificed.

She stared a minute at her fingers, which had not stopped tapping on the table.

I'm still missing something. What?

She went into the workroom, where Raeesha was lying naked on a pallet, surrounded by sorcerous implements. She lay in stasis, her face frozen in an expression of rage and indignation. The physical examination had been stressful.

Raeesha was no one, just an obnoxious teenager, a runaway. Would anybody care if she died? Would anyone even notice? Her own father wanted her dead. Even the turncoat Bandeluks wouldn't talk to her. And now, Singer had left her behind. What was she worth to anyone?

Am I to blame if the Prince decides to kill her? I'm not responsible for the Prince!

Her fingers had wandered over to a workbench arrayed with tools. The forefinger was tapping sharply next to the sacrificial knife. Annoyed, she picked it up.

As her finger touched the cold steel, she felt a chill, and her body shook as the realization came.

They're going to make me kill her!

She'd never killed anyone before, but she knew very well what she had to do: One began by excoriating the ventral torso, before making exploratory incisions in each of the major organs, beginning with the liver . . . but it would be kinder just to cut her throat and burn the corpse . . .

Raeesha was staring at her, face frozen in rage.

Can I really do this? She's just a girl!

What would the Old Woman say if she were here? She'd probably say what she always said: Shut up and do as you're told.

I need help!

She put down the knife and went back to the library. On the top shelf, under a layer of dust, was a row of thick books: Ferhad's "History of the Bandeluks". Behind them, she'd hidden the ancient leather-bound book from the Madlands. Pressed into the worn leather cover were letters of shining gold, which, translated from the archaic Kano language, said: "Field Manual for the Practice of Military Sorcery, 3rd Ed."

She laid it on the table and flipped the pages, looking for something, anything that could change the situation. There were many powerful spells under her fingers, waiting to be invoked. With this book, she could summon demons far more dangerous than Singer's pets, cause storms and earthquakes, or even spread virulent plagues. She'd never shared this knowledge with anyone.

It must not fall into the hands of Prince Krion, or any of his kind. That would mean the deaths of thousands.

But what exactly was the difference between killing one person and a thousand? That was something the Old Woman had never taught her. Now that she thought about it, her lessons were all about the how and never the why of magic. The Old Woman had kept some things from her. She remembered seeing places in her books where pages had been torn out. But this was one book the Old Woman had never touched.

She was getting to the back of the book. The margins here were full of the crabbed handwriting of the ancient sorceress Dariea, mostly notes on the various kinds of demons and their uses. Sometimes, loose bits of parchment were stuffed between the pages, for want of space. Lamya had already sifted through this part. There was nothing that could help her now.

She'd just turned the last page and was about to close the book in despair, when she felt an uneven surface inside the cover. Something had been printed there, but the letters were faded and no longer legible. She could feel indentations where they'd been. She got a piece of charcoal from the fireplace and began rubbing the page gently with it. Gradually, the antique letters took shape:

PRECEPTS OF POWER
Greatness does not come cheap.
It is a loan, not a gift.
You will bear the burdens of others, but do not carry their sins.
No reward is worth more than a clear conscience.
Everything has consequences. A price must be paid.
If you do not know the price, then it is too high.
Good intentions are your best protection.
Beware of making corpses. Beware of making slaves.

Do not destroy those you can compel, and do not compel those
you can persuade.
Do not look for enemies. They will find you.
You will make mistakes and suffer for them.
Others will suffer more. That is your greatest burden.
Let the gods be gods. Do not meddle in their business, and pray
they do not meddle in yours.
To lose your health or wealth is not the greatest tragedy. To
lose yourself is the greatest tragedy.
Remember that all things are born to decay.

Lamya read it all twice, and then a third time before it began to sink
in. She was looking at a thousand-year-old code for sorcerers. This
was what the Old Woman had kept from her!

*She just wanted a docile servant! She never told me what NOT
to do!*

The Old Woman feared this ethical code more than any wild
magic. It lay like a barricade in the way of her plans. This was the
page she'd torn out of all her grimoires, the one secret her servants
must never learn. Lamya had spent half her life in that bleak fortress, and she'd had no idea such a thing existed.

Thank the gods I got out even if it took a war to do it!

She snapped the book shut and returned it to its hiding place.
Now, she knew what to do. It was obvious.

An hour later, she'd finished fumigating the workroom and
chalking the necessary circles and symbols on the floor. The candles
were lit. The governing powers had been invoked. She could feel
them gathering, a circle of invisible faces waiting expectantly. She
picked up a wand for the final evocation.

"Put it down!" said a voice behind her.

She turned around in surprise. A masked man was standing in
the library door. He held a drawn bow. The arrow was pointed at her
heart.

"Put it down!" he said again, drawing the bow half an inch
more.

Lamya's heart fluttered, cringing away from the sharp point of
the arrow. She had only one spell ready, and it wouldn't stop arrows.
She put down the wand.

The masked man advanced two steps into the room. The arrow never deviated an inch from its target. "What are you doing?" he demanded.

How am I to explain this?

"It's harmless," she began, "a simple projection . . ."

There came a violent noise from downstairs, the crash of something heavy yielding to superior force. Then, before she could ask what was going on, there were screams and sounds of fighting.

She looked, aghast, at the masked man, who slowly shook his head. "Don't move," he said in ominous tones. "Be quiet. We have not long to wait."

Then there were feet pounding on the stairs and a *bang* as the door to the hallway flew open. Three more masked men charged into the room.

"There she is!" yelled the leader, waving a bloody dagger.

It took Lamya an instant to realize he was not threatening her, but Raeesha, who was lying helpless on the floor. Instinctively, she stepped between.

"Stop!" she said.

"Wait!" said the man with the bow.

But the man with the dagger wasn't listening. As he raised it, she grabbed at his wrist with both hands. The force of his rush

knocked her back. She tripped over Raeesha and fell with the assassin on top of her.

As he raised the dagger a second time, she spoke the words of evocation.

6: Bardhof

FROM: Hisaf, Captain, Kafra City Watch
TO: Prince Krion, Commander-in-Chief of the Allied Forces
SUBJECT: Incident on Khibaz Street

The incident took place sometime after midnight and was first reported shortly before dawn by a watchman who observed a broken door on a side street, but was unable to enter the premises because it was off-limits to civilians. The investigation was further delayed some two hours, due to the need for obtaining permission from the occupational authorities. The building is presently unoccupied. Four corpses have been removed and are in the possession of the army.

Initial inspection shows the door was broken in with great force. Blood and overturned furniture on the first floor indicate a violent struggle. Another door, on the second floor, was also broken, and there are further signs of struggle in the adjacent room, which was apparently devoted to sorcery. Fallen candlesticks and chalked symbols on the floor indicate a magical ritual was in progress at the time of the break-in.

The remainder of the building is undisturbed, except for an open skylight, possibly the point of egress for the intruders. There is no sign of robbery though an inventory has not been attempted. Neighbors report hearing no disturbance. Military authorities refuse to disclose any information concerning the house and its occupants. This effectively precludes further investigation by the city watch.

The conclusion of the preliminary investigation is that the disturbance was caused by the catastrophic failure of an experiment in sorcery.

"What do you make of that?" said Krion.

Lt. Bardhof sighed and scratched his head. "I don't know, my Prince. It's a rather vague report."

"Then allow me to cast some light on it. The building on Khibaz Street was the quarters assigned to Singer's Witch. She was investigating the rains of fire and of blood. Here is her report. She wrote it just an hour or two before she was attacked."

Bardhof's eyes grew wide as he read the report. "I don't know much about sorcery, but this sounds extremely dangerous."

"Yes! Yes, indeed! Someone is using this girl against me. She's like a dagger at my throat. We don't know when the next attack will come, or what form it will take. I was relying on the Witch to deal with this, and now she's disappeared. The girl too. And it happened in the middle of Kafra!"

Bardhof had never seen the Prince so agitated: He paced around the room of mirrors, staring at his reflection, first in one, then in the next. "I want you to look into this for me. Find the Witch. Find the girl."

"Yes, my Prince. Where shall I begin?"

"Begin with the watch report. Investigate the site yourself. Verify everything you can. Try to find any clues that could identify the attackers."

"Yes, my Prince."

As Bardhof turned to go, Krion thought of something else: "And don't go alone, this time. Bring a couple of guards. I don't want you disappearing too."

The Prince didn't say which guards I was to bring.

Kafra was a nest of spies and traitors. Who could he trust?

Bardhof turned toward the barracks that housed the Covenant Heavy Assault Group. He found them as they were lining up for lunch in front of a huge kettle of mutton stew and a small mountain of brown bread.

"I'm looking for Grimald and Murdoon," he told the mess sergeant.

"In the kitchen, sir. They were assigned extra duty for fighting."

With each other, most likely.

Looking in the kitchen, he had to choke back a laugh: The two big bruisers were on their knees, scrubbing pots and pans in a tub of soapy water. Both were completely clad in chain armor.

"Ho, you lazy louts! Don't you ever take that armor off?"

"We're practically naked, sir!" Grimald objected. He pointed with a soap-dripping brush at a pile of armor in the corner: breastplates, greaves, vambraces and other pieces normally strapped on over the chain.

"Put down those brushes, and pick up some manly weapons! The Prince has work for us to do!"

"Now that is a welcome order!" said Murdoon, tossing aside his brush. "Just a minute . . ." He went to get his gear.

"No time for that! Grab a helmet and an axe and go!"

Seeing a pair of the Covenant Heavy Assault Group with him, two-handed axes casually resting on their shoulders, people hurried to clear the street. Grimald and Murdoon came from the same place he did, a mining town high in the mountains. They'd been his schoolmates before the war. Both were rock-solid Covenant plebs and proud of it. He felt safer with them behind him.

Which is more than I can say for the Akaddians. They were happy enough to follow Basilius when he was in charge.

The house on Khibaz Street had seen better days: It was a shabby two-story affair with an old-fashioned, dark red roof and covered with tiles of the same color. These were cracked and, in places, flaking off to reveal a roughly-mortared stone surface underneath.

The house was shadowed by two larger buildings. Peering in the front gates, he saw each was built around a central courtyard, a style favored by wealthy Bandeluks.

The bedrooms are probably on the top floor and facing the inner courtyard. So the story that they heard nothing is plausible.

He made a circuit of the Witch's house. There were no windows on the first floor, he noticed. Those on the second floor were concealed by latticework, which was intact.

The house had three doors: a heavy front door, which was locked and apparently had been for some time, a little door in back, long disused, and another one on the side, which was recently boarded up. It had a small stoop and the protection of a wooden canopy. There were two baskets of stinking kitchen waste next to it. He told his companions to tear off the boards, so he could get a better look at the door.

It was easy to see it had been forced open. The latch was broken, and the wood splintered around a large central indentation. He ran his fingers over it. The indentation was smooth and regular. There were no marks of any blow except the one.

"What do you think did this?" he asked.

"Looks like a ram, sir," Murdoon said.

"As any fool can see," said Grimald with a smirk. "We have one with the siege equipment," he added.

And the Sappers do too, I expect. Could this be an aristo plot?

He studied the indentation. It didn't seem likely he could identify the attackers just from this one mark. Some Akaddian units had rams, maybe the Free Staters too, not to mention the city watch. And it wasn't hard to turn any log or beam into a ram.

But demons don't carry battering rams.

He gave the door a push and immediately caught his breath. He'd seldom seen so much blood in one place. It was spattered everywhere. The floorboards were coated with it.

The city watch had made a mess. Their boot tracks were all over the room, together with those belonging to the detail that had dragged away the dead guards. It was impossible to learn anything from the confused muddle of footprints.

Looking around, he saw the room was a kitchen. The remnants of last night's supper were still on the counter. In the middle of the room was a heavy table, surrounded by overturned chairs. It held a half-full wine bottle and some tumblers. Two other bottles, empty, lay on the floor. The room smelled of cheap wine.

So, they were whiling away the time with a little party when the killers broke in.

"Didn't waste much time on these guys," Grimald said.

"You should stop drinking on duty. Bad for your health," Murdoon added. He picked a bread roll from the counter, but put it back down when Bardhof glared at him.

The kitchen opened to a hallway, which was full of bloody tracks. Besides the fainter boot tracks of the city guard, he could make out at least three distinct sets of sandals, the common daily footwear of Bandeluks.

"Look at how wide they're spread," said Grimald.

"Yeah, they were really making tracks," Murdoon offered, provoking a groan from Grimald.

The tracks lead directly to a stairway, which brought them to another corridor. The doors here were closed except one, which was hanging from a single hinge. This, then, was the room of the "experiment in sorcery".

Bardhof peered nervously inside, but there were no lurking demons, only a small room that was empty of furniture, except for two small tables, one overturned. Candlesticks lay on the floor with a scattering of small implements, and more on the standing table. Presumably, these were tools of sorcery. He had no idea what most of them were for and decided to leave them where they lay.

In the center of the room was a pallet, surrounded by a chalked circle and mysterious symbols. "Either of you seen anything like this before?"

"No sir," said Grimald. "I'm guessing some spell-monger made those chicken tracks."

"I'm guessing you don't know any better than I do," said Murdoon.

"Wait by the door while I inspect the room."

Bardhof felt the back of his neck prickling as he approached the circle. It was as if something invisible were watching. The strange symbols seemed to invite him to step within.

Maybe the Witch forgot to dismiss something she summoned?

Anything seemed possible. He didn't dare to set foot inside the circle, but instead walked around it. There was a pillow, he noticed, on the pallet, and it still held the indentation of a human head.

Sgt. Raeesha?

Bending over to avoid stepping in the circle, he picked up a single, short black hair.

Is this hers? Maybe a sorcerer could use it to find her.

He laid the hair on his handkerchief, which he carefully folded and put in his pocket.

There was nothing more to do here. He moved on to the next room, which was paneled with bookcases and had a heavy desk in the middle. There was a stack of books on it, and more spread on the floor.

So this is where the Witch did her research.

The books on the desk and the floor were written in Bandeluki or another language he couldn't read, but some of the books on the shelves were in Akkadian. One title caught his eye: "An Introduction to Forensic Alchemy".

It wouldn't hurt to have a look at that one.

Flipping through the pages, he saw it had to do with the examination of corpses and identification of poisons. He stuck it in his pocket for future reference.

Inspecting the desk more closely, he saw some scribbled notes lying under a book beside two burned-out candles, and a pen and inkwell.

This must be where she wrote the report.

There was a bell pull in the corner. He pulled on it experimentally and heard a bell ring in a distant part of the house.

If she yanked this, it didn't do any good. The guards were already dead. What did she do when the attackers came storming in?

There were no obvious clues in the library. He moved on to the next room, a bedroom. A lingering scent of perfume greeted him. Women's clothing was casually draped on the furniture. There was some silver jewelry on a dressing table. The bed, he noted, had not been slept in.

Doesn't look like they came here. The Witch left this room yesterday and did not come back. So where is she now?

He took a brush from the dressing table. There were several long, black hairs tangled in it. He picked one and rolled it in a stocking, stuffing it in his pocket with the book and the handkerchief.

If they didn't come this way, how did they leave?

Cursing himself for a fool, he remembered the report had said something about a skylight. Stepping back into the library, he could see it, still open, about ten feet above his head.

If this is the "point of egress", how did they get up there?

He called in Grimald and Murdoon, and told them to climb on the desk, then to raise him up. Standing on their shoulders, he was just able to crawl out on the roof.

Thankfully, the roof wasn't very steep, but the tiles were old and loose. One, dislodged by his boots, skidded away and fell with a crash in the alley. As he bent down to steady himself, he could hear the old boards creaking under his feet.

A dangerous place to be climbing around! How did they manage it?

He had a closer look at the skylight. The glass window was lying on the roof next to the casement. From marks next to the latch, he guessed someone had used a knife to open it from the outside. There was a piece of rope tied around the casement, which had been recently cut.

So, someone climbs up here like a spider, pries open the skylight, ties off the rope, and lowers himself inside. Then he returns the same way, but is in too much of a hurry to close the window or untie the rope.

He untied it himself and inspected it. It was not, he saw at once, a ship's manila rope, but a thin, hand-plaited rope, made from some strange, pale fiber, most likely by a local craftsman.

Would a shopkeeper remember selling something like this? Or tell me about it if he did?

He tugged at the rope. It didn't seem very strong.

This is nothing but a clothesline. Not the kind of tool a professional would use. And it surely couldn't have supported more than one person.

He tied the rope around his waist and had a further look around the roof. It would be fairly easy to reach this point from one of the adjacent buildings, he saw, but getting back would be a problem. The easiest way to get down would be with the rope – and the fact that it had been cut would tend to rule that out – or else to drop onto the canopy above the door.

This was someone's "point of egress," but probably just for one person.

So how did the rest of them leave? Through the kitchen, most likely. Why then did the watch assume this was the "point of egress"? Presumably, they hadn't examined it closely. And before they tracked things up, they'd found no sign of captives being taken out through the kitchen.

That doesn't leave a lot of possibilities.

Bardhof sighed. The Prince was anxiously waiting for his report, and he wasn't going to like this.

FROM: Lt. Bardhof, Investigating Officer
TO: Prince Krion, Commander-in-Chief of the Allied Forces
SUBJECT: Incident on Khibaz Street

A second investigation has revealed some further information.

The break-in at the ground level was accomplished by three or four men using a ram. The guards, who had been drinking wine in the kitchen, were surprised and dispatched after a brief struggle. Another intruder entered alone, by means of a rope, into the library on the second floor.

There is no evidence of a supernatural agency in the initial attack. All indications point to a group of Bandeluks, most likely local residents, or at least familiar with the city. The coordination of the attack suggests military organization or training.

At the time of the incident, Mistress Lamya was engaged in a ritual of some kind in a room adjacent to the library. Sgt. Raeesha may also have been present though probably unconscious or spellbound on the floor.

The absence of blood shows neither woman was wounded during the attack, and there is no sign captives were physically removed from the building. All available evidence suggests the women were extracted by means of sorcery. Their present location is unknown.

Physical evidence secured includes hair samples from both victims and a length of rope used by the attackers. Examination by a trained sorcerer may reveal additional information.

Prince Krion was sitting in the room of mirrors, amid an untidy scattering of maps and papers. He ran his fingers nervously through his hair as he read the report. Finally, he threw it down in disgust.

"This is all you were able to find? Have you no other leads?"

"The attackers were very efficient, my Prince. They left behind no witnesses and very little evidence. I can try to trace the rope or locate the ram they used, but frankly, the chances don't look good."

"They were imperial agents, then?"

"If so, they're much better organized than I thought. It didn't take them long to locate the Witch. And they seemed to be quite familiar with the local neighborhood. I'm afraid I have no idea how they removed the women unless it were by sorcery."

Krion stood up and walked over to stare into one of the mirrors, his eyes twitching as they peered into the labyrinth of reflections around him. At last he said, "I've sent for another sorcerer, a Free Stater from Westenhausen, but it will take days for him to get here. And in the mean time, we're defenseless against magic."

Not a licensed sorcerer from the Royal College of Magic? You had to hire a stranger from Westenhausen? Have we fallen so low?

"I'm putting you in charge of the military police," Krion went on. "Take whatever precautions you can. Your new rank is Captain, and your initial budget is 500 thalers. You can draw it from the bursar whenever you like. Commandeer any building you want for a headquarters, and recruit whatever personnel you need from our forces or the locals. Just don't deprive me of Mopsus. I need him here."

Good, I have no use for that runt anyway.

"The city watch is yours to command. Register the citizens and issue them identification papers. Station sentries at all points of entry. No one gets into or out of the city without identifying themselves. Assign plainclothesmen to key locations. Arrest anyone who behaves suspiciously. You have my full authority to arrest and interrogate anyone up the rank of general."

Bardhof listened with his mouth open. It was a lot to swallow. *How in the name of all devils can I pull this off?*

"You have any questions?" Krion asked.

"When shall I start, my Prince?"

"Yesterday."

Grimald and Murdoon were waiting expectantly by the palace gate. "How did it go, sir?" Grimald asked.

"It went well. I'm a captain now. And both of you are ser-
geants."

Each looked at the other skeptically. "Really?!" they both said.

"Yes, really."

Bardhof stood by the gate for a moment, looking out over the
city. The afternoon sunlight gave everything a sinister, dark cast.
Ordinary people going about their business in the square created a
throng of shifting shadows. His eyes picked out a single figure, a
woman selling figs to passersby from a basket.

*Who are you? An imperial spy or just a harmless peasant?
How am I supposed to know? Gods help me!*

7: Rajik

He sat in the mud and wept.

How can I be so stupid!

He'd done it again. They'd told him his sister was pregnant and hiding among the foreigners, and he had believed them and assumed the worst. He'd gathered his friends and charged right in, not waiting for Hisaf to ask questions, but the Witch had tricked him and brought him to this awful place, where everything was filthy and smelled bad.

And now, the Witch said Raeesha was not pregnant, but infected with some kind of demon. And she was not hiding, she'd been kidnapped. He glanced over to where Raeesha lay among the reeds, naked and half-sunk into the swamp. She looked like she wanted to kill him, which she probably would, at the first opportunity.

He averted his eyes. A man should not see his sister while she was naked. "I'm so sorry," he whispered pitifully to himself.

"Good," said the Witch. "Let me up."

He'd forgotten he was sitting on her. He glanced at the Witch, who was lying face-down in the mud. Her fine silk robes were caked with filth. "Why should I?"

"For any one of several of good and persuasive reasons: I'm not your enemy. You attacked me when I was trying to help your sister. You will never restore her without my assistance. Nor have you any hope of returning home by yourself. Furthermore, it's your fault we're in this mess."

Rajik stood up and watched as the Witch shakily did likewise. "How is it my fault?" he said. "It was your stupid spell that landed us here."

The Witch was trying to wipe the muck off her clothing, but it only stuck to her fingers instead. She walked slowly, the gooey mud sucking at her feet with every step, to a small, lily pad-covered pool nearby.

"My plan was to project Sgt. Raeesha to one of the *elysian* planes, where she'd have been safe. But you disrupted the ritual and pushed us both into the circle, which wasn't intended for us. I don't know exactly why we came here, wherever this is."

Rajik looked around. There was nothing to see but reeds circling small, muddy ponds, a few hummocks tufted with grass and an occasional small, shrubby tree.

"We're somewhere west of Kafra. Near the Frog Creek village, I'd guess."

"Look behind you."

Behind him were more of the same swampy landscape . . . and also the ribs of some monstrous creature, at least a hundred feet long. Whatever it was, it had a lot of ribs. He could see a dozen of them sticking out of the swamp, some taller than he was.

"What's that?"

"If I could answer that question, I'd be closer to knowing where we are. All I can say for sure is the gravity has changed. Everything feels lighter than before. Also, you may have noticed, it's daytime now, and the sun is different."

He squinted upward to where the sun was approaching the noon position. The Witch was right. It looked orange and was bigger than he remembered.

"We're not in Kafra anymore," he muttered.

"We're nowhere you've ever been or heard of," she said. The Witch had finished washing and climbed out of the pool. Her robes clung to her body in a way that concealed very little. Rajik averted his eyes before, under great temptation, venturing another look.

This is not my sister.

She didn't attempt to cover herself, but instead stared at him until he felt his cheeks turning red and looked the other way. "So how do we get back?" he said.

"It would help if I knew where we were. Also, I need to find some equipment." She picked up a twig and waved it in the manner of a wand before discarding it and going to where Raeesha was lying. "I suppose we should start by taking Sgt. Raeesha out of stasis."

He looked upon the nakedness of his sister and felt his cheeks turning red again. "Get her some clothing first."

"Do I look like I have spare clothing? Give me your knife, and I'll create something."

"Create clothing? Is that another spell?"

"A spell to make clothing would be more than I could manage right now. But when I was a child, we didn't have much money. We had to make our own clothing, out of whatever we could find."

Without asking again, she took the knife from his belt and began cutting reeds, tossing them in a pile. "Give me an hour or two. Meanwhile, try to find food and some kind of a shelter."

No matter where he turned, there was nothing to see but the same stinking swamp in every direction. The only landmark was the bones of the whale-sized creature that had apparently died there, so he headed in that direction.

Progress was slow in the ooze that threatened to swallow him up with every step, and the bones were bigger and farther away than he thought. It took him nearly an hour to reach the spot, and when he got closer, he began to doubt they were bones at all. They were too uniform in size and shape, more like something man-made than anything natural. He reached out to touch one, and then jerked back his hand. There was a splinter in his finger.

This is wood, the ribs of a ship! How did it get here?

The wood wasn't as old and weathered as he expected. Looking more closely, he could see holes where the nails had been.

Somebody must have dropped it here in the swamp and stripped away everything they could: planking, decking, even the nails! So where's the crew?

He walked the length of the ship without finding any answer to that question. He was turning back, when he stubbed his toe on something buried in the muck. He picked it up, a small brass plate that had probably fallen off when the ship was scrapped. Wiping away the mud, he saw the familiar image of a lion holding a sword.

The Imperial Lion! This is a Bandeluk warship!

Now that he knew what it was, other details became obvious. There were notches in the frame for the benches where the rowers sat. Also, he could see some uprights that once supported the stern castle, where the steersman had stood. Near the prow, a rusty piece of iron sticking out of the mud proved to be the ship's anchor, something the salvagers probably found too heavy to remove.

He climbed up one of the ribs as far as he could and had a look around. From this small elevation, the swamp wasn't quite so flat and featureless. To the north, he could make out a low line of hills. Closer by, there was another wreck. This one was smaller and not so picked-over. It looked like it might be a fishing boat. To the west, he could see a thin column of smoke.

A campfire? Is there some-one else out here, in this awful place?

As he was trudging back to the Witch, he noticed something scurry away from his feet into the water. He splashed around until he got ahold of it, a squirming crab-like thing, but with a tail and too many legs.

A lobster-crab? Why have I never seen one of these before?

He found the Witch sitting on a hummock. She'd split fibers from the reeds and was weav-ing them by hand into a coarse-looking garment. He dropped the lobster-crab at her feet. "I found it in one of these ponds. I don't know what it is, but it looks like it might be good to eat."

"Cooking is such an adven-ture. I found some clams. They're everywhere." She pointed to a small pile she'd gathered. "What else did you see?"

He gave her the brass plate. "That thing to the southwest used to be a war galley. How do you think it got here?"

"I'll have to look at it more closely, but I assume it was by magic. Anything else?"

"Yes. There was a wrecked boat. We might be able to use it for shelter. And some hills to the north, and I saw a campfire west of here. I thought it would be bet-ter not to approach it alone."

"A wise decision. How do you like this?"

She held up her handiwork for inspection. It was a mass of coarsely woven plant fibers, like a sack, only open at the top and bottom to make a skirt. There was also a little braided belt of the same material.

"It looks awful. You want her to wear that? Where's the top?"

"I thought you might contribute your vest. I'm done weaving for today." She held up her red, raw fingers in evidence.

He took off the leather vest. "So, what are we going to do about Raeesha?"

The Witch walked over to where Raeesha was still nakedly raging at the sky. "I can remove the stasis quite easily. The hard part will be doing it without being murdered."

A few minutes later, they were both wearing fresh scratches and bruises, and sitting on top of Raeesha as she screamed and kicked at them.

"It was just a big mistake," said Rajik for the third time.

"TRAITOR!" screamed Raeesha.

"He's not taking my side, but I am taking his, and he's taking yours," said the Witch.

"You're just confusing her . . .OW!" said Rajik, as one of his sister's heels caught him in the ribs.

The Witch pushed Raeesha's face down into the mud until the kicking stopped, then raised it up again and while she was spitting mud said, "Listen! This is important! You aren't pregnant!"

"I'm not?" said Raeesha when she'd finished gasping for air.

What made her think she might be pregnant?

It didn't seem like a good time to raise the subject.

"It's much worse than that," said the Witch. "You're infected with a demon parasite. I think it caused the rains of fire and blood. I was trying to move you to someplace I could extract it safely when your brother came charging in."

"I was trying to rescue you," said Rajik. It was the best story he could think of. "We got you some clothes," he added.

"Where the hell are we?" said Raeesha as she washed and dressed herself.

"'Hell' is approximately correct. This is one of the demon worlds," said the Witch. "If I knew which one, I might find a way to bring us home."

"Demons? There are demons here? What happens if they catch us?"

"That would depend on what kind of demons they are. We'd do well to avoid them until we find out."

"This skirt is too short," complained Raeesha, tugging at it to make it longer, "and it's so rough and scratchy!"

"It was the best I could do," said the Witch, glancing at the sun. "If you're ready, I think we should get moving."

Following the Witch, they went hopping from hummock to hummock toward the wreck. Meanwhile Raeesha entertained them with many complaints:

She hated the swamp and especially the gnats that were swarming about them in the heat of the day. She hated the crudely woven skirt, which was like walking around in a basket. But mostly, she lamented the cruelty of fate.

"Everybody treats me like a stray dog. My father hates me. My mother ignores me. I thought I could trust the foreigners, but then they kidnapped me. Why is everyone so mean?"

"You must have chosen the wrong gender," said the Witch.

"I tried switching. I did!"

"And you really thought that would work?" The Witch seemed amused.

He came to her rescue. "You're a straggler," he said. "A soldier alone hasn't any chance."

"So I need an army?" said Raeesha.

"I'll keep my eyes open for one," said the Witch.

"We found a navy, at least," said Rajik.

They'd reached the wrecked galley. The Witch inspected it, peering through the green stone that hung always from her neck.

"It's been here at least a year," she said finally. "They used a summoning circle. But I haven't seen an entire ship transported this way before."

"Why would anyone do such a thing?" said Raeesha.

"Why would wreckers lure ships onto the rocks? They want the cargo, of course. And anything else they can get. Ah!"

She reached deep into the mud and plucked out a small, white stone. As she wiped it clean, Rajik saw it was inscribed with an arcane symbol.

"A summoning stone," the Witch said. "There must be more of

them. It was probably these that drew us here."

Following some trace visible only to her, she walked a few paces before reaching again into the mud and pulling out another stone.

"I need to find some equipment," she explained. "These used stones aren't much, but I haven't the facilities to make new ones. Where was that campfire you mentioned?"

"Over to the west."

"See if it's still there."

Rajik climbed up on the wreck a second time, but there was no sign of the smoke he'd seen before.

"It's gone," he said.

"Then whoever lit it is also gone," said the Witch, who was still searching the mud for stones. "It might be worthwhile to inspect their campsite. Think you can find it?"

"Maybe. But we'll never get there before dark."

"Then let's have a look at the other wreck."

The other wreck was much smaller, and it was broken into pieces. It was hard to tell where it came from or the nationality of the crew, whose bones were visible here and there in the mud.

After inspecting the site, the Witch said, "They tried it here first, but the parameters were off. It wasn't the kind of ship they wanted. Also, they brought it in too high, killing the crew. They just left this one where it was and tried again."

Raeesha pulled a human femur out of the mud. "It doesn't look like it's been chewed on. I guess they aren't cannibals."

"'Cannibals' would be the wrong word, in any case," said the Witch. "'Cannibals' would mean human beings."

"So what happened to the other crew?" asked Rajik.

"Enslaved, most likely. They were needed for some kind of work. It's why one summons demons."

"But we aren't demons!"

"This is their world. We're strange creatures brought by magic from a distant plane. What else would they call us?"

"You may be a demon, but I'm not," he said stubbornly.

"You can argue about that with the natives if we run into any," said the Witch. "See if you can turn that wreckage into some kind of shelter. I'll try to start a fire."

Raeesha, who'd been looking around the wreck, gave a cry of delight and pulled something out of the mud. As she washed it off, he saw her prize was a ragged piece of sail.

"What are you planning to do with that?" asked Rajik.

"What do you think?" She poked around among the bones until she found something else, a rusty fishing knife. Then, she sat down happily and began making a new skirt for herself.

The Witch was meanwhile carving symbols on a piece of dry wood. As she muttered over it, it burst into flames.

"Ah!" she said triumphantly. "I wasn't sure that would work."

She added sticks to the fire and began washing the clams for cooking.

"Isn't that dangerous?" said Rajik. "What if the demons see it?"

"We will have to take the chance. It isn't safe to eat strange food without cooking . . . or sometimes even with."

"You mean they could be poisonous?"

"That's another chance we'll have to take."

The clams proved to be quite tasty, but the lobster-crab had many tough bony plates and very little flesh.

"If this meal doesn't kill us, we won't starve," said the Witch, who was peeling away the bark from a tree branch to make a wand.

By now, it was getting dark. A cold wind blew in from the north, causing the reeds to rustle as if a horde of stealthy feet were creeping up on them. Rajik moved closer to the fire and pulled up the collar of his shirt.

The little shelter he'd cobbled together from wreckage didn't look very secure. He picked up a piece of wood and whacked the shelter with it, testing its heft as a club. It was a puny weapon, he decided, but better than nothing.

Suddenly, Raeesha said, "I'm getting sick!" She leaned over and coughed up everything she'd eaten.

He looked at the Witch in alarm. "Were those clams poison?"

The Witch shook her head in puzzlement. "I feel fine . . ."

As if this were a signal, something came *zip* out of the dark and struck the shelter next to where Rajik was standing. An arrow.

He fell to the ground and threw handfuls of mud on the fire. "What do we do now?" he muttered.

The two women said nothing, merely crouching as low as they could. More arrows came *zip-zip* through the darkness above their heads. One landed near him. He had a closer look at it. It was a short and crudely-fletched arrow with a stone tip, but it would certainly get the job done if the attackers managed to hit them.

Raeesha drew her knife. "Here's my plan. We play dead until they get closer . . . AUGH!" She kept trying to vomit, but she'd already lost it all.

The Witch, who'd rescued a coal from the fire, was holding it in her hands and whispering to it, ignoring everything else.

Suddenly, the ground began to shake. The mud under his feet, already soft, was turning into quicksand. He got up and clutched the shelter for support. The rain of arrows had stopped. From the darkness, he could hear shrill voices, which became loud and panicky as the vibrations from the tremor grew stronger.

In front of him, a hole was forming, from which a stream of mud emerged: at first a trickle, then a fountain.

"Close your eyes! Do it now!" said the Witch. "*Yejeb ala yekwon hnak dwy!*"

He closed them just in time. A brilliant flash of light burned red through his eyelids and left him blinking. The shrill voices in the dark had turned to screams.

"Follow me! Quick!" said the Witch, and she was off and running like an antelope.

He paused a moment to help

Raeesha, who was sinking in the mud, before pursuing the Witch.
She was already a hundred feet ahead of them and increasing the
distance with every step. Cursing, he followed.

After ten paces, he turned to see if Raeesha were following.
She was. Behind her, the fountain of mud had turned into a geyser.
The place where they'd camped was already buried in mud, which
piled up higher as he watched.

All around, small humanoid forms were staggering blindly.
Their shrill voices sounded like pigs being slaughtered. As he turned
to go, he almost ran into one, looking in the starlight like a pale-
skinned child with huge dark eyes. He struck it once with his club
and kept running.

The Witch had turned and was waiting for them, her face ghost-
ly in the starlight. The earth was no longer shaking. Back in the
direction they'd come, the shrill yells were dying down. Rajik could
see the vague outline of a hill that hadn't been there before.

"What in the name of all devils was that?"

"Later," said the Witch. "We must leave this place." She turned
to go.

After they'd been stumbling around in the dark for an hour,
a small, blue moon came out, covering the swamp with unearthly
light. It was shortly joined by a second moon, larger and yellowish
in color. The wrecked ships were far behind them now. There was
nothing to be seen but the endless swamp.

"Are you going to tell us what happened?" said Rajik.

"It was the demon," said the Witch. "That's what made Raeesha sick. The demon is getting larger and stronger. This excitement
must be stimulating it."

"But what about the earthquake?"

"The demon again. As it grows, it draws more and more foreign matter to itself. This time, it was underground, perhaps because
of the planetary circumference. We will probably never know what
it was, under all that mud. However, the tremors distracted the *efaryti,* and I was able to dazzle them with a simple cantrip."

" *Efaryti?* What's that?"

"The natives. I know where we are now. The *efaryti* are a species skilled in stealth and the use of poisons. Some are sorcerers."
She looked thoughtful. "It could be worse. I've had dealings with
the *efaryti.*"

"But they tried to kill you," said Rajik. "How could that be worse?"

"A slight misunderstanding. Trust me, there are things far worse than the *efaryti*."

"Then I hope we never meet any," said Rajik.

"If you know where we are, can we go home?" asked Raeesha.

"Not yet, but we're getting closer. The first thing we have to do is get that demon embryo out of you. It's growing faster than I thought."

Raeesha stared apprehensively at her midriff. "I think I can feel it moving sometimes."

"Good. That means it will implant itself in a cyst, so I can remove it. Unfortunately, we can expect more anomalies before then."

"Like the rain of fire? Or the mud geyser?" asked Rajik.

"There's really no way of knowing."

Exhausted, they huddled together and fell asleep. When they awoke, the sun was already a handsbreadth above the horizon, and the gnats were starting to buzz around. They decided to continue without breakfast in the direction they'd been going, to the south.

The longer they walked, the worse the swamp became. The hummocks were fewer now, and the pools of water were larger. When Raeesha took a sip of water from one, she said the water was brackish. Rajik climbed to the highest point he could find, which was no more than two feet above the water. From there, he could see a thin, blue line on the horizon.

"I think we're running out of swamp," he said. "Now what?"

The Witch glanced back the way they'd come. "We may be running out of time as well. But if you still want an army, there's one following us."

8: Singer

I wish Raeesha were here.

The girl was annoyingly unpredictable, but she had a talent for sorting out tricky situations. This one was especially tricky, and if mishandled, could end in hundreds of deaths.

He was staring at a sheer cliff, almost a thousand feet high, carved from the tableland by some long-vanished river. High above, he could see a tower and part of a stone wall, and above that, the imperial banner flapped defiantly in the wind.

From the distance, he heard the faint sound of jeers and taunts. The garrison, in their hundreds, seemed ready to defend their stronghold forever. If they had enough food and water, there was no obvious reason why they couldn't. A narrow path, wide enough for one camel, snaked up the face of the cliff. It was blocked at several points by large boulders. More boulders were poised on the edge of the cliff above, ready to fall on anyone who tried to ascend.

The road circled Gedij to the left and right, but neither route was safe, so long as the fortress was defended.

The Prince said I could just bypass it!

"What do you make of this, Baron?"

Baron Hardy stroked his long, blond beard. "A hard nut to crack. I doubt our siege weapons will be of any use unless we position them on that mesa."

"And then what? Even if we knock down the walls, we have no way of assaulting Gedij."

"Can your demons can scale the cliff?"

"They probably could if no one were dropping boulders on them."

"Well, that would seem to be the problem, then."

Singer checked the sky. The sun was no longer visible, sunken behind cliffs that lined the gorge, but he guessed they had another hour of light.

"Nothing to do here today. We'll camp and wait for the rest of the army to catch up. Station some sentries. I don't like all these cliffs, and I don't want any surprises."

In the morning, the Baron came to his tent. He had a boy with him, about twelve years old, filthy and ragged. He was darker skinned than most of the Bandeluks, and his curly, black hair stuck out in all directions.

"We have a prisoner, sir," Hardy said.

"How did we manage that?"

"The sentries saw him climbing down the cliff, just before dawn."

"He seems a bit young to be a spy."

"Indeed, sir. I thought you'd want to speak to him personally."

"Good guess," said Singer, and continuing in Bandeluki: "What's your name, boy?"

"Mangasar, effendi. "

"Call me Singer. Is Mangasar a Bandeluk name? You have a strange accent."

"I'm a fatherless child. I belong to one of the desert tribes. Or I did until they traded me for some goats."

"That was unkind of them."

Mangasar shrugged. "They had too many boys and not enough goats."

"I thought the Emperor had abolished slavery."

"He did. They call it something different now."

"Have you had breakfast, Mangasar?"

Mangasar looked surprised. "No one has asked me that for a long time."

Singer gestured to a table, where his own breakfast was steaming: a large bowl of porridge with raisins. Mangasar sniffed at it suspiciously before attempting a spoonful. But soon, he abandoned all restraint and gobbled up the entire bowl within a minute.

"That was good," he said, wiping his lips on his sleeve. "But I never saw porridge on an officer's table before."

"In this army, the officers eat what the men eat. How long were you in Gedij?"

"I didn't count the days, but it was almost two months."

"Whom did you belong to?"

"Capt. Bogra. He's a hard man, and he likes boys better than girls."

"They'd probably hang me if I did that. How did you escape?"

"They were looking for people going up, not down. I climbed down in a place they weren't watching."

"Could you go back if you had to?"

"I don't think so. The climb down was bad enough, and anyway, why would I go back?"

"I need to know at what points the cliff can be scaled."

"At none, if you mean by men with armor and weapons."

"How big is the garrison?"

"A hundred imperial troops. Twice that many civilians, but most of them men. They all have weapons and know how to use them."

"Where do they get their water?"

"Gedij is covered with gutters and drains. All the rain flows into a cistern. They say there's enough water down there for a hundred years even if it never rains again."

"And food?"

"This is a base for caravans into Berbat. For the last month, Capt. Bogra has forbidden the sale of grain and oil, so some of the tribes must be getting hungry. All that food is piled up everywhere, big sacks and jars. It will spoil before they eat it all."

"Tell me Mangasar, when this is over, where'd you like to go?"

That stumped him. Mangasar scratched his dirty head, in which Singer noticed lice were crawling. "I don't know. I just don't want to go back to Gedij."

Singer turned back to Baron Hardy. "This is a clever boy, a real find. Get him some clothing. Cut his hair and scrub him down. He has lice. After lunch, we'll climb the mesa and have a look at Gedij from that angle."

In the lengthening shadows of late afternoon, a small group of officers stood on the edge of the mesa and surveyed the fortifications from a distance of 300 yards. Now and then, a spent Bandeluk arrow struck near their feet, but far more fell to the bottom of the gorge.

"I'd feel more comfortable if we were fifty yards back," said Capt. Fleming.

"Go back then," said Singer, making no move. Fleming shifted nervously, but remained with the group.

Gedij was a well-constructed castle, covering the top of the plateau. At the north end was a great tower, about eighty feet high, a fortress within a fortress. There were also three lesser towers and several outward-projecting bastions, which would give the garrison a clear shot at anyone approaching Gedij. The curtain walls were twenty feet high.

"'Tis a most imposing fastness," said Sir Gladwood.

"I'm not much impressed," said Baron Hardy. "We could easily get over those walls with a few scaling ladders."

"If they were on the flat," Singer reminded him. "What do you think, Sgt. Littleton?"

The engineer was studying the fortress with an intense expression, his eyes darting here and there as if it were a puzzle he was determined to solve. When Singer spoke, he shook his head, seeming to come out of a trance, and said, "About thirty acres, all told. Most of it just empty space. Shelter for the caravans, I guess. There are some interior fortifications on the north end, to separate it from the campground. That's the strongpoint. With our onagers, we would need weeks to breach the walls."

"How would you go about attacking it?"

Littleton ran his fingers through his stubbly beard as he thought about it. "I'd start piling rocks to make a ramp, and then run a siege tower up to the walls. It would take three or four months, perhaps."

"Any other suggestions?"

The officers looked at each other uncertainly, but said nothing.

"This is what we're going to do," said Singer. "Littleton is going to throw up some fieldworks right here. Fleming will make his camp atop the mesa and cover the defenses with his crossbows. Shoot at anything that moves."

"Pretty hard to hit anything at that range," said Fleming.

"You can make them keep their heads down. We'll disassemble the onagers, haul them up the mesa and put the castle under continuous fire. No one in Gedij gets an easy night's rest until the siege is over."

"What about the siege crossbows?" said Littleton. He loved to fire the tripod-mounted monster crossbows, which could shoot an iron bolt half a mile.

"Don't waste your ammunition on stone walls. Place them around the fort to cover the approaches. No one gets in or out unless we let them."

"And the *fui* demons?"

"I have other plans for the *fui* demons. Fleming will assign you all the workers you need."

Baron Hardy stroked his beard thoughtfully. "If you don't mind my saying so, General, this looks more like a campaign of harassment than a real siege."

"Call it a contest of wills."

Lt. Gallites, who'd been listening with a puzzled expression, said, "May I ask what you plan to do with the demons?"

"No, you may not."

Two days later, Singer had a meeting with Capt. Duvil, commander of the Invincible Legion. Duvil was a tall man with a neatly-trimmed dark beard. He had the muscular build one would expect of a man who'd been carrying a pike since he was a youngster.

In the background, both men could hear the regular *thump* of catapult stones hitting the walls of Gedij. The garrison repaired the damage almost as quickly as it occurred, but the bombardment kept them too busy for other mischief.

Duvil had built a fine, walled camp with a ditch and ramparts, directly on the northern approach to Gedij, an important strategic point. Singer studied it for only a minute before saying, "Tear it down. Make your camp on higher ground, over there."

Duvil seemed ready to throw up his hands in frustration. "After all that hard work? What's wrong with it?"

"Like I said, it needs to be on higher ground. What if there's a flood?"

Duvil glanced at the cloudless sky. "Here? In this wasteland? If that happens at all, it won't be until spring."

"You want to take that chance? You have your orders, Captain."

Quietly fuming, Duvil saluted and went to give the bad news to his men. Singer decided to check on the *fui* demons, and found them digging a deep pit. There was a small mountain of tailings nearby, rocks and boulders Fleming's men were harvesting for catapult ammunition.

The demons swarmed around the pit like ants. It was hard to tell them apart. Singer had to wait a few minutes before he spotted Twenty Three, who was carrying a boulder as big as a human being.

"How's it going?"

"We will need *bzzz* a few hours *bzzz*, and more precise *bzzz* directions."

"I thought my orders were clear."

"Orders, yes *bzzz*. We need more *bzzz* information on the *bzzz* defenses."

"I'll see what I can come up with."

An hour later, he was back in his tent with Sgt. Littleton and the nomad waif, Mangasar, who now sported new clothes and a haircut. Sheets of paper and a quill pen were set out on the table.

"We need to prepare a map of the defenses," Singer said in Bandeluki. "Do you know what a map is?"

"It's a picture of a place on a piece of paper. Capt. Bogra has one on the wall."

"Yes, good. A map shows a place as the gods see it, from above. It's made to scale, so one inch on the map means ten feet on the ground. Or it could be a hundred feet, or even a mile, depending on the kind of map. The whole map is made to the same scale, so if the great tower in Gedij is twice as big around as a smaller tower, that's how it should look on the map. Are you following me?"

Mangasar looked uncertainly at the blank paper. "I think so," he said.

Singer smiled in encouragement, but he had deep misgivings. Could this illiterate nomad really draw a decent map?

"I'll start it," he said, picking up the pen. He sketched a rough diamond shape on the paper with a circle on one end. "This is what the plateau would look like to the gods, with the great tower on the north end."

Mangasar studied the drawing for a minute, before taking the pen from his hand. "No, it's not like that. It's shaped like the head of a camel. And the great tower is the ear of the camel."

Within a minute, he'd done his own map, an improvement on Singer's crude sketch.

Impressive! But where did he learn to use a pen?

"Very good," he said. "Show me where the other towers are."

"It's easy. This tower is the eye . . . and this one the nose . . . and here is the jaw, where we tie the bridle."

"Good, good. Can you draw the outer walls?"

"Oh, yes."

Another minute, and the main defense points were all there, as if drawn by a surveyor.

"Where is the cistern located?"

Mangasar frowned. "The gods can't see the cistern because it's dark and underground. But the entrance is here. I had to go down there often, to get water."

"And what does it look like down there?"

"Dark, very dark. It's like a big cellar, almost as big as the castle. There are stairs that go down into the water, I don't know how deep. You can't see the bottom."

"It extends under the great tower?"

"Oh yes, and under the tower of the eye as well."

Singer talked to him a bit longer, drawing out all the details the boy could remember before giving the map to Sgt. Littleton. "Go make some observations. Verify all the details you can. Check the scale."

Then he called in a messenger and said, "Tell the commanders to withdraw their sentries at dawn. No one is to leave camp after dawn until further orders, except for Capt. Fleming. Fleming's men continue their bombardment as usual."

The messenger saluted and left.

I like messengers. They don't ask too many questions.

Dawn found a small group of officers standing at the same place on the edge of the mesa. A group of Fleming's crossbowmen crouched behind an improvised rampart, waiting for the sun to provide them with targets. Singer had brought Kyle, his new Standard-bearer, with him. The silver-black Free State banner flapped above their heads.

"That flag will draw a lot of fire," said Fleming.

"It won't be a problem," said Singer.

The men shifted nervously as the sun rose over Gedij. No one but Singer had any idea what was supposed to happen. Almost an hour passed, and nothing did. The monotonous *thump* of stones striking the fortress continued like the beat to a doleful song.

"Keep your eyes on the cliff," he told Kyle. "You can see better than I can."

"Yes sir. Is there anything in particular I should be looking for?"

"You'll know it when you see it."

Only a few minutes later, Kyle pointed: "There! I see a trickle of water on the cliff. No, it's more like a stream."

Then, they could all see it, a stream of water jetting out of the cliff side, about half way down, as if under great pressure. As they watched, the stream grew in volume. With a sharp *crack* a boulder gave way and fell into the gorge. And then the water became a great torrent, and the cleft it was flowing from began to widen.

By now, the defenders had noticed the water and were peering down on it from the curtain wall. Singer couldn't hear what they were saying, but their voices sounded panicky and became hysterical as the wall itself slowly tilted, then fell over the edge of the cliff.

Enough water for a hundred years!

There was no stopping the flood. Frightened Bandeluks ran in all directions as the very foundations of Gedij cracked and slid into the cistern, which had become a huge sinkhole. To Singer's shock, the great tower crumbled like a child's sand castle and joined the avalanche of rubble pouring down the cliff.

No! I only told them to dig a tunnel underneath and drain the

cistern!

There was nothing he could do as, with a great tumult, fully half the plateau broke apart, and screaming Bandeluks fell among the debris. A great, riotous wave roared down the canyon, drowning it to a depth of ten feet. Of the fortifications on the north side, nothing remained but the tower of the eye. Then, as if in afterthought, it too fell over backward into the growing pile of ruins with frantic soldiers still clinging to the parapet.

Suddenly, everything was still. The water ebbed away. There was nothing to hear but a distant whimpering of terrified voices, as the surviving Bandeluks took stock of the disaster that had befallen them.

"Wow!" said Kyle.

This is not what I wanted!

Ignorant of Singer's plan, the officers took turns congratulating him.

"Gedij has fallen in just three days, and we didn't lose a man!" said Capt. Duvil in wonder.

"I did not expect this," said Capt. Fleming. "It exceeds any plan I could have devised."

"Entirely beyond my experience, which is considerable," said Baron Hardy, shaking his head in amazement.

Only young Lt. Gallites seemed disturbed by the wanton destruction. He turned and looked at Singer as if waiting for an explanation. Singer avoided his eyes.

Now I have another massacre on my head! There's nothing left to do, but pick up the pieces.

"Cease the bombardment," he said dispiritedly. "Let's go see what we have left."

Where a cliff had stood a few moments before, there was now a slope, which they found easy to climb. The broken and twisted limbs of Bandeluks were visible here and there in the debris. Occasionally, under their feet, they heard the faint, muffled voices of people trapped in the rubble and calling for help. Singer sent the *fui* demons to dig out those who could still be saved.

As they approached the remains of the fortress, a few shocked and despondent survivors appeared and quickly surrendered. Singer counted only twenty-five, out of a population Mangasar had estimated at three hundred.

So much blood! When will it ever end?

On top of the plateau, there was no castle left, only two small towers and a curtain wall between them. One of the bastions now jutted out of an abyss, protecting the empty air from any attackers. The former campground was still piled with sacks of grain and jars of cooking oil as Mangasar had reported.

"Looks like we have a windfall," Singer said.

"Right you are, sir," said Gallites. "Our supply problem has been solved, for the time being."

"How many of those jars can we carry?"

"I expect we can get most of them, but that would leave no space for the grain."

"Then take the oil, and leave the grain."

"May I ask why, sir?"

"No, you may not."

Singer tossed and turned half the night on his cot, tormented by the distant songs of men celebrating the easy victory, and especially by the unnerving chant, "SINGER! SINGER! SINGER!" which broke out all too often.

Now, they think I'm invincible! What happens when they learn they're wrong?

It had been a mistake to trust the *fui* demons. They were notoriously careless of human life. He suspected they'd deliberately destroyed the fortress, just to spite him. But there was no proof, and even if there were, what could he do about it?

Too late for regrets. I will just have to pretend I planned it this way.

He couldn't make it good, he could only make it look good. It was probably just as well no one cared about all those dead people.

No one but me! How can I live this way?

Eventually, the songs and chanting died down, and he fell into a troubled sleep with many dreams full of sly demons and falling towers. When he woke, the tent was bright with sunlight. The first thing he noticed was the dagger sticking out of his pillow, an inch from his nose.

Heart pounding, he jumped out of bed and reached for his sword, but the tent was empty.

Someone has been in here! Who?

He could ask the guards, but they would just say they'd seen nothing. What else could they say? He leaned over to take a closer look at the dagger. The hilt was finely carved ebony. When he pulled it out, he saw it was only six inches long, with a wavy blade.

Beneath the knife was a small piece of parchment with a note in the Bandeluki script:

> The Hierophant summons you! Come to Debel Kresh. Come now. Come alone. There is much to discuss.

Singer frowned. The message was clear: If he didn't come, the next dagger would not end up in his pillow. This threat had to be taken seriously.

That's how Amir Qilij died, in his own palace, with his guards all around him! This is some country for assassins!

He looked closely at the knife, which was double-edged and very sharp. When he tested the edge, he nicked his finger. As his blood dripped to the ground, he admired the little murder instrument.

Someone twisted an iron bar, and beat it flat, and twisted and beat again until he made this, a knife shaped like a serpent.

Still, the blade was very short and thin, not something he'd carry into battle. The hilt, too, was oddly-shaped and stunted as if made for someone with tiny hands.

This is no weapon of war, just a child's toy . . .

He called Mangasar into the tent. When the boy saw what he was holding, his eyes grew round. "A flame dagger! It brings doom to all who behold it!"

"Why are you afraid? It's only a knife."

"It belongs to the Spectral Slayers! They come unseen in the night, and leave death everywhere! No one escapes them!"

"But why would the Spectral Slayers be interested in me?"

"They serve the god of death! He has marked you out! Your fate is sealed!"

"Mangasar, you don't know me, so I should explain a few things. I was promoted to commander when a demon took my predecessor's head. I stepped into the place he left vacant. My successor will do the same. We're not like the Bandeluks. When one falls, another replaces him. We serve the god of war, and death is only his servant."

He turned and brought the dagger down sharply on his own helmet, which was lying on a table. The flame dagger broke into pieces. He tossed the hilt aside.

Mangasar glared at him, outraged. "No one who defies the Hierophant escapes death!"

"It would simpler to say that everyone dies. You may go."

9: Erika

Damn, damn, damn, damn, damn!

Seen from the docks on the river, the Akaddian capital city of Elohi was immense. It was built on a mountain, and it dominated the surrounding countryside, with its five stacked rows of city walls, each with its own gates and towers, sheltering terraces crowded with residences, shops and inns, whose peaked roofs sometimes poked out among the crenellations. Above them all was the glittering royal palace, which seemed to be made of polished silver as the sun reflected brilliantly from the many glass windows of its great hall.

Somewhere up there, presumably near the top, was the home of Duchess Thea. It would take the entire day to reach it if she could manage it at all with the heavy travelling bag in her left hand and the heavier bag of cloth samples in her right.

I need help!

The docks were crowded with rough-looking sailors and longshoremen, all occupied with their tasks. They brushed rudely past her without saying anything, sparing only a brief, lecherous glance when they took note of her at all. There was no one she could ask for assistance.

Seeing no alternative, she lifted her bags and picked her way among the crates, barrels, coils of rope and other obstacles which left only a narrow path between her and the shore. Ahead of her, seated a little above the crowd, she could see a tallish individual, whose red box coat and top hat identified him as a coachman.

Gods be praised!

The coachman stared vacantly into space, showing a lordly disdain for the stream of humanity that flowed past, a disagreeable rabble beneath his notice. He also ignored Erika, even when she loudly cleared her throat.

"Are you for hire, sir?" she said finally.

The coachman looked down imperiously at her. "I am not," he said. "But my coach may be, to appropriate clients. You would not seem to be one of those."

"Appearances may be deceiving. My business is with the

Duchess Thea."

"Really?" he said skeptically. "You don't look like one of her servants. They're a snooty little clan and always impeccably dressed. You look more like a shopkeeper."

That came painfully close to the truth. Erika realized she didn't cut an impressive figure in her soiled travel suit and especially while carrying two heavy bags. Fortunately, a solution occurred to her.

"How much?" she said simply, offering a handful of silver.

That brought him around. "I couldn't charge you less than three krones. The Duchess has a big pile on the Promenade, near the Palace. It will take me over an hour to get there. The horses will be exhausted."

What an outrageous price!

"Done," she said, and not waiting for him to help her, shoved her bags into the coach, then climbed onto the seat beside him.

"What are you doing?" he said, his face red with indignation.

"Sitting down. Do you mind? There appears to be plenty of room."

"But a lady does not sit with the coachman! It isn't done!"

"A minute ago, I was a shopkeeper, but now I'm a lady? Stop telling me who I am and what I should do, and start earning your fee!

"I'd be much obliged," she added, "if you would point out the local landmarks, as I'm a stranger here. And also tell me anything you may know about the Duchess Thea. There's another krone in it if your information is helpful."

It soon became obvious the coachman had hardly ever seen the Duchess Thea though he had sometimes driven her servants around the city and even overheard their gossip, but nothing of much interest to Erika. However, as a guide to Elohi, he was voluble and enthusiastic:

"On our right is the King's Rest, so called because King Amyleus once spent the night there though some say it was only a brief assignation. You will find inns that are equally reputable and a good deal cheaper on Koral Street. . . .

"The structure to our left is the Temple of Narina. As you can see, the steps are infested with beggars, some of them also talented pickpockets. There's a side entrance for persons of quality though you wouldn't gain admittance there, dressed as you are . . .

"That fountain is called the Three Ladies because of the ancient statuary, which is older than the city itself. It's said to be a Moietian shine, but no one really knows for sure. The water, which is quite palatable, comes from a natural spring . . .

"That narrow street to the side is Klipper Lane. It's home to the city's best jewelers. The guards strictly control entry and observe all visitors. You would need an introduction to get in. Thieves are never arrested on Klipper Lane; they simply disappear. The massive wall behind it belongs to the Upper Reservoir . . ."

Erika encouraged him with smiles, nods and occasional exclamations of wonder. An older man, he found her company so charming he sometimes forgot what he was doing and had to be prompted to get the coach moving again. It was almost two hours before they arrived in front of a stately-looking building fronted with eight marble columns, the mansion of Duke Claudio and Duchess Thea.

The coachman insisted on carrying her bags to the door. He tipped his hat courteously when she paid him off and departed with a friendly wave, whistling pleasantly to himself.

I seem to have brightened his day. Let's see what I can do with the Duchess Thea.

The mansion had an elaborately-carved double door eight feet tall. Erika raised the heavy brass knocker, which was in the form of a balled fist, and let it fall on the metal plate. It made a resounding *clunk.*

She'd waited over a minute and was wondering whether to knock again, when a panel in the door, which she hadn't noticed before, suddenly flew open, and a stern-looking elderly man looked down at her.

"If you're the new upstairs maid, you should use the rear entrance," he said, "and you will need to wash and change your clothing before I can present you to the housekeeper."

"I'm not the maid, I am Lady Erika of Tidewater, and my business is with the Duchess. I have a letter of introduction," she said, offering it.

His blue eyes narrowed suspiciously when he saw the grimy, creased letter, but widened when he recognized the seal. He snatched the letter from her hand and, without another word, shut the panel in her face.

That did not go very well.

There was nothing to do but sit on her bags and wait for the butler to come back. She watched elegant couples strolling among the great and lofty mansions and the shrubby, little, over-pruned trees of the Promenade. Apparently, this was the place to be in Elohi. She noticed most of the women were clad in fine satin.

Not much of that for sale! Looks like I may have an opportunity!

After ten minutes, the butler opened the door behind her and announced, "The Duchess awaits you in the drawing room."

As she reached for her bags, he impatiently brushed her hand aside and said in the manner of one correcting a child, "I will take those, madam."

Take them to where? I guess I shouldn't ask. But at least I'm a "madam" now!

The dark paneling of the entry hall was decked with weapons, suits of armor and banners. Some were centuries old, but all seemed ready for immediate use. Her heels rang hollowly on the parquet floor as she strode between the relics of old battles.

The Duke and Duchess haven't forgotten where their power really comes from.

The "drawing room" was a separate wing, larger than most of the city's homes, illuminated by French doors that looked out on a garden ornamented with fantastic topiary. The Duchess Thea awaited her, a stately woman of middle years, made taller by her elaborate blonde coiffure. She wore a lacy tea gown and was clutching a crumpled letter. Erika knew exactly what it said, under all the smudges and water stains:

Dearest Thea!

I must once again rely on you to assist me in an affair of the heart. This young woman, Erika by name, is my wife by a secret marriage. She has some fabric she wishes to sell and also some entertaining stories that may enliven your soirees, but her work is really a matter of great importance. I would be most grateful if you would consider her your protégé until I am able to return and relieve you of the inconvenience. Your loving brother,

Clenas

The Duchess startled Erika by bending in a deep curtsey.

What? Oh, a princess out-ranks a duchess, of course. She's testing me.

Her curtsey was equally deep. "Please, your Grace," she said modestly, "you mustn't show me any deference. I'm travelling incognito, as you can see."

The Duchess stood and inspected her. "I do see. A perfect disguise," she said without a hint of irony. "I'd have taken you for a common tradeswoman."

Erika felt her cheeks getting red. "You must excuse my appearance, your Grace. I've come directly from the front in Chatmakstan, am without a maid and have had no opportunity to replace my wardrobe."

The Duchess raised one eyebrow. "What were you doing at the front, may I ask?"

"I was making my own small contribution to the war effort by nursing the sick and wounded. I had the honor of attending your brother, Prince Krion, during his recent indisposition."

The Duchess smiled maliciously. "I heard something about that. It's really true, then, that only a witch can find the way into his heart."

So, Krion isn't her favorite brother.

"His heart is a closely-guarded fortress, and I made no attempt to storm it, by witchcraft or other means. As soon as he'd recovered sufficiently, he invited me to display my patriotism somewhere else."

"Or in other words, he ungratefully expelled you as soon as he was able. That does sound like Krion. What brings you here?"

"I was moved by the suffering of your countrymen and mine, in that awful place. They're far from their homes and loved ones, and plagued by shortages of every kind. I'm sure your Grace appreciates the logistical difficulty of supplying so large an army far from home."

The Duchess' blank stare suggested she hadn't thought about it much.

Let's see where I can go with that.

"With Prince Clenas' encouragement," she continued, "I've devised a modest plan whereby the wives and sisters of our fighting men can make a real contribution to the war effort, without the hardship of travelling to Chatmakstan, or enduring Prince Krion's uncertain temper.

"As you know, there is a shortage of fabric for dressmaking. Silks and satins were imported from the Bandeluk heartland, but this trade is now closed to us. I have, however, discovered a product native to Chatmakstan that the natives call *pamuk,* but I would prefer to christen Patriot Silk. This fabric is as fine as it is strong and is quite suitable for summer dresses or undergarments.

"I've brought some samples, with which I hope to introduce this product here in Elohi. If the ladies of Akaddia can be persuaded to adopt Patriot Silk for their dresses, it will improve the balance of trade. Because, you see, the funds thus generated may be used to advance the war effort: Ships bearing fabric to Akaddia could carry supplies in the opposite direction, for the relief of our soldiers and the civilian population as well."

Would that really work? I think it might!

The Duchess frowned as if she were trying to solve a problem in higher mathematics. "That all sounds rather promising," she said finally. "But I wonder what my husband would say about it."

" I'd be delighted to explain it to him. The importation of Patriot Silk will mean a new source of revenues for the Exchequer. The crown will, of course, collect its share of the trade, in both directions."

Making your own purse that much heavier.

The Duchess looked uncertain. "I don't believe we're quite ready to discuss the matter with my husband. I'd like to inspect your fabric personally and also hear what my dressmaker says about it.

"In the meanwhile, I suggest that you dress for dinner. Lukas will show you to your room. I'll ask my maid to pick out two or three dresses that may be suitable for a private dinner with the family. We will speak of this later. Until then, I'd advise you not to mention it to anyone."

"I am most grateful." She could only curtsey and go where the butler led her, to a small but plushly-furnished room on the second floor. Alone, she danced around it for a moment in elation.

I'm in! I'm in! I'm in!

10: Raeesha

The demons were looking at her and squeaking among themselves. One of them kept poking her in the stomach. She brushed the small, clawed hand away, and a minute later, it did it again. She shifted uncomfortably, but there was no escape.

Beside her, Rajik was cheerfully stuffing himself with the food the demons had served, mainly flatbread with stewed tubers and the omnipresent clams. There was also a pitcher of flat ale, from which he drank liberally. She was still queasy at the thought of something moving around inside her and barely touched the food though it seemed wholesome enough.

At the other end of the hall, the Witch was engaged in squeaky conversation with the demon matriarch, a huge, fat *efaryt* heavily decked in strings of beads.

At least they're talking and not trying to kill us.

She wasn't sure why the demons had brought them here at all, to this miserable village of grass huts crowded together on a small hilltop. They were taken to the central hall, which was like the other huts, only bigger.

Instead of killing them, the matriarch had spread a feast before them and offered one word of tortured Bandeluki: "Welcome!" It was the only comprehensible sound any of the *efaryti* had made. Raeesha didn't see how the Witch could make any sense out of their weird bat-noises, much less pronounce them, but she suspected magic had something to do with it.

She's probably offering to sell us to them, in exchange for passage back to Kafra.

She glanced suspiciously to where the Witch had gotten in a fierce argument with the matriarch. The bat-noises were becoming loud and painful to the ears. Even the other demons stopped eating and turned to look.

Finally, the Witch stood up and headed for the door. The matriarch grabbed her by the ankle, but instead of jerking her roughly, made soft, chirrupy noises that sounded almost like an apology. The Witch sat back down.

The demon poked her in the stomach again. She slapped its hand away.

"What's wrong with this thing?"

"Besides being a demon?" said Rajik, chewing on the clam roll he'd made for himself. "He thinks you're cute. This is the language of love."

"How do you say 'go away' in the language of love?"

"Easy," said Rajik when he'd finished swigging some more of the ale. "Do what heartless women always do. Crush his hopes by ignoring him."

The demon poked her again.

I should have known better than to expect any help from Rajik.

The Witch and the matriarch were getting friendly. They made cooing noises at each other instead of harsh squeaks. As Raeesha watched, the matriarch hugged the Witch, then sliced her thumb with a knife, allowing the blood to run into a cup on the table. The Witch repeated the gesture, mixing her blood with the demon's. Each took a small sip from the cup. They hugged again.

I guess that means we have a deal.

Picking her way among the feasting demons, the witch approached them with a satisfied look on her face. "It's a reciprocal pact," she said.

"What does that mean?" said Rajik, who'd drunk too much ale. "Are we going home?"

"Not quite yet. But they were impressed with our magical powers and especially with the earthquake. These *efaryti* are called Ghost Feet. They have enemies called Wind Bags, whom I promised to destroy."

"What?" said Raeesha and Rajik together.

"The Wind Bags can fly. They raid this place and take slaves, then go back to the hills. It was they who wrecked the ship."

"These Wind Bags sound dangerous," said Raeesha. "How are we supposed to destroy them? And why should we anyway?"

"I don't know how. We will have to think of something. As for why, I was able to obtain some important concessions in exchange."

"Like what?"

"They promised not to kill us."

"We're going to fight a bunch of demons, just so another bunch of demons promises not to kill us?"

"It seemed like a good enough reason. But this pact is reciprocal, meaning they can't break it without injury to themselves."

"And neither can we?"

"Naturally. But in the end, we can go home."

"How do we get there?" said Rajik, who was finding this hard to follow.

"I haven't worked that all out yet. But now we have more resources. The first thing is to get rid of the demon embryo before it causes more trouble."

The *efaryt* next to Raeesha poked her again.

This is very annoying.

"Why does it keep doing that?"

"It's just curious. It can see your navel, but doesn't know what it's for. There's some speculation."

"Tell it to go away!"

"I don't think that would be wise. I've only just completed some difficult negotiations . . ."

"Negotiate this!" Raeesha dumped the ale pitcher on the demon's head. The other demons broke into a loud chittering that sounded like laughter as it scurried away.

"Now you're communicating!" said Rajik.

"Yes, I think I like this language of . . . WUP!"

The demon had come back and poured the contents of a pot on her head. It contained nothing nearly as palatable as ale. Rajik held his nose and backed away from her. The malicious laughter of the demons was loud in her ears.

"Better go wash that off," advised the Witch. Raeesha fled without another word.

At the bottom of the hill was a pond. She threw herself in and soaked until she could no longer smell the filth the demon had thrown on her.

Floating in the warm water and staring at the pale purple sky, she felt her body relax. The terror and misery of the last few days gradually drained away. No matter what else happened, this place was peaceful and even pleasant. She could feel the cool wind that blew down from the hills, causing the reeds to rustle . . .

Wait!

She jumped up and went to the place where she'd heard the reeds. There were three half-grown demon sprats crouching among them and glaring at her resentfully. One held a primitive wooden bow, but made no move to draw it.

Oh, did I spoil your game, little Ghost Feet?

She took the bow and inspected it: This was no Bandeluk recurved bow, just a bent stick, crudely shaped with a knife, with a string twisted from plant fibre. Even the Chatmaks had better bows than this.

She'd lost her thumb ring, but the string wasn't hard to pull. Experimentally, she nocked one of the stubby, stone-tipped arrows and drew it as far as it would go, aiming at a nearby tree stump.

Thunk!

A square hit in the middle showed Umar's archery lessons hadn't been forgotten. She gave the sprat its bow back and pointed at the stump, an obvious dare. The demon sprat glared fiercely at the stump and pulled the bow string as far as it could.

Swish!

The arrow overshot the stump and disappeared among the reeds. The sprat hissed, while its companions chittered scornfully. Raeesha gave the bow to a second demon sprat, who also missed.

I see what they're doing wrong.

No one had taught these demons to shoot properly. They just

pulled the nock to the cheek, holding it with the thumb and fore-finger. She showed the bow to the third sprat, who seemed appre-hensive. Having just heaped derision on its companions, it now ex-pected some abuse in return.

She pointed at the bow with her finger until she felt sure it was watching, then slowly raised it and aimed with the nock at her ear and three fingers wrapped around the string.

Thunk!

The third sprat took the bow and tried to hold it as Raeesha had.

Thunk!

Chortling gleefully, the victorious sprat waved the bow, the proof of its superiority. The other two, having observed the trick, tried to take the bow away. Raeesha gave it to the one who'd fired first.

Half an hour later, she'd moved a hundred feet away from the target, and all three sprats were hitting it regularly. However, they were nearly submerged in a crowd of newcomers, immature demons who fought with each other for turns with the bow.

If only I could get them to stand in line!

Occupied with this problem, she paid no attention to what was happening above her on the hill until the Witch sharply cleared her throat. Beside her stood a crowd of demon grown-ups, who were watching in fascination.

"They want to know what magic you're using with the bow," said the Witch.

"Tell them my navel is a magic eye that makes arrows fly straight, and they must not to touch it if they want to defeat the Wind Bags."

11: Bardhof

This just keeps getting worse.

He was standing in one of the Amir's well-equipped torture chambers under the Temple of Justice. It was dark. The room was illuminated only by a small lamp at the clerk's table and the great heap of glowing red coals in front of his latest victim. Naked and hanging from the ceiling by his thumbs, which had been tied together behind him, his toes barely touched the floor, doing nothing to relieve the agony that must be screaming from every joint in his body.

But from the victim's mouth came only a babble: whimpers, protests and prayers, which the translator didn't bother to repeat.

This is the most stubborn one yet.

He was certain the man had valuable information. He'd been caught with false papers and a list of the ships in the harbor, written in Bandeluki and hidden in his turban. Bardhof himself had had a taste of what he was experiencing, having found this old, forbidden torture in a history book and experimented upon himself. He couldn't tolerate this interrogation method for more than a few minutes, but somehow, the little Bandeluk had been standing there for half an hour and, despite the sweat pouring down his scrawny body, showed no sign of breaking.

Will Narina forgive me?

It didn't bear thinking on. He'd already interrogated dozens of people and sent most home with nothing worse than a bad scare and a warning against breaking the curfew or whatever else had led to their arrest. But now that he actually had some solid evidence against a suspect, the man was being mulish, and he was tempted to try out some of the torture implements – pinchers, thumbscrews and things dreadful to contemplate – that lay in easy reach.

I didn't join the army so I could be a torturer.

Of course, no one cared what he wanted. He'd sworn loyalty and obedience to the Prince, and the Prince demanded quick results, no matter how they were obtained.

Grimald, sweating heavily under his chain shirt, was hitting the man on the thighs with a leather strap. He'd been at it for over fifteen minutes and had raised welts on half the spindly body. But the prisoner hardly even seemed to notice, and big Grimald was getting tired.

"Leave off, it isn't doing any good."

As Grimald gratefully relaxed, Bardhof moved closer to the victim, so close he could feel the oven-like heat from the great brazier, in which iron torture implements were glowing. He didn't understand what the man was saying, but it had a rhythmic, repetitive quality, like a chant.

This was clearly a professional. He'd been trained to resist interrogation and was probably doing some kind of mental exercise to shield himself from the pain. Bardhof felt sure wouldn't get any results unless he could find a way to break the man's concentration. More pain would obviously not do it.

There was a beaker of water on the clerk's table. He grabbed the victim's hair, tilted his head back and poured water down his throat. The man coughed and sputtered in surprise, then drank eagerly. Bardhof let him have his fill.

Then, while the man was still confused, he held his face close and looked in his eyes. "I thought you were a reasonable fellow, and so I spared you the treatment you undoubtedly deserve," he said.

There was an unfortunate pause while the translator – a plump, middle-aged Covenant man named Hingaft, who'd been conscripted from a merchant vessel – nervously repeated his words in Bandeluki. Barhof heard the *scratch-scratch* of the clerk's pen as he added to the transcript.

"But now, we're getting close to supper time, and I refuse to miss a meal for the likes of you. So I'll make this quick."

He reached over with a gloved hand and took glowing hot pincers from the brazier. He held these an inch from the man's face.

"I'm going to take your nose. If you still don't speak, I will take an eye. Then the other one. In the end, you will tell me everything I want to know."

The man's eyes widened as the hot iron approached. At the first touch, he screamed, and Hingaft grabbed Bardhof's arm. Barhof was about to tell him to let go, but the plump translator was now busy, trying to keep up with the frantic babble coming

Liz Clarke 2014

from the prisoner's mouth:

"I know nothing! I'm just a courier! I was to take pieces of paper from a barrel near the docks and leave them under a brick behind the temple! That's all!"

He didn't endure so much of torture just for that.

Hingaft was staring at him now, blue eyes full of hope that the confession was enough. But of course, it wasn't.

Bardhof grabbed Hingaft by the throat and yelled at him in the Covenant dialect, a language no Bandeluk was likely to know: "LISTEN! TELL HIM I'M ANGRY BECAUSE YOU INTERFERED! TELL HIM YOU ARE AFRAID NEITHER OF YOU WILL GET OUT OF THIS ALIVE! YOU UNDER-STAND?"

Hingaft didn't need much encouragement to look frightened. He nodded vigorously. Bardhof turned his back and examined the torture instruments while Hingaft whispered feverishly to the prisoner.

Feeling no need to hurry, Bardhof picked out the most gruesome device he could find. A testicle crusher, maybe? He didn't recognize it, but the prisoner did because he promptly emitted another flood of Bandeluki.

"He got his orders from a place on Aleskafy Street," said

Hingaft, who was now sweating as profusely as the prisoner. "He couldn't see who gave them because of the grill on the door, but there were three brass stars on the lintel, and there's only one like it in Kafra."

Both the prisoner and the translator stared at him in dread as he played with the torture instrument a moment longer. Perhaps it was a tongue extractor; he still wasn't sure.

Let them sweat a minute longer.

Finally, he said, "That's enough for now. Return him to his cell. And send the doctor to see him. We may have more questions later."

As the prisoner was led away, Hingaft approached him with the desperately hopeful expression of a starving mongrel. "Please Captain, I beg you to excuse me. I can't take any more of this."

"If I can take it, then you can. Follow me."

This is getting a lot nastier than I expected.

He had the uneasy feeling it would get even worse before the night was over.

Half an hour later, he stood in front of the house with three stars above the door, while the city watch formed a cordon around it. They didn't inspire much confidence. The watchmen were dressed in blue uniforms and armed only with truncheons. They looked around nervously in the dim light as if something were about to jump on them.

Turncoats. Hired thugs. Loyalty doubtful, morale hopeless. No use in a real fight.

Besides the watch, he had only his personal staff with him. He'd sent a runner to the Heavy Assault Group, but there was still no sign of reinforcements.

He studied the building he was waiting to storm. A three-story, tiled masonry structure, there was little distinguish it from dozens of others, except for the stars on the lintel. The windows on the first floor were heavily barred, and the solid, wooden door was bound with iron.

He turned to Hisaf, who was critically watching his men while fingering the hilt of his sword. "Do you know who lives here?"

Hingaft translated: "A gem dealer named Omin. I don't know much about him."

"You should." He turned to Grimald and Murdoon. "What do you think is keeping them?"

"Suiting up," said Murdoon.

"Yep," said Grimald. "Takes most of an hour to strap on all that gear."

"Unfortunately, we don't have . . ." A sudden, bright glow from a third-floor window caught his attention. It was followed by a cloud of smoke that streamed skyward.

"FOLLOW ME! WE'RE GOING IN!" he yelled to everyone and no one. Drawing his saber he charged the front door . . . and came to an embarrassed stop. The door, of course, was locked.

"Allow me, sir," said Murdoon, throwing his weight against it.

"Idjit!" said Grimald as Murdoon bounced and fell on his rump. He drove the spike on the back of his axe into the door jamb and, pulling the handle for leverage, tore it open. There was a faint *tink* as an arrow, fired from within, glanced off his helmet.

Bardhof charged inside and felt the light touch of a second arrow as it whizzed past his ear. There was a pile of furniture in front of him. Men with bows crouched behind it. He vaulted the barricade at the lowest point, meanwhile slashing at a bowman, who dropped his weapon and grabbed his face, blood streaming between his fingers.

Now there was a broad staircase before him. Not waiting to see what happened behind him, he charged directly up, taking the stairs two at a time. A third arrow clattered as it flew past him and bounced down the stairs.

On the second floor were two frightened-looking women dressed like servants, who shrieked as they saw his bloody sword. He brushed past them and continued up the stairs. Below him, near the entrance, he could hear screams and the sounds of fighting.

On the third floor, there was a landing with five doors. He picked the one nearest the window where he'd seen the flames. The brass knob burned his hand as he threw the door open. A choking cloud of smoke surrounded him. He could see nothing in the room but smoke and flames, and indistinctly, a still form lying in the middle of the floor. He shut the door to keep the flames from spreading.

Whatever was in there is gone. He must have spread lamp oil around, lit it and then killed himself.

The landing was filling with smoke, but there were still four doors left. The first opened into an elegantly furnished bedroom. Seeing nothing of interest, he tried the second one, which proved to be another room like the first.

The third room was a small study with a bookcase on one wall and a desk against another. A young man was slouched over the desk. Blood pooled on the floor beneath him, dripping from the knife hilt in his back. It didn't take Bardhof long to see he was dead.

Some clerk or secretary, he was hard at work when his boss came in and stabbed him.

The room had been ransacked. Half the books were on the floor. The desk held nothing but a stack of blank paper and some writing instruments. He checked it for secret compartments, but found nothing.

Wait. If this man was working when he died, then what was he working on?

He grabbed the corpse by the collar and pulled it away from the desk. Beneath it lay a blank sheet of paper. Disappointed, he was turning to go when he noticed a strange odor.

Lemons. Why does this room smell of lemons?

He grabbed the inkwell and dashed the contents on the floor. No ink spilled out, but something that looked and smelled like lemon juice.

Invisible ink!

He picked up the blank sheet and sniffed. It too reeked of lemons.

They were using lemon juice for invisible ink. Whatever document the clerk was transcribing is gone, but the killer overlooked the copy underneath the corpse.

He carefully folded the paper and put it in his pocket. As he stepped back onto the landing, he had to cough. There was smoke everywhere. It was pouring from under the arsonist's door.

Only one door remained, and it was locked. He threw his weight against it, but without effect.

Forget it! I'm not getting killed over this!

It was hard to breathe. His eyes were running, and he could barely see where he was going as he made his way back to the staircase. At the top of the stairs, he bumped into Murdoon, who was coming up.

"Are you all right, sir?"

"Fine . . ." He coughed. "Let's get out of here."

There was a haze of smoke now on the second floor and no

sign of the maids, who must have seen the folly of lingering. On the first floor, he was surprised to see Hisaf with a bloody sword in his hand. Even more surprisingly, several watchmen had followed him into the building.

"Get your men out of here. Call the fire brigade."

"Yes sir!" said Hisaf in passable Akaddian, before repeating the orders in Bandeluki.

Hisaf is tricky. Does he really know nothing about the death of Amir Qilij?

At the moment, he had more urgent matters to deal with. The watchmen had herded some prisoners together in the street and were tending to their wounds. Another watchman was kneeling by a prostrate figure who had an arrow in the chest. It was Hingaft. Bardhof could see he was dead.

He paused for a moment, expecting to feel some compassion for the man who'd briefly served him, then died so senselessly, far from home. But he felt nothing; his compassion was burned out. All he could think was:

Now, I have to find another translator, on top of everything else!

Behind him, shrill screams announced the presence of a woman at a third-floor window. Some of the watch moved in that direction, but there was no way to reach her. The whole building was enveloped in flames. He glanced indifferently at the desperate figure.

You'll just have to jump or die, lady. I have no time for you.

FROM: Capt. Bardhof, Investigating Officer
TO: Prince Krion, Commander-in-Chief of the Allied Forces
SUBJECT: Incident on Aleskafy Street

Acting on information obtained from a prisoner, members of the military police, assisted by the city watch, raided a suspect house on Aleskafy Street. Evidence from prisoners suggests it had served as the headquarters of a spy ring dedicated to domestic surveillance, independent of the local government and perhaps unknown to it.

The resident spymaster killed himself and his chief assistant, and set fire to the building before it could be assaulted. A prisoner named Anahita, self-identified as a courtesan, said he was a native of Kosizar, living under the name Omin and posing as a gem dealer. She was unable to provide further details.

An intercepted document suggests the spy ring was engaged in monitoring allied shipping. Its further activities are not known in detail, with one notable exception:

A letter written in invisible ink, found in the burning building, reports recent contact with an allied officer, known by the code name "Creeper". This person claimed to represent a clique or faction that was prepared to offer the Empire a truce, in event of a change in the allied command. No further information on this group is presently available.

"Hmm," said Krion, who was casually munching on his breakfast as he read the report. "They don't give up easily. We just buried Basilius, and already someone else wants my job."

"Yes, my Prince," said Bardhof, staring hungrily at the fruit, bread and cheese spread out before his commanding officer. – He'd missed both supper and breakfast. – "And their plot is already so far advanced, they're ready to approach the Bandeluks with a peace offer."

"There may be some problems with that," said Krion, taking a sip of strong, black tea. "I wonder who this Creeper is. That name is suggestive."

"Or possibly misleading. We found no clues to his identity."

The Prince unconcernedly nibbled on some grapes as he replied, "I'm sure something will turn up. How's your work going otherwise?"

"In general, quite well. We've disabled the principal enemy spy network in this region. But . . ." – He paused. – " . . . there is as yet no sign of Sgt. Raeesha or the Witch."

Oh that," said Krion. "I should have told you. My new sorcerer says they will no longer be a problem. Based on his investigation, they were both transported to a distant plane of existence."

"So he plans to bring them back?"

Krion looked surprised. "Why would he do that?"

12: Nergui

I hate Seserils!

It didn't help that he, Nergui Pasha, had himself been born to the steppe people. As a boy, they'd sent him with a tribute caravan to the capital, where he had the fortune to serve as a page in the imperial palace, before being selected for military training.

Now he was the *mushir,* the high commander of the imperial army, with three horse tails on his standard and over a hundred thousand men under him, but the years were all swept away as he watched the mounted column approaching over the plain. Unwelcome memories from his childhood came flooding back: yurts crowded with unwashed bodies, endless battles with fleas, meal after meal of yogurt and greasy mutton.

From the distance, the Seseril horde was just a formless mass, befouling the landscape with a cloud of reddish dust. But as it came nearer, he could pick out the Khan's vanguard: squat warriors on shaggy steppe horses, clad in silk and mail. They were riding, he saw with great annoyance, under a standard with four horse tails.

His horse stamped impatiently, unaccustomed to standing around for so long. Other horses were doing likewise, he noticed, but his men kept them in check, and the formation held. To receive the Khan, he'd gathered an honor guard of 20,000 mailed lancers, half *sipahis* from the provinces and half his own elite *kapikulu.* Behind them stood the many-towered city of Kosizar, the imperial capital, and he was determined that none of the unruly auxiliaries from the steppes would set foot there.

Illiterate horse butchers! Liars and thieves!

The Seserils were drawn naturally to war like flies to shit. Under the pretext of doing a loyal vassal's military service, the Khan had led his horde through two imperial provinces. They'd helped themselves to crops and cattle, and doubtless expected to be quartered through the winter at imperial expense. Seserils couldn't be counted on in a real battle, but they'd certainly seize every opportunity to gather loot, no matter from whom.

The Seserils were upon him. The Khan's vanguard halted a

hundred feet away. Units of the regular cavalry, dressed in padded leather coats and fur hats, and carrying spears, fanned out to the right and left as if arraying themselves for battle. In the middle, he could see Hulegu Khan himself, a fat man, gorgeously arrayed in red silk and gilded mail, holding a fly whisk in his hand.

The fat man beckoned with the fly whisk, bidding Nergui come.

They pile insult upon insult! Now he expects deference from his own commander!

Patience exhausted, he spurred his horse and went forward with only his personal bodyguard behind him. Not waiting for the Khan to speak, he said, "His Imperial Majesty bids me extend to you his greetings and make you welcome."

The Khan flicked his fly whisk as if a bothersome insect were before him. "I thank his Imperial Majesty for his greetings," he said, "and look forward to making my obeisance."

"The Emperor is unfortunately occupied with affairs of state and cannot grant you a personal audience," Nergui said. "We've prepared a campground for you and your men to spend the night. Tomorrow, my men will escort you on the road to Saramaia, where our forces are gathering to

face the enemy."

The Khan grinned slyly. Both men knew no military operations were expected until spring. Nergui was just inviting his troublesome guests to leave.

"Please convey to his Imperial Majesty my dutiful wish to make the traditional obeisance of our people to the imperial throne and renew our historic bonds. Also, my men are tired from their long journey and will need several days' rest before they can continue. And of course, as loyal subjects, they're eager to see the imperial city."

Ten thousand dirty nomads wandering around the capital, stealing from shopkeepers and molesting women? Never!

Nergui gritted his teeth as he pondered his response. It would be difficult to move the Seseril horde if it simply refused to go . . .

In the brief silence, he heard a sound like a woman crying. Near the back of the Khan's vanguard, he could see some veiled women mounted on ponies.

He brought his wives too?

Spurring his horse, he forced his way past the Khan's guards. Behind him, he could hear rich curses in Seseril and in Bandeluki as his men followed him. From somewhere ahead came a *slap,* and the crying ceased.

The veiled women were staring at him. He rode up to each one and looked her in the eye. Round faces with the heavy-lidded eyes of the Seserils looked back, some frightened and some curious, but most with studied indifference. Those in back, he saw, were bunched together as if trying to hide something behind them.

He pushed past them and saw a young girl, no more than fifteen, who looked at him with round, brown eyes that were red with tears. He ripped away the veil. Although her face was heavily painted, it definitely belonged to a Bandeluk. She'd probably been kidnapped from some village along the way. Her terrified expression suggested she didn't regard him as her savior.

This child just sees another damned Seseril!

A plump eunuch was pointing a spear at him. "This woman is the personal slave of Hulegu Khan!" he said officiously.

Nergui grabbed the spear from his fat hands and broke it over the pommel of his saddle. "SLAVERY IS FORBIDDEN! WHO SCORNS THE EMPEROR AND DEFIES HIS JUST COM-

MANDS?"

His men drew their swords, and the Khan's guards did likewise. It wouldn't take much to start a battle. Nergui knew how it would go: He and his bodyguards would be cut down, but then the 20,000 mailed lancers, who were watching from a short distance, would charge furiously and butcher the Seserils. Not one would see his native steppes again.

The Khan swiftly ordered his men to put away their weapons. "My apologies for the disturbance," he said, no longer waving his fly whisk about. "I don't know how this young woman came to join us. I will investigate the matter tonight, before we depart for Saramaia. You can be sure the culprit will be punished according to the law."

Now he wants to leave before I uncover any more of his crimes, which are doubtless many.

"The Khan is wise," he said simply.

Taking the girl with him, he rode back to his own lines. He decided to give her 100 piasters from the war chest and send her home. The money would suffice for a dowry large enough to tempt some peasant into a quick marriage, and thus the matter would be settled quietly. Of course, he'd have to forego the pleasure of seeing Hulegu Khan impaled, but he knew from bitter experience there was nothing to gain by pursuing the case any further.

I wonder who he intends to punish. Some witless scapegoat, no doubt, maybe the stupid eunuch who blurted out the truth.

He was still watching the Seserils file into their assigned camp, when a messenger rode up on a lathered horse. "Respects from Col. Sardar, *mushir.* He urgently requests you visit his headquarters."

Being insulted by the Khan wasn't enough? Now a mere colonel orders me around!

But he knew he'd have to swallow the loss of face. Col. Sardar, the head of imperial intelligence, was the most feared man in the Empire, and he wouldn't summon the *mushir* unless it were a matter of grave importance.

"Tell Col. Sardar I will see him as soon as I've discharged my present duties." After waiting two minutes, he made an excuse and left.

Col. Sardar was a small, thin man dressed in the simple, knee-

length coat and leggings of an infantry officer. He snapped to attention as Nergui, still wearing his gaudy parade armor, clanked into
the office. It was hard for him to believe this obsequious little man
was the dreaded imperial spy chief, someone who collected incriminating files on all the chief officials.

He looks more like a village priest than a soldier.

"As you were, Colonel. What do you have for me?"

Sardar clapped his hands, and guards brought in a chained prisoner, a young man dressed in the ragged uniform of a frontier regiment. He was badly bruised and trembling with fear.

Seeing the *mushir,* the prisoner threw himself to his knees and
raised his manacled hands in appeal. "Pasha! You must save me!
I've done nothing!"

One of the guards cuffed him. Nergui waved him back and put
on a sympathetic face. "If you've done no wrong, you will not be
harmed," he said. "What do you have to report?"

"Just repeat the story you told me," said Sardar menacingly.
"Don't leave out a word."

The young man spoke hesitantly, as if he were afraid he wouldn't
be believed. "I'm Pvt. Dalir, 3rd Company, 2nd Frontier Regiment.
We were stationed at Gedij. Two weeks ago, a large enemy force
came and surrounded our position. I don't know how many there
were, thousands at least. And they had demons with them.

"We weren't afraid because the castle was impregnable and besides, well-stocked with food and water. On the second day, they
began pounding us with their siege weapons. Huge stones fell on us
day and night. But we stood our ground and repaired the damage as
best we could. There seemed to be no real danger.

"On the morning of the fifth day, it was my turn to stand watch
in the south tower. I heard a loud noise and then screams. When I
turned to look, I saw the whole castle falling. The earth split open
and swallowed it up, every stone, and the garrison with it. In a minute, it was all gone.

"There were scarcely a dozen of us left, and we could do nothing to oppose the foreign army when it came climbing over the rubble. I saw an officer in a golden helmet. It was Demonslayer. He's a
frightful man! Just to look at him made my blood turn cold!

"But all he said was, 'I think you have suffered enough.' And
he let us go."

"Just like that?" said Nergui incredulously. "He just let you go? Nothing else?"

The young man licked his lips, perhaps expecting another beating. "There was one other thing. He gave us food for the journey."

Col. Sardar reached behind his desk and opened a dirty sack, from which he extracted a partially-eaten loaf of bread. The bread was stale, but Nergui could see it wasn't baked by any Bandeluk.

Nergui shook his head in wonder. "Enough," he said. "Take him away."

The guards hauled the prisoner away though he kept looking over his shoulder, hoping to the last for a reprieve.

"No matter how we question him, he always tells the same story," said Col. Sardar.

"Can you confirm it?"

"My scouts have not yet returned."

"And if they tell you the fortress is destroyed?"

"Then the foreigners have a terrible new weapon."

Nergui felt dizzy for a moment as if the earth were shifting under his feet.

This can't be true!

"That makes no sense! If they had such a weapon, they'd have used it to take Kafra!"

"They didn't wish to destroy Kafra. They needed it as a base."

"Then they'd have saved it for some important target, not an isolated trading post like Gedij."

"I believe the weapon is new to them. They're still testing it."

"Where did you get that information?"

"Think, *sir,*" said Sardar. He managed to make the word sound like an insult. "The first thing they did after laying siege to Kafra was to attack Barbosa, an old fort in the middle of nowhere. There was nothing there but that crazy old witch and her servants."

The Witch of Barbosa!

He remembered the frightful stories they told about her. He'd always dismissed them as fairy tales, but now, they were suddenly gaining substance.

"And one thing more," Sardar continued, "a weapon of great power. It was all hushed up centuries ago, but I searched the archives until I found it: An ancient Kano demon was imprisoned there."

Nergui's head was spinning. Old legends were coming to life

around him. He felt like sitting down. "Why did no one tell me about this?"

"Few knew, and fewer cared. The demon was immensely powerful, but it hadn't twitched in a thousand years. It was like a dormant volcano, there under the castle. The witch was supposed to keep it quiet, and she did until now.

"Then this Demonslayer appeared as if by magic and took Barbosa on the same day. They must have been well prepared. Barbosa fell without a struggle. A few weeks later, we had these strange reports of fire and blood raining down on Kafra.

"The city was already in enemy hands, so they had no reason to attack it. Perhaps the demon was restless, or perhaps they hadn't learned to control it properly. But now they have."

"I've seen sorcery and demons, but nothing more dangerous than a line of spears held by determined men."

"You've fought many battles, *sir,* but I expect you've never seen the earth open up and swallow a whole fortress. This is the weapon that brought down the Indo Empire, and we have no defense against it."

Sardar paused a moment, waiting for these words to sink in. The silent moment stretched into a minute as Nergui considered the possibilities. Suddenly, his armies all seemed useless, their weapons no better than sticks and stones.

"There must be some way to counter this demon," he said finally.

"Sorcerers are working on it now. So far, they've only established the demon is no longer in Barbosa. They can't locate it anywhere."

"And the witch? What does she say about it?"

"Barbosa has been occupied by the enemy, *sir,*" Sardar reminded him. "That source of information is no longer available."

"So, the enemy has captured a weapon that can destroy whole castles, and there's nothing the mighty Bandeluk Empire can do about it? That cannot be!"

"It can, *sir.* Even if we manage to find the thing, there may be no way to dismiss it. No charm can protect us. I believe the enemy must have planned this long in advance.

"Ask yourself, *sir,* why they would attack an enemy several times greater than their puny kingdom if they didn't plan some kind of a trick? And now that the secret is out, they free their prisoners and even give them rations, so they will spread fear and panic."

"That much, at least, we can deal with," said Nergui. "Do not let the prisoner speak with anyone, not even his own family, and not even the guards if you can prevent it."

"I can," said Sardar. His eyes narrowed in a cruel way that made even battle-hardened Nergui uncomfortable. "But there will always be rumors. We can't lock up everyone."

"Spread your own rumors. The commander of Gedij took a bribe to surrender the fortress. Have his family arrested."

"You can consider it done, *sir,* but we still have no defense against this weapon."

"But we do have months to prepare. The foreigners won't attack until spring."

"Even if we had a century, it would do no good. This is the weapon that destroyed the Indos. There may be no defense possible."

Sardar leaned forward, in the humble posture of a servant reminding the master not to forget his gloves. "If I may make a suggestion, *sir,* the only defense is an attack. Demonslayer and his army are in Berbat. It would take weeks to withdraw them. If we attack now, we can defeat the foreigners before they can use their weapon a second time."

"Impossible! The army is not yet assembled, and the passes are closing soon!"

Sardar smiled, barely concealing his contempt. "And that little cavalcade of 30,000 today, was that nothing? That alone is equal to the enemy forces in Kafra. I believe you could be there next week if you wished, *sir.*"

Nergui felt a hopeless panic, as a hanged man must, when there's nothing but air under his feet.

Sardar is a desk soldier! He thinks he's clever, but he knows nothing of strategy.

"Kafra is fortified, *Colonel.* It can't be taken with cavalry. And there's no way to transport siege equipment through the passes before the snow. Our forces would be trapped in an enemy province, cut off without supplies or reinforcements. It's suicide!"

"My agents have looked into this," said Sardar, producing a sheaf of reports. "The Prince you're so afraid of is a young man, headstrong and overconfident. He imagines he's a military genius. He attacked the late Amir with a weaker force and won. He overcame a rebel army with a few squadrons of cavalry. Now, he thinks he can't be beaten. In point of fact, he never has been."

"Then he hasn't been a soldier very long."

"Long enough to have a very high opinion of his own abilities. If you cross over the mountains now, in whatever numbers, he won't wait to share the glory with Demonslayer. He will attack at once, counting on his genius to overcome you. But . . ." – Here he put on a flattering smile. – " . . . he does not yet know the quality of the *mushir,* a man who has grown old on the field of battle, who has humbled far better generals. Strike now, *mushir,* and you will win."

Sardar was driving nails into his coffin. A suggestion from him was as good as an imperial decree. Sardar was a man who could unseat ministers with a few sly words and, according to rumor, assassinate imperial princes with impunity. And now, he was convinced he could read the mind of an enemy commander he'd never even met.

Nergui temporized. "You're asking me to risk the whole Empire on the draw of a single card. I will have to think it over. The scouts haven't returned. This may be nothing but a rumor. It would be prudent to wait."

"Then wait, *sir.* But don't wait too long."

13: Singer

I wish Raeesha were here.

She had a way of lifting him up when he fell into a dark pit of depression, like the one that held him now. He was surveying the village of Gulhan, or rather the few blackened mud brick walls that marked the place where the village had been. The wooden buildings were all reduced to ash. Even the olive trees had been cut down and burned. There were no corpses to be seen, but a horrible stench came from the village well.

"They must have known we were coming," he said, pointing toward a pair of feluccas that were sailing back and forth off the coast, watching.

"Indeed, sir," said Baron Hardy. "They can't fight us on land, so they employ a scorched earth strategy."

"Look!" said Kyle, pointing to a distant column of smoke. The small group of officers stared at it silently. They all thought the same thing: The pirates were already burning the next village.

"I could be there in a few hours," said Baron Hardy.

"They will be gone by then," said Lt. Gallites. "This race we cannot win."

"What are we to do for water?" asked Capt. Fleming.

"I'll tell the *fui* demons to dig us a new well, upstream of this one," said Singer. "Or better, several of them. We need water for the horses too."

"We can't just let pirates depopulate the whole coast," said Capt. Stewart.

"When you think of some way of stopping them, let me know," said Singer.

"But they can't beat us this way," said Capt. Duvil. "They'll give it up when they see it does no good."

"The pirates have a different idea of what is good," said Gallites. "They rely on terror and intimidation."

"They take us for cravens?" said Sir Gladwood.

"No, but they would slow us down and discourage anyone who might help us. And they add to their own forces. Those ships . . . " –

He pointed to the feluccas. – ". . . were once fishing boats. I expect some of the crew, also, were fishermen, who have no choice but to join the pirates now that their homes are destroyed."

"Why do you know so much about pirates?" asked Singer.

"I come from a naval family. It's in the blood."

"If you're our naval expert, then tell me what those are." Singer pointed to some wooden structures that were visible in the water not far from the shore.

"I don't know, sir. I'll have a look."

Gallites rode into the water until the waves were washing around his horse's knees, then rode back. "Small boats," he reported, "most likely from the village. Any boats too small for their fleet, they sank near the shore."

Singer thought about it for a moment. "Haul them out and fix them up. Any that can be transported, we're taking with us."

"May I ask why, sir?"

"No, you may not."

That evening, Singer called Gallites to his tent. "Lieutenant," he said, "you ask more questions than the rest of my officers put together. Am I to conclude Prince Krion sent you to spy on me?"

To Singer's astonishment, Gallites smiled and then began chuckling.

"Did I say something funny?"

"Not really, sir," said Gallites, choking back his laughter. "But I believe the Prince sent me here because he thought I'd been sent to spy on him."

"Who are you spying on then?"

"No one. But there is a certain tension between the Prince and the Royal Navy, which is not yet under his authority, but is nonetheless occupied with the transport of supplies for what many in the Admiralty consider a pointless expedition."

"Really? Why pointless?"

"No one says so openly, but it's more or less common knowledge the Prince instigated this war, based on false reports of a pending Bandeluk attack. His real aim, it's generally believed, was further his own advancement, in view of the age and infirmity of King Diecos."

Singer had long suspected as much, but from the lips of an

Akaddian officer, it became more than just a suspicion. "That's all very interesting, but what does it have to do with you?"

"To be candid, sir, I seem to have fallen between two stools. My father, the Count of Langonnes, is no younger than King Deicos, and in the normal course of events, I might be expected to succeed him. But my family, which is well-connected with the Admiralty, was so concerned for their heir, they would have made me an ensign and assigned me to a revenue cutter or some other duty they considered safe.

"I managed to evade their scrutiny long enough to volunteer for the army, but I did not entirely escape. They simply had me assigned to the supply corps, and here I am."

"So why all the questions? Are you really a supply officer?"

"For the time being, sir. But my father is not well. In the event of his death, I will become the Count Langonnes, too lofty a title for a lieutenant in the supply corps. If I prove myself in battle, I can expect a promotion and a command of my own. I'm not ready for that."

"You're about as ready as I was. You want me to teach you how to be a general? I hardly know myself."

"I think a bit of practical experience would improve my self-confidence."

"You seem to have as much self-confidence as anyone around. But if you really want to see some action, I can't help you. There isn't much happening at the moment."

"And yet, you ordered me to assemble a fleet of small boats."

Singer waved a hand dismissively. "A good commander is prepared to take advantage of opportunities. Any pirate vessel that anchors too close to the shore may be in for a surprise, some dark night."

"I hadn't thought of that! Is this where the Spindrift Marines come in?"

"Maybe. I've not yet found much use for the marine detachment. What good are marines without ships?"

"As much good as any infantry, I should think."

"They're light troops. They can't stand up to the Bandeluks."

"I think that depends on how you deploy them, sir. Marines are trained to fight in all kinds of terrain: hills, swamps and forests."

Singer thought it over . . . and lightning struck.

I've been looking at this wrong!

"Now you've given me an idea," he said. "When you're done with your boats, hand over the supply job to your assistant and report to Capt. Baldwin."

"May I ask why, sir?"

"Of course."

14: Gallites

This is so humiliating!

He'd started at the head of the column, but as it continued its all-night forced march, up increasingly steep, narrow and winding goat trails through the hills, he kept falling farther and farther back until now he'd reached the end of the formation. He couldn't catch up with the rest of the company, and he couldn't fall behind any further because there was a grizzled sergeant in the rear whose duty it was to give any stragglers helpful encouragement or else a sharp kick, whichever seemed more expedient. The marines had a fixed rule to never leave anyone behind even if it was only a foreign supply officer who was tagging along as an observer.

They'd issued him the basic marine equipment: a steel cap, a mail shirt, a light crossbow that had a handle so that it could be fired one-handed, a shortsword and a buckler. He also had a week's rations, a water bottle and a blanket in his pack. But no one had given him any boots, and his riding boots were raising huge blisters on his heels. He had the strong impression that complaining would do no good.

Besides the sergeant, there was no one in sight but a young private with a twisted ankle, who was grimly limping along with the help of a stick. He looked as humiliated as Gallites felt. The rest of the marines were pounding up the trail ahead like champion athletes. Occasionally, he could hear a faint *clink* from their armor and equipment.

"I see you have some extra gear," he said by way of conversation.

The sergeant, who had a massive battle axe on his back, merely grunted. Gallites had noticed all of the marines were carrying something extra: axes, bows, coils of rope, entrenching tools, firepots and medical supplies, among other things.

He tried again. "Won't it slow us down to carry so much extra?"

The sergeant spat. "This is a light pack," he said. "Most of our gear is in the wagons."

Seventy pounds of gear wasn't what Gallites would have called light, but the marines were probably used to more. He went to see if the limping private was any more talkative.

"What's your name?" he said.

"Finley, sir. I have the honor to be named after Capt. Finley, the famous pirate chief."

"That's an honor?"

"On the Spindrift Islands, it is. Finley was a great captain from the glory days a hundred years ago, before the Hallanders came and persuaded him to give up pirating."

"How did they manage that?"

"It involved a length of rope."

"So Capt. Finley was hanged?"

"Aye, sir. Him and some other folks who are dead but not forgotten. We learned a valuable lesson from that: Pirating is wrong. We were not too clear on that point before. We also learned rope is mighty useful stuff. We carry some wherever we go."

"For the pirates, you mean?"

"For whoever needs it. We're mighty generous with the rope."

"Marines take no prisoners?"

"We do, sir, if anyone wants them. But no one wants pirates."

"You two, stop jawing and get moving!" said the sergeant.

Gallites was about to remind him to speak more respectfully to superior officers, but he decided to bite his tongue instead.

Six hours later, he was having a terrible nightmare: He was staggering down a mountainside, totally exhausted, in the dark of the night. There was blood in his boots, but he couldn't stop because of a demon who kept pushing him from behind. His tongue was sore from being bitten.

Now the dream was getting worse. He kept stumbling past marines who were lying dead on the ground. Suddenly, he ran into the insanely cheerful Capt. Baldwin, who put a hand on his shoulder. "Enjoying the hike, Lieutenant? Why don't you get a little shut-eye. I'll wake you up if there's any action."

And now, he was lying down among the dead marines, only they weren't dead, but asleep . . .

Someone was slapping him in the face. It hurt. He wanted to

tell him to go away and let him sleep, but the marine grabbed him by the collar and lifted him up.

"The captain wants to see you right away. Sir."

His neck wasn't working right; it kept trying to nod. He thought he'd only dozed off for a minute, but the sky was turning red with pre-dawn light, so he must have slept for some time. The marines were standing around and checking their gear. He pulled himself to his feet and staggered down the trail to where Baldwin was waiting.

The captain shook his head when he saluted. "No saluting in the field," he said. "You'll get me killed with that shit."

"Oh. Sorry, sir. What did you wish to see me about?"

"We're going to try to lure the pirates to our position. Do you speak Bandeluki?"

"Some."

"See if you can manage some Bandeluk war cries when the fighting starts. You can join the special squad on the ridge there." – He pointed to where a small group of marines wearing native costumes and holding Bandeluk horse bows were standing. – "But take off your helmet and keep your head down. They won't loiter here if they smell marines."

"Yes sir."

Still sleepy and wondering what was going on, Gallites climbed the ridge and peered over the edge. The first thing he saw was a charming little fishing village in the early dawn light: a cluster of huts, mostly cobbled together from driftwood, in a small inlet surrounded by olive trees. Smoke was starting to rise from some of the chimneys as the villagers prepared breakfast.

The second thing he noticed were the masts of tall ships emerging from the mist across the bay.

Pirates!

As the ships bore down on the unsuspecting village, he counted them: a four-masted barque, three schooners, a brig, several feluccas and a big dhow, perhaps a supply vessel.

Is this all they've got? Where are the rest?

It was hard to understand how so small a fleet could cause the Royal Navy such woe. The barque was the only real warship of the lot. With ballistas mounted fore and aft, it was clearly a match for any royal frigate. It looked like a Covenant-built vessel . . .

It's the Black Ansel!

"It's the what?" said Baldwin. Gallites didn't know he'd said it aloud.

"The Black Ansel was a ship that refused to surrender at the end of the Covenant war. It just disappeared. Guess we know where it went now."

"I remember that," said Baldwin. "Tanilhan was the captain, wasn't he? If I were him, I'd have disappeared too."

"Right you are, sir. There's still many an Akaddian sailor waiting to settle scores with Tanilhan."

Still unnoticed by the villagers, the larger ships were launching boats. The feluccas apparently intended to beach.

"About two hundred pirates in the landing party," he said.

"Won't be any problem," said Baldwin, grinning. He had four times that many men behind him. "Hold your fire!" he said to the squad of turbaned men. The rest of his company was waiting out of sight behind the ridge.

A woman came out of one of the huts with a water jar and went to the village well, not turning to look at the sea. The pirates were now a hundred yards from shore. Having filled her jar, she was turning to go, when she noticed the fleet of boats entering the inlet. She opened her mouth as if to scream, but an arrow from one of the boats caught her in the chest, and she fell, her water spilling on the ground.

"Hold your fire!" Baldwin repeated.

Gallites no longer felt sleepy. He could feel his heart going thud-thud like a snare drum as the pirate boats crept toward the beach. His fingers were twitching, eager to do something, anything. The marines on the ridge with him also shifted nervously, but no one loosed an arrow.

Down in the village, a man came out of a hut, perhaps to see where his wife had gone. He saw the pirates and yelled something, before three arrows knocked him over. The boats had now reached the shore. Pirates spilled out onto the beach, drawing their weapons.

"Now! Fire! War cries!" said Baldwin.

The squad of disguised marines plucked their horse bows. Gallites belatedly tried to think of a good Bandeluk war cry, but the only thing that occurred to him was the word for "fire", so that is what he yelled:

"FIRE! FIRE! FIRE!"

A light patter of arrows fell among the distant pirates, injuring none. Villagers were now emerging from the huts. Seeing the pirates, they ran in all directions. The pirates shot some and chased after the others.

"More war cries!" said Baldwin.

"FIRE! FIRE! FIRE!" yelled Gallites in Bandeluki, as loudly as he could.

Now, an arrow hit one of the pirates in the knee. He sat down heavily, staring at the wound in surprise. The other pirates paused to see where the arrows were coming from.

"FIRE! FIRE! FIRE!" repeated Gallites, not waiting for orders.

An arrow struck another pirate in the chest, and he went down. The other pirates pointed at the small group of turbaned figures on the ridge above them and yelled angrily, a babble of indistinct voices. In the light of the rising sun, Gallites could see them clearly now. Most were dressed as ordinary sailors, but others looked like Bandeluks, and a few wore faded naval uniforms.

"Now we see if they take the bait," said Baldwin, grinning wolfishly.

Some of the pirates began returning fire, but their arrows fell short. One pirate yelled in pain and began hopping around. There was an arrow sticking out of his foot.

The others reached a decision. Leaving the villagers for later, they charged up the slope at the disguised marines, who were still firing down at them.

"Ready your weapons!" said Baldwin to the marines waiting below. Those with crossbows cocked them. Fifty men with axes gathered below on the trail, ready to greet the visitors.

Gallites remembered he had a crossbow and cocked it. While he was doing that, he heard a sound like a knife cutting a melon. One of the marines beside him fell, an arrow sticking out of his turbaned head and a look of astonishment on his face.

"Right!" said Baldwin. "TAKE YOUR POSITIONS! FIRE AT WILL! AXES FORE!"

With a loud yell, the axe men raised their weapons and charged down the trail. Crossbowmen joined their comrades on the ridge. Bolts descended on the pirates like a shower of hail.

Gallites had heard the Spindrift Marines could get off four aimed shots a minute, but the estimate seemed much too low. The

sky was full of bolts. He raised his shaking hands to fire at a pirate archer, who was taking aim at one of the axe men. The archer went down, but whether it was his bolt that felled him or one of the others, he never knew.

He bent over to cock the crossbow for another shot. When he raised it again, he could only see the backs of the pirates, not so numerous as before, who were running toward their boats. He didn't pause to take careful aim, but loosed into the thick of them and prepared another round.

When he looked again, the slope below was covered with dead pirates. The only live ones in sight, probably the first to flee, were piling into a single boat and rowing away as fast as they could, while crossbow bolts continued to rain down, now less accurately because of the range.

"CEASE FIRE!" said Baldwin, who grinned cheerfully. "I like to leave a few alive, so they can spread the news. Let's go have a look at them."

The marines picked their way down the slope, pausing now and then to finish off wounded pirates where they lay groaning or crawling about. They were wretched-looking men, Gallites thought, ragged, unkempt and underfed.

No one becomes a pirate if

he has better opportunities.

It occurred to him he'd been yelling the word for "burn", not "fire". No one seemed to have noticed.

The surviving villagers, now that the battle was over, wandered back to their homes, some going from one corpse to another in search of loved ones. Piercing wails broke out when these were found, a dismal chorus that grew ever louder.

Down near the beach, the axe men had gathered a handful of prisoners, all locals, who'd dropped their weapons and fallen to their knees. As he came nearer, Gallites could hear them pleading for their lives:

"Mercy, effendi!"

"I'm but a poor fisherman!"

"They forced me to join them, I swear it!"

"I've never killed anyone!"

The marines, none able to speak Bandeluki, merely looked amused. One turned to the captain. "What shall we do with them, sir?"

"Beats me," said the obstinately cheerful Baldwin. "Let's ask the jury."

"Talk to the villagers," he told Gallites. "Tell them we'll kill the prisoners or let them go, whatever they decide."

Gallites climbed up on the prow of a felucca and banged his buckler with his sword to get attention. One by one, the mournful, tear-stained faces turned to look at him. He kept the speech short:

"GOOD PEOPLE! WE COME AS FRIENDS! THESE MEN WHO ATTACKED YOU SAY THEY ARE ONLY POOR FISHERMEN WHO WERE FORCED TO JOIN THE PIRATES. WE ARE STRANGERS AND CANNOT JUDGE THEIR GUILT. THAT LIES WITH YOU. SHALL WE KILL THEM OR SPARE THEM? WE AWAIT YOUR ANSWER."

There was a brief silence as the villagers, standing amid the bodies of family members, regarded the prisoners, who were kneeling miserably a short distance away. No one spoke.

Then a woman who'd been clutching a dead child put it down gently to pick up a stone, which she hurled at the nearest pirate. The other villagers began to do likewise. The pirates screamed. Some tried to cover themselves and others to flee, but inside a minute it was over. The pirates all lay still.

"Saved us some rope," commented a young marine, who Gallites recognized as Pvt. Finley.

Gallites, feeling shocked and not knowing what else to say, asked, "How's your ankle?"

"Good news, sir. The doc says it isn't broken, so I'm good to go. Will you be coming on our next little hike?"

"Maybe if it's an easy one."

"This was an easy one."

Out in the bay, the Black Ansel was weighing anchor.

15: Erika

"May I introduce my protégé, Lady Erika of Tidewater?"

The Duchess had said it for the fiftieth time, and it sounded exactly like the first. The gnome-like, balding man she was being introduced to was the Honorable High Court Justice Megabastus, a name already fading from her memory, together with a long string of others, all blurring and running together:

Thehonorableeuclesmasteroftheroyalmintsirwellbournethaneofcornwickandambassadoroftremmarkandhiswifeladyodeliahisexcellencygeneralpotamusretiredandhiswifeeuthensiatherighthonorablechalcabuscountofmyteliaandhiswifecountesssolenathehonorablecouncillorhalitotisandhiswifepornillatherighthonorablepimplefaceandhiswifeburstinggirdlesirstaresatmybosomandladyshrillgiggletherightignoblesirbelcherandladysmellsofsherry . . .

Regardless how disagreeable they might seem, she greeted them all with a smile and a curtsey, even when this put intolerable strains on the tight, white lace gown the Duchess had given her.

I have to wear her one of her old cast-offs from three seasons ago, and she takes all my samples!

Standing next to her, the Duchess was wearing a gaudy, rainbow-colored creation her dressmaker had put together from Erika's *pamuk* samples. It was obviously the wrong season for such a gown if there were a season for something that looked like it had been constructed by a demented quilt maker.

("But how will I sell my fabric if you take my samples?" she'd said, despairing. "Don't worry about that," the Duchess had replied. "You don't really want to be seen peddling merchandise around town, do you? That's not how things are done here.")

No matter how outlandish it appeared to Erika, every lady who passed down the reception line complimented the Duchess' gown in extravagant terms: "Gorgeous!" "Stunning!" "Fantastic!" "Superb!" And they all asked where she'd gotten the fabric. "My own little secret," the Duchess always replied.

I guess I found out who sets the fashion in Elohi.

Erika had often wondered what mysterious person decided

what was in fashion and what was out. Now, she was standing next to the very source, the high oracle of fashion.

But still, she hasn't mentioned the pamuk!

At the head of the reception line, while Erika was doing her endless smiles and curtsies, the Duchess' plump and phlegmatic husband, Duke Claudio, mechanically shook hands and responded to all greetings with a passionless, "Welcome." He barely tried to disguise his boredom.

Finally, when the stream of visitors had tapered off, the butler announced everyone on the guest list had arrived.

"Excellent!" said the Duchess. "We may proceed to the drawing room . . . Don't scowl like that, dear, a lady must keep her composure."

"Excuse me, your Grace," Erika said, "I have some difficulty remembering the names of your guests."

"The important thing is that they remember you. Just try to be decorous, and make sure that you aren't forgotten."

Decorous? I'm about to pop out of this dress, and I'm sure they wouldn't forget that!

As they stepped into the drawing room, the crowd interrupted their conversations. The men bowed and the women curtsied. Erika felt rather important until she realized they were all greeting the host and hostess. No one seemed interested in her except for a red-faced young gallant in a dazzling military uniform, whom she vaguely remembered as Capt. Sclerosis.

I should have known I'm not the guest of honor.

Before she could get on with the meet-and-greet, a plump young woman who'd somehow stuffed herself into an unfashionable black satin gown, which fit her as the skin fits a sausage, grabbed her elbow and hustled her into a corner. While Erika wondered who she was and whether she ever plucked the hair on her upper lip, she launched into a rapid monologue:

"Hello! I'm Camilla, the Duchess' secretary, and I'm ever so eager to meet you because they've kept you closeted all by yourself, and it's very hush-hush, so I probably shouldn't be saying this, but aren't you a friend of Prince Clenas?" She leaned forward with the eager hopefulness of a squirrel who expects to receive a peanut.

"You could say that," Erika answered hesitantly. "We met in Chatmakstan when I visited the front."

Camilla squealed and clapped her hands. "I knew it! I knew it! You have to tell me all about him! I've heard so much about his adventures. We hardly speak of anything else. And you were actually there! You must have seen some of his famous exploits! Is it true he struck off the head of Gen. Basilius with a single blow?"

Something about Clenas makes Akaddian women crazy. But this dumpling wouldn't even interest one of his footmen.

"I can't say I witnessed that," she said carefully. "I was in a different part of the field, with Prince Krion."

Camilla made an impolite noise. "Krion! He's a fraud! Where would he be without Clenas? In a cage, that's where! Clenas wins all the battles, and Krion claims all the victories! But one day soon, everyone will know the truth! It's not far off!"

She looked around and then leaned even closer, as if to impart some deep secret. "Clenas has many admirers in this city."

Most of them women.

"So I understand."

Camilla nodded solemnly. "Well, enough of that. A word to the wise. I've already said too much. But I simply must introduce you to my friends, somewhere we can speak in confidence . . . Wait! The Duchess gave me a message for you. Capt. Scolinus, you've met him?"

Oh, so that's his name.

"Briefly. We were introduced."

"He's a very influential man, the head of the Palace Guard. He can help us a great deal. It's important you make a good impression on him. Spare no effort to win him over. 'Do not disappoint us!' the Duchess said. 'Do not disappoint us!'" With that, she left.

If people were judged by their servants, anyone would assume the Duchess was an idiot! Whatever was she babbling about?

She went to look for Capt. Scolinus, but then a bell rang and the doors to the banquet hall opened. The Duke himself appeared as if by magic at her side and with a courtly bow, offered her his arm. She took it and was escorted into the banquet hall, the others following in some order of precedence unknown to her.

This is an interesting turn of events!

The Duke had never taken a personal interest in her, and his wife was apparently pulling his strings because he merely deposited her near the lower end of the table, where a waiter offered her a chair.

It's like I'm an actress in a play, but no one has shown me the script!

The procession of guests into the hall seemed to go on forever since each had to be escorted to a specific place at the table. Erika took the opportunity to study the banquet hall, a cavernous structure a hundred feet long. Waiters stood attentively with their backs to either wall, and above them the portraits of noble ancestors looked down on the scene, illuminated in silvery light by a series of crystal chandeliers hanging from the vaulted ceiling.

Is this a dining room or a temple to the gods?

The table was covered with a seamless damask cloth about 80 feet long. It must have taken a master weaver years to create. On it stood rows of small cut-glass dishes and bowls holding pickles, olives and celery. Plates with bread rolls and exquisite little marmalade jars lay within easy reach of each guest. Before her was an elaborate table setting that included four wine glasses and a bewildering display of polished silver knives, forks and spoons, some of which she'd never seen before.

Is that thing a celery fork or an oyster fork? How am I supposed to know?

Fearing she'd commit some hideous social blunder, she sat bolt upright with her hands in her lap and smiled at the guests as they came in. The table filled mainly from the other end because the most important guests sat near the Duke, but eventually Capt. Scolinus appeared, uncomfortably escorting an axe-faced matron in a dark silk gown six seasons out of fashion. He took his place to Erika's right, with the matron on the other side.

I guess the pieces are all in place. But am I a queen or a pawn? And who moves first?

Unfortunately, the first move was taken by the matron, who, charmed by the young captain, began telling him about her children, particularly a young and apparently marriageable daughter, whom she wished him to meet.

While Erika was trying to think of a way to get his attention, she was startled by someone whispering intimately in her ear: "Hello, Miss Boobies!"

It was Philocratus, the Duchess' teenaged son, who had the delusion he was irresistible to women and dedicated himself to making his mother's maids miserable. To Erika's dismay, he took the place directly to her left. And then, his equally obnoxious younger brother Amphitus was seated opposite. He grinned evilly at her.

She learned closer to Philocratus and whispered, "No games! This is important business!"

He nodded and said loudly, "Sure! Why not tonight?"

This drew a raised eyebrow from the Duchess, who was taking her place at the end of the table. "I was just asking your son if he had an interest in the classical theatre," Erika explained.

The Duchess seemed mildly surprised. "Then you're having more luck with him than I ever did. It's hard enough to get him to use proper grammar. But of course, there will be no time for the theatre tonight. Perhaps another occasion. I understand the Elohi Players are putting on 'Mostellana' next week."

"Oh! We mustn't miss it!" said Erika. "That's one of my favorites!"

My favorite for taking naps in the theatre.

Philocratus kicked her under the table. Smiling sweetly, she ground her heel into the top of his foot, a method Halland women sometimes used to discourage rapists. He grimaced.

"Oh, don't make faces," said the Duchess. "It's only three hours. Surely, you can sit still that long?"

The servants were filling their glasses with an aperitif. Duke Claudio stood and offered a toast to "His Majesty, the King". Everyone stood and said, "The King!" before taking a modest sip. Capt. Scolinus, however, drained his glass and upon sitting, had it filled again. He seemed, at once, to be in a better mood.

Seeing her chance, Erika said, "You enjoy the wine?"

"I confess to enjoying wine of any kind, but the Duke's cellars are the best in the city," he replied. "You are, then, that mysterious young Hallander, whom the Duchess favors with the title 'Lady'? I had the impression that Halland was a republic where all citizens are considered equal."

"We are, but some of us are more so."

"So then, I'd venture to surmise you're from one of those fabulously rich families of merchant princes?"

"I'm afraid we're more like merchant baronets."

Scolinus, who was now working on his third glass of wine, laughed as if he'd heard a great witticism. "You're charmingly modest," he said. "But I saw the Duke bow quite low when he offered you his arm, and he seldom bends over unless it's to pick up a bag of gold."

"I think his Grace may be more impressed with my future prospects than my present circumstances, but I'm not at liberty to discuss them at the moment."

"Ah, an heiress! I knew it!"

At this point, the waiters brought in an oyster soup, and Erika was distracted by loud slurping sounds coming from her left. The hatchet-faced matron took advantage of this pause to inject herself into the conversation.

"You should know, Miss, although Capt. Scolinus bears no title, he stems from one of our most noble families, the dukes of Potiana."

Am I now rebuked for being too familiar with one of my betters?

Scolinus, who was half way through a glass of the white wine that had replaced the aperitif, merely shrugged. "Yes, I do have an excellent pedigree from that old and somewhat threadbare house. It doesn't come with any income or a career unless one wishes to be a soldier. And anyone can be a soldier."

"But surely," said Erika, "it's commendable that you rose on your own merit?"

"If you want to call it that. I happened to be in the middle of the action during the Battle of Dolwyk when the enemy rushed us. My pikemen stood firm against the Covenant axes, and my superiors were watching. But some of my friends, who were no less brave, chanced to be in the wrong place at the wrong time, and we left them on the field."

There was an awkward silence. Either Scolinus was overcome by tragic memories, or the wine was making him maudlin. He stared despondently at his soup, ignoring the ladies at his elbows.

This tippler is the influential man the Duchess is so eager to impress?

To Erika's relief, the waiters brought out the fish course. But just as she was taking her second mouthful, Philocratus leaned close and whispered in her ear, "Before you get too attached to that braggart soldier, you should remember drinkers aren't much good in bed."

Philocratus had also been enjoying the wine. Under the table, his hand was on her knee. He gradually moved it up her thigh and into forbidden territory. Erika grabbed a finger and twisted it sharply backward.

"You bitch!" he gasped.

Erika didn't let go. Instead, she leaned closer and whispered, "Do you want your mother to see where you have your hand right now?"

"Just wait . . . AAAAGH!" Erika had twisted his finger back further. Philocratus was almost doubled up with pain. The Duchess turned to stare at him in astonishment.

"Oh, dear!" said Erika, her voice filled with anxiety and concern. "I think he may have swallowed a bone!"

"Did he? I'll have the cook's head!" The Duchess barked orders to the waiters: "Take him to his room at once! And send for the doctor!"

The disturbance attracted some attention, but was quickly submerged in the bustle of the waiters who brought out the main course. Knives flashed in the corners of the room as carvers sliced up huge roast birds on the sideboards.

When Erika received her slice, she saw it consisted of several birds stuffed one inside an-

other: a hen in a duck, the duck in a capon, the capon in a goose and the goose in a swan. It was hard to tell exactly how many layers there were, but she felt sure an unfortunate hummingbird lay somewhere at the heart of it.

It must have taken days to prepare all this!

The matron had given up on the drunken captain, who was picking at his food as if it were a kind of hors d'oeuvre served with the drinks. Erika couldn't even guess how much wine he'd consumed. As soon as his glass was empty, a waiter filled it up again.

How am I supposed to make a good impression on someone deep in his cups?

She turned to the Duchess, but she was busy giving instructions to the headwaiter. As she wondered what to do next, Erika felt something small and moist land between her breasts. The Duchess' unruly younger son had flicked an olive into her décolletage. She covered herself with a defensive napkin.

"Ha!" said Scolinus. "Want me to fish that out for you?"

Not so drunk as I thought. He must have an enormous capacity for alcohol.

"Not right now if you please. Perhaps later?"

"Whenever you like."

"We shall have to make an appointment. In the meanwhile, I'd treasure a small keepsake of our meeting. Perhaps one of those gold buttons?"

"Anything for the ladies," said Scolinus, cutting one off with his fruit knife.

"Thank you," said Erika. Meanwhile, a waiter had placed a wobbly-looking confection in front of her, which she tentatively identified as a panna cotta covered with a mosaic of red and blue berries.

Across the table from her, Amphitus was about to plunge his spoon into this treat, when a large gold button landed in the middle of it, splashing him with gooey pudding and decorating his face with berries.

"HA!" said the drunken captain, pointing. All eyes turned toward the boy, who looked around in bewilderment, pudding dripping from his face.

"How many times have I told you not to play with your food?" scolded the Duchess, who hadn't noticed the hostilities. "Go to your room!"

"That was quite droll," said Scolinus. "Dinners in Tidewater must be very lively."

"It depends on who's invited," said Erika. "But I'd rather hear more about your military career."

"Not much to tell," said Scolinus, who was sampling the dessert wine. "I was going to take part in the invasion, but my creditors decided otherwise. They managed to stick me in a post that wouldn't involve any great risk to their investments.

"And so old Epidarus is ordering my pikemen around in Chatmakstan, and I'm stuck scheduling watches and inspecting boots, except when I'm drafted for some official function, where I have to stand to attention while the King entertains us with one of his rambling speeches. It's the most boring job you can imagine."

"Perhaps we can find some way to liven it up. Let's stay in touch."

"Yes, let's do that."

As the waiters removed the last of the plates, the Duchess stood and tapped on a wine glass with a silver spoon.

"I have an apology!" she announced. "Several of you were kind enough to compliment me on my new dress and inquire where I obtained the fabric. Selfishly, I've kept that information to myself.

"But now I will make amends. The cloth is a previously unknown fabric, booty from the province of Chatmakstan. As much as I'd like to take the credit for its discovery, it properly belongs to a young woman of my acquaintance, Lady Erika of Tidewater, who's brought it here at considerable personal risk. She tells me she has a small supply she wishes to offer to her friends through a trading house under the patronage of my son Clenas.

"And despite my understandable protests, Lady Erika has chosen to honor this new fabric with the name Duchess Silk. I anticipate it will soon be indispensable for ladies of fashion."

As the men wandered off into the drawing room, some of the ladies clustered around the Duchess for another look at her dress and others around Erika, hoping for more information on the new fabric and when it would be available. Erika could only say, "You can expect an announcement soon." Several women slipped her visiting cards, asking to be personally notified, and Erika told them they would be.

The more they struggle to get ahold of it, the better!

After the last inquisitive guest had been ushered out the door, the Duchess took Erika aside and grilled her. "Well? How did it go?"

"Very well, your Grace. There seems to be a great demand for *pamuk . . .*"

The Duchess frowned at her as if she'd said something stupid. "Not that, I meant with Capt. Scolinus."

"You said I should make a good impression, and I doubt I could have made a better one. He thinks I'm a wealthy heiress."

"Did you know a servant found one of his buttons in my son's dessert?"

"Oh, yes. He was rather tipsy, your Grace. But the point to which I would draw your attention is that the captain is a drunkard and deep in debt. His career is as good as over. When our heroes return, they'll pack him off to some remote garrison where he can quietly drink himself to death. You needn't dangle women in front of him. Capt. Scolinus is for sale, and I doubt he will reject your first offer.

"But," she added searchingly, "I can't possibly imagine what you would want with such a person."

"Thank you for your assistance."

The next morning after breakfast, the butler announced a visitor was waiting for her in the drawing room. There, she found a tall and dignified gentleman whom the butler introduced as Mr. Herminius of the Mercantile Consortium.

Herminius got straight to the point: "I understand you're the agent responsible for the distribution of Duchess Silk?"

"That would an indelicate way of putting it. The Hikmet trading house is a new firm operating under the patronage of Prince Clenas and engaged in the export of native fabrics as supplemental finances for the war effort. The Prince requested my assistance, since I was travelling to Elohi, and they had as yet no permanent representative here."

"I see," said Herminius impatiently. He looked as if the doctor were giving him a particularly disagreeable nostrum to drink.

He thinks I'm just another stuck-up aristocrat.

"But that need not concern you. I am, in fact, authorized to sign sales contracts on behalf of the Hikmet trading house, which is the sole supplier of Duchess Silk."

"Ah. And may I see some of this much-discussed new product?"

"Of course. Unfortunately, my samples were sacrificed to produce an exhibition gown for the Duchess. I will have to ask her dressmaker to bring down what she has left."

It turned out most of the fabric was still there though there were many missing pieces. Herminius examined each sample in turn, tugging at it to test for strength, putting it under a magnifying glass to count the threads and dunking a scrap in a bowl of water to see if the dye ran.

Finally, he said, "Most remarkable. I've never seen anything like it. Of course, it's not nearly as fine as real silk."

"I think you will find it quite acceptable for the summer season. The ladies here are clamoring for it." She showed him her collection of visiting cards.

"How much can you supply?"

"At the moment, we have 300 bolts of the first grade and 200 of the second ready for 30 day delivery. Another batch will be available in a few days. We expect to have a total of eight batches completed in time for the summer season."

"And how much would you want for all of it?"

Erika's jaw dropped. "All? You want an exclusive contract?"

Herminius nodded. "I think you can readily see the advantages of a central distribution. We will control the supply and therefore the price, without any lengthy negotiations. The stores will all send their orders here. You need only ship us the merchandise."

"But . . ." Her mind was whirling. "But . . . if we're to bind ourselves to an exclusive contract, we would have to demand an exorbitant price . . ."

"How does three thalers a bolt sound?"

It sounds ridiculous! I'd hardly pay that for the finest silk!

"Six for the first grade, five for the second."

"Done. I'll have my secretary draw up the papers."

That was too fast! I could have gotten more!

"Wait a minute! I will need a deposit! I can't conclude an agreement of this scale simply on a handshake!"

"Fine. We will make an advance payment for the first shipment

. . ." – He paused a moment to calculate. – ". . . of 2,800 thalers. You can expect to find a deposit under your name in the Royal Bank of Akaddia within 24 hours."

When the papers were signed and the guest had left, Erika sat down heavily in the empty room and allowed her body to relax into an unladylike sprawl. She felt drained, almost as if she'd given birth. With so much money, she could buy out most the fabric stores in Halland.

So this is how they do business here! So this is how one becomes the owner of fine mansions!

Now she could have anything she wanted. But the first thing she wanted, no, desperately needed, was a stiff drink. She reached for the bell pull to summon the butler.

After lunch, the butler brought her three sealed letters. She went to her room to read them privately. The first was written on the elegant, gilt-trimmed stationery of the royal palace:

Dear Erika,

It has been many a long day since I enjoyed myself so much as when I shared your company at the Duke's dinner party. Your beauty and your wit are captivating. I can hardly wait to see you again. With your permission, I would like to call on you tomorrow. Perhaps you would care for a tour of the palace? My position, though sometimes tedious, allows me access to even the most private places. The war has separated me from my friends, but I would be most honored to consider you a new one.

Anxiously awaiting your response,
Capt. Scolinus

Well, I guess I hooked him.

Under other circumstances, it might be a tempting invitation. That is, it might have been, were she not married to a royal prince and were the captain not a hopeless drunkard. As she read the situation, Scolinus would soon come to pay her a visit, but be greeted instead by the Duchess, who had some sort of proposition for him.

I wish I knew what's going on . . . but maybe it's better not to know.

The second letter was a note, written in a woman's hand on pink stationery:

Dear Erika,

Following our tête-à-tête, I consulted with the Duchess with regard to your situation, and we agreed you should be brought up to date on current developments. I have arranged for the use of an appropriately inconspicuous conveyance, which will await us at the rear entrance after breakfast tomorrow. The driver is a trustworthy family servant and also somewhat deaf. We shall then be able to exchange confidences at our leisure, and I will introduce you to certain persons whose acquaintance you may find advantageous.

Yours truly,

Camilla

Having read the letter, Erika blinked incredulously and read it again. Was this the same bubbly little busybody who'd accosted her last night?

Camilla is no fool, but she certainly played me for one! What kind of a game is this?

Still shaking her head, she put aside the second letter and opened the third one, which was written in block letters on anonymous white paper:

DEAR LADY ERIKA,

DO NOT TRUST THE DUKE. YOU HAVE BEEN BETRAYED AND ARE IN GRAVE PERSONAL DANGER. MEET ME AFTER DARK BY THE THREE LADIES, AND ALL WILL BE REVEALED.

A FRIEND

16: Rajik

He kept sinking in the mud.

All around him, the *efaryti* lay among the reeds, up to their eyeballs and motionless as stones. They were in their element. Rajik, however, felt quite certain he didn't belong here, in this desolate swamp, particularly on a night when the blue moon made everything look strange and the silence was so deathly, he could hear himself breathe.

He squirmed uncomfortably as the mud tried to swallow him up. His struggles caused a small rustling among the reeds and drew resentful looks from the *efaryti,* who seemed offended by his clumsiness. He wondered if Raeesha, who was hiding a short distance off to his right with another demon pack, had the same problem.

The Witch, of course, was on the hill somewhere, warm and safe and, for all he knew, asleep in bed. The stakeout was her idea. The Wind Bags, she said, attacked on still, moonlit nights, and it should be possible to set an ambush for them. But this was their third attempt, and nothing had happened, except the lack of sleep was making him groggy.

Rajik began to wonder if the Ghost Feet were playing some kind of demonic trick on him. Obviously, they were enjoying this more than he was. How could he even be sure there were any such things as Wind Bags? The description they'd given him was so vague, he could only imagine flying monsters bigger than houses swooping down from the sky. How was he supposed to fight that?

He clutched the bow he'd made from a sapling. Since he had no skill as a bowyer, his weapon wasn't much better than those used by the *efaryti,* just a little bigger. He had only the one weapon, but he did have a hundred Ghost Feet with him and their archery was much improved. He'd worked out some hand signals, which they seemed to understand, but whether they'd pay any attention in the dark and in the middle of a fight was still an open question.

How did I get into this mess?

It seemed totally unfair he was stuck in the middle of a swamp all night with a bunch of demons. And now, it was getting chilly.

Maybe sinking down into the warm, soft mud wasn't so bad after all. He could hardly drown in water a few inches deep, and the demons would pull him out if he got stuck.

He turned his head to look up at the stars. He couldn't recognize a single constellation, but to kill time, he started to give them names. This one looked like a sword, and that over there like a horse's head. That one was like a water jar, and the other had four sharp points, like a diamond. Now, he saw a constellation like the Amir's palace, with its golden dome, and while he stared in amazement, he saw a Bandeluk war galley rowing by, its oars churning up the sea of stars . . .

"Pssst!"

Something was poking him sharply in the ribs. He rolled over and found himself sputtering, face down in the water. He must have fallen asleep. Crouching next to him was the demon he'd christened Long Ear, one of the few he could recognize. It pointed with a clawed finger at the yellow moon, which had appeared on the horizon behind a small cloud.

Though he squinted, he couldn't see anything special about the moon. It looked just like it had the night before, perhaps a bit fuller, but now it was obscured by the cloud . . .

That's not a cloud!

It was moving too fast, and it was getting bigger. This cloud seemed to have sharp edges, and there were things hanging from it on ropes . . .

A ship! A flying ship!

He pinched himself in case he was dreaming again, but as it approached, it became more and more obvious he was looking at some kind of a ship without sails, floating high in the air. Lying in the mud beside him, he could hear Long Ear hissing softly to itself, a sound full of malice and hatred, as if it recognized an ancient enemy.

So this is what they tried to describe. No wonder we couldn't understand them!

As it came nearer, it grew huge, almost eclipsing the moon. If this were a ship, it was the biggest he'd ever seen. And then it grew larger still, blotting out the light as it hovered above the dark village. Cables were lowered with objects that looked like the anchors of a ship. Rajik could feel his heart hammering. Talking about this was one thing, but actually doing it was something quite different.

According to the plan, the villagers were to wait for the Wind Bags to attack, then flee and lead them into an ambush. Meanwhile, the Witch was supposed to cast some kind of spell that would prevent them from flying away. Rajik wondered if everyone had gotten the message. He looked over to where Raeesha and her demon pack were waiting, but he could see nothing in the endless bog.

The flying ship descended slowly. He could hear a distant whirring as if great wheels were spinning around. Then, suddenly, dozens of ropes were dropped, and shadowy figures came sliding down. All at once, there were lights in the village and he could hear shrill screams as the unarmed villagers, doing a good imitation of a panicky mob, streamed out of the huts and toward his position.

Where's the Witch? What's she doing?

There was nothing he could do but lie still and watch as the villagers, pale in the moonlight, fled from the sinister, dark figures that pursued them. Meanwhile, he noticed, the flying ship had begun to glow: A pale nimbus surrounded it, which grew steadily brighter, and it started to descend with a jerky motion as if out of control. He could hear the great wheels turning, but they seemed unable to correct the sudden fall. It was caught like a fish in a net. The giant ship was heading toward the ground.

Ha! Now we've got them!

He was almost ready to give the signal to fire, when he heard a soft noise to his right as if someone were retching.

No! Not now!

The excitement must have stimulated the demon embryo. Some new calamity was about to happen, and there was no way to prevent it.

The earth began shaking. The *efaryti* squealed in fear, as those who were standing fell on their faces. The great flying ship, which had descended almost to the surface, suddenly dropped. There was a series of loud *crunches* as the straw huts of the village collapsed. Then, the ship bounced skyward. The glowing nimbus around it flickered and went black.

What happened to the Witch?

He had no time to worry about her because now rain was falling on him from out of a clear sky. The water was cold and had a salty taste. From his right came shrill screams. A geyser of water had sprung in the air. It rapidly grew into a column that seemed to fill the sky. Terrified Ghost Feet ran in all directions, some even toward the attackers.

The rain of salty water was now a torrential downpour. The swamp rose around him. He had no choice. If he didn't stand up, he'd drown. He could no longer see any of the Ghost Feet except Long Ear, who was crouching beside him and hissing like an angry cat. Rajik gave it the signal to follow and moved toward the hill.

The water was getting deeper. It was freezing cold. Rajik's toes became numb, but not before he felt something scaly brush against them underwater. Salt water was pouring down the hillside like a river, and the current threatened to sweep him off his feet.

Then, without any warning, the rain suddenly stopped, and he could see once again. He was standing knee-deep in a cold, salty lake. *Efaryti* splashed around, some with bows and some without. A hundred yards behind him, two of the little demons were helping Raeesha to her feet.

On the hill, there was no village left to be seen, just mounds of straw and earth. The flying boat was raising its cables and ropes. Attached to some of the latter were struggling forms he took to be captive Ghost Feet. There was no sign of the Witch.

He stood there helplessly, as the flying ship gained altitude and sailed away serenely into the night. The ambush had turned into a rout, a complete disaster.

Now what do we do?

Morning light found a despondent group of *efaryti*, with two humans, sitting among the remains of their village. The straw huts were completely flat; it was hard to see where they'd been. Many of the Ghost Feet were missing, among them the matriarch. The Witch was nowhere to be found.

Some of the demons poked through the ruins, salvaging whatever they could. Small, pitiful piles of possessions were gradually assembled: stone tools, pots containing grain, baskets full of tubers, woven reed mats. The mood was listless. Around the barren hill, their ponds and gardens were full of salt water.

Demon sprats gathered clams in the water. The clam shells were already open; the salt had killed them. Here and there, they brought in some of the strange fish that had washed up: bizarre creatures with huge eyes, scales like armor and teeth like daggers. Raeesha picked one up, examined it critically, then began gutting it. Seeing what she was doing, the Ghost Feet started to gather sticks for a fire, and before long a fish fry and clam bake were in progress.

The demons gorged themselves with single-minded determination, not knowing when they'd have another chance. Hunger satisfied, they sat on the remains of their homes in a kind of stupor. Without the matriarch telling them what to do, they seemed completely lost. But it was obvious they couldn't stay here. The Ghost Feet village was done for.

Raeesha sat by the dying fire, finishing off the clams. She seemed to have recovered from her fateful nausea the night before.

"What do you think we should do?" he asked.

"I want this demon out of me, and I want to go home, and for either one, we need the Witch," she said. "Let's go and find her."

"I think the Wind Bags must have gotten her." He pointed north, the direction the flying ship had taken.

"Then we need to go kill some Wind Bags."

Nearby was a heavy wooden mallet the *efaryti* used to pound the reeds into fiber. Raeesha picked it up and smashed an empty pot.

Then all eyes were on her.

Pulling an arrow from her quiver, she pointed it to the north and made the sign for attack. That was all it took. The Ghost Feet began hissing softly. The hisses grew louder, turned into indignant squeals, then shrieks of rage. The mob of demons stood and shook their weapons in the direction of the hated Wind Bags. Now they knew what they wanted: They wanted revenge.

Toward evening on the next day, they came to a river. Rajik had had no idea it was there, this muddy, winding estuary. It was at least a hundred yards across and no telling how deep. The Ghost Feet could probably swim it, but they'd have to leave their possessions behind, and food was already in short supply.

For lack of any better plan, they turned and moved upstream, hoping to find a place to cross. After an hour, they saw a boat anchored near the opposite shore. A pair of *efaryti* were working the water with their fish spears. They turned to stare suspiciously at the intruders.

That looks a lot like the reed boats the Chatmaks make.

The Ghost Feet shouted with their shrill voices at the fishermen and gestured for them to come over, but got only what sounded like jeers in response. One of the strangers bent over and presented its buttocks. After some further acrimony, the fishermen raised anchor and paddled away upstream.

"That did not go very well," said Rajik.

"At least they aren't Wind Bags," said Raeesha. "No one fired at them, and we could have."

"Some other tribe, then."

"If they aren't going to help us, let's hope they don't get in the way."

The next morning, they found the path blocked by an *efaryti* village, somewhat larger than that of the Ghost Feet. It was built on a small rise above the river and protected by a stockade decorated with a large collection of skulls. Rajik half expected to see human skulls among them, but they all belonged to the familiar local demons.

Don't mess with us, is what that means.

Villagers armed with spears, axes and bows crowded the edge

of the stockade, looking down at the approaching Ghost Feet.

"How do we tell them we just want to go by?"

"Maybe we could ask him to translate," said Raeesha, pointing to a bearded head, wearing a Chatmak turban, which had appeared among the *efaryti.*

"What in the name of all devils is he doing here?"

"I can only think of one way of finding out." She signaled the Ghost Feet to wait and, slinging her bow over her shoulder, walked up to the palisade. Rajik trailed behind.

The face above the palisade stared at them incredulously. "How did you people get here?" he said in Chatmaki, adding, "You look like Bandeluks."

"You found us out," said Raeesha. "But we're just trying to get home."

"You have a way to get home?"

"If we did, we wouldn't be here, but yes, we do know of a way home."

"You better come inside," said the Chatmak.

A few minutes later, they were in a wooden hut in the village, sipping something that tasted only faintly like tea. The building, Rajik noted, was made of dressed timber, better than anything the Ghost Feet could boast of, and furnished with wooden stools and benches, besides decorative woven hangings on the walls. There was an iron-headed axe by the door.

I thought the efaryti *were ignorant, but maybe we happened to land among a bunch of primitives. Just my luck.*

"We were out fishing," said Iyad, as he called himself. "It was a perfectly normal day until a waterspout suddenly grabbed us and whirled us in the air and dumped us here. My comrades held onto the boat, but I was thrown clear and splashed down in the swamp, so I was the only one who survived."

"I think we found your boat," said Rajik. "There was a Bandeluk warship too."

"Yes, I was coming to that. I was so stunned I could hardly move, and I had no trouble playing dead while the demons sniffed around, but after awhile, I saw they'd brought in another ship, a big one, and were hauling off the crew in chains. And then a big flying thing came and picked them up, along with the salvage.

"I thought I must be going crazy, but I followed them because it was the only thing I could think of, and so I came here. These demons (they're called Head Counters) grabbed me and made me chop wood for them, but eventually, I learned a bit of their lingo and was able to show them I could make reed boats and some other things they found useful, so they gave me this house and set me to work."

This man must have been saving up his Chatmaki for a long time.

"It was a Witch who brought us here," said Raeesha simply. "And she promised to bring us home, but then the Wind Bags grabbed her, so we're going to get her back."

"I hope you're ready for a stiff fight. The Wind Bags aren't keen on negotiations."

"Yes," said Rajik. "They totally destroyed the Ghost Feet village. There's nothing left of it."

"Bad news. Very bad, for the Head Counters. The Wind Bags used to come here for their slaves until they found easier targets. We may be looking at a war."

"We already are," said Raeesha. "The whole Ghost Feet tribe is on the warpath, and us with them. We were hoping the Head Counters would help us out, or at least let us pass through."

"I can talk to them about it," said Iyad skeptically. "But I hope you have a better plan than to go after the Wind Bags with a ragged mob of Ghost Feet. The Wind Bags have a big fortress up in the hills. If they were easy to clean out, the Head Counters would have done it years ago."

"Of course we have a plan," said Raeesha confidently.

Not unless she just thought of one!

17: Bardhof

This is a new low, even for military intelligence.

The Amir's archive, in the basement of the palace, was a dark and musty place, crowded with shelves and cabinets full of documents, reports, assessments, notices and correspondence. Some documents, the oldest ones presumably, were in wooden crates in the back. Others, the newest, were scattered around in random stacks and heaps, or simply lying on the floor where the archivist left them, before he died during the siege.

Anahita stared at the jumbled paper warren with distaste. "What are we doing here?"

"You say you can read. Start reading," said Bardhof.

"Salak!"

He didn't know what that meant, but it sounded rude. Recruiting a captured Bandeluk prostitute for clerical duties violated several military regulations, he knew, and probably some ethical and moral standards as well. But his Bandeluki was still quite poor, and translators were hard to find. Anahita was the mistress of three languages, which she frequently used to complain.

"My father sold me to a brothel when I was twelve," she said. "They taught me to please men, to sing and dance, to play instruments and to recite poems. But mostly just to please men."

"Good, then you should have no trouble pleasing me."

"They never taught me to read government documents."

"It isn't that hard," said Bardhof, taking one at random from where it was lying on a desk. "What does this say?"

Anahita studied it, frowning as if she were sizing up an impecunious customer. "It's a summary of tariff revenues from the port," she said.

"See, that wasn't so hard. What about this one?"

She took a bit longer with the second document, which contained many crossed-out words and marginal scribbles. "A letter to the Emperor, congratulating him on his 37th birthday," she said finally.

"This is like your job," said Bardhof. "The more you do it, the easier it gets." He reached for another piece of paper.

"And your job? Is it getting any easier?" She pressed her body against his. "Are you sure this is what you want me to do today?"

He pushed her away. "Yes, quite sure. If you don't like working here, I can move you back to the prison."

Her eyes widened. "You are not so cruel!"

"Little you know. I'm practicing to be a pimp."

She glanced at the third document, before tossing it aside. "A furlough for an officer due to a death in the family. How can you find anything this way?"

"I can't. But you can. We're just looking for your old friend Omin. You already know him."

"I already told you, he was never a friend, only a client!"

"Whatever you call him, he's in here somewhere. No one lives and dies without leaving some traces."

She flung her hands skyward, a gesture of helplessness. "But it's such a big place! He could be hiding anywhere!"

"You're good at finding men. It's your job."

"I seldom go looking for any specific man and certainly not in a place like this!"

So what does one do with a prostitute who refuses to work?

One could reach for the whip, or . . .

"How much do you charge your customers?" he said.

"It depends on who they are and what they want. A common sailor is two piasters. They don't expect much. An officer is five, more for a high official. Perverts are extra."

"Fine," he said. "I will pay you two piasters for every document you find that mentions Omin. The gem merchant Omin, not anyone else by that name."

She gestured at the piles of documents. "But where am I to start?"

"Anywhere you like. If you don't find him in one place, try another. I will be back in a few hours to see how you're doing."

He closed and locked the door, but not before a parting *"sal-ak!"*

When he returned two hours later, he found Anahita lounging, with a bored expression, at a desk that held a small stack of papers. "You owe me ten piasters," she said.

Already? You're clearly wasted as a prostitute.

"Only five customers, out of such a crowd?"

"It was a slow day. I'd gladly earn more piasters if I could, but there's nothing here. These are mostly just financial records. The great Amir didn't care about anything but money."

Then you have something in common.

"Let's see what you found."

She held up three documents. "He three times paid a tariff on shipments of garnets from the Nonus trading house in Kingsport."

"Garnets? Are they popular here?"

"Hmmpf. Baubles for peasants. Who'd want garnets if he could have emeralds and pearls?" She fingered her own pearl necklace.

"Might be worth looking into. What else?"

She held up two documents. "Omin paid a tax of 40 piasters on his house and 40 piasters also the previous year."

"Only two years? The tax records go back no further than that?"

"They do, but the house belonged to someone else, a goldsmith named Toygar."

Interesting: gold and gems. No one is surprised to see a jeweler or goldsmith in a big house with extra security.

"What do you have on Toygar?"

"Nothing. You didn't ask about Toygar. I get no piasters for

Toygar."

"Then we may need another search."

"You will have to pay me extra," she said sulkily, "for being a pervert."

The records of the city watch showed identity papers had been issued to a goldsmith named Toygar, who lived on Kuyumcu Street. They found the old man in his modest shop, industriously hammering away at something behind a counter covered with gold rings, bracelets and necklaces. He put down his tools and bowed respectfully when Bardhof entered, but less respectfully to Anahita. When Grimald and Murdoon entered, he gasped and turned pale.

"We just need to ask you some questions," said Bardhof reassuringly.

"Effendi, this is not my war! I'm just a civilian! I'll tell you whatever you want to know!"

"That's what I like to hear."

Bardhof took Grimald aside privately and said, "I think Murdoon might be tempted to filch some of this gold. Keep an eye on him."

Then he whispered to Murdoon, "Grimald is so greedy, I'm afraid he may try to snatch the gold. Don't let him out of your sight."

As he followed the old man behind the counter and into his living quarters, he left the two soldiers standing in the shop. Each glared suspiciously at the other.

Toygar's living room was small, but comfortably furnished with rugs and cushions. An old but dangerous-looking sword hung on one wall. After the customary cups of tea, he told the visitors his story:

"I served the old Emperor many years. When he died, Col. Sardar was appointed chief of intelligence, and I was sent to Chatmakstan. In those days, it was a kind of backwater. Nothing ever happened here. Older officers were posted to Kafra for a few years of easy duty, before collecting their pensions. But I never got mine.

"There's this old summer house on Hajar . . ."

"Where?"

"Hajar is an island south of Kafra. No one lives there; it's all rock and sand. But years ago, Prince Beyazid liked to spend his summers . . ."

"Who?"

"The Emperor's eldest son and heir. Was. He renovated the old summer house and moved in with his friends and had parties and went sailing around in his *gulet* . . . "

"His what?"

"A *gulet* is a ship like a big dhow, a kind of a yacht. He used to cruise along the coast and pretend to be a sailor or a fisherman, or whatever he liked."

"That sounds harmless."

"I thought so. But Col. Sardar disagreed. He said Prince Beyazid was entertaining foreigners. He thought there might be some kind of treasonous conspiracy and ordered me to investigate. So I placed a reliable man named Evrim on the island and told him to watch the Prince and record all the comings and goings."

"And?"

"And nothing. Evrim reported the prince sometimes entertained visiting merchants and ship captains, and asked questions about the countries they came from or had visited, but didn't disclose any secrets. I don't think he knew any. His trips in the *gulet* were to remote beaches and coves, wherever the fishing was good and the girls were pretty. There was no treason, no conspiracy. I wrote a report to Col. Sardar and told him that."

"And then?"

"And then he dismissed me, just one year short of my pension! I had to take up my old trade, which I fortunately knew well enough, so with my savings and a bit of hard work, I was able to open a shop . . ."

"Yes, that's too bad. What happened to Prince Beyazid?"

"He drowned a few months later."

"Drowned? His ship sank?"

"No, that was the strange part. They found him floating in a canal in the capital."

"He was assassinated?"

"Maybe. Beyazid was always a good swimmer, and how could he end up in a canal? It sounds suspicious. But no one really knows."

Somebody knows!

"We'll have to have a long talk about Col. Sardar sometime."

"I'll tell you what I know, but it's second-hand. I never worked closely with him."

"So Omin took over your office?"

"Yes."

"And he handled things differently?"

"I really can't say. He was a stranger from Kosizar. We hardly even met."

"During your time here, did you gather foreign intelligence?"

"Not much. We were primarily interested in domestic surveillance. There were always little intrigues between the sheikhs and unrest among the peasants. Nothing very serious, though. I had a couple men watching the docks and the foreigners, to pick up rumors. They didn't learn much. No one dreamed the Akaddians were going to invade. Who would invade a place like this?"

"But someone warned the Amir the foreigners were coming, days before the landing."

"I heard that. Everyone heard that. But who told him, I have no idea. It was long after I was dismissed. No one cares about an old man like me."

"Did you ever hear of Gen. Basilius?"

"Not until he landed with the troops. No, not one word."

"Have you ever heard of someone called the Creeper?"

"Never."

"Have you ever heard of the Nonus trading house in Kingsport?"

"I don't think so. But there are a lot of trading houses that do business here."

Bardhof sighed. This investigation was going nowhere.

"What about this island? What happened with it?"

"So far as I know, it's still there." Toygar smiled timidly at this little joke.

"And the summer house?"

"Still in the same place."

"Who lives there now?"

"No one unless Evrim is still there. I don't know what happened to him."

"Why would he still be there?"

"He was the caretaker. And still is unless Omin reassigned him. I haven't seen Evrim for a long time."

"You think Omin just left him there? Why would he do that?"

Toygar shrugged. "Maybe they didn't get along."

There has to be more to it than this. Is this man telling me the whole story?

It didn't seem worthwhile torturing an old man who probably didn't know anything. At least not while there were other lines of inquiry.

"While I'm here, perhaps I'll buy something for my friend Anahita. It happens I owe her some money."

"Just the cash, please," said Anahita.

Assholes!

He'd spent an unproductive hour in the naval headquarters, where he was told, over and over, no ships were available for a trip to Hajar, and any such orders would have to come from the base in Kingsport. Also, they had no information on Hajar, except what the charts said, that it was a desert island, presumed uninhabited.

But that can't be true! Do they really know nothing about the prince and his summer house?

Looking toward the harbor, he saw a felucca coming into port with a load of fish. "Let's see who that is and whether his boat is for rent," he said.

"Most things are, at the right price," said Anahita.

A few minutes later, they were standing on the dock, talking to the owner, a man named Guner. "He says he's from the village of Yalniz," said Anahita. "He heard pirates were burning the villages, so he came here. He wants to know where you're going."

"Hajar. It isn't far away. Tell him we're only going for the day."

"He says he can't go there. Hajar is an imperial preserve. A trip to Hajar means a trip to heaven."

"Tell him the Emperor isn't watching. Tell him I'll pay 20 piasters."

"He calls you cheap. He says he can make that much fishing."

"Offer him 30 then."

"He says 35. And he wants me as part of the deal."

"Tell him he'll have to negotiate with you separately."

The felucca had only a single sail. It was about 25 feet long, small enough that Grimald and Murdoon had to sit in the center for fear of tipping it over. It stank of fish, and it tended to pitch and rock in the choppy waters off the coast. Anahita was soon seasick.

Multilingual curses accompanied a colorful breakfast of cheese, to-matoes, carrots, cucumbers and olives over the side.

As they drew closer, Bardhof saw Hajar was a volcanic island. The parts that weren't rock were sandy. Guner, seeking a landing place, found the inviting beaches were guarded by jagged shoals with many cross-currents that made any approach hazardous.

It was almost noon before they found a small inlet on the south side, with a single quay. Rising behind it, like the teeth of some monstrous creature, were the blackened ruins of a once-palatial building.

As they docked, a ragged figure came running out of the ruins. Looking as scrawny as a beggar and frantic as a fugitive from justice, he fell on his knees and launched into a babble of Bandeluki.

"He calls you effendi. And he begs you to take him away from this cursed place," translated Anahita.

"Ask him what happened here."

"He says pirates came in the night and took away the boat and the crew. They looted the house and then burned it down. He's had nothing to eat but mussels and rainwater for weeks."

"Ask him his name."

"Evrim," said the kneeling man. That required no translation.

"Tell Evrim he's a lucky fellow. Tell him we're going to be great friends."

FROM: Capt. Bardhof, Investigating Officer
TO: Prince Krion, Commander-in-Chief of the Allied Forces
SUBJECT: Counterespionage

Further investigation reveals the Bandeluk spymaster Omin had contact with Akaddian sources. A former operative named Evrim, found on the island of Hajar, reports several meetings on the island in the last two years between Omin and naval officers. The identities of these officers have not been determined.

Omin also had correspondence with the Nonus trading house in Kingsport regarding the purchase of garnets. The Nonus trading house is part of the Merchantile Consortium controlled by Duke Claudio.

Prince Krion glanced at the brief report quizzically before passing it back to Bardhof. "What do you expect me to do with this?" he said.

"I expect nothing, my Prince. I'm merely reporting the progress of my investigation."

"It does not appear to have progressed to any conclusions."

"Unfortunately, the naval authorities have been uncooperative, and Kingsport lies outside my jurisdiction."

"So your next step would be . . .?"

"Referring the case to Elohi for investigation."

"That might mean asking the culprits to investigate themselves."

"What of the judicial authorities?"

Krion waved a hand impatiently. "What of them? Do you have any criminal case you could present to the courts?"

"Not yet, but there is clear evidence of treasonable communications with the enemy."

"By whom? Is there any actual record of what these unnamed naval officers were doing in Hajar?"

"Not here. Maybe in Kingsport."

"Could they have been doing something perfectly innocent? Coordinating anti-piracy efforts, perhaps?"

Bardhof licked his lips. He felt sure this had nothing to do with anti-piracy operations, but how could he prove it? "Further investigation . . ."

"Will have to wait. I'm not in any position to make demands on the Admiralty right now."

"But this Nonus trading house . . . "

"Could simply be doing what it always does, trading. You have any proof to the contrary?"

"Not yet, but there must be records . . . "

"Under the control of Duke Claudio, who's someone else I can't afford to skirmish with. Take this report and file it. We have a war to fight."

Bardhof was turning to go, when the Prince stopped him as if he'd remembered something important. "Did you learn anything further about this mysterious person, the Creeper?"

"No, my Prince."

"Ah. I guess that's not terribly surprising."

Crestfallen, Bardhof left the palace with the feeling the jokes about military intelligence were not without merit. For all his efforts, he was no closer to finding the Creeper.

"You look like you're in need of consolation," said Anahita, who was waiting outside. "For that, I can offer you a special rate."

18: Nergui

Everything was going wrong, and now he had a headache.

It was not enough he was forced to wait an hour in the small, dark and stuffy council room with people he hated. For this occasion, he was obliged to wear the turban of the *mujahid,* the warrior, which represented a shroud. It was heavy as an iron helmet and wrapped extremely tight, so it wouldn't fall off when he bowed to the Emperor. Every pulse of blood brought a sharp pain to his head, which felt like it would explode.

I could hardly devise a better instrument of torture!

It was some comfort that Vizier Yasin, sitting next to him, was wearing an even bigger turban and was sweating like a pig in his embroidered ceremonial robes. Two of the Emperor's personal servants, deaf-mutes most likely, were lazily stirring the air in the chamber with fans made of peacock feathers. There was no one to encourage them since the Emperor Ahmed, as usual, was late.

Nergui entertained himself by imagining how much fun it would be to impale Yasin. The Vizier, he knew, had been sucking money from the military budget, supplying the army with swords that broke, uniforms that dissolved in the rain and food that was barely edible, while he and his cronies got richer and richer. Regardless of his complaints, Yasin was untouchable because he'd allied himself with Hervika, the Favorite. Doubtless after some generous bribes, she'd persuaded the Emperor to overlook his faults.

By no coincidence, Yasin was seated opposite Prince Murad, Hervika's son, the heir apparent. A boy of only 13 years, he owed his position to the sudden death of his half-brother, Prince Beyazid. Nergui believed Col. Sardar had played a role in that, but there was nothing he could do about it. There was nothing anyone could do.

Yasin, Hervika and Sardar, what a pit of serpents!

Aside from two of Yasin's lickspittle ministers, the only other person in the room was Adm. Haluk, and Nergui expected no help from him. Twenty-five years before, the aging admiral had crushed the Hillinese fleet with his war galleys and ever since had thought of little but bigger and more magnificent war galleys.

It was no good pointing out his galleys were useless in the stormy western ocean, where a different kind of navy was needed against the foreigners. Nor was Haluk moved to action when some of his mighty warships disappeared without a trace while on routine patrols. He simply confined his precious galleys to port, where they made an impressive display of military power and were otherwise completely worthless.

May the gods help me! Have I not always served the Emperor faithfully? Why then am I brought low by this miserable pack . . .

His bitter thoughts were interrupted by a faint breath of air, followed by sound of a door closing. Someone must have entered the small chamber behind the throne, which had a lattice through which one could secretly observe the proceedings. The law said no woman could attend a meeting of the war council, but Hervika was a law unto herself.

Then a gong sounded as the Emperor entered, accompanied by two of the palace guard. The councilors all bowed until their noses almost touched the ground. Nergui felt an explosion of agony as the blood rushed to his head, but at least the turban stayed in place. The gong sounded again, and he was permitted to sit up, something he did with a sigh of relief.

The mighty Emperor, Chosen of the Gods and Master of the World, didn't inspire any feelings of awe. Ahmed was paler and flabbier than when Nergui had last seen him, taking the inevitable decline of middle age with alarming speed. He stared for a minute at the council, blinking in befuddlement as if he'd forgotten what to say.

Has she been giving him opium again?

A hushed whisper was audible from behind the lattice as his Favorite prompted him. The Emperor nodded and began to speak:

"Our loyal subjects," he began, "we call on you, in this troubled time, to advise us what measures to take against the vicious foreigners who have swarmed over our westernmost province and murdered our servant Amir Qilij. We trust, with your counsel, we may soon put an end to this scourge. Let our honored *mushir,* who has so many times brought us victories, begin by sharing his observations."

That was his cue. Standing with his head respectfully bent toward the Emperor, he began. "Your Imperial Majesty! I am delighted to report the raiders in Chatmakstan present no serious danger to your Empire. The foreigners do not number more than 40,000 and are confined to a narrow strip of land. They won't be able to cross the mountains until spring, by which time 120,000 of your invincible soldiers will be waiting for them.

"Nor can the meager resources of Chatmakstan long sustain them in their present position. They must either advance recklessly into certain defeat, or else take their shabby plunder and flee from your just retribution. You need not bestir yourself. Only raise your little finger, and they will fall before you."

There was another hushed whisper from behind the lattice. The Emperor said, "What then of this new weapon, which has already destroyed the fortress of Gedij? Would it not be wiser to attack now, before it can strike at us again?"

Sardar! You will ruin us all with your scheming!

Nergui shifted uncomfortably. "We've only recently received reports of this weapon. No one has seen it. Its nature is unknown. We would be foolish to risk our army by crossing the mountains before winter, on the basis of such uncertain reports."

Now, to his surprise and alarm, young Prince Murad began what was obviously a rehearsed speech. His mother, Nergui saw with irritation, had decked him in fine silk robes, heavily embroidered in gold. His turban bore a ruby like an enormous drop of blood on his head.

"Perhaps the *mushir* has grown old. Perhaps the little trip over the mountains is now too much for his aged bones. Perhaps he would prefer to spend the winter comfortably in his headquarters rather than in the field, facing the enemy.

"Our Empire is a sacred gift of the gods! If we allow it to be trampled under the feet of heathenish foreigners, we must expect their wrath! This insult is not to be tolerated! If no one else is willing to defend the Empire, then send me! My years may be few, but my spirit is strong! Let me show them what a son of the Emperor can do!"

A mere boy to lead the army? Madness!

Nergui felt as if he were sinking into an abyss. Sardar must have persuaded the Favorite that an attack would bring an easy victory, for which her son could claim the credit. Murad was primed with emotional pleas to convince his suggestible father he should lead the attack. And what argument could prove him wrong?

While Nergui was still searching for words, Adm. Haluk rose to speak. He began in the reasonable manner of one who comes to smooth over differences. "The prince's words have moved us all, and his courage is most praiseworthy. But surely it would be foolish to dismiss the *mushir* so lightly when he's proved his worth in many battles?

"Let each do what he does best. If the Emperor sends his own son to lead the army, they will be inspired to such heroism that nothing can withstand them. Who could do less when an imperial prince rides in the van? But let the *mushir* assist him with wise advice and counsel, to avoid the snares of the enemy."

"The admiral speaks well," said Yasin, and his toadies nodded their agreement.

They're all against me!

He was the only one in the room who understood the military situation and perhaps the only one who didn't know the war council was rigged in advance. The Favorite would promote her son as savior of the nation, and he'd be left to take the blame if things went wrong, as he felt sure they would.

"This sounds like an excellent plan," said the Emperor, who by now probably thought it was all his idea. "Has anyone something to add?"

"Yes," said Yasin. "If I may venture one thing more, to ensure victory in this crisis, we will need a total commitment. The whole population must be mobilized. Shirkers and defeatists cannot be tolerated. For this reason, we should declare martial law immediately."

That would give Sardar almost absolute power! Does Yasin even know what he's proposing? Does he care?

"So ordered," said the Emperor. "Let the *mushir* draw up the necessary decree for the vizier's signature. The council is adjourned."

As he left the chamber, Nergui ripped off the turban and tossed it aside. It no longer just represented a shroud, it had become one in fact.

No one needs more than one shroud!

I wonder if the foreigners have a war god as ugly as this one?

It was his custom, whenever he felt troubled, to put on the tunic of a common soldier and go sit in the chapel, the quietest place on the base. Here, he was seldom disturbed though he always had the menacing statue of Savustasi, the war god, looking down at him. Today, his mind was full of pain and confusion, and he couldn't take his eyes off the statue. Savustasi stared back as if he wanted to say something.

That I'm going to die? I knew that already. The gods were never much help to me, but if I ever needed them . . .

An elderly priest came in to light the incense. He paused to mumble a prayer in front of the statue. Noticing Nergui sitting dejected in the corner, he walked over.

"Is something troubling you?"

Good, he doesn't recognize me. I might as well talk to him. Where's the harm?

"Nothing you can help me with. I've given my whole life to the Emperor, fighting for him in many battles. Now, I'm going to war again, and this time I won't return. What was it all for?"

The last words were something he hadn't meant to say. They came directly from the heart.

The aged priest nodded as if he'd heard this before and offered some familiar platitudes: "The Emperor does not expect from any man more than he's able to give. You are his soldier, and he is your Emperor. The one is helpless without the other."

"I have nothing left to give! My wife died years ago. I have only a daughter, and he took her for his harem! He, who had hundreds of women, took my only child! I can't even bid her farewell!"

The priest, taken aback by this outburst, retreated into aphorisms. "Those whom the Emperor has chosen to honor . . . hu . . . ah . . . umm . . . mmm . . ." He stared slack-jawed, unable to speak.

Is he having a stroke?

The old man bent over to look closely at him. His eyes were now piercing, his voice, deep and rich. It resounded through the empty chapel. "Don't be a fool! The gods have not forsaken you! You think you're weak and helpless, but you are all-powerful! What do you have to fear? Your life is not ending, it has only begun! Don't throw away this blessing!"

Startled, Nergui blinked. "What? What are you saying?"

The priest looked around in helpless confusion. "I have . . . have said something? I . . . I . . . must go. Duty calls. Gods be with you." Without another word, he scurried out of the chapel.

"Thank you for the advice," Nergui said to his departing back. "You have given me much to think on."

Dearest Enkhtuya,

I am called away for another war and may not be able to write again soon. I can only humbly apologize if I have neglected you. Please believe that I love you with all my heart and always tried to do the best for you though it was little enough.

I must ask you, this one time, to aid me with a matter of some urgency. Please deliver this message as soon as you can to the Emperor's Favorite, Hervika. I have no other means of communicating with her.

"Most fair and beloved Hervika! I cannot express what joy I take in the honor of being entrusted with your son, the hope of our nation! Fear nothing! I will show him all the care and protection he deserves! Trust me, his welfare is in safe hands, for I too know what it means to lose a child.

"Your loyal servant,
"Nergui Pasha"

He studied the letter thoughtfully a moment Would Hervika understand this message? She was, by all accounts, an intelligent woman.
The story he heard about her was she'd been taken from a pirate
ship, before Haluk presented her as booty to the Emperor. It was
never clear whether she were a captive seized by the pirates or part
of the crew. Or was it both? For a woman like her, it wouldn't take
much to ingratiate herself with some pirates.

No one knows who she is, but she has the whole Empire in her
hands!

Whoever she was, Hervika clearly could adapt herself to changing circumstances, and circumstances were about to change a great
deal. He sealed the letter.

Sardar seemed surprised by the sudden appearance of Nergui
and a dozen of his personal guard in the intelligence headquarters,
but he quickly returned to his fawning manner. "Greetings, *mushir,*
to what do I owe the honor of your visit?"

"There are some new developments. I need to speak to the prisoner, Pvt. Dalir, immediately."

"May I ask what this concerns?"

"I don't care to repeat myself. You will know it all soon enough.
Just take me to him."

Sardar nodded. "As you wish, *sir.* But he's deep in the isolation
cells below the surface. It will take some time."

"Then we should go to him without further delay."

Sardar's headquarters was a sprawling building. The long,
snaky corridor he chose headed toward the center. Nervous clerks
and messengers scampered out of the way when they saw the dreaded intelligence chief accompanied by the *mushir* and his armed
guards. Something big was obviously going on, and it was safer not
to be a witness.

"I'm concerned there may be a breach of security," said Nergui. "Are you quite certain no one is able to speak to Pvt. Dalir?"

"Very much so, *sir.* The cell is completely soundproof. The
guards aren't permitted to open or even to approach the door. The
prisoner receives nourishment through a tube from the floor above,
which is serviced by a deaf-mute. It's much like being in the grave,
except of course, that he's still alive. Temporarily." He grinned cru-
elly.

"Who has the keys?"

"I do." Sardar produced a ring of them.

"There's no other key?"

"None."

"But men can be bribed, and locks can be picked. Our enemies are clever. In the future, there will be some of my own men standing guard at all times."

"As you wish, *sir,* though I assure you, it's quite unnecessary."

They descended for what seemed a very long time down a twisting, narrow stair. A turnkey at the bottom admitted them into a dank tunnel that branched into several side passages, each separated from the other. Sardar lit a torch and beckoned him into one of them. Before long, they came to a door.

"Are you sure you want to station men down here, *sir?* It's not a pleasant place to serve one's time."

"My men understand the importance of this work. Just open the door."

There was a loud groan from the hinges as the massive door swung open. It was at least a foot thick.

No good screaming and pounding on this door!

Nergui wasn't prepared for the stench. Comfort was not a priority here. Dalir, pale and blinking at the light, sat on a heap of rough sacking. He was chained by the neck to the wall. "Pasha?" he said hopefully.

"I cannot speak to him this way! Unchain him at once!"

"Yes *sir.*" Sardar seemed annoyed at having to give the prisoner any more consideration than absolutely necessary.

Dalir pulled himself shakily to attention. Though pale and trembling, his health had apparently not suffered much.

He's young. A few good meals, with some sunlight and exercise, and he will be fine. Physically, at least.

"Private, I'm reluctant to take you from your duties here, but I happen to have a vacant position on my staff, and I'd like to know if you'd be interested in it."

"SIR?" said Dalir and Sardar simultaneously. Nergui noticed Sardar's voice had lost its sarcastic edge.

"Naturally, I don't expect you to change your post without any incentive," he continued. "This comes with a promotion, making you a sergeant. Well?"

His mouth gaping in astonishment, Dalir fell to his knees. "I'd be honored to serve the Pasha in any way he chooses."

Sardar was staring at him as if he'd suddenly gone mad. "Is THIS why you've . . ."

Without another word, Nergui grabbed him and threw him hard against the wall. As he fastened the iron collar around the stunned man's neck, he said, "Yes, to answer your question, it is. Also, I'm promoting you to general. And you are not to leave this position without further orders."

Vizier Yasin frowned, his brow furrowed as he read the proclamation carefully, line by line. It was the most reprehensible document Nergui had ever seen, and even though he was the author, he'd gladly have burned it.

The decree of martial law placed all civil authorities under military command. Men of military age could be conscripted without notice, and private property could be commandeered without any appeal. Defeatists and malingerers were threatened with the death penalty.

"Sardar has seen this?"

"Not yet," said Nergui. "He's been promoted to general and assigned new duties that occupy his attention."

"A general already? Well, he certainly does move fast. And so must we, I suppose," said the vizier. He sent an aide to fetch his seal. "You don't have any problem with this, I hope?"

"Of course not. Any loyal citizen should be honored to make sacrifices for the Emperor."

"Good, good," said Yasin amiably. He signed the document and pressed his large, ornate seal on it. "Shall I order it distributed?"

"No need. I've already dispatched copies to every military post. And I've prepared additional copies for the civil administration."

"Excellent. Will there be anything else?"

"Just one additional thing," said Nergui, as one of his guards rolled up the parchment and tied it with a ribbon. "I'm conscripting you for military service."

Yasin blinked as if he failed to understand. "I beg your pardon?"

Nergui turned to his men. "Take the recruit to the barracks. See that he's shaved and fitted with a uniform. He's to be enrolled in the training regiment."

"Wait!" said Yasin, much alarmed, as the soldiers took him by the arms. "Is this a question of money?"

"Of course not. You have no money. I'm commandeering it for the war chest. My men are in need of supplies and equipment."

"The Emperor will hear of this!" wailed Yasin, as he was hustled out the door.

"Eventually, I'm sure."

But I wonder who's going to tell him.

Nergui sighed. The three poisonous serpents that plagued the Empire – Sardar, Yasin and Hervika – had all been defanged, for the time being. He could now devote himself to external enemies: the Akaddians and their allies. He was already starting to feel a bit sorry for them.

19: Lamya

They built this place from the top down, and they left out the middle!

The wicker cage the Wind Bags had shut her in was hanging from a big inflated sack or bladder, which was levitating above her without any magic. All around were similar structures, most much larger, floating in air. She could see laundry hanging from some of them, and juvenile *efaryti* gawked at her from the windows. The flying ship that had brought her here was tethered some distance away.

The door to the cage was unlocked. She pushed it open for a better look at what lay below. She saw at once she was a hundred feet in the air, and there was no ladder or rope within reach.

Unless I invent a flying spell, it looks like I'm stuck!

Spread out below her was a settlement in a small valley. The trees had all been felled, replaced with rows of shabby-looking huts, which she presumed were slave quarters. Human and *efaryti* figures scurried around among them. Smoke rose up from several forges and smelters. There was a huge pile of mine tailings at one end of the valley; workers were adding to it as she watched. In another place, slaves were cutting stones from a quarry and stacking them to build a high stone wall, which was gradually replacing the crude stockade made of rough-hewn timber and salvaged lumber.

Fascinating! The Wind Bags must be a tribe of flying nomads who anchored their homes here and decided to stay. But what do they want with me?

Before she could think of any plausible theories, the cage jerked sharply and began to descend. Looking down, she could see a winch, cranked by a gang of *efaryti,* was pulling in the cable that tethered it. A few minutes later, she was standing on the ground, surrounded by a menacing circle of Wind Bags holding spears.

"Please excuse our caution," said one of them, speaking in a shrill Bandeluki, "but we never had a sorceress before. They call me Whip Hand. I'm the slave boss here." Whip Hand did indeed have a nasty-looking whip in its belt, but apparently didn't feel the need to use it at the moment.

It doesn't know I understand its language. I better keep that to myself.

"My name is Lamya," she said in Bandeluki. "Don't mind me. I was only passing through."

"I'm afraid that wouldn't be possible right now. We require your assistance with a few things. Please come with me."

Lamya felt the sudden urge to grab Whip Hand by its scrawny neck and kill it.

The pact! I must find a way destroy the Wind Bags! But not now.

"By all means," she said calmly.

The slave huts were made of lumber scraps, apparently whatever had been lying around, and were hammered together without care or craftsmanship. Here and there, she could see slave crews, some human and some *efaryti,* building new ones. Their labor became hasty and even frantic when they saw Whip Hand was looking at them. Many bore marks of the lash.

It wouldn't do these people much good to rebel. Their masters are watching, out of reach, far above! And that stockade looks like it's meant to keep people in, not out.

Before long, they came to an open space, where a huge air sack was anchored close to the ground. A two-story house made of wicker hung from it on cables. Ladders to the ground provided easy access.

This looks a lot like the flying ship. But why isn't it flying?

As they approached one of the ladders, Whip Hand took her by the arm and held its whip before her face. "This is the home of Sky Lord, your master," it said in its squeaky voice. "You must show him respect, or he will give poor Whip Hand much work to do. You understand?"

She wanted to strangle it with its own whip. "I wouldn't wish to cause you any inconvenience," she said.

Climbing the ladder, she found herself standing in a workroom. Some humans were hammering and filing metal things on benches. Others were sitting at tables, assembling components into what looked like pumps and valves. Elaborate technical diagrams hung from the walls. Nearby was the finely-crafted wooden model of a flying ship. She turned to study it.

"That's the Model 3," said a shrill voice behind her. A hunched and elderly *efaryt,* wearing a finely-woven purple robe, had appeared and was staring obsessively at the wooden model.

"You're standing in the Model 2," it continued. "It was too large to be maneuverable. The Model 1 met with a bad end. And now . . ." – It raised its voice in shrill accusation. – " . . . you almost destroyed the Model 3!"

It grabbed her by her clothing and pulled her until she was looking closely into its eyes. "HOW DID YOU DO IT? HOW DID YOU BRING DOWN MY AIRSHIP?"

She felt like using the nearest stool to break its head. "It was just an improvisation," she said. "I had only a simple spell for catching birds, but I changed a few parameters, and somewhat to my surprise . . ."

"A BIRD-CATCHING SPELL!" said Sky Lord, for that was surely the name of the aged *efaryt* that was screaming and waving its fists. "THE MODEL 3 FAILED THE TEST OF A SIMPLE BIRD-CATCHING SPELL!"

It grabbed the wooden model and threw it on the ground, then kicked it across the room. When its wrath abated, it turned back toward Lamya and began speaking in a more reasonable, though still very squeaky, voice. "My assistants are imbeciles, the slaves sabotage everything, and the Model 3 is deficient in every way! Underpowered! Hardly any lift! Nothing for weaponry!"

"That sounds bad," said Lamya. "But I don't see what I . . ."

"You must help me!" said Sky Lord. "You killed the chief sorcerer. He was in the observation gondola when the Model 3 hit the ground."

"But I don't know anything about . . ."

"What do you know, then?"

Lamya felt more and more like killing Sky Lord. "I pursued several fields of study," she said evenly. "But the main focus was on demonology."

"Aha! Demons! Just what I need!" said Sky Lord. He pulled her over to where an intricate technical diagram was hanging. "What do you make of this?"

It looked like a massive star chart with all the visible stars of a night sky, but formed into strange constellations, which were drawn in different colors, overlapping each other. "I have no idea," she said honestly.

"That's the Model 4. It will have 75% more lift than the Model

3 and an airspeed at least ten knots faster. There are 12 self-inflating gas cells, each with its own remote valves and pressure gauges, eight torque-adjusted, variable-pitch fans, a buoyancy compression condensate ballast system, gyroscopic stabilizers . . ."

It went on for several minutes, describing the features of its invention, pointing to this section and that of the technical diagram. Rapt with its vision, Sky Lord seemed to have forgotten about Lamya, who simply stood and stared in confusion.

This demon is either a genius, or completely demented, or maybe both!

"ARE YOU PAYING ATTENTION?" Sky Lord clearly suspected she wasn't. A sharp poke from behind by Whip Hand reminded her why she was here.

"Absolutely!" she said. Privately, she wondered whether it would be better to murder Whip Hand first and save Sky Lord for later, or the other way around.

"Then the central design problem should be obvious."

Sky Lord hissed with frustration as Lamya's blank look suggested it wasn't. "Come with me!" it said.

Prodded ungently by Whip Hand, she followed it down a passage into the forward part of the grounded airship. At the end was a small room with many windows, full of strange controls and instruments: There were not one, but three ship's wheels, beside rows of levers, valves and gauges, and many things Lamya didn't recognize at all.

"There!" said Sky Lord. "Even a hairy demon can see the problem now!"

Lamya shook her head. "It's too complicated."

"Exactly! We've rebuilt the Model 2, streamlining, adding fans, extending control surfaces and making numerous improvements, based on our experiments with the Model 3. But the end result is an airship that neither the *efaryti* nor the hairy demons can pilot effectively!"

"So . . . you want to simplify the controls?"

"That would be a good plan for the Model 5, but unfortunately, I'm working under a deadline." With a clawed finger, it pointed at its heart, or the place where Lamya supposed its heart must be. "This is my last airship. And there is no one to replace me as designer. It will just have to do.

"Everything depends on this. The prototype is nearly finished. All I need from you is a pilot."

"You mean a demon? I don't know of any demon that . . ."

"Not a problem! Just use the parameters I give you. If the first one is no good, we'll summon another."

"But blind summoning is very dangerous . . ."

"Which is why you're going to do it while I watch from a distance! And since you're an expert, you may recognize the spell I'm about to lay on you." Taking a small knife from its belt, Sky Lord pricked its thumb.

SPLAT!

The demon, a huge, gelatinous creature, landed with some force in the pit where Lamya had made her circle. Stunned for a moment, it seemed to recover and began reaching out with a myriad exploring tentacles. Lamya retreated hastily toward safety, before she realized there wasn't any; the Wind Bags had pulled up the ladder.

As the tentacles wrapped themselves around her ankles, Sky Lord, who'd been watching it all from the edge of the pit, gave a signal, and *efaryti* archers fired at the monster, turning it into an oversized pin cushion. The demon twitched a few times and then lay still.

"You've failed again!" said Sky Lord sharply. "That was too big, and it wouldn't have lived an hour in the open air!"

"But I used the parameters you gave me," Lamya wailed, distraught.

"Well, they were the wrong ones! As soon as we can clean up this mess, we're trying again! This time, reduce the mass requirement by 25% and exclude aquatic creatures. And lower the elevation eight feet."

"Even if I find your perfect demon, we may have no way to communicate with it!"

"Leave that to me. How do you think I learned your preposterous language?"

Ladders were lowered for *efaryti* slaves, who clambered down with knives and buckets to remove the gooey remains. Lamya took advantage of the pause to climb up and find some rags to wipe off the stinking demon slime.

The new pact, to protect, defend and obey the Wind Bags, had partially neutralized the old one, to destroy them. She still had an urge to kill Sky Lord, but that felt like a natural impulse, and the compulsion to obey him was strong.

I will just have to wait for a better opportunity.

THUNK!

The man-sized demon, coming out of nowhere, knocked her over, before flying into the wall of the pit. Frustrated, it tried to climb the wall with its dozen spiny legs, before falling back down.

The demon turned to confront Lamya, who was getting to her feet. It folded its wings into its carapace and raised its claws threateningly.

As it stared at Lamya with the motley-colored collection of eyeballs that sprouted from its head in all directions, Lamya could do nothing but stare back. Neither of them liked what they saw.

Snap!

Without further hesitation, the hideous insect unfurled its wings and, with a great buzzing sound, flew out of the pit and into the purple sky. A few belated *efaryti* arrows went wild or struck it without any visible effect. Lamya sat down and rested her head between her legs. Her nerves were shot. Her hands would not stop trembling.

This gets worse and worse!

Sky Lord yelled down at her, "Didn't I tell you to exclude winged creatures?"

"No, you did not," she answered resentfully.

"Well you should have! It's obvious! Why do I have to think of everything? Get up and try it again!"

"Let me prepare a stasis spell to immobilize it. This way is much too dangerous."

Sky Lord considered the question a minute, before replying: "I see what you mean," it said grudgingly. "We might kill a promising specimen before we have a chance to examine it. But no tricks, or you know what will happen!"

Maybe I should just summon a fire demon and get it over with!

The next demon arrived in the circle without violence, merely collapsing as if it had suddenly been tripped. Large, snaky arms reached out as it tried to steady itself, and two big fishy eyes peered around, taking in its new surroundings.

It had pulled itself into a crouching position and started to make quizzical gurgling sounds, when Lamya tapped it with a wand and froze it in stasis.

Sky Lord climbed down a ladder to inspect the latest victim of its aeronautical ambitions. "Much better!" it pronounced, touching it here and there with a wand. "Good eyesight, eight limbs, a distributed cerebral system, everything we need!"

"It looks like an octopus," said Lamya. "They can't live out of water."

"I thought I told you to exclude aquatic creatures?"

"I did. I thought I did. But this is creature is unknown to me. Maybe it's amphibious."

"Well, it will just have to try hard to live out of water. Unless you want to summon something else?"

"No, no. Let's see what we can do with this."

Forgive me Mr. Octopus, or whatever you are, I just can't take any more summoning!

"Don't understand," said Talkypus, as Lamya called it. The new demon was standing, or rather hanging, in the control room, clinging to one of the rings Sky Lord had added so it could move around more easily. Its soft, gurgling voice formed the Bandeluki words with difficulty. Sky Lord had injected it with a concentrate distilled from the brains of human and *efaryti* slaves, which added to its language skills, but hadn't given it a throat that could do anything with the shrill Efaryti phonemes.

"It's basically quite simple," said Sky Lord. "The large wheel before you works the rudder, controlling the left and right motion of the ship. These wheels control the forward and rear elevators, which move the prow and the stern up and down. The smaller wheels are for adjusting the trim . . ."

"I don't think it understands the basic operations," said Lamya, who was getting interested despite herself. "You better explain the trim later."

"Don't interrupt me!" said Sky Lord. "I was making an important point!"

Talkypus grabbed the central wheel and spun it. "Won't move," it commented.

"You moved the rudder," said Sky Lord. "But the ship won't

move without the fans."

Talkypus studied the array of throttle levers, before deciding to move all eight forward at once, using several of its arms. "Doesn't work," it said.

"First, we have to heat up the boiler, and we can't do that without priming the water pump from the ballast."

Talkypus' arms writhed among the valves, opening some and closing others, apparently at random.

"At least it seems interested in learning," said Lamya. "Maybe in a few weeks . . ."

"I can't wait that long! There's only one way to teach it to fly, and that's the way we teach children to swim!"

"How do you teach children to swim?"

"We throw them in the water!"

This will be interesting: an oversized and overly complicated flying ship designed by a mad demon, assembled by truculent slaves and piloted by an amphibious octopus, assisted by an enchanted sorceress . . . what could possibly go wrong?

"That's right," said Sky Lord, "Just keep turning slowly in circles. Try to stay at the same altitude. And notice, as the ship turns, the compass is turning too . . ."

The ship was cruising at a thousand feet altitude. Sky Lord had taken advantage of a clear day for some practice maneuvers. Talkypus had learned the controls with amazing speed and was now being coached on navigation.

Since no one was paying her any attention, Lamya drifted over to a window and looked around. She could see a river stretching out before her. The swamp, she now realized, was a delta near the river's mouth. From this height, it didn't look nearly as vast as it did from the ground. She couldn't see the Ghost Feet village, but there was a stretch of wooded hills to the west she hadn't noticed before and a great expanse of ocean to the south.

Nowhere did she see a city or a paved road or any sign of civilization, beyond a few clusters of huts, or patches of fields. There were no ruined fortresses or crumbling monuments to lost empires.

This world is young.

A world like this, she thought, belonged to whoever claimed it. The empty hills and forests could never resist an invader, and primitive tribes like the Ghost Feet were hardly any obstacle.

But the Wind Bags had stolen a lap on their rivals through the genius of Sky Lord, who'd turned their drifting balloons into flying ships. This ship, she realized, could travel hundreds of miles in a day. The Wind Bags could land it wherever they liked and take whatever they coveted. And they coveted everything.

If I left this world and came back in a hundred years, would there still be different tribes here, or would it all belong to the Wind Bags?

The words of the ancient sorcerers' code came back to her:

You will bear the burdens of others, but do not carry their sins.

Was she responsible for the Wind Bags now? She was no longer just a slave. She was becoming more like a collaborator, or even a trusted confidante. She glanced over to where some of the guards were standing, peering out a window and commenting on this landmark and that. No one noticed her.

When did they lose interest in guarding me? How soon before they set me to guarding someone else?

This was all happening with alarming speed. A few weeks ago, she was in Kafra, and not long ago had made a pact with the matriarch of the Ghost Feet.

What happened to her? Why don't I know? And why don't I at least feel curious?

Perhaps Sky Lord's spell was stronger than she thought. Or maybe she'd succumbed to the lure of power and, worse, the greed for secret knowledge. Those were the two fatal weaknesses that had corrupted so many sorcerers who could never have enough power or knowledge . . .

Glancing out the window, she noticed the ship had drifted over the ocean. Sky Lord was apparently too occupied with navigation to watch where it was going. She walked back to the rear window to see how far they were from shore, and there she got a shock that sent her running back the full length of the ship.

"TURN IT AROUND!" she yelled, rushing into the control room.

Sky Lord looked up in irritation. "What . . ."

"JUST DO IT! TURN IT AROUND NOW!"

Sky Lord hesitated a second before turning to Talkypus: "Do what it says."

But Talkypus had not waited for further orders. Alarmed by the yells, it had turned the rudder as far as it would go. As the ship swerved sickeningly, Lamya grabbed for a ring, sharing it momentarily with Talkypus, who was also thrown off balance.

Through the windows, she could see the distant shore coming into view, and just above the horizon was a dark line. "Thunderheads! They're blowing in from the north!"

Now it was Sky Lord's turn to become excited. "Full speed!," it said in its squeaky voice. "Full speed! Take us home!"

Talkypus didn't need any further encouragement. It jammed the throttles forward. The whirring of the fans, which was audible everywhere on the ship, became a loud roar as the ship raced to beat the approaching storm. No one needed to be told what a crash at sea meant.

But the wind was now working against them. Even at full speed, the airship's progress was maddeningly slow. Looking out the window, Lamya could see its shadow on the ocean, barely crawling across the waves.

Though only minutes passed on the clock, it seemed to take hours for the ship to cross the beach, and by then turbulence was shaking it. Dark, wispy clouds

flew past them, outriders of the storm, and they were getting thicker and thicker. Soon it would no longer be possible to see the ground.

"Take it down to 400 feet," ordered Sky Lord, and Talkypus complied with a sharp dive that put Lamya's heart in her throat. As they cleared the cloud layer, she saw they were now cruising over the swamp. An intermittent drizzle obscured visibility, but she could see flashes of lightning in the hills ahead of them.

When the ship came in view of the Wind Bag town, she saw that it was burning.

20: Singer

Lt. Gallites was waiting next to some fresh graves at the edge of the village. He looked paler than Singer remembered him.

"How did it go? Were you wounded?"

"No sir, just a bit tired from the march."

"But you saw some action?"

"Right you are, sir, enough to satisfy me for awhile. We lost four marines, and there are some wounded in the huts over there. Eleven dead villagers."

"And the pirates?"

"I counted 182 dead on the ground. Six or seven got away."

"That was a good day, then."

"Honestly, sir, I'd have to call it the worst day of my life."

"Your life is not yet over, and you will have some worse ones if you stick with the army. Where's Capt. Baldwin?"

"He took his company on ahead, in case the pirates attack the next village."

"Not much chance of that. We spotted them sailing south. They probably need to replenish their crews in Mirajil."

"That would be their obvious next move, sir. Perhaps Capt. Baldwin just likes to do forced marches."

"Or likes to kill pirates. He lost a brother in Mirajil years ago."

"He's a good man to take the lead, then."

"Negative on that. I need him to give his marines a rest so I can move up the cavalry. It's bad for their morale when the infantry outruns them. Is there somewhere here we can pitch our tents?"

"There's a creek about a mile down the road. Someone's goat pasture. I don't suppose they'd mind if we use it."

"I'll talk to them. It doesn't hurt to ask."

He dismounted and led his horse toward the village. Civilians were coming out to look at the approaching cavalcade. Singer noticed an old man leaning on a stick by the road.

"Who's in charge here?" he said in Bandeluki.

"I am, effendi."

"Good. I understand there's a goat pasture near a creek, on the other side of the village. I'd like to camp there tonight if you have no objection."

The old man, his face lined with many seasons, stroked his thin, white beard for a moment as he took in the thousands of heavily-armed foreigners who were bearing down on his defenseless village. "And if I say no?"

"Then we'll just have to camp somewhere else."

"Effendi, you can stay there a hundred years if it pleases you."

"Hopefully, we won't be here that long. However, I am entrusting you with four of my men who fell defending your village, and I'd ask you to see the graves are tended. They may be here even longer than a hundred years."

"It will be an honor."

That night, as he was turning in after supper, he was startled to find Mangasar waiting for him in his tent. The boy was wearing a long, loose coat over a white robe, which Singer guessed was normal clothing for the desert tribes. He bowed respectfully as the General entered.

"What? You again? No knife this time?"

"I'm seldom without a knife, General, but in this case, the Hierophant has given me a letter and a personal message to deliver: He admires your courage and hopes to work with you in the near future."

"The Hierophant is a more reasonable fellow than I supposed," said Singer, taking the letter.

"He's very reasonable, General, but he's accustomed to dealing with men who are less so."

The letter was written on a single sheet on parchment, in an elegant Bandeluki script:

Honored General,

According to my information, the imperialists plan a surprise attack on your forces in Chatmakstan before the snows. I would advise you to reverse your course and return to Kafra in all haste.

I am prepared to offer you the assistance of 2,500 seasoned warriors, conditional upon your promise to liberate the province of Mellik, the traditional homeland of our people, which is occupied by the imperialists.

I have entrusted this letter to a capable person who can also bear your reply.

Your servant,

Hovannes, Hierophant of Jassarra
And Lord of Debel Kresh

This is big news if it's true. But how do I know Mangsar isn't making it up? He could be in league with the pirates, for all I know!

"Does the Hierophant do this often? Entrust important secret messages to 12-year-olds?"

Mangasar smiled. "I'm older than I look. You may have noticed I can move through an armed camp without challenge and cross dangerous stretches of desert without escort. What I said about the Spectral Slayers was not entirely a fable."

There may be something to that.

"But how do you know what the Bandeluks are planning to do?"

"You have been at war with them for a few months. We've been fighting them for 800 years."

"You don't seem to be winning."

"We have survived, which is more than your army could do in a place like Berbat."

I suppose I'll have to concede that.

"But how do you know my promise to liberate Mellik is worth anything?"

I'm not too sure about that myself!

"The Hierophant has seen it in the stars."

Stars, now? He answers my questions with riddles. Maybe if Raeesha were here, she could explain some of this.

"Even if every word of this is true, you have to understand I'm not a king or a prince. I'm a soldier; I just follow orders."

"Then perhaps you need some new ones."

Surely, this is no child. And if he's telling the truth about that, then what about the rest of it?

"Just a moment." He left the tent long enough to tell a guard, "Tell Lt. Gallites I want to see him urgently."

Gallites arrived a few minutes later, still buttoning his tunic.

How are you feeling, lieutenant?"

"I'd feel better if I could spend the whole night in bed, sir."

"But you can travel?"

"Without any doubt."

"Good. You remember Mangasar?"

Gallites glanced at him. "The slave boy from Gedij?"

"He's a good deal more than that. Look what he's brought me."

Gallites studied the letter a minute before turning to Mangasar. "You're full of surprises, young man."

Managasar grinned. "You have no idea."

Singer said, "I need to get this letter to Prince Krion right away. Do you think you could take it by boat?"

"I don't see why not if the pirates are gone. With one of these feluccas, I could be in Kafra in two days if the winds are favorable."

"Good. Take Mangasar and all the wounded who can be transported. I don't want to leave them in a place like this."

Mangasar shifted uncomfortably. "I've never been in a boat before," he said.

"Think of it as a chance to add to your many abilities."

They caught up with Baldwin two days later. His marines had halted near a spit of land that extended some distance into the ocean. Singer could see a ship anchored offshore.

"What's up, Captain?"

"I wish I knew, sir, but that's the Black Ansel, and it's bad news."

"A pirate ship, then?"

"The worst. It's Capt. Tanilhan's ship."

"Tanilhan? He's still alive?"

"I assume so, sir. He wasn't among the dead. And I won't count him out until I see the corpse."

"But we have no definite information he's here?"

Baldwin grinned. "Unless I miss my guess, that's him right there."

Baldwin pointed to the land spit where a longboat had been beached. Singer could make out two men beside it. One bore a red-gold flag.

"Isn't that an old Covenant flag?"

"The aristo war banner. All the pirates fly it now."

"But most of them aren't from Covenant. So, a flag of convenience?"

"Not for Tanilhan, it's not." He smiled as if at some private joke.

"Looks like they want to parley."

"Sir, I would not advise you to parley with the pirates. They're surely up to some mischief. You could hide a dozen men behind that longboat."

"Pirates are always up to mischief, but that doesn't mean they won't parley. I'm not very clear as to their intentions and would like to find out."

"It would be healthier just to kill them first and worry about their intentions later."

"I'm not here for my health. Stand down. Give your men some rest. They've done their part and a lot more. Let the cavalry take point for awhile. I'll be back shortly."

He rode back, past the riders of Hardy's company, to where the seven-foot *fui* demons were striding along in formation. Singer had discovered the horses moved faster with the *fui* demons behind them, and no pace the horses could set seemed to tire the demons.

Singer signaled for them to halt. He took the three-bladed pole weapon from Twenty Three's claws and replaced it with the army banner.

"We're going to a parley. For today, you're my Standard-bearer."

"Yes *bzzz.*" The demon didn't seem to appreciate the honor.

A few minutes later, they were back at the head of the column. Singer told his men to wait while he went forward on foot with Twenty Three. There were a number of nervous, sidelong glances, but experience had taught them it was unwise to question anything the General wanted to do.

As they got nearer, Singer could see more clearly the men who were waiting for him. The one with the banner looked like an ordinary sailor, but the other was an imposing, grey-haired gentleman in a faded naval uniform. He was holding something that glittered like polished brass in the sun.

A spyglass. I wonder what he makes of my demon?

If Tanilhan were intimidated by the demon, he gave no sign of it, merely raising his spyglass occasionally to get a closer look at

Singer.

Suddenly, Twenty Three said, "Demonslayer! *bzzz* There are *bzzz* men hiding *bzzz* behind the boat!" It sounded excited.

"Just call me General."

There was a brief pause. "I have *bzzz* no weapon, *bzzz* General."

Twenty Three's inhuman, buzzing voice sounded almost plaintive.

My horrible demon is afraid of losing its horrible life? Maybe this would be a good time to make some rules.

"Listen carefully," he said. "You must trust me. It will all be correct. But you must do exactly what I tell you, swiftly and without hesitation. Do you understand?"

"Yes *bzzz.*" The demon's voice held no trace of emotion, but its great, clawed feet went *clump clump* as they tore up the wet sand, in powerful and remorseless repetition.

As they drew close, Tanilhan lowered his spyglass. "Have I the honor of addressing Gen. Singer?"

"You do. And you are, I presume, Capt. Tanilhan?"

"Yes. I've heard a great deal about you, General."

"And I of you, Captain."

"Nothing bad, I hope."

"That would depend a great deal on your point of view."

"I like that helmet you're wearing."

Why this small talk? What's holding him back?

"And you have a pretty little spyglass. What was it you wanted to discuss?"

"You seem to have marched a great many troops into my little corner of the world. I hope you're not wasting the trip."

"Thank you for your concern."

"You understand there's no way to attack a navy with an army?"

"That had crossed my mind."

"And even if you storm the walls of Mirajil, which in a thousand years have never been breached, my fleet will only move somewhere else?"

"I've never heard pirates were inclined to suicide."

"Then perhaps you'd care to explain the nature of your mission?"

"I would not."

"Or cannot?" Tanilhan's voice took on a pleading tone. "General, you're being used against your own people! The Free States are a scattering of little republics that cannot preserve their independence unless they stand firmly together, and certainly not when their best troops are squandered in far-off deserts! When this war is over, what will be left of your army?"

Whatever I can save.

"That remains to be seen."

"And you would live to see it? Your men fallen in foreign wars, your country brought under the Akaddian yoke? Is that what you want to see?"

"I will see what is to be seen."

"If I'd waited to see what the royalists planned for me, I'd have been hanged! You think you'll fare any better? I never wanted anything but my country's independence!"

This is the infamous pirate chief everyone is afraid of? He expects me to feel sorry for him?

"And yet, there are plenty of your countrymen on the other side."

"Traitors bought with Akaddian gold!"

"Poor people who never got a thing from your Covenant but hard work, hunger and the contempt of arrogant landowners."

"They were free men who sold out their country for a few crusts of bread!"

"If you think freedom is worth more than bread, then you've never been very hungry."

"And you have? You wear the Prince's gold on your head!"

"Oh, it's the gold that caught your eye?" Singer took off his helmet and threw it down on the sand. "There's your gold. Take it if you want it. I'm not here for the gold."

"You self-righteous prig!" Tanilhan now waxed scornful. "What in the name of all devils do you think you're doing here?"

Suddenly he grows bold!

"I'm here because the High Council of the Free States sent me here, and I'll go when they send me somewhere else."

"That will be too late! Listen to me! You have an army and I have a fleet. The royalists are busy with their stupid war, and their coasts are undefended. If we were to land in Covenant with a small force, we could raise a huge army in no time. The most radical

plebs are already here, under the Prince's banner."

"And what would we do with this grand army, assuming we could raise it?"

"Whatever we like! Akaddia is defenseless! We could take Kingsport! We could take Elohi!"

"And then what?"

"Anything! There's gold enough in Akaddia for anything you want!"

"How quickly the conversation turns from freedom and independence back to the subject of gold. If that's all you want, take this . . . " – He kicked his helmet. – " . . . and go."

Tanilhan bent over to pick up the golden helmet. He admired the snarling demon face, the glittering ruby eyes. "This is a very nice present you give me. And you want nothing in return?"

"Since you ask, I fancy that little spyglass of yours. I think I'll just take that."

Tanilhan laughed. "You really are a fool! All this talk of the brilliant young General! Demonslayer! Such nonsense! Listen, FOOL! I'm not here to exchange banter or trade gifts! I'm going to put things on a very different footing! SHOW HIM, MEN!"

Six pirates wearing threadbare naval uniforms stood up from behind the longboat. They were aiming crossbows directly at Singer.

Finally he shows his true face. What more do I need?

Tanilhan continued, sneering, "And tell your demon that if it takes a single step, you will be the first to suffer for it!"

"I'll tell him," said Singer. Without turning around, he said, "Twenty Three, take off your mask."

21: Erika

"But I didn't do anything!" she said as they slammed the cell door in her face. She'd been saying the same thing over and over to everyone she saw since they snatched her off the street. It was starting to dawn on her that no one cared what she did or didn't do. They were just paid to carry her away and lock her up.

She ran to the window and saw she was at least five stories above the ground. There was no way down even if she could squeeze between the heavy iron bars. The few people she saw in the dim courtyard below looked like guards or soldiers of some kind. Screaming would probably do no good.

The cell contained a narrow bed, a chair, a small table with a pitcher and wash basin, and a chamber pot. There was only one door, and it had no handle on her side. But it did have a grill.

As she went to have a look, she heard a voice coming from the hall. "This one is a woman! And she's a quite a belle!"

"Oh, lucky you," said another voice. "I'll probably never even get to see her."

"How we can call ourselves a brotherhood anymore?" complained a third voice. "Maybe a colloquium?"

"I'm not even sure what that means," said the second voice.

Standing on her tiptoes, she could peer through the grill. On the other side of the hall was another door with a grill. An old man was looking at her through it. The other speakers were out of sight down the hall.

"What are you talking about?" she asked.

"You, of course," he said, "our newest companion. I'm Judge Kratos. The other gentlemen are Master Diomedos and Gen. Tissander."

"My name is Erika," she said. "What is this place?"

"Young lady," said Kratos, "you have the honor of being enrolled in a most exclusive brotherhood."

"Colloquium," said someone she took to be Diomedos.

"Society," suggested Tissander.

"But to give it a more vulgar name," continued Kratos, "you're in prison, specifically the High Prison of Omoris, an establishment dedicated to a very select clientele."

"But I didn't do anything to be in prison!"

This provoked general laughter.

"It's not actually necessary to do anything of a criminal nature," said Kratos. "You were probably just inconvenient to someone else's plans. I, for example, made the mistake of ordering an audit of the Exchequer. That was three years ago, and I'm still waiting for the audit."

Diomedos said, "And I failed to lift an enchantment from Prince Krion, which he took as a personal slight. Honestly, I don't believe anyone could have removed it unless they knew the key. Also, I cut off his finger, on the orders of Gen. Basilius. I still don't know why; I told him it would do no good."

"And I had the misfortune to be second in command when Basilius killed himself," said Tissander. "So it was I who surrendered his force to Krion and was treated as a rebel. The third in command, Grennadius, happened to be the first to surrender, and he was promoted. It could just as easily have gone the other way."

"But I never did anything like that!" said Erika. "I was just negotiating a trade agreement for Prince Clenas!"

"That does sound like a bit of a puzzler," said Kratos.

"The real puzzle is how that young profligate got interested in trade negotiations," said Tissander.

"There was a pretty face involved," said Diomedos.

"Ah, that would explain it."

"There's also a great deal of money involved," said Erika thoughtfully. "If I don't have it, someone else may."

"Where was this fortune when you last saw it?" asked Kratos.

"In the Royal Bank of Akaddia."

"Then I'd expect it's safe. No one is going to raid the RBA; everyone owes them too much money. They'd probably overturn the dynasty if they called in all those loans."

"The King's treasury isn't half so safe," said Tissander, "at least with Duke Claudio in charge."

"I could break out of here more easily than into the RBA," said Diomedos.

"That would appear to be a moot point," said Kratos.

"But then I really have no idea why I'm here!" wailed Erika.

"Our colloquium can take up the subject in the morning," said

Diomedos. "It's getting rather late."

"Yes," said Kratos. "I declare an adjournment. We will have plenty of time to discuss this later."

"How long am I going to be here?" asked Erika.

"Now that," said Kratos, "is a question I can answer with some precision. No one in living memory has ever been released from the High Prison of Omoris."

Erika went to the bed and lay down. She felt lightheaded as if she might faint.

This can't be real!

She woke up as if from a nightmare. But as she blinked sleepily at the sunlight, she was dismayed to see the barred window of the night before. Looking out the window, she saw the same bleak court-yard, but now she could make out some of the surrounding country-side. From her position, she guessed she was in a tower somewhere on the edge of town. She had a splendid view of the river and could even see boats moving back and forth, but with a shock, she realized they were going places she might never see again.

There was a slight noise at the door. Someone was sliding a tray through a slot underneath it. Closer inspection revealed it held two slices of bread, a small hunk of cheese and a quartered apple.

This is supposed to be breakfast? At least I won't have to worry about gaining weight!

When she was done with the meager breakfast, she found Kratos was already waiting behind his door. "I've given some thought to your situation," he said. "And I believe we may require more information to clarify it. For example, where are you from? Do I detect a Hallandish accent?"

"Yes, I'm from Tidewater."

"I knew it!"

"An easy guess," said Diomedos, who joined the conversation. "I should give her elocution lessons. You know how Hallanders struggle with diphthongs and mix up the long and short vowels."

"I don't want elocution lessons, I just want out of here!" said Erika.

"You will have to accept the aid we are able to give," said Diomedos rather stiffly.

"Oh, don't be hard on the girl," said Tissander. "Of course, she wants out. Who doesn't?"

"I think we should return to the agenda," said Kratos. "How do you happen to know Prince Clenas? Bear in mind, there is a clerk at the end of the hall who writes down everything we say."

"You think anyone reads all that stuff?" said Tissander.

"Better safe than sorry," said Kratos.

"Everyone knows about me," said Erika. "At least, everyone in Chatmakstan. Basilius accused me of witchcraft and locked me up, before Clenas sent some people to get me out. They practically fought a war over me!"

"So you're the witch?" said Tissander.

"I'm not a witch!" said Erika indignantly.

"Technically, she's right," said Diomedos. "A witch is someone who engages in unlicensed and forbidden sorceries. I investigated that charge myself and found very little evidence to support it."

Kratos said, "In my experience, the charge can sometimes carry a lot more weight than the actual evidence. Perhaps someone still believes her to be a witch."

"In that case," said Diomedos, "the Royal College of Magic would begin an inquisitorial process. There would be no need to resort to a carte blanche."

"What's a carte blanche?" said Erika.

"It's very likely why you're here," explained Kratos. "A carte blanche is a personal order from the King for the arrest of a suspect for reasons of state without the usual judicial process."

"But I never even met the King!"

"And he's probably never heard of you. I think I may say, without any treason – You getting this, clerk? – the King is very advanced in years and tends to sign any piece of paper they put in front of him."

"Who is 'they'?"

"Anyone with access to his person."

"You mean someone like Capt. Scolinus?"

Tissander broke in. "That drunk? No, you can scratch him from the list. He wouldn't have the balls for something like this."

"Watch your language," said Diomedos. "There is a lady present."

"Carte blanche is normally a privilege of the royal family," Kratos continued. "That would mean one of the four princes, the

Duchess Thea or possibly Duke Claudio."

"That's right," said Tissander. "There are only six real possibilities, and we can exclude Clenas and Krion because they're in Chatmakstan."

"Correct," said Diomedos. "And Vettius hardly ever leaves his estates."

"That leaves Chryspos, Thea and Claudio," said Kratos. "Do you have any connection with them?"

"Not with Chryspos," said Erika. "I've never met him. I thought Thea was my friend. She put me up in her home and called me her protégé."

The men all chuckled. "She's had a lot of protégés," Tissander explained. "That's what she calls Clenas' lovers. Do you remember that little freckle-faced creature who . . ."

"I don't think the lady needs to hear that story," said Diomedos.

"But she's the one who presented me to society! Just two days ago, she held a big banquet and introduced me to a lot of important people."

There was a brief silence.

"Certainly an odd thing to do if she intended you should disappear," said Kratos. "You've done nothing since to offend her?"

"I had a scuffle with her son Philocratus. He made some improper advances, and I was forced to defend myself. It's possible I may have broken his finger."

"Where exactly was this finger at the time?" asked Tissander.

"An improper question," said Diomedos, "and we really don't need to know the answer."

"Indeed not," said Kratos. "If the Duchess wished to punish some such transgression, she would have many means available short of carte blanche. That is usually reserved for treasonable offenses."

"But I don't have any treasonable offenses!"

"Perhaps nothing you or I'd consider treason. But the royals have their own definition, which is not to be found in any law book. What exactly is your relationship to Duke Claudio?"

"I only spoke to him two or three times. He didn't seem interested in me."

"But this trade agreement, would it affect his interests?"

"It might. It's worth a lot money."

"How much?"

"Thousands of thalers!"

"Who were you negotiating with?"

"The Mercantile Consortium."

"Aha!" said Tissander. "Everyone knows Claudio is up to his elbows in that."

"Did the negotiations go well?" asked Kratos.

"Very well. We agreed to an exclusive contract that would give them a virtual monopoly on the summer fabric trade for Akaddia, Covenant and the Free States as well."

"And now that you're here?"

"I don't know. There's a deposit sitting in the RBA, but I never sent in the order. The Mercantile Consortium won't be getting any product.

"It's possible," she added with some misgivings, "they may think I absconded!"

"Even if you had, it wouldn't change your situation here," said Kratos.

"It sounds as if the good Duke won't be pleased with your incarceration," said Diomedos.

"You think he could get me out?"

"I'd assume not," said Kratos. "Even if he were quite sure where you are, the High Prison isn't in any court's jurisdiction. And your name was never entered into the prison rolls. Officially, you don't exist."

"Unless the King issues a general pardon," said Tissander. "Then everyone goes home."

"I think we can discount that possibility," said Kratos. "It hasn't happened in over a century. A general pardon would be an inconvenience to a lot of important people, including Duke Claudio. I'm pretty sure he doesn't want to see me again, for example."

"Eliminating Claudio reduces the list to just one," said Diomedos.

There was a silence that seemed to drag on and on. Finally, Erika broke it. "You mean Prince Chryspos?"

"That's one person we prefer not to discuss," said Diomedos.

"The prince controls the civil administration, except for the Exchequer," explained Kratos. "He controls this prison."

"I don't see why that's a problem," said Tissander "What more can he do to us?"

"He could throw us in the oubliettes!" said Diomedos.

"What for? Even if we say terrible things about Chryspos, no one outside this prison will know. Except for one person."

Tissander raised his voice. "Hello, clerk! Are you there? You might want to take a break. We're about to say some impolite, incriminating and possibly treasonous things about Prince Chryspos, calumnies so vile that he may well decide to silence us forever! And if he silences us, he may find it prudent to eliminate you as well!"

There was the distant sound of a door opening and closing.

"I've heard that many times," said Kratos. "He's allowed short breaks to relieve himself."

"So we won a few minutes," said Tissander. "We should make use of them."

"Chryspos is at odds with Krion," said Diomedos, "and more so with Claudio and Thea."

"But surely, he wouldn't use a carte blanche just to break a trade agreement," said Kratos. "There must be something more important at stake."

"Perhaps he's taking a hostage," said Diomedos.

"Against whom? Claudio?"

"No, against Clenas."

"But Clenas is just a foolish young idler," said Tissander. "Why would he need a hostage against Clenas?"

"Clenas is second in command of the army," said Diomedos.

"Ah, it's becoming clear," said Kratos.

"Not to me!" said Erika.

"It's classic," said Tissander. "One pins the knight in order to advance the pawn."

"I still don't understand."

"The finger I took from Krion must have been a back-up, in case the coup failed," said Diomedos. "Any sorcerer who has the finger could use it to lay spells directly on Krion. Of course, I'm referring to the kind of forbidden magic that leads one to be burned in the public square."

"But who has the finger now?" asked Tissander.

There was the sound of a door opening and closing.

"As I was saying, Chryspos is a wonderful fellow," said Kratos.

"The very model of a virtuous young prince," said Diomedos.

"They really should name something after him," said Tissander.

Erika went to the chair and sat down. Her head was spinning with plots and counterplots, and visions of black magic and daggers in the dark. Elohi was much more dangerous than she thought. Chatmakstan was probably safer.

All I ever really wanted was to marry someone nice and earn a decent living!

The next morning, she woke to the sound of hammering in the courtyard. Looking out the window, she saw some workmen banging away at a wooden structure.

I wonder what they're building?

All at once, inspiration struck. She ran to the grill, yelling, "LOOK! THEY'RE BUILDING A SCAFFOLD!"

"What, a gallows?" asked Kratos, much disturbed. "It's on the other side! Tell me what you see!"

Running back to the window, she pressed her face against the bars and said, "You see it?"

As she'd hoped, the voice that answered was Diomedos. "No, silly girl, they're just fixing

the stairs . . . ”

"Wait!" she said. "Can they hear us?"

"From the window? Unlikely. What did you want to say?"

"Could you get a message to Prince Clenas?"

Diomedos thought about it for a moment.

"Maybe," he said, as one who has grave reservations, "if I can catch one of these pigeons. But why should I? If they find out, it's the oubliettes for certain!"

"There's going to be a coup. I heard them talking about it. Claudio wants to get rid of Krion."

Is that really true? I think it might be!

"Of course he does. A lot of people want to get rid of Krion. But even if it's true, it doesn't help us. Clenas is far away. And besides, the last coup didn't come off very well."

"Clenas is coming here! I'm sure of it! We just need to tell him where I am."

"I've seen him chase a lot of women, but none so far as that."

"But I'm his wife! We were married in a secret ceremony."

"Clenas was never one to respect the institution of marriage."

"You didn't see him. He fought for me, alone against a hundred men!"

"And lost."

"But then he raised his standard against Basilius when he had only one squadron against the whole army!"

Diomedos was silent.

"And Basilius is dead," she added.

"There may be something to what you say," Diomedos admitted.

"And besides that, he has thousands of thalers waiting under my signature in the RBA!"

"Now that is a very strong argument indeed," said Diomedos. "Very well, I'll see what I can do."

Erika went back to the grill. "Sorry, my mistake! They're just working on some stairs. What did you want to talk about today?"

22: Bardhof

Bleary-eyed, he stared at the pile of reports in front of him. He'd read them all at least twice: reports from the informants he'd planted in every neighborhood, inn and public place. They were full of chit-chat about the black market, complaints about the occupation and accusations against petty criminals, but not one said anything about the Creeper.

Grimald was snoring in the corner. Bardhof didn't bother to wake him; there was nothing for him to do. Anahita's head rested on the table. Her black hair lay all around, and her regular breathing suggested if she wasn't asleep yet, she soon would be. Bardhof started to pour another glass of tea, but found the pot was empty.

Why am I doing this? There's nothing here!

He picked up the Creeper file, which still contained only the single letter. It mentioned the traitor just once and gave no clue to his identity. "Creeper" was just an empty name, a mystery. He stared at the name on the file, which was in Akaddian and Bandeluki, and traced with his finger the swirling foreign script he could barely read.

This has got to mean something! It didn't just come out of nowhere!

He shook Ahahita's shoulder.

"Hmmpf?"

He pointed to the name. "What does this say?"

"What I told you, creeper, someone moving close to the ground."

"Say it in Bandeluki."

"Surume." Anahita rested her chin on her hand. She was ready to fall asleep again.

"Could it mean something else? Maybe a plant creeper, a vine?"

"No, that would be a different word."

"What about creepy, like a ghost?"

"No, no, no. No ghosts. Please." She was starting to nod off.

He grabbed her hair and pulled her head back, so he was looking in her eyes. "Think! Is there anything else it possibly could be?"

"Huh. Surume. A name, maybe."

"A name? Why didn't you say that before?"

"Bandeluk name. You wanted a foreigner."

"What kind of a name?"

"Name is name. Old name. Not common."

"You know someone named Surume?"

"No. Don't think so. Don't ask names."

"Could it refer to a place?"

"No. Just name."

"A historical person? Someone famous?"

"Never heard of him." She yawned and tried to lay her head back down. Bardhof decided to let her sleep.

Whoever chose this name had a reason even if it were frivolous. I just need to find it!

By noon the next day, he was no closer to finding the Creeper, but feeling a good deal more frustrated. The records kept by the city watch included only two people named Surume. One of them turned out to be the doorkeeper for a rich family on Draper Street. Bardhof had gone in with Grimald, Murdoon and several of the city watch, searched the whole house, interrogated everyone and learned absolutely nothing about Omin or the Creeper.

If those people weren't anti-royalists before, they certainly are now!

The second Surume listed his occupation as "merchant", which could mean anything, but the address was on a side street in one of the poorer sections of town, so he was probably just a shopkeeper at best. Arriving at the home, he saw it was on the second floor of a house that was at least a century old and, to all appearances, had never been repaired in all that time.

They rushed up the stairs with Grimald and Murdoon in the lead and burst in on a young woman with two small girls, who were sitting at a table shelling peas. The peas spilled and rolled all over the floor.

Grimald and Murdoon had a quick look around and reported there was no one else home. Meanwhile, the woman stood up, pale with shock and fear, in her shabby little apartment, while the two girls clung to her skirts.

"Ask where her husband is," he said to Anahita.

"She asks what you want with her husband."

She still wants to defy me? Perhaps this requires a different approach.

"Tell her you've made a complaint against Surume. Tell her he owes you money. You've come to collect."

"But he doesn't . . ."

"Just tell her."

The young mother took the news with a look of astonishment, which soon turned to rage. She launched herself at Anahita, striking with her fists, so Murdoon had to restrain her. The children broke into loud wails.

Unperturbed, Anahita continued to translate. "She calls me a filthy whore. She hopes I choke on this money. She calls me a loathsome animal. She wishes I should die an unclean death . . . "

"Ask her again where her husband is."

Anahita slapped her hard in the face, so she ceased storming and broke into helpless tears.

"She says he's on Hamilad Street, selling his shish kabobs. She hopes you give him a good thrashing. She wonders how she could marry such a man . . . "

"Thank her for her cooperation."

Now, I've broken in like a thunderbolt from the blue and shattered their peaceful lives, and what have I learned? Probably nothing!

There was a shish kabob seller on Hamilad Street, just a few paces around the corner from the burned-out spy nest on Aleskafy Street. Bardhof left Grimald, Murdoon and the watchmen behind, and took Anahita by the arm.

"Today, you're my girlfriend."

"I usually get paid for that."

"Today, you're the kind of girlfriend who doesn't get paid."

"Oh, a dummy. Whatever you say." She buttoned up her blouse.

They strolled casually down Hamilad Street, not in any particular hurry. "Are you hungry?" he asked.

"Not yet."

"Wrong! You're very hungry. You're begging me for a shish kabob."

Anahita could have appeared on any stage. As they approached the street vendor, she pointed to his grill and said, "Please! I'm famished! Why do we have to wait for dinner?"

"Well," he said reluctantly, "I don't like to buy things from strangers off the street, but maybe just this once. Ask him how much they cost."

"He says two for a piaster."

He handed over the money, noting the man was young and thin. His shish kabobs, however, looked good: grilled goat meat with tomatoes, onions and peppers.

His customers probably eat better than his own children.

After a bite, he said, "Tell him I like his shish kabob."

Eager to please as any spaniel, the young man grinned and nodded.

"Flirt with him. Make conversation. Ask for his recipe."

Bardhof ate his shish kabob and watched the two Bandeluks chatting. The young man was healthy, but not very imposing. He looked exactly like a typical street vendor, his skin darkened from standing all day in the sun. His clothing was worn and patched. It would probably be a waste of time interrogating him. Still, Omin had some reason to steal this name for a secret code.

Now, Anahita made some kind of a joke, and Surume laughed.

Mopsus!

He'd served with Lt. Mopsus a long time. They were both part of Krion's staff. Among his other annoying habits, Mopsus had an odd, girlish giggle that sometimes broke out at inappropriate moments. Though they were different in many other ways, Surume and Mopsus shared the same distinctive laugh.

That's got to be it!

"Enough," he told Anahita. "Thank him for his shish kabobs. Time to go."

He was just turning away, when he thought of something else. "Tell him when he goes home tonight, to tell his wife the whore lied. He doesn't owe money to anyone. The police apologized for the mistake and gave him this in compensation."

He handed Surume a gold coin stamped with the well-known image of King Diecos. They left him standing in the street beside his grill, staring in amazement at the gold coin in his hand.

This is about the last place I'd have looked for spies.

The barracks where he'd lived for over two months was formerly the home of the Amir's palace guard. By military standards, the accommodations were luxurious. Both he and Mopsus had rooms on the second floor.

"I need your master key," he told the sergeant on duty. "Police business."

"Yes sir," said the sergeant. "But I'll need it back soon. I expect to be relieved in an hour."

"No problem. My men are Sgt. Grimald and Sgt. Murdoon. They'll just stay here with you for awhile. If anyone asks, you're trying to find quarters for them."

The barracks were quiet, the loudest noise being his feet on the stairs. Most of the soldiers were on duty or asleep.

This has got to be the easiest burglary ever attempted.

He tapped softly on Mopsus' door, but got no response. This time of day, Mopsus was usually at the headquarters. Letting himself in, he saw Mopsus had been to the bazaar. There was a fine, thick carpet on the floor and a few of the big cushions the natives seemed to love and some colorful wall hangings.

He likes it soft, my friend Mopsus. Perhaps he has some income on the side?

He searched the desk without finding anything but a bundle of letters from the man's family. He skimmed a few. They didn't appear to have any connection with the case, so he left them where he found them.

A closet held only the standard uniforms, all clean and well-pressed. Reaching under the bed, though, he felt something out of place, a metal surface. Feeling around with his fingers, he found a handle and pulled it. A very solid-looking strongbox slid into view.

Now this looks interesting!

The strongbox, of course, was locked, and it was of a type he'd never seen before. Perhaps it had been made in Kindleton or one of the other Free States. He doubted the local Bandeluk locksmiths would be able to open it, at least not without damaging the lock.

Frustrated, he pushed the strongbox back under the bed for later and had a look at the bookshelf. Mopsus had eclectic reading habits. There were several novels besides popular histories and books of an erotic nature. Bardhof flipped quickly through some of them without seeing anything of interest. There were also some reference books on the Bandeluki language, which he passed over.

One book drew his attention: Lindus' "Principles of Cryptography".

Now why would he be interested in a technical subject like that?

"Principles" looked a bit dog-eared. Someone had spent many hours with it. Passages inside, explaining the different cipher codes, were underlined for future reference.

It looks a bit suspicious, but he could always explain it as a hobby or part of his staff work.

Returning Lindus to its place, he noticed one other item on the shelf: a plaster bust of Prince Krion.

Why does he need a bust of someone he sees every day?

Closely examined, the bust seemed to be one of the cheap, familiar ones that were sold in every Akaddian town. As he turned it over to check the base for a maker's mark, he heard something rattle inside. After a bit of shaking, a finger-sized roll of paper fell out. He laid it out on the desk.

The paper had nothing on it but two columns, one of letters and the other of numbers. The letters were alphabetical, but the numbers seemed to be totally random. For example, the letter A was on the same line as 77, whereas B was next to 36.

A cipher code! Mopsus has been practicing! But where did he get this particular code?

The Bandeluks, he knew, preferred invisible ink to ciphers. The alphabet, also, was Akaddian. There were none of the special characters one saw in Hallandish. So, whoever had created the code was Akaddian, and he probably intended to communicate with another Akaddian, or at least someone who could read that language.

Of course, the code alone doesn't prove anything. I haven't found any treasonous messages written in code.

Bardhof looked around the desk until he found a blank sheet of paper, then copied the code and returned it to its place in the bust of Prince Krion. He had a last look around the room, but saw nothing else of interest, so he left and locked the door behind him.

A short distance down the hall was his own room, and he needed no special key for that. He sat down at his desk and composed a short message, which he then turned into random-looking strings of numbers using Mopsus' code. Deciphered, it looked like this:

URGENT TO RECONSIDER PEACE OFFER
MEET TONIGHT AT EIGHT IN GOLDEN LION
WEAR A WHITE GLOVE ON YOUR LEFT HAND

He sealed the letter in a plain, white envelope and went downstairs.

Grimald and Murdoon had gotten in a game of cards with the duty sergeant, who, to judge by the pile of coins in front of him, was doing very well.

"Sorry to interrupt your game, men, but it's time to go." He returned the master key to the desk sergeant and gave him the envelope. "Put this in Lt. Mopsus' box, please. It's confidential. If he asks where it came from, you don't know."

"Yes sir."

A few hours later, he Grimald and Murdoon were crowded into a dark doorway down the street from the Golden Lion, a posh establishment much favored by officers, visiting merchants, diplomats and foreigners generally. The evidence Bardhof had so far collected was weak, he thought, but if Mopsus showed up at the appointed time in the appointed place with a white glove on his left hand, he'd have some explaining to do. Bardhof was already looking forward to the interrogation.

Shortly before eight, he spotted Mopsus coming from the direction of the palace. He seemed to be affecting a casual manner, while keeping a watchful eye on his surroundings. Pausing in front of the Golden Lion, he looked around as if he were expecting something, but seeing nothing out of the ordinary, took a white glove from his pocket and started to put it on.

At that moment, one of those unpredictable quirks of fate occurred, which have spoiled many a good stakeout. Across the street from Bardhof, a woman opened her kitchen window momentarily to throw some dirty dishwater in the gutter. Bardhof and his men were briefly illuminated.

Down the street, Mopsus, who already had a glove on his left hand, put one on his right as well and waved at Bardhof as one who greets an old friend. He walked up boldly to the group.

"Good evening, Captain. A bit nippy tonight, isn't it?"

"I hadn't noticed. What are you doing here?"

"I've been looking all over for you!" Mopsus pulled the letter from his pocket. "Someone left this for me at the barracks, but I can't make heads or tails of it. It seems to be just a random jumble of numbers. Perhaps a secret message of some kind? I thought you might want to see it."

Bardhof took the letter. "Don't worry, I'll get to the bottom of it."

"I'm much relieved. Good evening, Captain." Mopsus left, but not without a girlish giggle.

23: Gallites

They were beating around Cape Dire when he saw the pirate ship.

He'd chosen a felucca small enough to handle alone. He had no experience with this type of vessel, but it was enough like a sloop that he felt sure he could manage it though the lateen rig took some getting used to. This choice now appeared to be a serious mistake. There was no way the felucca, hardly bigger than a longboat, could outrun the two-masted vessel behind them.

"What is it?" said Mangasar, momentarily forgetting his seasickness.

"I don't like the cut of his jib," said Gallites, pointing.

"You don't like the what of his what?"

"It's pirates," he said simply.

"Is that a schooner?" asked Pvt. Humbert. He was sitting amidships, nursing a wounded leg that seemed to pain him every time the boat tacked.

"I think it's a yawl," said Gallites. "But whatever it is, it's trouble."

He'd been fighting a strong north wind that made tacking difficult, especially with the lateen rig. The felucca kept shipping water and, even with Mangasar and Humbert bailing, it threatened to soak Sgt. Westcott, who was lying wrapped in blankets, unconscious with a septic gut wound that was likely to kill him soon if he got no better care than what the combat medics could provide.

Of all the lubberly crews I've ever seen, this has to be the worst!

"Are they chasing us?" asked Mangasar, wide-eyed. The boy seemed brave enough on land, but had yet to find his sea legs.

"They may not have spotted us yet," said Gallites. "But they will soon. And they're taking a northerly course."

"Why don't we just land somewhere until they go away?"

"Here?" Here pointed to the shore where the wind was driving six-foot breakers against the rocks. "And if they put ashore, we could never outrun them with two wounded. Our best odds are with the boat."

"We're going to lose him anyway," said Mangasar, pointing to Westcott.

"Maybe, but we're not losing anyone without a fight." He was happy these comments were in Bandeluki, a language neither of the marines could understand.

"What are you talking about?" asked Humbert.

"I said they aren't getting us without a fight."

"Damn straight!" said Humbert, patting his crossbow.

Two crossbows against a whole pirate ship?

The future looked grim, no matter what he did. For a moment, he considered turning back, but the pirates were gaining, and they'd surely catch him if he turned around. The best chance was to round the cape and hope for better winds on the other side.

Mangasar stared at the pirate ship, which kept gaining while they beat into the wind. "We should pretend to be fishermen," he said.

"Then they could kill us without a fight. Pirates are everyone's enemies, fishermen included."

"They just lost a lot of men. They probably want to replenish their crew."

"Join a pirate crew? I'd rather just die fighting."

"I'd rather not die at all."

"Then stop yakking and start bailing, or we won't need any pirates to kill us."

They cleared the headland half an hour later. The wind wasn't much better, but he was able to take a starboard course without much tacking and gain some headway on the pirates, who were still struggling past Cape Dire. The shortest route north to Kafra was directly into the wind, and his present course would take him to the Dead Cliffs, so-called partly because of bleakness of the high, dark cliffs that hung remorselessly over the waves, but also because they offered no refuge to storm-tossed sailors.

With the Dead Cliffs before me and the pirates behind, I'll be trapped like a lobster in a pot.

It was still possible an Akaddian patrol would show up, or he could find a shoal to cross that was too shallow for the pursuing vessel. But the Royal Navy was busy elsewhere, and looking for shoals was a dangerous business.

For the time being, he concentrated on driving the boat through the waves. It kept heeling to leeward and threatened to broach. But before long, he noticed the wind, which had been blustery and from the north, was abating and shifting to westerly. The waves, too, were less violent.

Soon, he was running before the wind. He began jibing back and forth for additional speed. The pirates, he noticed, were sailing almost dead downwind.

Either that's a green crew or a skeleton crew, or else they feel very sure of their prey.

If the pirates hadn't replenished their crew, his chances of out-maneuvering them were that much better. On the other hand, the Dead Cliffs were looming up in the distance, so his options were severely restricted.

Now that he had a closer look, he could see the pirate vessel was neither a schooner nor a yawl, but the big dhow he'd seen earlier. Actually, he had no word for the vessel, which was longer than any dhow he'd ever seen and had a narrow beam, a low profile and a deep keel. He thought it was a sharp-looking vessel and might have liked to sail on it, were it not already crewed with pirates.

The Bandeluks are better shipwrights than I thought.

With a ship like that, the pirates would probably have caught them already if not for the green crew, and they were sure to do so before long. On the other hand, with that keel . . .

Feeling he had no choice, he turned into shallow water. The wind was dying now, and the gentle swells weren't much of a threat, but the tide was going out, and there was danger of running aground. He raised the centerplate.

"Think you could climb the mast?" he asked Mangasar.

Mangasar studied the mast, which was twelve feet high and had small wooden handholds for climbing. "I can, but what am I to do up there?"

"Look out for dangerous rocks. If you see one point at it, so I can go around."

"Very well."

He glanced at the pirate ship, which hadn't changed course. As he expected, it didn't dare follow him into the shallows, which were perilous enough for the felucca, a boat without a fixed keel.

Climbing the mast was a challenge for Mangasar, as it swayed back and forth with every wave. Meanwhile, Gallites found it harder and harder to hold course without the centerplate. The boat kept drifting to port; the ebb tide was sweeping it into deeper water.

Mangasar reached his perch and pointed excitedly at a rock he'd spotted. Gallites saw it too, a nasty, jagged tooth to port that seemed to be getting bigger with every trough. The tide was moving them directly toward it. He turned to starboard and felt a shock as the boat ground suddenly to a halt, the prow striking against something underwater.

There was a shriek as Mangasar fell into the sea with a great splash and flailing of limbs. Gallites released the sail and the useless rudder and went in after him. The boy, he knew, couldn't swim.

The current knocked him off his feet and spun him around. He was helpless, floundering, disoriented and still trying to stand up in the shallow water, when a wave slammed him into a rock. He clung to it desperately and looked around for Mangasar.

The boy, he saw, was caught in a rip current and being swept out to sea. There was no way to reach him by swimming, but the ebb tide had exposed a sand bar, and he made for it. He ploughed across the sand, then down into the current. The undertow sucked at his ankles. He grabbed at the boy as he came by splashing and thrashing, caught a handful of his loose robe and hauled him back to the bar.

Mangasar crouched on the sand, cold and trembling. When had he finished coughing up water, he said, "You saved my life."

"Comes with the job. You're safe now. Wait here until the tide's out."

He went back to the boat, which had come to rest on the bar. It was not stoved in, as he'd feared, but could probably use some caulking. Humbert was bending over Westcott, who was still unconscious.

"How is he?"

"Worse. The fever is worse."

"Sorry. I can't do much for him here. I guess I'm not the seaman I thought I was."

"You'll do until someone else comes along. I thought we were dead back there."

"We aren't out of trouble yet." He turned to look at the pirate ship, which had taken a northerly course. Someone standing on the stern waved at him. He waved back.

"How long are we stranded here?" asked Humbert.

"Six hours, more or less, until the tide comes in. Try to get some rest." He went to open the supply chest.

Sgt. Westcott died in the night.

Dawn found them becalmed in a fog. Westcott's body, wrapped in blankets, lay amidships, serving as ballast until they could find somewhere to bury him. The felucca wasn't equipped with oars, so Gallites sculled as best he could with the rudder. The sail hung listlessly, making no more contribution to their progress than Westcott did.

"The fog will burn off in a few hours, and the wind will pick up then," he said.

"How do you know?" asked Mangasar.

"I don't. But that's what usually happens."

"Won't the pirates see us?"

"I don't believe they'll come back soon. I don't know why they were headed toward Kafra, but it's nothing to do with us."

He was glad no one asked how he was navigating. The correct answer, he suspected, was "very poorly". The only thing he had to steer by were the low swells that passed, headed toward the shore behind him. As best he could judge, he was headed northwest, into open water.

It was eerily quiet. There was nothing to hear but the soft sound of the rudder stirring the water. Nothing was visible more than a few feet away from the boat. The presence of the dead man didn't encourage conversation, so they sat silently, each wrapped up in his own thoughts.

After awhile, Gallites thought he must be falling asleep because he heard distant voices calling from the mist. But Humbert and Mangasar were looking around, so they must have heard them too. He silently put a finger to his lips. The voices gradually became louder. They were speaking in Bandeluki, and he could make out a few words, then a whole conversation:

"How do we know Evrim is still there?"

"Where could he go without the boat?"

"He may not even be alive."

"Why should he be dead? Did anyone see him killed?"

"But what could he do for us? There's nothing left."

"You have some better plan?"

"Let's go to the Heartland Sea."

"We'd never get past Mira-jil."

"If we did get home, they'd only make soldiers out of us."

"Conscript able-bodied seamen? What for?"

"They don't need sailors. The navy is doing nothing. And they always want more warm bodies for the army."

"What's the difference between a whore and a general?"

"Tell me."

"A whore makes cold men warm, but a general makes warm men cold."

These don't sound like pirates, but the Bandeluks may not be any friendlier. Better to avoid them.

The voices were getting louder, but it was hard to tell where they were coming from. He turned to port. And then, suddenly, it loomed up out of the fog: a two-masted vessel of Bandeluk make and rigging. He turned the rudder back to starboard.

He heard a loud *click.* Humbert had cocked his crossbow. Gallites gestured for him to put it down.

Someone onboard the Bandeluk vessel, now barely 50 feet away, said, "Did you hear something?"

"Nothing."

"I'll go look."

"You think they found us?"

"I don't see anything."

The vigilant sailor had apparently gone to the other side of the ship. They could hear him moving around on deck. Gallites sculled as fast as he could into the fog bank.

"I told you it was nothing," somebody said. "They'll never find us in all this fog."

Looking over his shoulder, Gallites could no longer see the mystery vessel. It had vanished like a ghost into the mist.

That was close! They must have hove to, waiting for the fog to lift.

Now came a faint stir of wind. The sail, which had hung apathetically from the mast, began to billow. Gallites, who'd completely lost his sense of direction, chose a course athwart the wind, hoping to put some distance between himself and the Bandeluks before the fog lifted. He could hear the babble of foreign voices fading behind him.

A short time later, he broke out of the fog and found himself on a westerly course. The Bandeluks were still in the fog bank behind him, but as the southerly wind picked up, he assumed they wouldn't be concealed for long. He decided to risk a dash across the open sea. He turned the prow north, let out the sail, pulled up the centerplate and began scudding before the wind.

As the wind gained force, the felucca began moving at a remarkable speed, faster than he'd have expected for a boat of this size. This, he saw, was the great strength of the felucca: whatever its other shortcomings, it could take a following wind and run with it.

To the east, the fog lifted to reveal the Bandeluk ship. Surprisingly, it took a north-easterly course, ignoring the felucca.

Maybe they just weren't interested in us.

He'd assumed the pirate vessel following them from the south was in pursuit, but now it seemed the crew weren't pirates, and they happened to be sailing on the same course for reasons of their own. Were any of the reckless maneuvers of the previous day necessary? He decided to keep his doubts to himself.

"Looks like we gave them the slip," said Mangasar.

"That's how it looks," he said.

Now, thanks to this miscalculation, he'd embarked on a dangerous course, running before the wind on the open sea in a small boat. The felucca began pitching alarmingly as the swells grew stronger. He was afraid it might capsize. Accordingly, he lowered the centerplate and took a more conservative course, paralleling the mystery vessel.

"Are we chasing them now?" asked Humbert.

"I think we should keep an eye on them," he replied. "I'd like to know what they're doing in these waters."

"That's what I'd call a gutsy move, sir!" said Humbert, much impressed.

Gods help me! I don't believe I'm fit to command a rowboat!

Gallites had expected the southerly wind would blow him straight to Kafra, but he'd forgotten about the island in between: Jahar? Something like that. It was just a spot on the map, but now it had become the most important place in the world.

One could go around the island to port or starboard. The mystery ship, now far ahead, had taken the starboard course, up the relatively safe channel that led to Kafra. But that way was now closed to him. The wind had increased to gale force. Huge swells were driving the boat before them. It was impossible to maneuver. A wise but useless bit of nautical lore crossed his mind:

A wet sheet leeward in the gale means lose the mast or trim the sail.

An insane, horizontal rain of wind-driven foam pelted them. Humbert and Mangasar were bailing desperately, but he could see they'd never make it to the channel.

The only real chance was to beach the boat on the island. Wiping the spray from his eyes, he scanned the shore for a landing place and was pleased to see a beach dead ahead. There was, however, a line of breakers in between. As he drew nearer, he saw ten-foot waves were breaking over a reef.

To strike a reef in such waves meant certain death. The only hope was to catch a timely wave that could carry them over the reef. But such a stunt would take great skill and incredible luck, a legendary feat of seamanship if he accomplished it and a quick burial at sea if he didn't.

A long shot, but the only one I've got.

He raised the centerplate. When his companions saw that he

was steering directly for the breakers, they both turned to look at him, aghast. He grinned to show a confidence he didn't feel and gestured with the flat of his hand as if to indicate he'd slip through a channel, one that none of them could actually see. Not reassured, they braced themselves for impact.

The waves got higher as he approached the shore. By chance, one caught the boat and pushed it ahead, faster and faster as it peaked. But it was now obvious the maneuver he planned was unworkable for any boat larger than a dory. The felucca was simply too long. While its stern rode the crest, the prow was sinking into the trough, so the boat tilted forward. The rudder was already in the air. Abandoning any attempt at steering, Gallites simply clung to the tiller for dear life.

As the crest rose behind him, the prow struck the rocks with a loud *crunch*. At that moment, Westcott made the move that saved them: The 200-pound corpse slammed into the mast, tilting the boat still further. The following wave completed the work, as the whole boat did a forward somersault, flinging its contents into the surf.

Stunned by the sudden immersion, Gallites tried desperately to swim, before noticing the water was only two feet deep and becoming shallower as the wave ran out. He'd been thrown completely over the reef. Looking around, he saw Mangasar struggling in the surf a short distance away and pulled him ashore.

Mangasar fell to his knees and bent over to kiss the sandy beach. "May the gods curse me if I ever set foot in a boat again!" he declared.

"If you're so friendly with the gods, beg them to forgive your rash oath because we're stranded on an island," said Gallites. Then he went to look for Humbert.

The marine was sitting on the beach a short distance away and clutching his injured leg. Gallites could see fresh, red blood trickling between his fingers. But before he could inspect the wound, Humbert waved him off, saying, "First, save him."

He was pointing at the cold, stiff figure of Sgt. Westcott which, shorn of its blankets, was rolling in the waves.

"Of course." He grabbed the corpse by the collar and hauled it up on the beach, then went to tend Humbert's leg. The wound, he could see, had broken open and probably needed new stitches, but there was nothing he could do at the moment except change the dressings and hope the bath in sea-water would prevent an infection.

Sometimes that works, and sometimes it doesn't.

He put on a cheerful face for Humbert and said, "I think you'll be fine." Seeing the felucca's rudder had washed ashore, he broke off the tiller and gave it to Humbert for a walking stick until they could find something better.

Meanwhile, Mangasar had been collecting debris from the wreck and piling it up to make a fire. Gallites was about to tell him not to waste his time because the wet wood would never burn, especially in such a wind, when the boy leaned over and breathed on it. The wood instantly burst into flame. Mangasar stripped off his clothing to dry it.

That's a neat trick!

"Think you could teach me how to do that?"

"It's a trade secret. I may owe you my life, but how much is that worth? Ask for something else."

"I'll let you know when I think of something."

If that's a trade secret, then what's his trade? It might be better not to ask.

Naked, Mangasar looked very different. He still had the rounded face of a child, but his body was lean and wiry. And he had scars as if he'd been in battle. Some of the scars looked very old, and some seemed to be from wounds that should have been fatal.

I think I'll just get him to the Prince and let the Prince ask the questions.

"Are we going to camp here?" asked Mangasar as he dressed himself.

"Can't. The tide will put this beach underwater." He pointed to the jagged rocks that lay above it. "And the shore here isn't very inviting. I suggest we gather whatever we can salvage and have a look around."

"We need to bury the sergeant," said Humbert, who'd just come limping to the fire.

"Of course."

They found a shelf of volcanic rock that was split by deep fissures, lowered the body into one of them and piled rocks on top of it.

"We have no food or shelter, and it's getting dark," complained

Mangasar. "Why are we wasting time with a corpse?"

"Because he earned it."

"Is there anything you want to say?" he asked Humbert.

"I'm not good with words, so I'll just say he was a brave marine and a loyal friend, and he died of wounds he got in honorable battle, and he never once complained, even when he was dying. And I hope the gods deal gently with him because he's already had enough hardship."

"Amen."

Mangasar, who'd understood none of this, asked, "Where do we go now?"

"Our best bet is to follow the shore east toward the channel because walking the beach is easier, and we're more likely to find shelter there."

They walked slowly because Hubert's leg was paining him. The wind gradually abated, and the clouds broke in the east. A waxing moon appeared and favored them with its light.

"What place is this?" asked Mangasar, who'd been looking around with misgivings and clambering up on rocks for a better view.

"It's what it looks like, a desert island. No one lives here, but if we get lucky, we may find some water and a place we can sleep."

"How do we get off?"

"We'll just have to hope the gods haven't forgotten about us."

"You're a religious man?"

"We all are when the storm winds blow."

"It's not always wise to rely on the gods."

"Is there someone else around who can help us?"

"What about those people over there?"

Mangasar was pointing to a faint light that had appeared up the beach to the north. It was hard to tell exactly where it was coming from because a rocky headland concealed the source.

"That's an excellent question!"

They climbed up the rocky ridge. From there, they could see the source of the lights: The mystery ship was tied up at a quay, which was in a small cove. The Bandeluk crew had lighted lanterns and were sitting around the deck, talking to each other. He couldn't hear what they said, but it seemed to be an argument of some sort.

Those boys are a long way from home.

"I don't know if we can take them," said Humbert. "We lost our crossbows in the surf."

A curvy knife appeared, as if by magic, in Mangasar's hand. "I can dispose of them," he said, "though it would be easier to wait until they're asleep."

"Please don't," said Gallites. "That's a two-masted ship, and it's going nowhere without a crew. Just wait here while I talk to them." He repeated the comment in Hallandish for Humbert.

Working his way around the end of the cove proved easier than he thought. Soon he was following a gravel path that branched left to a ruined building and right to the quay. He walked up to the gangway without being noticed.

The Bandluks were passing a bottle around and complaining to each other about the cruelty of fate:

"There's no safe port for hundreds of miles!"

"Well, we can't stay here. The pirates took everything they could and burned the rest."

"And Evrim has disappeared."

"We should probably go look for him."

"Where? You think he's hiding in the rocks?"

"I don't know where he is, but we won't be seeing him again."

Gallites stepped down into the light of their lanterns. The Bandeluks stared at him in blank-eyed astonishment as if he were a ghost that had appeared out of nowhere. The one holding the bottle dropped it with a shattering of glass. A strong-smelling puddle of arrack spread over the deck.

"Good evening, gentlemen," he said in Bandeluki. "My name is Gallites, and I'd like to charter your boat."

24: Raeesha

And I thought it would be hard to manage a bunch of Bandeluk girls!

The column of *efaryti* behind her stretched over a mile and must have numbered at least a thousand though there was no way to tell how many were warriors and how many were spectators. Small bands of demons kept joining without anyone's invitation or permission. Apparently, there were a lot of *efaryti* who had scores to settle with the Wind Bags.

She'd improved her system of hand signals though only the Ghost Feet were much good at recognizing them. Besides the hand signals, she'd mastered just one Efaryti word (if you could call it that): a sharp whistle that brought any demons within earshot running.

She envied Rajik who, under Iyad's tutelage, had learned to make a few chirps, clucks and squeaks the *efaryti* could understand. But she was already occupied trying to organize the demons in groups, keep them moving in the same direction, find campsites and handle the distribution of food. The *efaryti* had a tendency to wander off whenever they saw something interesting or felt like taking a nap and to show up only for meals.

She made the biggest demon in each group the leader and put it in charge of the food distribution. Since the *efaryti* weren't generous about sharing, this contributed to unit cohesion, but didn't prevent incidents like the one yesterday, when nearly a hundred *efaryti,* dissatisfied with the progress of the expedition or the distribution of food or possibly something else, suddenly decided it was time to go home. She had no way of stopping them. Apparently, discipline was not a concept familiar to the *efaryti.*

She was, however, getting better at recognizing some individuals, especially the one she called Big Stick, who'd assumed the authority to follow her around and attempt to translate her gestures into the Efaryti language and to smack anyone it regarded as a troublemaker with its big stick. It wasn't always clear whether she was leading the march, or Big Stick was leading it according to orders it claimed to receive from her. She thought it better not to inquire too closely.

At the end of the column came Iyad and the Head Counters, who were better organized and had thick leather hides strapped to their bodies as armor. The presence of Head Counters cut down on desertions because it was dangerous for a member of a different tribe to be found alone under circumstances where it might be considered fair game for head-counting.

Iyad had advised them to follow a stream up a wooded valley where he said the flying ships couldn't spot them. She had hardly any idea where she was, aside from the occasional mechanical whirring sounds she heard above the treetops, which suggested she was nearing her goal.

A little after lunch on the third day, the column halted for no reason she could see. The Ghost Feet were talking excitedly among themselves, but she couldn't understand a word. She turned to Big Stick, who simply drew its finger lengthwise along its stomach, a gesture she hadn't seen before.

She rushed forward to the vanguard, Rajik's scout group, and found them standing around a tree from which an *efaryt* was hanging by its feet, covered in blood. The cause of death was easy to see: It had been cut open and gutted like a goat.

Rajik stood next to the corpse, looking unhappier than she'd seen him for a long time. "That was Long Ear," he said glumly. "He was teaching me their language. He got a little ahead of the group, and suddenly he wasn't there anymore. Then we found him like this."

"Wind Bags?"

"No. I can't tell what they're talking about, but it isn't Wind Bags."

She grabbed the nearest *efaryt*, said "Iyad," and made the gesture for "come." The messenger went running off to the rear of the column. It would take twenty or thirty minutes for Iyad to get here, she calculated.

"If not Wind Bags, who?" she asked.

"I don't know. There are many tribes. This must be one of them."

"Did you look for tracks?"

"Oh yes, there are lots of them. See for yourself."

The path ahead did seem to have a great many *efaryti* tracks, some very recent. But they all looked the same to her eyes. She couldn't make sense of them. The only thing she knew for sure was, a large body of *efaryti* had been here recently.

While she was studying the tracks, Rajik came and said, "Well?"

"Well what?"

"What do you think we should do?"

"Find whoever did this, and make sure they don't do it again."

"A good plan if we can do that. I'm not sure where to look."

The Ghost Feet were peering nervously in all directions. They'd drawn their weapons and seemed to expect a monster to jump out of the woods. If they knew where to find the enemy, they gave no indication of it.

Raeesha said, "My best guess would be your friend Long Ear ran into an ambush. When the attackers were done, they headed back upstream to set another ambush."

"Why would they do this? Are they trying to scare us?"

At that point, Iyad came running up with some of the Head Counters behind him. He took one look at the corpse and said, "Gut Eaters!"

"What's that?" asked Raeesha.

"Another tribe. They eat the entrails of their enemies. They think it gives them magical power."

"Are they working with the Wind Bags?"

"They aren't friends with anyone. They wander through the hills, take prisoners wherever they find them and slaughter them like goats. Our column must have drawn their attention. Sheer bad luck."

"Can we chase them down?"

"We will be doing well if we can chase them away. It isn't easy to find Gut Eaters in the woods."

"What about all these tracks?"

"They'll lead you into an ambush or else a dead end. Our best bet is to stick together. Don't let them pick you off alone."

I'm sure the General could think of a better plan than that. But what would it be?

Looking around, she saw she was in a narrow place with steep, rocky hills on either side. There was a thick growth of forest everywhere.

They're probably watching us right now!

"What if we retreat?"

"Then they'd follow us and harvest stragglers. They don't give up their prey so easily."

"Our position here is too exposed. The Gut Eaters have all the advantages. Go back to the fork in the stream, the one with the clearing. Wait for me there."

"We'll lose the rear guard if we do that."

"I am the rear guard."

A few minutes later, she was leading a skittish mob of Ghost Feet downstream with the help of Big Stick, who zealously whacked anyone who lagged behind or wandered away from the column. Big Stick, she thought, would make a fine babysitter.

Shepherding her little demon pack downhill was no difficult task, especially as they seemed eager to go. The problem was controlling her nervousness. She clutched the bow in her hand, but she doubted it would be of much use against the Gut Eaters, or that the Ghost Feet would protect her. Once the *efaryti* started running, they ran.

She hadn't felt the demon moving around in her belly for some time, but she knew it was still there, and if she let her fears overwhelm her, her heart would race, and then the demon would cause another disaster.

Whatever happens, I must stay calm.

But that was hard, when she could hear the rustling of dead leaves and the occasional snap of a twig behind her. It sounded like the Gut Eaters were growing in number, but whenever she turned to look, there was nothing visible but the trees and shrubs.

To give herself courage, she sang an old Bandeluk song she remembered from childhood:

Come, put aside your woes and fears,
Take up instead your bows and spears!
Go in the woods without delay,
Have some fun and kill some prey!

No mercy for the big-eyed deer,
For goose and grouse we shed no tear,

Boar and bear are going to die,
Their blood will spurt and flesh will fry!

Women, light the kitchen fire!
The hunt is done, the men come nigher,
Bringing many a bird and beast,
Set the table and spread the feast!

The Ghost Feet had all stopped. They were staring at her, agape. It suddenly occurred to her she'd never heard them make music of any kind.

They must think it's a magic spell!

She waved them forward to continue the march, and when they didn't go at once, Big Stick began helpfully to whack the nearest ones. Reluctantly, they continued down the trail, pausing occasionally to look over their shoulders and see if some sort of wizardry were in progress.

The song made her feel better. The Gut Eaters seemed to hesitate, but soon the distant rustle of footsteps behind her was audible as before. And now that the afternoon shadows were lengthening, the enemy came nearer.

I have their attention, good, but I need them to keep their distance.

Walking down the path with no undue haste, she took note of the natural cover around her.

That bush there looks like a real good one to hide behind.

The rustling kept getting closer. After a hundred feet, she suddenly whirled and fired an arrow into the bush she'd noticed before. There was a loud squawk.

Got him!

The Ghost Feet celebrated with gleeful chittering, and some loosed arrows into the brush. She gestured for them to continue along the path.

No fighting! Not yet!

She noticed her heart was beating faster than it should, so she concentrated on relaxing.

Breathe slowly! Think nice thoughts!

The casualty they'd taken discouraged the Gut Eaters for only a few minutes. It was getting darker, and the rustling was louder. On the other hand, they were approaching the bend in the stream where a tributary split off. Hopefully, Iyad and the Head Counters were waiting in the clearing ahead.

She picked another bush, walked past it, then whirled and fired. This time, there was no rewarding squawk, and the gleeful chittering came from the dark forest behind her. The Gut Eaters were more numerous than she thought. Certainly, they outmatched her little pack of Ghost Feet, and from their jumpy demeanor, she guessed the Ghost Feet knew it too.

Breathe slowly! Think nice thoughts!

There was a light flickering among the trees ahead.

The Head Counters must be making camp. Are they ready for a fight?

The Ghost Feet had noticed the light too, and they began moving faster. Anything to get out of the dark forest! Big Stick squeaked and threatened with its stick, but the group was breaking up, the fastest ones taking the lead.

I can't hold them anymore!

She signalled for the Ghost Feet to run, which they were more than willing to do. She followed them for a few paces, then whirled and fired at a surprised *efaryt* who was emerging from behind a tree. It went down with an arrow square in the chest. She walked slowly backward a few paces, waiting for more of them to appear.

Breathe slowly! Think nice thoughts!

She was quite alone now. Even Big Stick had deserted her. Downstream, she could hear a babble of shrill voices, as the Head Counters greeted her little Ghost Feet pack. She turned and dashed a few steps down the trail, then whirled again, bow in hand.

But now, she had too many targets. Dozens of Gut Eaters were emerging from the shadows, holding spears, their bodies smeared with stripes and dabs of war paint. She fired one last, wild arrow and turned to go . . . but tripped on a root and went sprawling. The Gut Eaters were almost on top of her.

This is it!

She stuck her fingers in her mouth and whistled as loudly as she could. Immediately, there was a whizzing sound, as hundreds of Ghost Feet, who'd concealed themselves in the wooded hills to the left and right fired their bows. The air above her head was thick with poisoned arrows, like swarms of angry bees. She decided to stay flat on the ground.

Breathe slowly! Think nice thoughts!

There were a number of loud shrieks, followed by thumps, as bodies hit the ground. The corpse of a Gut Eater came tumbling down the path beside her, an arrow in its eye.

Breathe slowly! Think nice thoughts!

From the other direction now came a pounding of feet and shrill war cries as the Head Counters charged up the path with spears and axes. She concentrated on lying very still.

Breathe slowly! Think nice thoughts!

There were more shrieks, and ghastly ripping sounds as sharp stone and iron edges tore through living flesh. The feet and legs of struggling *efaryti* were all around, one actually stepping on her in its haste to get at the enemy.

Breathe slowly! Think nice thoughts!

The terrible sounds of battle gradually diminished and moved away uphill. The Gut Eaters had decided to beat a retreat. Then came distant squeals and shrieks of desperation as they discovered Rajik and his scout group blocking the path behind them.

Breathe slowly! Think nice thoughts!

Lying on the grass in the

dusk was relaxing, and she no longer felt the urge to get up and join the battle. The physical and emotional strain of the last few hours had drained her reserves of energy, and the fading bedlam no longer seemed as important as the memory of that day many years ago, when her elder brother Alim had, to her delight, lifted her onto the back of a horse and let her ride around the courtyard . . .

Something was poking her. She opened her eyes and saw Big Stick, who was bending over her with a torch. It kept making the sign for "come."

She sat up. It was very dark now, but she could see bodies lying everywhere the torchlight could reach. Most of them, she noted, were Gut Eaters, and many were missing their heads. Big Stick grabbed her hand and pulled to get her moving. They followed the path upstream, tripping now and then on the corpses that lay scattered in the brush.

After an hour, she saw the light of a campfire. Coming closer, she could see Rajik talking with Iyad amid an attentive circle of *efaryti.*

"Raeesha!" cried Rajik as he jumped to his feet. "I thought you were dead! Where were you?"

"I fell asleep."

"You fell asleep during a battle?"

"It was all I could do. I had to lie still and control the demon." She added for the benefit of Iyad, "I'm cursed with a demon that always causes a disaster when I get too excited. There have been earthquakes. You can ask Rajik or the Ghost Feet."

Rajik simply nodded. Iyad was taken aback. "Why didn't you mention this before?" was all he could say.

"If I had, would you have come with me? But that's over now. I wasn't sure I could control the demon. But now I know I can, and that is bad news for the Wind Bags."

"Just in time," said Rajik. "We've done some scouting. They're on the other side of that hill. Come and see."

They climbed up the crest of the hill, from where, in the moonlight, Raeesha could see a stunning spectacle. Scores of big bags hung in the air. Beneath some of them, distant lights were visible.

It's like a floating city!

Below the air bags, she saw, was another city, but this one was mainly just small, dark huts surrounded by a wall. Crude wooden watchtowers dotted the perimeter.

"The slaves are in the lower section," said Rajik. "The Wind Bags have hundreds of them, maybe thousands. They themselves live in the flying part. That wall has a very strong stone gateway, but most of it's just a stockade, and I think we could scale it."

"Assuming no one tries to stop us?"

"Well, yes."

"And assuming no one shoots arrows down on us."

"That too."

"So how do we get in?" asked Iyad.

"Through the front gate. I'll trick them into opening it and then create a distraction while Rajik and the Ghost Feet slip over the stockade. Then your Head Counters can rush in."

"Won't they see us coming?"

"Not if we're clever. We need a dark night, or some rain or fog."

"So we wait and pray for bad weather?"

"We won't have to wait long, just till the next night there's an overcast, or the moons haven't risen yet."

Iyad glanced up at the starry sky. The blue moon had set, but the yellow one was still hours from the horizon. "I think it may be several days until the next moonless night," he said.

"Then we'll have to trust to luck."

"And if that fails?"

"We make other plans."

The next morning dawned bright and clear. There was no sign of a helpful rain cloud. An hour after sunrise, a huge airship rose from the Wind Bag town and, with a great whirring, turned and flew away to the south. It was bigger than any ship Raeesha had ever seen.

"What is that thing?" she asked in astonishment.

"I haven't seen it before," said Iyad. "It looks like the Wind Bags haven't been idle. They're preparing some new surprises.

"I'd hate to think what a ship that size could do to the little Head Counter towns," he added thoughtfully.

"I thought the last one was big," said Raeesha. "But it wasn't half that size."

"And it completely destroyed the Ghost Feet village," said Rajik. "I think just by accident. They weren't even trying."

The *efaryti,* she noticed, had fallen silent. They'd stopped their usual squeaking and chirping. The threat posed by the giant airship was obvious to all of them.

The day was hot and muggy. There was hardly a breath of wind. Raeesha had nothing to do but sit and stare at the Wind Bag town. It was bustling with activity. Air bags were raised and lowered, wicker cages on windlasses picked up visitors and supplies. Slaves scurried around below, adding stones to the wall. Columns of smoke rose in several places: Some, she guessed, came from cook fires and larger ones from smelters or forges. Slag and offal were dumped below the walls.

And these are the same race as the Ghost Feet?

Of course, they weren't the same at all, she realized, any more than she was the same as a Chatmak or a Hallander. The race didn't count for much. The only thing that mattered was that the Wind Bags had taken something from her, and she wanted it back. She felt drowsy from lying in the warm sun and gradually fell asleep . . .

Rajik was shaking her. "Look over there!" he said.

Blinking sleepily, she could make out a dark line of clouds to the north. The breeze, she noticed, was picking up.

"Iyad says it's a storm," said Rajik. "This could be our chance."

"How long before it gets here?"

"A couple hours."

She returned her scrutiny to the *efaryti* town, where the air bags were being lowered in anticipation of the storm. "See that ridge to the left?" she said. "Do you think you could move the Ghost Feet behind it without being seen?"

"I think so, but I'll have to leave right away."

"Good. Leave me Big Stick and its pack. Take the rest. Wait behind the ridge until I give the signal."

"What's the signal?"

"You'll know it when you see it."

She moved down the hill, to where Iyad was talking to his Head Counters. "Their guard is down," she said. "Rajik and the Ghost Feet are moving into position. I'll try to infiltrate a pack near the gate. When the weather closes in, I'll create a diversion. Hopefully, we can take the gate and hold it until your Head Counters get there."

"That sounds risky."

"This is all very risky, but so far, we have the advantage of surprise. There will be a disaster of some kind, perhaps an earthquake. I don't know exactly. But we're expecting it, and they aren't. They don't expect any attack, and when one comes in the middle of a storm, with their airships on the ground and a mob of angry slaves at the door, they'll be defenseless."

"Things don't always work out the way you plan them," said Iyad.

"Things never work out the way you plan them. There are a hundred things that could go wrong, but two hundred that could go wrong for the Wind Bags. And we don't need everything to go right."

She pointed to the Head Counters, who'd circled around, listening to the conversation without understanding it. "Look at them! They just won a battle. They wiped out the Gut Eaters and counted many heads. They're flushed with victory. They feel invincible."

"None of that will help if you can't get the gate open."

"Leave that to me. If the gate is not open, you and your Head Counters will at least be in no danger from the Wind Bags."

The Ghost Feet camp was empty except for Big Stick and its pack. She led the little band of demons on a winding path through the hills to a drainage ditch she'd noticed, which ran up a slope toward the Wind Bag town. By crouching low behind a rock outcrop, they were able to drop one by one into the ditch without being seen.

By now, an intermittent drizzle was falling. Peering over the edge of the ditch, she could see the town only indistinctly. Presumably, any sentries would also have trouble seeing her. The storm clouds were getting closer. Great, towering thunderheads rolled over the hills, with bolts of lightning among them.

That's a bigger storm than I expected. I better move fast!

It occurred to her the drainage ditch was a bad place to be during a thunderstorm, so she tried to increase the pace. But the ditch wasn't ideal for walking. Its muddy, stinking bottom prevented her from moving as fast as she would have liked.

Heavy drops of rain were starting to fall as she reached the Wind Bag town. Peering over the edge of the ditch, she could see the gate, a forbidding structure guarded by several Wind Bags equipped with spears and torches. They didn't seem to notice her.

Lightning flashed in the north, briefly filling the landscape with a glaring white light. She hurriedly ducked back down as the thunder rolled. Her heart was pounding like the galloping of a horse.

Did they see me?

If they'd seen her, there was nothing she could do about it. The storm would be here any minute. She didn't know if Rajik and Iyad were ready, but it couldn't be helped. There was no time left.

She made the sign for "wait" and climbed out of the ditch. Walking with what she hoped was a casual saunter, she approached the gate. The Wind Bag guards looked down, baffled by her sudden appearance at their door.

"Hello up there! Will you open the gate?" she yelled in Bandeluki.

The guards simply stared at her. Probably, they'd sent for someone who could speak Bandeluki. It was a couple minutes before the new face arrived, and by then, both the wind and the rain had grown stronger. The guards' torches sputtered.

The new face above the gate was an *efaryt* who carried a whip. It glared suspiciously at Raeesha. "Who are you, and what do you want?"

"My name is Raeesha. I'm a stranger here. I just want shelter from the storm."

The Wind Bag chittered softly to itself. "My name is Whip Hand. I bid you welcome. We already have many guests, but there's always room for one more."

As the gate opened on well-oiled hinges, she saw Whip Hand had come down to greet her, along with the guards. She took a cautious step backward.

"Why all the spears? Is this how you greet guests?"

"They're for our protection and yours. These hills are full of dangerous outlaws and savages. Come! Supper is waiting!"

She continued backing slowly away, her heart racing. There was a cold, nauseous feeling in her stomach. The storm was upon them. The wind whipped her hair back and forth. Her clothes were becoming sodden.

"What's the whip for?"

Whip Hand advanced boldly. "Funny you should ask!" It barked an order, and the guards rushed forward.

Run, but not too fast!

She turned to flee. She could hear, above the storm, footsteps getting nearer. The guards' torches cast flickering shadows before her. Her breath was coming in gasps. Her stomach churned as if there were a living thing inside that was trying to get out.

Now or never!

She stopped and whistled as loudly as she could before falling to her knees. A convulsion of nausea overcame her.

25: Krion

If he doesn't stop talking soon, I'm going to fall asleep.

His newly appointed chief engineer, Col. Lessig, had a lengthy presentation on his plans for the fortifications around Kafra. He and his aide, Lt. Radburn, had covered the table in the mirror room with an enormous, detailed chart, showing all the bastions, redoubts, ravelins, sally ports and other features that Krion felt sure would never be needed.

How likely is it the Bandeluks would actually attack us here?

Krion had already endured Lessig's droning voice for an hour, with no end in sight. No one had bothered to tell Lessig his precious fortifications were a make-work project to keep the troops from getting bored and restless over the winter. But it would certainly not do to suggest they were anything less than the highest priority.

Everything must be urgent, urgent, urgent! If it isn't urgent, it doesn't get done!

Pleased with his fancy new uniform, a promised bonus in gold thalers for completing the project on schedule and the hint of a possible barony, Lessig had approached the project with the enthusiasm of a pig at the feeding trough. But his aide seemed to be depressed and irritable.

I like to see happy faces in my headquarters. Perhaps I can find Lt. Radburn something to do in Berbat.

Next to Krion, his own aide, Lt. Mopsus, was paying close attention to Lessig and zealously taking notes. Capt. Bardhof, however, seemed to be less interested in the fortification plans than in Mopsus. He kept glancing over to see what he'd written.

It's nice having subordinates who watch each other.

Krion noticed, without much concern, he hadn't actually heard anything Lessig had said for the last five minutes. He returned his attention to the chief engineer, who was praising a system of moats, now almost complete:

" . . . and by incorporating part of the abandoned diversion canal, we were able to complete the enclosure of Fort Nine in record time. There remain, however, the sluice at Fort Ten and the vent system at Fort Twelve . . . "

At this point, a guard timidly knocked at the door and announced, "A messenger has arrived from Gen. Singer."

Anything but more engineering reports!

"Show him in." Krion was surprised to see Lt. Gallites enter, sunburned, with three days' beard and a uniform that looked like it belonged to a shipwreck survivor. He was even more surprised that he was accompanied by a 12-year-old boy dressed as a nomad.

I thought I had got rid of him. He better have a damned good reason for this!

"Lieutenant, I entrusted you with the provisioning of the Free State Contingent, which is much in need of your services."

"My apologies, sir. Gen. Singer gave me an important message to deliver. I was the only officer available for the assignment."

He laid a dirty-looking envelope on the table. Krion noted with displeasure it had already been opened. He glanced nervously at the inhuman Ragman who was standing quietly in a corner, but the Ragman wasn't even looking at Gallites; its attention was focused on the boy.

"What is the nature of this message?"

"It's from the Hierophant of Debel Kresh, who warns of a pending attack and offers an alliance."

"Very well, go ahead and read it."

"It's in the Bandeluki tongue, which I will translate."

Honored General,

According to my information, the imperialists plan a surprise attack on your forces in Chatmakstan before the snows. I would advise you to reverse your course and return to Kafra in all haste.

I am prepared to offer you the assistance of 2,500 seasoned warriors, conditional upon your promise to restore the province of Mellik, the traditional homeland of our people, which is occupied by the imperialists.

I have entrusted this letter to a capable person who can also bear your reply.

Your servant,

Hovannes, Hierophant of Jassarra
And Lord of Debel Kresh

There was a brief silence, which was broken when Lessig dropped the dagger he'd been using as a pointer. "My fortifications aren't complete!"

"Then I'd suggest you return to your work immediately," said Krion. It's even more vital than before."

"We will redouble our efforts!" promised Lessig, as he and his aide rolled up their chart.

At least I got rid of them for awhile!

Turning to Gallites, he said, "Am I to understand that this message was addressed to Gen. Singer?"

"Right you are, sir. Gen. Singer is our commander in Berbat, but he thought it would exceed his authority to enter into a foreign alliance."

So he knows his place, or perhaps just how to pass headaches on to his superiors.

"This mysterious Hierophant, what can you tell us about him?"

"Very little, sir. However, I've brought the original messenger with me, in case he can answer your questions."

Krion looked at the brown-faced boy, who was obviously in want of a good meal. The Hierophant's messenger simply stared back at him, giving no sign he understood what was being said.

It doesn't look like I can expect a lot of answers from him. Someone handed a note to this urchin and told him to give it to Gen. Singer. Why should I believe this fairy tale?

"Ask him who he is and where he's from."

"He says his name is Mangasar, and he's from Debel Kresh."

"Ask him to describe Debel Kresh."

"It's a city in the desert of Berbat."

"What kind of a city?"

"It's an oasis city in a valley with desert all around. It's smaller than Kafra."

This informant isn't very informative. But what can one expect from a child?

"Ask him about the Hierophant."

"He's the high priest of Jassarra and leader of the Melliki people."

"Who are the Melliki?"

"The former inhabitants of Mellik, driven out by the Bandeluks."

"How many troops does the Hierophant command?"

"All told, around 2,500."

So far, he hasn't said a thing I didn't know before! This is a waste of time.

"Ask him if he can carry a message to the Hierophant."

"Certainly."

"Tell him I swear I will return Mellik to the Melliki. Tell him I expect the arrival of his troops."

This time, Gallites hesitated a moment before translating. "Sir, he says he will convey your message, but you should not expect the troops."

"Why not?"

"He says the Hierophant has seen your stars."

The meeting adjourned, Krion asked Bardhof to remain and discuss a security matter. "This letter was in the mail bag from Elohi. It's addressed to Lt. Mopsus. There was no return address."

Bardhof seemed surprised. "I didn't know we were intercepting correspondence!"

All the better, so I can enjoy reading yours!

"Ordinarily, I pay no attention to such things, but this one was in code, which aroused some suspicions."

Bardhof glanced at the letter, which seemed to be a meaningless string of numbers. To Krion's astonishment, he then pulled a piece of paper from his pocket and began to decode it:

WE ARE READY TO MOVE
L UNDERWAY WITH THE PAPERS
G IS RECALLED
SEE THAT HE HAS THE NECESSARY ITEMS
C

Krion reached back to scratch the awkward place between his shoulder blades, which always itched when conspiracies were afoot. It had been bothering him for days, and now it had become a torment.

C is who? Chryspos? Claudio? And what about G? Grennadius?

It didn't seem likely either Chryspos or Claudio would attach his name to a message of this kind. G might be any one of a dozen officers, and he couldn't even begin to guess who L might be.

Then he thought of something else. Turning suspicious eyes toward Bardhof, he asked, "How is it you happen to have this code in your pocket?"

Bardhof seemed embarrassed. "A long story, my Prince. Information from Bandeluk sources identified Lt. Mopsus as the likeliest suspect for the traitor known as the Creeper. I took the liberty of inspecting his quarters and found this code. I was, however, unable to link it to any treasonable communications. Until today."

"And you kept this information from me?"

"My investigations had not yet risen above the level of suspicion. There was no evidence that would justify an arrest. And you specifically said you wished to retain Lt. Mopsus."

Did I? Of course I did.

"Let that go for a moment. My new sorcerer has intercepted a second message, this one attached to an enchanted bird and addressed to my brother Clenas. What do you make of it?"

He handed Bardhof a thin roll of paper with a message written in plain Akaddian though in a small, crabbed hand.

Beloved Clenas!
Though innocent of any crime, I was taken from the street and confined in the High Prison of Omoris. Please, please, please come and save me!
Your faithful,
Erika
P.S. First lot sold. Exclusive contract with MC. 2,800 thalers in RBA.
P.P.S. I love you with all my heart!

Bardhof shook his head in puzzlement. "This is the accused witch? The script is in a man's hand. I could almost swear I've seen this handwriting before, but I don't know where."

"But the content?"

"It's rather a muddle. A hasty note, possibly dictated. 'MC' could mean the Mercantile Consortium, Duke Claudius' operation, which owns the Nonus trading house. That name that came up in the Creeper investigation. 'RBA' is obviously the Royal Bank of Akaddia.

"But 2,800 thalers is an enormous sum, far beyond the resources of the alleged witch, possibly even beyond those of Prince Clenas. The 'exclusive contract with MC' suggests Claudio may be the ultimate source of these funds. Perhaps it's a smuggling or black market operation."

Didn't Clenas send me a report on the "economic development of the conquered areas" or something like that? I should have paid it more attention. I had no idea so much money was involved!

"Are you suggesting that my own brother, who's famous for his profligacy, has masterminded an extensive criminal enterprise under my nose without alerting anyone?"

Bardhof shifted uncomfortably. "I have no direct evidence implicating Prince Clenas. The private affairs of royal princes aren't usually subject to police investigation.

"I've monitored the activities of the black market, but they don't appear to be of such a scale. My efforts have been mainly focused on counterintelligence and particularly the investigation of the Creeper case."

"You think Clenas may have some connection with the Creeper?"

"It's too early to say. I might suggest the interrogation of Lt. Mopsus would reveal some further information."

My dear, little Mopsus, always so solicitous of my needs! And so very, very discreet. Whatever would I do without you?

"Not yet. One kills a snake by striking at the head, not the tail. Arresting Mopsus now would simply announce the plot has been discovered. Place him under observation."

"What shall we do with these secret messages?"

"We'll pass them on to the addressees, exactly as if they were never intercepted. Wait and watch for the response."

"What are we going to do about the Bandeluks? Shouldn't we put the troops on alert?"

"That would also make the Bandeluks aware their plans have been discovered. There's more advantage in letting them invade Chatmakstan rather than crossing the mountains to attack them on ground of their choosing."

"But shouldn't we at least recall Gen. Singer?"

"No. Singer is making a valuable contribution where he is. There've been no pirate attacks in weeks. And if I recalled him now, it would do no good. He couldn't possibly get here before the Bandeluks."

Bardhof was starting to look confused. "Are we then to do nothing?"

Krion smiled at him indulgently as if he were a faithful but dull-witted servant. "I didn't quite say that."

26: Nergui

In western Saramaia, hard by the slopes of the Kessifan Mountains, was a high plateau called Melatya. It provided summer pasture for numerous herds of sheep and was otherwise of little interest, except for the rare moments in history when it became a place of strategic importance. This was one of those moments.

Nergui had pitched his tent on a small hill near the old caravan road that led to the pass. Nearby were the camps of his beloved *kapikulu* corps, and spread out around them were the other divisions of the Bandeluk army: firstly, the provincial *sipahi* cavalry, second only to the *kapikulu* in their splendor, and next to them the *yayas,* or foot soldiers. Among the *yayas* were trained specialists – mountaineers, sappers, engineers, medics, signalmen, surveyors, barbers, cooks, saddlers and more – besides the *deliba* corps of freed criminals, who were allowed to win pardons by serving as shock troops.

The camp, which was half a mile in area, included thousands of supply wagons and uncounted numbers of camp followers. The Seserils were separated in their own camp as were the other auxiliaries, mainly Tamirids and Astrakans. In all, nearly 100,000 troops and hangers-on were camped on the plateau. Water was short and sanitation rudimentary, but no one expected stay for long.

Nergui inspected the camp and saw that it was good. The armor was burnished. The weapons were sharp. The troops were well-trained, and their officers seasoned and professional. The slow rot that infected the Empire, so obvious in Kosizar, did not reach here. With this army, he felt confident he could crush any enemy.

The problem, of course, was the imperial army was in Saramaia, not Chatmakstan, and he'd be lucky to get even half of them over the mountains before the snows, not to mention the supplies. And he had no siege weapons. The Emperor had assigned him a very dangerous mission. Still, seeing so many spirited and disciplined troops gathered amid a forest of flapping banners, he felt his spirits soar.

He noticed, far above, an eagle circling in the thin mountain air, in search of its prey.

If only I could borrow your eyes for a moment. What a spectacle lies below you!

As he returned to his tent, he saw a visitor waiting, Tutku Wali, the provincial governor. Tutku, a morose, grey-bearded man had come under a standard with two horse tails and with a retinue of twenty men. This, then, was no casual visit.

"Greetings, Wali! I hope my little operation is placing no undue strains on you?"

"Greetings, *mushir.* It is that I wished to discuss. Perhaps in your tent?"

"As you wish," said Nergui amiably and led the dour official inside.

If Tutku Wali had expected some privacy in the command tent, he was disappointed. Staffers were everywhere, receiving and dispatching messengers, consulting maps, updating rosters and performing logistical calculations. Col. Dundar, the chief of staff, was waiting nervously with a sheaf of reports, but Nergui brushed him aside and led his guest to the corner of the tent that served as his office and private quarters. It held a folding table, two camp stools, a cot and campaign chest.

"Sit down, Wali. Please forgive the rough accommodations. In the field, one can't afford much luxury. Can I offer you some raki?" He produced a bottle of the potent drink from the chest and began pouring a generous glass.

"Not right now, thank you. My business is pressing."

"But I rarely have an opportunity to sit and relax these days, so I hope you will excuse me if I indulge myself." He downed the glass in a single gulp.

"*Serefe!* I don't wish to take you from your duties, but I'd like to remind you what contributions Saramaia has made to your campaign."

The raki was having its desired effect. Petty annoyances were banished. He smiled cheerfully at the governor. "You don't wish to waste my time, but you do wish to discuss some things that are already well known to both of us?"

"Not at all. I'm not here to complain, but . . ."

"But you have a complaint?"

Tutku's face turned red. He suspected he was the object of mockery. But the staff officers pointedly looked elsewhere, and Nergui continued to smile warmly at him.

Tutku decided it would be wise to pretend he'd heard nothing untoward. "I merely wished to say we have ungrudgingly contributed thousands of troops and hundreds of wagons of supplies, as our duty requires, but I'm surprised the *mushir* has also conscripted many people unfit for military service, namely, conjurers, wise men, mediums, fortunetellers and the like."

"And I'm surprised the Wali is interested in such persons."

"These petty magicians provide us with useful services. They bless the crops, help people find lost articles, console the bereaved and resolve marital disputes."

"Also dispense poisons, traffic with demons, lay curses and swindle the gullible. Why not get straight to the point? I believe you have a particular interest in an individual named Azuzub, your wife's favorite astrologer?"

Tutku assumed a visage of aloof dignity. "Why do you say that?"

"A person by that name resisted conscription, threatened to curse my recruiting officers and boasted of his powerful political connections. He went so far as to predict dire consequences for myself if he were not discharged immediately."

Tutku said nothing. He clearly regretted declining the offer of a strong drink.

Nergui continued, "You need not be concerned, Wali! I was about to discharge him anyway. Upon examination, he proved to be barely literate, with no talents except for drawing up meaningless charts and making vague prophecies.

"For the remainder, I will retain those conscripts who show any talent, but just for a few months. They need only repeat a simple ritual my staff sorcerer will teach them and will never come in contact with the enemy. In the spring, I will return them to you as soon as the passes open."

Assuming always that I return myself.

Tutku stood up to go. "I see now my worries were unnecessary. My people are clearly in the best of hands."

"You can rely on me, Wali."

When the governor had left, Col. Dundar presented himself again with his armload of reports.

"What news, Colonel?"

"Only the best, *mushir.* Our scouts have detected no new enemy troop movements. They plainly don't expect an attack. However, they do continue to strengthen their fortifications."

"I believe the fortifications may be less of an obstacle than expected. Have you prepared an order of march?"

Nergui took the document and laid it out on the table for closer study. "It looks good, but with one change." Taking a pen, he crossed out the Seserils where they appeared in the middle of the column and added them to the front.

Dundar was shocked. "Are you serious, *mushir?* Are those flea-bitten nomads to lead the army?"

"That's not how I'd put it. *I* am leading the army. The Seserils are preceding it as an advance guard."

"Would it not be better to keep them in the middle, where we can control them?"

"I'd prefer to keep them directly in front of me, where I can watch them. They're not much use in a pitched battle anyway. I expect they'll take the first opportunity to go off on a looting expedition, which is fine. At the least, they will be a distraction for the enemy."

Dundar went from surprise to indignation. "You mean to loose 10,000 robbers and rapists on an imperial province?"

"Nothing of the kind. Chatmakstan is a rebel province. The Chatmaks are taking arms against us. Very soon, though, we may find them turning to us for protection. Then, we may condescend to rein in the Seserils."

If there are any Seserils left. Or any Chatmaks.

"But how are we to maintain communications?"

"We don't. We're cutting them off. The Seserils are good for only one thing, which is pillaging. Let them pillage all they want. Then we won't have to waste any supplies on them. Supplies are going to be short."

"But if you're declaring Chatmakstan a rebel province, then the Mantis Mandate . . ."

"Is in force, yes."

Dundar swallowed. "*Mushir,* this is a very different campaign than what I planned."

"Your campaign would have failed to thoroughly eradicate the enemy, which is why I'm changing it."

"The Khan won't like this."

"I will explain it to him in terms he will understand. Is there anything else?"

"Just one thing, sir. You have a letter from your daughter Enkhtuya."

Dearest Father,

Do not imagine even in dreams that I feel any bitterness toward you. You have provided for me as well as any man could and are not responsible for the unyielding fates that have twisted my destiny.

You need have no fears for me. Of late, Hervika has added me to her circle of favored intimates, so I am no longer burdened with drudgery, and my situation has become much more bearable. Her message follows.

"Honored *mushir!* I am much relieved to hear you're taking such good care of my son. These kindnesses cannot go unrewarded. You should know, therefore, I have placed your daughter under my personal protection, so that she may receive the same loving care you're showing to my boy. I hope also you will encourage him to write me more often, as he is somewhat thoughtless about writing letters.

"Your friend,

"Hervika "

Nergui sighed. Hervika had as good as threatened to harm his daughter if anything happened to Prince Murad. It couldn't be helped. As ruler of the harem, she was personally untouchable. By now, though, she probably knew what had happened to her erstwhile allies, Sardar and Yasin. She also knew, whatever her influence at court, it didn't count for much with the army, particularly when the army was in Chatmakstan. So, she was protecting her interests as best she could. At least, she hadn't turned openly against him.

But there will be a reckoning to pay when I return. If I return. And of course, it would be better not to if I lose the prince.

He was still formulating a reply, when another visitor demanded his attention. He recognized the prince's tutor, a man named Ufuk.

"*Mushir!* The prince is spending too much time in his tent. He needs to engage in martial exercises to prepare for the campaign."

"Agreed. Give him some martial exercises."

"I will require some assistance with that. He needs to practice with the bow."

"I'll have them set up an archery butt. Anything else?"

"The prince is accustomed to firing at live targets. His mother believes only living targets can prepare him for the experience of battle."

And I expect she'd know.

"Fine. I'll have the men catch some rabbits for him."

"Rabbits are not worthy targets for the prince. In the capital, we received a supply of convicts from Col. Sardar."

What have they been teaching this boy?

"You want human targets? I have no one to spare. He'll have plenty of human targets when we cross the mountains."

"Couldn't you just round up some peasants or something? What about all those convicts in the *deliba* corps?"

This is really too much!

"Very well, you win. I will find a living target for him to shoot at."

Not far from the camp was a gorge cut by a stream that flowed down from the mountains. He sent Sgt. Dalir and two men to set up a shooting range.

An hour later, he arrived with Prince Murad. He'd discovered, to his disgust, the boy had no campaign uniform and only one very flashy and impractical suit of armor. At the moment, he was wearing the same gold-bedecked silk robes he wore at court.

Dalir was waiting with his men, holding a bow. A hundred yards away, a naked man was standing, his head covered with a hood. His hands had been tied behind his back, and his feet were hobbled with a length of rope.

"Only one target?" said Murad. "One won't be enough for much practice."

"Apologies, your Highness! One was all we could find on such short notice," said Nergui. "But don't worry, after this, we will have some other martial exercises for you."

Murad took the bow and raised it, but then lowered it again. "I can't shoot a standing target. Tell your men to whip him and make him run around."

"No need." Nergui took the bow and yelled, "HEY YOU! GET

MOVING! WE ARE STARTING THE ARCHERY PRACTICE!"

He fired an arrow so it landed between the man's legs. Blinded by the hood, he jumped away from the sound. Nergui passed the bow back to the prince.

"It's good sport. See how close you can come without hitting him."

The human target jumped and danced as the prince's arrows whizzed by. He attempted to shout something, but Nergui had taken the precaution of gagging him. Some of the arrows were coming very close indeed.

The boy isn't a bad shot. I may make a good soldier of him someday if I can keep him away from his mother.

Eventually, the prince's target dodged to the right when he should have gone to the left. He folded up with an arrow in the belly. Nergui sent one of the soldiers to finish him off.

"Good shooting, your Highness! And look, your new uniform has arrived."

A messenger was coming from the camp with the package he'd sent for. The prince opened it, only to stare at Nergui in bafflement. It was a plain private's uniform.

"Honors and glory aren't so easily gained in the field as at court, Highness. I suggest you wear this for awhile, before you're ready for something else."

"I am *not* wearing that! It's in no way suitable . . ."

Nergui struck him on the thigh with the bow stave.

Whack!

"This is treason! I will have your . . . "

Whack!

Unaccustomed to such treatment, the prince struggled to avoid unmanly tears. "I demand to see my tutor!"

"Ufuk? He's over there," said Nergui, pointing. "Somebody shot him. I've already found you a better tutor. Sgt. Dalir will take charge of your military education, starting immediately."

He turned to Dalir. "Get him properly dressed and run him twice around the camp before supper. Use the rod if you must, but try not to leave any scars. Afterward, we'll get together and help him compose a nice letter to his mother. She worries about him."

For supper, Nergui had arranged an invitation for a private meal in Hulegu Khan's tent. The Khan had erected a pavilion for himself, larger than the command tent and much better furnished. Carpets and silk cushions were scattered around in abundance. Golden lamps hung from the tent poles.

Supper consisted mainly of a large, fat sheep, doubtless filched from some peasant. Hulegu insisted, as a mark of respect, in cutting off the greasiest parts and presenting them to his guest. Silent, veiled women plied them with wine. Someone was playing a two-stringed Seseril fiddle in the background, behind a hanging partition.

After they'd stuffed themselves with mutton and enjoyed a couple glasses of wine, Nergui got to the point:

"The incident in Kosivar troubles me, Khan. We must not let it come between us. We should set an example for the troops in burying our differences for the common good. In this light, I've brought a small gift."

He clapped his hands, and a soldier brought in the bundle of silk garments he'd confiscated from Prince Murad's tent. "I'd like apologize for the scare I gave the ladies and thought they might enjoy some of these."

Hulegu picked through the bundle like an expert rag merchant, admiring the fine silk weave and testing the weight of the gold threading. Then he turned his cunning eyes to Nergui. "This is a fine gift. I'm sure the women will be much pleased."

And now, he's waiting to see what I want in return.

"Have you ever been to Chatmakstan?"

Hulegu shook his head.

"I was there once as a guest of Prince Beyazid. Don't believe the stories about it being an impoverished place. The Amir was always poor-mouthing his province to avoid paying his fair share of taxes. The truth is very different. While he complained about the beggary Chatmaks, he was putting a golden dome on his palace. You can see it from the pass."

With the word "gold", the Khan's eyes narrowed. Nergui had captured his attention.

"Chatmakstan was the center for trade with all the western countries, and for centuries, the sheikhs there skimmed a share of everything that passed through. They all had grand villas with wine cellars and dozens of harem girls at their call. Their granaries were bursting, their fields crowded with fat sheep and cattle. It's a province ripe for plundering."

Hulegu leaned forward. "And of all this wealth, I expect my valiant warriors can claim their share?"

Greedy men are so easily deceived!

Nergui put on a skeptical expression. "I hadn't thought of that! The *kapikulu* will naturally expect the place of honor, and the *sipahis* customarily follow them. Also, the Tamirids and Astrakans are demanding a place in the van. It may be a week or more before the Seserils can take their turn. By then, the best pickings will surely be gone."

Hulegu favored him with a foxy smile. "But my men deserve a better reward for all their sacrifices! Can't you, my good friend, find some way to help them?"

Now we get down to the haggling.

When he left the tent half an hour later, he still felt an urge to puke up the greasy mutton, but he'd gained 2,000 piasters for the war chest, and the Khan was telling his men to saddle up early in the morning, urging them on with stories of the riches that awaited them in Chatmakstan.

Nergui paused and raised his eyes to the stars. The night was clear. A cool breeze blew down from the mountains. He felt the blessings of the gods upon him.

The omens couldn't be better.

This will be an excellent war, something for the history books.

27: Rajik

Why does this keep happening to me?

He was face down in the mud again. He'd been there half an hour already, and nothing had happened except that the sky was darker, the rain was heavier and the thunder was louder. The occasional flashes of lightning revealed no movement on the stockade, so the guards were probably as cold, wet and miserable as he was. They'd taken shelter in their watchtowers, leaving stretches of the wall unguarded. They hadn't even bothered to haul up the ladders, he noticed.

That corner where the bracing is, it wouldn't take me a minute to climb up there . . .

He didn't dare to move. Raeesha said to wait for a signal, and unless lightning and thunder were signals, nothing had happened.

His Ghost Feet were in position and ready to attack. Three groups would fire on the three nearest towers. Meanwhile, he and a small pack would sprint for the stockade, the weak place he'd found where it was being repaired, and climb up. Then, they only had to finish off the guards in the nearest tower and take the ladder.

It was a good plan. It ought to work. He looked to his right and left. The Ghost Feet were all staring intently at the enemy stronghold, weapons in their hands, impatient to get inside . . . and then the ground began to shake.

The signal!

He clung to his perch on the ridge and waited for the shaking to stop. But it didn't stop, it got even stronger. The Ghost Feet, though they were by now hardened earthquake veterans, squeaked excitedly to each other. Loud, frightened screeches came from the stockade, where the watchtowers were starting to sway back and forth.

As the shaking continued, he could feel the earth beneath him giving way. It was sliding downhill! Desperately, he grabbed a small tree sticking out of the rocks nearby. The stubborn tree roots held him in place for the moment, but he found he was now dangling over a cliff where the hillside had been.

From where he hung, he had a good view of the landslide,

which was gaining force as it descended. Great boulders, loosened by the quake, rolled down the slope toward the stockade. Frantic yells and screams were coming from every direction, punctuated by bursts of thunder. One of the watchtowers tipped over like a drunken man and fell to the ground.

He had no time to appreciate this small triumph because the tree root that supported him was coming loose. It gave way with an audible *snap*. He dropped a few feet, slid down the scarp, hit a boulder, fell off, and then he was rolling down the slope with the rest of the debris. A few terrifying seconds later, he landed on a pile of rocks and dirt. As he struggled to get to his feet, more earth and rocks rained down on him.

And suddenly it stopped. The ground was no longer moving. He was standing knee deep in a pile of debris a few steps away from the stockade, which now had a huge breach in it. His body was covered with bruises, but nothing seemed to be broken. To his joy, he saw his bow was lying nearby. He could, through the rain and wind, hear unhappy squeaks and cries of woe.

This is it!

He whistled to summon the Ghost Feet, and they came, at first hesitantly picking their way through the landslide, then more eagerly, with squeals of excitement as they saw the breach in the stockade. Rajik gave the "attack" signal, and they poured in together as a mob, all plans forgotten.

Inside, the Wind Bag town was a mess. Half of the slave huts had fallen over. Small fires sizzled in several places. Bewildered human and *efaryti* slaves emerged from their huts. Some poked around in the collapsed buildings to help those trapped in the wreckage, while others stood and stared agape at the mob of armed Ghost Feet streaming past. An occasional arrow came *zip* from the remaining watchtowers or from the air bags above, but in the rain, the defenders had little chance of hitting anything.

The Ghost Feet wandered in all directions, greeting lost friends and taking pot shots at any defender that showed itself. Rajik went along with the crowd. His plans had only brought him to this point; he wasn't sure what to do next.

Suddenly came a chorus of angry yells and shrieks from his left. He moved in that direction, the nearest Ghost Feet following him. He hadn't gone far before he saw a line of Wind Bags equipped with spears. They advanced through the ruins, killing anyone they could catch. The terrified slaves fled before them. Someone was beating a gong.

Bong! Bong! Bong!

Rajik whistled as loudly as he could, then let loose with the bow. The first arrow went astray, but the second hit a Wind Bag full in the face, and then the arrows began to multiply as more and more Ghost Feet arrived on the scene. Inside of a minute, the Wing Bags gave up and retreated in the direction of the gong, leaving several dead on the ground.

Bong! Bong! Bong!

Rajik gave the "attack" signal and yelled "To me!" in Bandluki, then in Chatmaki and, for good measure, in Hallandish. A mixed multitude of Ghost Feet and slaves pursued the fleeing guards, the slaves stopping to pick up fallen spears or anything else that could serve as a weapon. It was hard to see much in the rain, but the alarm was getting louder.

Bong! Bong! Bong!

Because of the rain, he didn't see the building until he was almost on top of it. A solid two-story wooden affair, it looked like a guardhouse or armory. The last Wind Bag slipped inside as he watched and slammed the door. A bolt clicked. Guards with bows appeared in the second-story windows and began firing at the attackers. On the roof, the gong continued to sound.

Bong! Bong! Bong!

Rajik spotted a foreigner who was holding a miner's pick, apparently the only weapon he could find. He pointed him toward the door, which soon resounded to a series of smashing blows. Alarmed, the defenders leaned out of the windows to get a shot at the pick-wielding slave, but this exposed them to arrows from the Ghost Feet. Rajik went to look for a battering ram.

Bong! Bong! Bong!

Not far away, two of the *efaryti* had the same idea. They were trying to pull a roof beam free from the ruins of a hut. Rajik called over a couple Bandeluks to help, and the five of them tore it loose. Then they carried it back to the door, where the foreigner with the pick had fallen, an arrow in his leg. Rajik could see lamplight shining through the holes the pick had made in the door.

Bong! Bong! Bong!

The five with the beam ran at the door.

Crash!

Suddenly, Rajik was standing in an entry hall crowded with surprised Wind Bags. They were so jammed together, there was no space to use a weapon. He grabbed the closest one by the head and twisted. There was a satisfying *snap* as its skinny neck broke. Then there was no more opportunity for fighting as a wave of attackers came pouring in the door. The rush of the crowd jammed both the attackers and defenders flat against the walls.

Bong! Bong! Bong!

Rajik found himself standing between two squirming Wind Bags. Feeling around with his one free hand, he touched a cold metal latch and pushed it. A door behind him flew open, and he fell into an adjoining room. He rolled and got to his feet just in time to glimpse a retreating Wind Bag run upstairs. He whistled and then yelled "Here!" in Bandeluki, but there was no need. The attackers were already rushing for the stairs.

Bong! Bong! Bong!

The surging crowd forced him into a corner. He could only watch the revenge-hungry humans and *efaryti* push by. From the floor above came shrieks and the sounds of fighting. Directly over his head, a corpse went *thud* as it hit the floor. The alarm gave its last *bong* as it was thrown into the street.

Suddenly, it was quiet. There was nothing to hear but moans from the wounded and the shuffling of feet as the victors looked around their new property for anything useful. Rajik noticed he'd lost his bow and went back to the hall to look for it, but he couldn't find it among the mangled corpses. He picked up a spear and stepped outside.

The rain wasn't as heavy as before, though the thunder continued to roll. Arrows were falling from the floating city above his head with more accuracy. Ghost Feet archers ducked and weaved among the slave huts, firing back. Here and there, air bags pierced by many arrows fell, their occupants hauled out screaming and butchered on the ground. It was less like a battle than a massacre.

I guess we won.

To the west there was glow in the sky as if the sun were coming out. The sky, however, was still overcast. He stared at the phenomenon for a minute, before he realized he was looking at a great fire.

A fire? In this rain?

It suddenly occurred to him he'd seen no sign of Raeesha. He ran toward the growing blaze. The Wind Bag town was in complete chaos, full of collapsed buildings, fallen watchtowers and deflating air bags. A cloud of fine dust fell, mixed with the rain. He rubbed some between his fingers and sniffed at it.

Ashes! Where's Raeesha?

Ahead of him, he could hear the sound of fighting. The stone wall, he saw, was still largely intact despite the quake. A small group of Wind Bags was making a brave but pointless stand to defend the gate, which had collapsed to rubble, from someone on the other side.

He climbed up onto the rubble heap and hit the nearest Wind Bag with the butt of his spear, causing him to fall forward into what he now saw was an assault group of Head Counters. As two of the Wind Bags turned on him, he struck one with the butt and then the other with the point of the spear. The wounded defender clutched the spear as it fell from the rubble, wrenching it from his hands.

Then there was no one left to fight. The remaining Wind Bags dropped their weapons and ran in all directions. A stream of Head Counters clambered over the rubble and ran after them. He pushed his way past the *efaryti* and went to look for Raeesha.

He didn't get far before he found the source of the fire: A jet of flame was rising from the ground, throwing a cloud of ash into the air. As he watched, a stream of glowing, molten rock emerged and ran down the side of the ash cone that was growing around the vent.

A volcano!

Raeesha was nowhere to be seen. However, he did see Iyad, who was urging his Head Counters into the town. Rajik ran over to him.

"Where's Raeesha?"

"Over there." Iyad pointed to the slag heap where the Ghost Feet had dragged her, away from the volcano and the fighting. "Where is this Witch you keep telling me about?"

"I don't know. I didn't see her in the town. Maybe Raeesha knows."

They ran to where Raeesha was lying, gripping her stomach in pain. "It's stronger now," she said. "I can't control it anymore. That big fire is a volcano. We have to move." But she was obviously not going anywhere unassisted.

"Forget the volcano, where's the Witch?" said Rajik.

"If she isn't in the town, I guess she's up there." Raeesha pointed to where the giant airship was bearing down on them.

28: Singer

This little spyglass is very handy.

He and an advance party were surveying the defenses of Mira-jil. The town was on a peninsula blocked by two cyclopean walls, one after the other, that shut it off from the mainland. The walls, he noted, had very narrow gates, which were packed with boulders and debris.

Behind the walls was a shantytown built of driftwood and timbers salvaged from wrecks. A ramshackle series of docks jutted out into the harbor. At the moment, these were being torn up to build barricades on the landward side. The defense preparations struck him as haphazard and desultory. The pirates were apparently not expecting any imminent attack. Their ships, however, had already left the harbor, which put them beyond his reach.

"Looks like they want to make a stand," said Capt. Baldwin, who grinned as if he'd found a nice place for a picnic and a swim.

Singer passed the spyglass to Sgt. Littleton. "So long as they don't have to fight too hard for it," he commented. "They can always pull out by sea."

"Why haven't they done that already?" asked Capt. Fleming.

"Because your puny army hasn't the slightest chance of taking Mirajil," said Tanilhan, who was tethered on a leash. "I know it, Singer knows it and the accursed Akaddians who sent you here certainly know it."

"I don't think you're the best person to judge our capabilities," said Baron Hardy.

"But I find Capt. Tanilhan's opinions interesting now that his mind is no longer preoccupied with the subject of gold," said Singer.

"It isn't about gold, it's about freedom!" said Tanilhan.

"I'll let you know when we have some to spare. What do you make of it, Littleton?"

The engineer lowered the spyglass reluctantly. "It's a very fine instrument, sir. Wonderful magnification. I'd like to take it apart and have a look at those lenses."

"I meant the defenses of Mirajil."

"Oh. The walls are hopeless. Can't go over them, can't go around, can't go under and can't go through. I surmise that they were originally part of a much larger structure . . ."

"Interesting, but how do we get in?"

"The weak point is the harbor mouth. In a month, I could build a causeway across it, and then we could march right in."

"And what do you expect the defenders will be doing in the mean-time?"

"I can't say, sir. What I'd do is construct a wall to block the causeway."

"So, we build a causeway, and then we have to get past a wall?"

"It wouldn't be much of a wall if I read this right. These pirates aren't exactly master builders, and they don't have a lot of construction materials."

"They aren't stupid. If they see the town can't be defended, they'll just leave."

"They may have trouble finding another port to shelter them," said Baldwin. "They haven't made a lot of friends."

"What's to stop them from joining with the Bandeluks?" asked Hardy.

"Too much blood on their hands," said Baldwin. "They've probably killed more of the Emperor's subjects than we have."

I wish Raeesha were here. She'd know more about that.

Littleton was dreamily staring into space, his mind already wrapped up in the new project, planning how long the causeway would be and how wide, estimating the depth of the harbor, calculating the tons of earth and rock, and the labor force he needed to move them.

At least, it will give the men something to do.

"Well," he said, "I haven't heard any better ideas . . ."

"I have a better idea," said Tanilhan. "Go home while you still can. Look to the defense of your own lands and forget this mad quest to conquer the Bandeluk Empire."

"Didn't I say Tanilhan is full of interesting ideas? How would you like a staff position, Captain?"

"A what?" Everyone, including Tanilhan, was staring at him incredulously.

"You can't be serious, sir!" said Baldwin.

"Oh, I'm serious. Find a big wooden staff and plant it on the

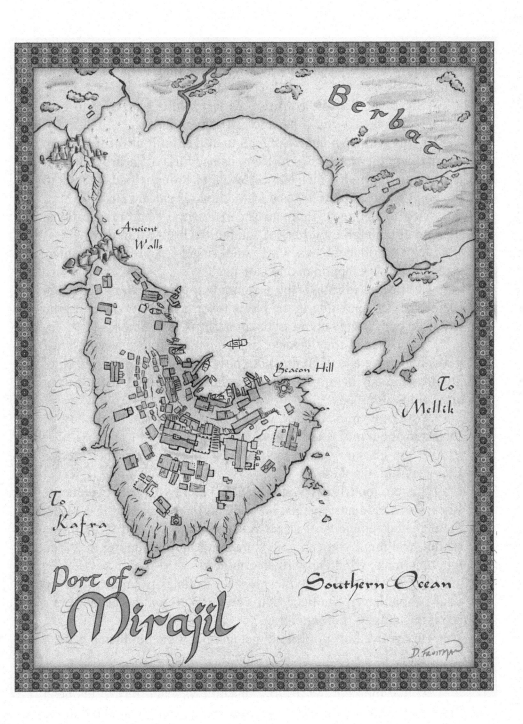

beach. Then tie the captain to it so he can watch the siege."

"Good morning, Captain, how do you like your new position?"

"Terrible. They make me pee while standing here," said Tanil-han.

"Since you broke the arm of the last soldier who tried to give you a latrine break, you'll have to put up with it."

It was two days later. Singer's men had built a fortified camp overlooking the beach. The *fui* demons had turned a nearby hill into a stone quarry, from which a line of wagons brought loads of rock to the point where Littleton was constructing his causeway.

Tied to his post, Tanilhan sneered at the siege preparations. "You really think they'll just let you build a bridge into town?"

"Not a bridge, a causeway," said Singer. "And I will be interested to see how they intend to stop us."

He peered through the captured spyglass. Nothing much seemed to be happening in the pirate town, except a wooden frame had been constructed at one end, across from the point.

"I had hoped they'd make some attempt to rescue you, but I guess they have a new commander now. The legendary pirate chief Tanilhan already belongs to the past, and the new boss doesn't want any competition."

"You said yourself, they aren't stupid. But if you think they've forgotten about me, you're mistaken."

"They treasure you in their hearts, but won't risk their necks. Can't say I blame them."

"Listen, fool! I was a naval officer before you were even born! I beat the Akaddians, against all odds, in three great battles! I took the defeated remnants of a lost war and made them a force in the world! You think you can gain something by humiliating me? You will only make my men more determined!"

"I can't honestly say the prospect troubles me much. Maybe your people haven't noticed you standing here on the beach. Let's see if this attracts their attention."

He removed his golden helmet and put it on Tanilhan's head. *Gods! He looks six inches taller!*

"How does it fit, Captain?"

At that moment, he heard a distant *crack* and turned his head in time to see something fly across the harbor mouth and land in the water a short distance from where Littleton's men were working.

"What was that?"

"That, my ignorant young friend, is called a springal. One winches back a length of timber, so it's bent to maximum tension, then releases it so it strikes the butt of a spear and sends it flying."

Singer studied the device with his spyglass.

"Interesting. Doesn't seem to be very accurate."

"Just wait."

The second shot from the springal landed in one of the wagons that was carrying rocks to the point. Littleton's men scattered and took cover.

"Not so big and tough now?" asked Tanilhan. "You haven't begun to see what my men can do."

"Then I suppose we can expect some lively entertainment."

The next morning, he was back on the beach at dawn, just as the first light was striking the roofs of Mirajil.

"Sorry to get you up so early, Captain, but I thought you'd like to see this."

Tanilhan, again wearing the golden helmet, squinted at where Littleton had erected a small wooden tower near the point. A thin cloud of smoke from a charcoal fire was visible.

"This is your big weapon? You think you can protect your workers with a wooden tower?"

"It's a rather special tower. We built it extra solid."

"I don't care how solid it is," said Tanilhan. "It's not going to extend your causeway."

"You'll have to wait a few minutes for that. They're still heating the irons."

As he spoke, there was a distant *crack,* and a spear from the springal landed just short of the tower.

"It takes them awhile to get the range," said Tanilhan.

Another *crack* and a second spear flew across the harbor mouth, higher but wide of the target.

"They also have to find the windage," added Tanilhan.

The third spear hit the tower with a *thunk,* but no visible damage.

"So much for the springal," said Singer. "I think we can expect some return fire before long."

He hadn't finished speaking, when a red-glowing object flew from the top of the tower and struck the wooden springal. Singer raised the spyglass in time to see a tongue of flame appear where it hit.

That," he explained, "is a siege crossbow, a good bit more accurate than your springal. It fires iron bolts which, when heated, tend to set things on fire."

A cloud of smoke was now rising from the springal. The crew hurried to fetch some water, but they hadn't returned before a second red-hot iron bolt struck. The wooden frame was soon consumed.

"I'll see your springal and raise you one tower," said Singer.

He awoke in the night to the sound of yells and running feet. The whole camp was in commotion.

Kyle stuck his head in the tent. "Sir! The enemy is attacking!"
Have they come for Tanilhan?

He threw on a mail shirt and went to look. It didn't take long to see the flames rising from Littleton's tower. He studied it with the spyglass. There was a ship beached near the point, and it was ablaze. The sea wind had carried the flames to the tower. Despite Littleton's vigorous efforts at fire-fighting, it couldn't be saved. A pall of tarry smoke was flooding the camp.

He turned the spyglass to Mirajil, where lights were dancing about, held by celebrating pirates. From across the bay, he could hear them chanting:

"TANILHAN! TANILHAN! TANILHAN!"

"What are we going to do, sir?" said Kyle.

"Nothing. Tonight, there's nothing to be done. Wake me up if anything else happens."

He returned to his cot.

When he visited Tanilhan the next day, he found the old pirate in a jubilant mood. "I trumped your tower with a fire ship!" he chortled.

"I think I can replace the tower more easily than your men can replace the ship."

"Bah! That old brig? Barely seaworthy! And you won't find a lot of trees around here for your towers."

"That's why we're starting work on a stone tower. You won't

have much luck setting it on fire."

"But I notice work has stopped on your causeway."

"There'll be plenty of time for that. The army isn't going anywhere until Mirajil is destroyed."

"Or the army is."

"That's what I like about pirates, always so optimistic."

There was a distant *crash* from Mirajil. Peering with the spyglass, he could see a wooden building was being torn down.

"Looks like they mean to destroy their own town. To keep it out of my hands?"

"Fool! They're gathering materials for more siege engines."

"After what happened to the springal? That's what I'd call an ill-conceived plan."

"They're doing fine so far. I taught those boys well." Tanilhan was glowing with pride.

"Too bad you never taught them to respect other people's lives and property."

Tanilhan spat. "You are conquering whole provinces."

"Perhaps we should take a survey of the natives and ask them which of us they'd prefer."

"What do you think they'd answer with you holding a knife to their throats?"

"If that's your theory of government, it's no wonder you ended up tied to a post. You couldn't even hold the lands you were born with."

"See if you do any better with these treacherous Akaddians lording it over you!"

"I could hardly do any worse."

Another *crash* came across the water from Mirajil.

"There won't be much town left for them to defend, at this rate," said Singer.

"The town's not important, fool. The town can be rebuilt."

"Only if there's someone to rebuild it. Now if you will excuse me, I need to see how work on the tower is coming along."

"Don't get attached to it. You've had some bad luck with towers."

Littleton's men were busy with shovels, digging a large, circular pit.

"What are you doing, Sergeant? I wanted a tower, not a dungeon."

"Yes sir, but to build a tower, we first need a foundation."

"What kind of a foundation?"

"In this soil, given the level of the water table, I'd estimate 20 feet deep."

"Any chance you could make it smaller?"

"Not for a six-story tower."

Littleton was getting that dreamy look again, visualizing the beautiful tower he was going to build, an architectural marvel. He'd all but forgotten about the siege.

Let's try a different tack.

"You know we're only going to demolish it?"

"What?" Littleton looked like a man who is told that, due to a supply shortage, he would have to eat his beloved pet dog.

"When the siege is over, the tower will serve no purpose. We can't just leave it behind for the enemy to occupy. The only lasting sign of our presence will be the causeway." He gestured toward the harbor mouth. "That great stone causeway will still be here thousands of years after we're all dead, a monument to the art of a master engineer."

Littleton blinked as if he were awakening from a dream. His vision of a beautiful tower had been replaced with a beautiful causeway. "Of course, sir," he said. "I'll get on it right away."

"But who's going to build the tower?"

"My assistants can handle it." He turned to the closest one. "Moffit! You take over here. The rest of you, come with me."

The unfortunate Moffit was left standing bewildered in the middle of the empty construction site while the others went off to resume work on the causeway. Singer walked up to him.

"Pvt. Moffit, have you ever built a tower?"

"Not exactly, sir, but I was in the building trade back in Tidewater before the war."

"Think you could build one now?"

"Not the kind Sgt. Littleton was talking about. He wanted dressed stone with waterproof harling, groin vaults and corbelled brattices . . ."

"That isn't going to happen. Is there some kind of fieldstone around here you could just stack up to make a tower?"

"Plain dry stone? Yes sir, I noticed a basalt outcrop a couple miles back. Of course, it would be a devil of a job to move it . . ."

"Not a problem. I'm assigning the *fui* demons to you. Just tell them what stones you want and where to stack them. All I need is a plain stone tower, two stories high and big enough to hold a siege crossbow."

Moffit looked apprehensive. "It shouldn't be much trouble, sir, except I don't know how to supervise demons . . ."

"The boss demon is called Twenty Three. I'll introduce you. Just tell it where to put the stones. Let me know if they give you any trouble, and I'll spank them for you."

"You really love those demons, don't you?" Tranilhan was frowning at the new tower, which had already ascended to eight feet.

"No more than you," replied Singer

"But you find a lot of things for them to do."

"I'd rather find some way to get rid of them."

"Easy. Send them on a suicide mission."

"That would be incorrect."

"What?"

"You wouldn't understand."

"I understand that you could never have overcome me without the demons."

"Don't be too sure. Never is a long time."

"You're full of noble talk, but still you associate with demons."

"I associate with a lot of people I don't approve of. Pirates, for example."

"What's that about? Trying to make a good citizen of me?"

"I'm not that big a fool."

"Think you can extract some military secrets?"

"You know any?"

"One or two, maybe."

"But nothing worth your life, or you'd have told me already."

Tanilhan laughed. "You really don't know much about me."

"I know you're greedy, treacherous and cruel. The cause you claim to be fighting for was lost years ago. You could have retired in obscurity, but your vanity wouldn't let you. You crave admiration and love to dominate people, and yet you'd sacrifice every single one of those pirates you're so proud of to save your own neck. I know you, Tanilhan."

"Then why do you waste words with me?"

"You make a better conversationalist than the demons. But I'm starting to find this discussion tedious." He focused the spyglass on Mirajil. "What do you suppose they're doing over there?"

"How would I know? I can't see."

"Looks like they're building their own tower . . . no, wait, it's a trebuchet."

"They surprise me."

"The springal didn't surprise you."

"That's mainly a naval weapon. A trebuchet is big and powerful. You could never mount it on a ship. It outranges your little siege crossbow, and it will certainly smash your tower."

"It isn't ready yet. They're trying to cobble it together out of driftwood . . . no . . . that looks like the mast of a ship."

Tanilhan peered curiously across the water. "Really? Where did it come from?"

"A schooner, I think. They're scrapping it for the timbers."

Tanilhan shook his head in wonder. "My brave, brave boys."

"Brave, or perhaps just reckless. Their real power is in ships. Without ships, they can't even retreat. They must love you more than I thought."

"No, no, I see what it is now. Schooners are everywhere. They can always get more schooners. Mirajil is worth more than any schooner."

"You said the town wasn't important."

"I changed my mind. It's like an unsinkable ship. Now that they're determined to hold it, your tin-pot army has no chance."

"Don't bet on it. They don't have a trebuchet yet. It's not the kind of thing a bunch of amateurs can assemble out of scraps. I'm not even sure I could build one. It would take weeks."

"And what makes you so smart? They've already destroyed one tower, and your causeway is going nowhere."

"Then I will have to exercise the virtue of persistence."

Two days later, not much had changed: The tower was complete, and the causeway had been extended a few yards. Littleton had put up wooden siege mantlets to protect the workers from archery, setting them on wagon wheels. As the causeway advanced, so did the mantlets.

Singer went to see Tanilhan again. "How's it going, Captain?"

"Dead boring. Just kill me now."

"Sieges tend to get a bit dull in the middle. But I expect things will pick up soon."

He surveyed Mirajil with the spyglass. "Now, that's interesting. The trebuchet seems to be progressing much faster than I expected. They should be able to raise the beam before long."

"Ha! And you said it would take weeks!"

"They're taking some shortcuts. They razed a building and used it to make a base for the frame, which is made from a ship's keel. The mast has been trimmed to make a beam, with an anchor for a counterweight. Also, they're using a ship's capstan to crank it. Pretty clever."

Tanilhan seemed to grow in stature. The helmet was helping. Even tied to a post, he was the picture of the legendary commander who'd crushed the Akaddians.

"That's more than clever, General! That's what free men can do in the face of tyranny!"

"They haven't actually tried to use it yet. Firing a trebuchet is trickier than it looks. You might want to wait a bit before declaring victory."

The next day, the trebuchet was ready to fire. The pirates cranked back the beam with the capstan, raising the counterweight. Singer watched as a boulder was laid in the sling. "Looks like a 200-pounder," he said.

"Let me see!" Tanilhan was stretching himself as far as the rope allowed to get a better view.

"You'll see it well enough if it works. I'll spare you the humiliation if it doesn't."

A pirate pulled the trigger holding the beam in place. The stone soared skyward, then whipped around and smashed into the ground directly in front of the trebuchet. The beam splintered into pieces as the frame fell over. Singer could hear distant yells and curses from the crew.

"They need some practice releasing the sling," he commented.

"IDIOTS!" yelled Tanilhan. He was ready to flog the lot of

them.

"Don't be too hard on your men. They've probably never fired a trebuchet before."

"I wouldn't gloat, General. They'll finish their trebuchet before you finish your causeway."

"Really? It's smashed up pretty badly. Think they'll sacrifice another ship? They don't have many left."

"They will sacrifice whatever they have to."

"Suits me," said Singer. "The more they sacrifice, the better."

Two days later, the pirates were ready to try again. This time, a stone flew through the air and fell near the point, splashing Littleton's causeway workers with seawater. They beat a hasty retreat.

"Ha!" said Tanilhan, "I told you they wouldn't give up! Your tower is doomed!"

"Maybe so," Singer admitted. "But it takes an hour to load that thing. I'll just have the men stand down for awhile."

"And then what? Are you planning to swim to Mirajil?"

"There are few other things we may want to try first. The forces of tyranny aren't done yet."

"You're wasting your time. You still have no idea what my men are capable of."

"I've seen what they're capable of. That's why I want them dead."

29: Bardhof

"It says Mopsus is moving in the direction of the harbor," said Anahita. "He has a metal box. Evrim is following him."

Bardhof shakily put down the teacup and pushed himself away from the desk. He'd stayed awake two days for this moment, but Mopsus hadn't left the vicinity of the palace. Now that he was making his move, Bardhof wasn't sure what to do.

His newest recruit, Evrim, was remarkably skillful at surveillance, but he spoke no Akaddian, while Bardhof's Bandeluki was marginal at best. And he felt nervous about the growing number of Bandeluks in his headquarters.

On the other hand, I trust the Bandeluks further than the Akaddians. At least, they aren't going to stage a coup.

Another problem was Evrim couldn't make arrests. Bardhof mentally laid a straight edge on the map of Kafra, trying to trace a path between the palace and the harbor. The latter bordered half the city. Mopsus' destination could be almost anywhere, and there was no way to get more precise information from a note carried by a runner.

Moreover, if Mopsus suspected he was being followed, he could take a circuitous route, perhaps doubling back or even going in circles to elude anyone behind him. Wherever he was going, there were dozens of possible ways to get there.

Bardhof's instinct was to seize Mopsus and interrogate him, but the Prince had instructed him to place the man under observation. To make an arrest, he'd need something more incriminating than just a stroll around Kafra. But he didn't have much time.

"Send the runner back to Evrim with a note I'm going to the harbormaster's office. It has a good view of the harbor. If Mopsus meets someone or goes to ground, send a messenger."

The harbormaster's office was on the fourth floor of a tower on the east end of town. Its many windows looked out on the docks, quays and anchorages that were numbered on a chart on the wall. A naval petty officer sprang to attention when Bardhof entered.

"As you were. Any unusual activity?"

"No sir, hardly any traffic at all today."

Bardhof looked at the public docks. Even on a slow day, they were full of people: sailors on liberty, street vendors, prostitutes, merchants awaiting shipments, customs officials, porters hoping for fares, and the usual beggars and idlers, some of them his own paid informants. There was no sign of Mopsus.

If he's up to no good, he'd hardly do it in front of so many witnesses.

To the south were military docks. A glance was enough to see nothing was happening there. He'd set up the security himself. No one got in without being logged.

On the north side of the harbor were the fishing docks, where security was laxer. Most of the docks were empty since the Amir burned the fishing fleet. And this time of day, the fishermen would be out fishing. However, Bardhof noticed a small boat tied up at one of the docks.

"What's that?" he asked the petty officer, pointing.

"Looks like a jollyboat, sir."

"I can see that. What's it doing there?"

The man shifted uncomfortably. "I don't know, sir."

"Aren't those docks reserved for fishing boats?"

"They are, sir, but it's rather difficult to track all the small craft, the tenders, liberty boats, bumboats, skiffs and scows . . ."

And smugglers. And the occasional spy.

Bardhof made a mental note to tighten harbor security. The jollyboat was too far away to see distinctly, but there seemed to be someone sitting in it. Waiting for Mopsus to arrive? If Mopsus did arrive, Bardhof was too far away to do anything about it. There was, however a customhouse near the fishing docks; that would be the best place to lie in wait.

"I have some business in the customhouse. If anyone comes looking for me, tell them that's where I went."

"Yes sir."

The customhouse was a rundown brick building conveniently close to the docks. It had doubtless served the same function under the Amir. There was no one inside except two Akaddian clerks, who began to industriously shuffle papers around when Barhof entered, to prove they were earning their salaries and not merely killing time between ship arrivals.

Barhof ignored them and went to take a closer look at the jollyboat from a window. It was, he saw, a brightly-painted rowboat of Bandeluk make. Two Bandeluk sailors sat inside, exchanging a leisurely conversation.

That doesn't look like a covert operation. But on the other hand, what are they doing here?

He addressed one of the clerks. "Are there any Bandeluk vessels in the harbor, aside from the fishing fleet?"

"Enemy vessels? No . . . wait." He checked a list on a chalkboard. "We have one vessel of Bandeluk construction at anchor, the Avare."

"Who's the listed owner?"

"It's registered to a Lt. Gallites, assigned to the Free State Contingent."

Singer's messenger! If this is his boat, then he may be buying provisions or something equally harmless. But why, then, isn't he at the military docks?

"What's the cargo?"

"None listed. Official business, you understand. No tariff was paid."

Bardhof had a sinking feeling. If this boat were from the Avare, it might have nothing at all to do with Mopsus. Gallites could simply be ducking out for a quick shore leave, ignoring the bothersome security regulations.

While he pursued this red herring, the real suspect was getting away! He went back to the window. The sailors didn't seem in a hurry to go anywhere, and there was no sign of Mopsus. It was already an hour since the message from Evrim.

If Mopsus were coming, he'd be here already.

Why was there no messenger? Frustrated, he stepped outside, almost running into a Bandeluk boy who was coming in. It was the same runner Evrim had sent before, and he was holding another message.

I'm such a fool! I left directions with the harbormaster, an Akaddian, to give to a Bandeluk, and neither spoke the other's language. No wonder it took so long to find me!

He passed the note to Anahita, who translated it. "It says Mopsus is in the Golden Lion. Evrim is waiting outside."

Is Mopsus just having dinner? Then why bring the strongbox? He must be delivering it to someone!

The Golden Lion was a hangout for foreigners, the ideal place for meeting an agent without creating suspicion. But a Bandeluk like Evrim couldn't just casually wander in without being noticed.

"Send Evrim a note saying I'm coming and to keep Mopsus in sight."

Let's hope I can get there in time!

The messenger dashed off, followed at a more deliberate pace by Bardhof, with Grimald, Murdoon and Anahita behind him. Although he'd have liked to run, Bardhof knew it would attract too much attention.

As they approached the Golden Lion, he saw the street was empty, except for a shoeshine man, who was sitting by his portable footrest and waiting for customers.

Am I too late?

He turned to Anahita. "Ask that man if he's seen anyone pass by recently."

Anahita merely glanced at the shoeshine man before answering. "I expect he has. That's Evrim."

Bardhof blinked his bleary eyes. Was the lack of sleep affecting him, or was he just naturally stupid? "Well, ask him what he's seen."

"He says Mopsus went in half an hour ago with another man, a military officer."

"Any idea who?"

"He says not, but it looked like someone important."

"Walk down the street as if you're looking for customers. Glance in the door and tell me if you can spot him."

Anahita sauntered down the street with a casual swaying of hips, calculated to draw the attention of every male in the vicinity. After a minute, she came back and said, "Don't know him. Some big shot. Had his back to the door."

This is my last chance! If I don't break the case now, I never will!

"Listen up. This is what we'll do. I'll stand right here and get my boots shined. Grimald stands beside me, waiting his turn. Murdoon, you stand over there, on the other side of the door, with Anahita. You're a client, but she wants too much money. Haggle. When they come out, we'll grab them. Wait for my signal."

And then, for what seemed like an impossibly long time, nothing happened. People went in and out of the restaurant, Bardhof's heart jumping every time someone emerged. Evrim shined one boot, then the other and finally the first one again. Anahita demanded a higher price, then a lower one, and then back to the higher one. An officious young officer threatened to report Murdoon for consorting with prostitutes until Bardhof waved him off.

The tea was taking its toll. Bardhof felt as if his bladder were about to burst. He was wondering whether he had time to run into an alley and relieve himself, when Mopsus came out the door, red-faced from at least two glasses of wine and paying little attention to his surroundings. He was obviously not expecting trouble.

"NOW!"

Murdoon grabbed him by the right arm, turned him around and pinned him against the wall. As the second man emerged, Grimald took him by the collar. But this one was alert. He dropped the strong-box he'd been carrying, grabbed his sword and, spinning around, struck Grimald in the face with the hilt. Stunned, the big man tottered backward, reaching for his axe.

Bardhof, who'd stepped forward to help Grimald, found himself looking at the business end of a very sharp cavalry saber held by Prince Clenas. The point was inches from his face.

"Halt!" he said. "Apologies, Highness!"

Clenas looked at him through narrowed eyes, the sword point not wavering in the slightest. "What in the name of all devils do you think you're doing, Captain?"

"My abject apologies, sir! My men were trying to intercept some black marketers. It must have been a false tip. We certainly didn't expect to meet you!"

"Really? Do I look like a black marketer?" He kicked the strongbox. "You can inspect that if you want. It's just some personal papers Mopsus was holding for me."

"No sir. I'm sure there'll be no need to search your personal effects."

"I'm happy to hear it! Remember what they say, 'Curiosity killed the cat!'"

Bardhof answered despondently, "Actually sir, I'm more accustomed to think of myself as a dog."

He sent the others home and told them to report in the morning. The investigation was over, a failure. He felt certain a treasonous conspiracy was in progress, but he could do nothing to stop it. Bone-weary, he went to his room and threw himself on the bed.

Sleep did not come. His mind was still buzzing with the Creeper case. What had he done wrong? He must have missed something, or it wouldn't have turned out this way!

Eventually, he dozed off into restless dreams full of mysterious messages and girlish giggling. Mocking faces danced before him as if he were shuffling a deck of cards.

Cards!

He sat up with a jerk and reached into the drawer where he kept an ordinary deck of playing cards. He looked through it until he found the Joker, which he laid on his desk.

There's Mopsus, alias the Creeper.

Next to the Joker, he laid the Knave of Spades.

His friend Omin, the Bandeluk spymaster.

Above the Knave, he laid the King of Diamonds and below, the King of Clubs.

Omin's other friends, Claudio and the Admiralty.

To the right of the Joker, he laid the Knave of Hearts.

His Highness, Prince Clenas.

Above Clenas came the Queen of Hearts.

The alleged witch, Erika.

After studying the cards for a moment, he turned the Queen so it touched the King of Diamonds.

We know they're in bed together, at least in a commercial way.

He examined the arrangement of cards with the growing feeling one must be missing. Picking through the deck, he found the Knave of Clubs and placed it next to the King.

Gallites and his naval connections.

The pattern still looked wrong. It wasn't symmetrical. He moved the Knave of Clubs so it was next to the Knave of Hearts and turned it to touch the King of Clubs.

That must be it! Where was Clenas taking that strongbox? "G is recalled. See that he has the necessary items."

He threw on his uniform and went down the hall to where the adjutant, Col. Eubulus, was sleeping. After a minute's banging on the door, Eubulus opened it, looking very annoyed.

"Well? This better be important!"

"It is, sir. Have any officers been recalled recently?"

"You woke me up to ask me that?"

"Please, sir! It's urgent. Just one question, and you can go back to bed."

Eubulus yawned. "If you really must know, yes. It was Lt. Gallites. His father died." He slammed the door in Bardhof's face.

I've got him!

Tearing out of the barracks, he ran past the surprised sentries and into the morning light of Kafra. He sprinted through the nearly empty streets until he came, sweaty and panting, to the harbormaster's office. A different petty officer was on duty.

"Quick, tell me if the Avare is still in port."

The surprised man pointed out toward the mouth of the harbor. "That ship has sailed, sir."

A two-masted ship of Bandeluk make was just passing the jetties.

"Is there any way to stop it?"

The man shook his head. "Not unless you sent a frigate after her, and there are none in port."

"What do we have in port?"

"Of naval vessels, there are only three troopships from Kingsport. They came in shortly after dawn."

Bardhof saw the third one was just tying up at the military docks. The first two were already disembarking passengers: Soldiers in polished armor formed up in orderly ranks on the docks.

Royal Marines!

"Who's in charge of those men?"

"At the moment, that would be Adm. Leucos, sir."

"L underway with the papers." This is it, the coup!

Leaving the clueless petty officer behind, he ran down the stairs and into the street. People were out and about now: laborers going to work, vendors setting up their stalls, children playing. He ran heedlessly past them all, racing to get to the palace, where he arrived exhausted and out of breath.

The guards were all gone, replaced with a group of the inhuman Ragmen. As he ran up to the door, one of them stepped into his path, a hulking, stinking creature that looked like it had been patched together from scraps of burlap and sackcloth.

"The Prince is occupied," it said in a voice like a small child's.

"Tell him Capt. Bardhof is here. Tell him I need to see him immediately."

"The Prince is occupied," it said again, the dark, glassy eyes staring at him expressionlessly.

"This is of vital importance! There is a coup underway!"

"The Prince is occupied." Did he imagine it, or was there a hint of mockery in the thing's voice?

Behind him, he could hear the stamping, rhythmic footsteps of men marching in formation.

They're coming!

Krion was probably at breakfast in the atrium, which had an open roof. Barhof yelled as loudly as he could: "MY PRINCE! THIS IS CAPT. BARDHOF! OPEN THE DOOR!"

There was no response. The unblinking, glassy eyes of the Ragman continued to stare at him inscrutably.

The sound of marching men was getting closer. Bardhof yelled again: "MY PRINCE! THERE'S A COUP! PLEASE OPEN THE DOOR!"

Finally Krion emerged, still brushing breakfast crumbs away with a napkin. He had two more of the Ragmen behind him. "Well,

Bardhof? What's all the fuss about?"

"Adm. Leucos has landed with a force of marines . . ." He turned to point and saw they were already at the gate. Marines armed with pole weapons filed in to the right and left as Krion watched unconcernedly. Their leader presented himself, a portly officer of distinguished years in a gold-trimmed blue uniform.

"Good day, your Highness. I am Adm. Leucos. You are hereby relieved of command, by the order of King Diecos."

He presented a document bearing the royal seal. Krion glanced at it incuriously, before passing it to Bardhof. "I suppose that means I shall have to move out of the palace, then. Such a bore."

"This document is already being distributed to every commander in the theatre."

"Make sure you get them all. They're rather scattered about, you know."

"Prince Clenas has been appointed commander of the army. May I ask where he's to be found?"

"At this hour, probably still in someone else's bed."

The admiral's face was getting red, but he could hardly accuse a royal prince of insolence. "I don't believe you understand the gravity of the situation, your Highness."

"Perhaps you should explain it to me, then."

"Our affairs have reached a critical juncture. This position is unsustainable. The whole Kingdom is in danger. Prince Clenas will be taking us on a new course . . . "

At this moment, a messenger dressed as a marine came galloping to the gate. He dismounted and reported to Adm. Leucos. "Sir, Prince Clenas is not in his headquarters. No one knows where he is."

"Surely someone must," said Krion. "But if you really can't find him, Gen. Grennadius would be the next in command. He spends most of his time in a nice little villa on the north shore."

"Go inform the general," said Leucos, throwing Krion a suspicious glance.

Hardly had the last messenger left before another one presented himself. "Sir, I am unable to locate the Brethren. Their camp is empty. I was told they pulled out last evening."

"Pulled out to where?" said Leucos, looking pointedly at Krion.

"I'm sure I don't know. They do have these little field exercises from time to time. Helps to keep the men in shape."

Adm. Leucos seemed to be on the verge of apoplexy. "You really have no idea? The Brethren are under your personal authority. You mean to suggest they wandered off without telling you?"

"It's a big army. I can't keep track of everyone. That's what adjutants are for. Go ask Col. Eubulus. He's still the barracks, I believe."

The messenger was sent to find Eubulus. Meanwhile, Krion had become bored and impatient. "Is there anything else I can help you with, Admiral? If not, I'd like to finish my breakfast."

Leucos was steaming with anger and frustration. "I should hardly think this would be an appropriate time . . ."

He was interrupted by another messenger, this one dressed as a naval petty officer. "Sir! An officer has been murdered! A patrol found him in the harbor!"

"Whom, may I ask?" said Krion.

"According to his papers, it's a Lt. Mopsus. It appears he was stabbed."

Krion seemed shocked. "Mopsus! He's really dead? He was one of my most loyal officers. I'm sure Capt. Bardhof will want to investigate this."

"We'll conduct our own investigation," said Leucos, glancing at the unshaved and disheveled Bardhof. "And we'll certainly question Capt. Bardhof about it."

At this point, a messenger in a cavalry uniform came in on a foaming horse. He rode straight to the Prince and might even have ridden him down, had not a Ragman stepped in between. The horse shied, frightened by the stink of the unnatural creature.

When he'd recovered his breath, the newest messenger said, "Sir! The enemy is advancing! They've overrun our outposts!"

Prince Krion gazed serenely to the east, where a column of smoke from a burning village was becoming visible. "Oh dear," he said, "This is all so unexpected."

30: Lamya

"What happened?"

She was stunned by the sight of the Wind Bag town, covered as it was with a glowing cloud of smoke and steam, shot through with flashes of lightning. A great fire had sprung up near the gate. Half of the buildings had collapsed. Some of the air bags had fallen from the sky.

"Another slave uprising," said Sky Lord, its voice shrill but unperturbed. "They rebel and rebel, but always, we put them down."

"You may have more trouble this time. Look! The town is in ruins."

"Then they will just have to rebuild it. This is good news, the perfect opportunity to test the condenser system."

"The what?"

"It's a high-energy shunt."

"A what?"

Sky Lord didn't answer. Instead, it opened the door to the crew cabin and yelled in Efaryti, "Raise the collectors! Lower the cathode!"

Lamya was fixed to the window, staring at the chaotic scene. The lightning was worse now. It danced around the growing column of smoke from the great fire. The ship shook with the turbulence and peals of thunder. In the town, the remaining air bags, one by one, were wrenched from their moorings or had their cables cut. They drifted off in all directions.

The Model 3 airship, its fans turning at full power, rose from the town and ascended almost to the cloud layer, before a lightning bolt struck. In seconds, it disappeared in a huge, fiery explosion. Burning fragments rained down on the town.

THAT is where we're going?

"I should have retrofitted the Model 3 with a condenser system," said Sky Lord. It sounded merely a bit disappointed.

"What are we going to do?"

"You are going to sit down and be quiet while the pilot takes us over the center of town."

Lamya sat down, but then stood up again.

I didn't have to obey! The spell must be weakening!

She hurriedly sat down before Sky Lord noticed. From a window, she could see more details as they approached the town: The gate had collapsed. There was a breach in the stockade. Some of the watchtowers had fallen over. A number of small fires were burning here and there, despite the rain. She could see armed bands of humans and *efaryti* moving among the ruins.

BOOM!

There was a blinding flash and a blast of thunder. The whole ship shook.

We've been hit by lightning!

When she could see again, there was no evidence of any damage to the ship. Sky Lord peered down from a window and exclaimed, "Excellent! Keep us hovering over the target area."

That's what the "condenser system" does: It collects lightning and directs it to the ground!

So long as the storm raged, Sky Lord controlled a weapon of immense power, one that it gleefully put to use.

BOOM!

BOOM!

BOOM!

BOOM!

She could only close her eyes and hold on to her seat as one bolt of lightning after another shook the vessel. The urge to kill Sky Lord was back, stronger than before. Raeesha must be somewhere nearby, she realized. The demon flux was interfering with the control spell. But if the lightning killed Raeesha, the cyst might also be destroyed, leaving her as Sky Lord's slave forever.

I have to do something NOW!

Between flashes, she ventured a look at the control room. Sky Lord was dancing around triumphantly, squeaking, "IT WORKS! IT WORKS! IT W . . ."

Raeesha had touched Sky Lord with her wand, freezing it in stasis. Opening the door to the crew cabin, she yelled in Efaryti, "Lower the collectors! Raise the cathode!" She wasn't exactly sure how it worked, but hopefully they'd turn off the lightning before they realized the orders weren't from Sky Lord.

When she turned around, she saw Talkypus staring at her with its big, fishy eyes. Its eight arms still rested on the controls, but they weren't moving. Talkypus was waiting for an explanation.

"The master told you to do what I say, and I say you should find a flat place and land the ship."

Talkypus didn't stir. "Why?" it said in soft, gurgling Bandeluki. Talkypus had never asked that question before.

Uh-oh! If the spell on me is broken, then so is the one on Talkypus!

"Because we're in great danger, and I want to get us out of it. And then, I'll send you home."

"You promise?" It stared at her with enormous, woeful eyes.

"Yes, yes! I promise!"

That was pact enough for Talkypus. It turned the wheel and revved up the fans. The airship headed toward a barren place on the edge of town, a dumping ground for slag and rubbish, where it gradually descended.

"Lower the anchors!" yelled Lamya, and the crew scurried to obey. The giant ship settled a few feet from the ground. Looking out the window, she could see *erf-aryti* and humans converging on the site, eager to retaliate for the lightning strikes. It suddenly occurred to her there was going to be a battle, and she'd be on the wrong side.

She turned to Talkypus.

"Some things are going to happen. But you must not become excited. Just stay here, and I'll be back shortly. You understand?"

"Yes." Talkypus seemed willing to trust their agreement, or perhaps it simply saw no alternative.

Next to the door was a spring-wound alarm bell, to warn the crew of a fire or collision. She tripped it.

CLANG! CLANG! CLANG! CLANG! CLANG! CLANG!

She screamed as loud as she could and ran the length of the ship, yelling in Efaryti, "GET OUT! GET OUT! IT'S GOING TO EXPLODE!"

As she hoped, the crew, already unnerved by the explosion of the Model 3, fell into a panic and followed her to the rear cargo ramp. Someone pulled a lever, and the ramp fell, opening a path to the ground. The terrified Wind Bags flooded out and directly into the path of the approaching Ghost Feet. Arrows flew among them as they scattered.

When the last Wind Bag was gone, Lamya rubbed the tip of her wand until it burned as bright as a star and walked half-way down the ramp. She waved the wand so everyone would see her.

"HEAR ME, GHOST FEET! OUR PACT IS FULFILLED. THE WIND BAGS WILL TROUBLE YOU NO LONGER. NOW IT IS YOUR TURN. LET US DEPART IN PEACE."

I just hope they don't know the spell is broken!

She needn't have worried. As soon as she said the Wind Bags were defeated, the *efaryti* burst into joyful squeaks and squeals. Some began to dance and caper about in revelry, while others climbed up the ramp to inspect the captured airship.

Fearing an unpleasant incident if they encountered Talkypus, Lamya retreated to the control room. She turned off the alarm and, turning to Talkypus, said, "All is well, but there are visitors here now. Bolt the door when I leave, and don't open it until I come back."

"Must leave soon," said Talkypus. It waved a tentacle at a window, through which she could see the fire. It was growing larger, throwing up great quantities of smoke and cinders, some of which were collecting to form a hill.

A volcano!

"Yes, we certainly will, but first I need a few minutes to collect some people. Don't forget to bolt the door."

Efaryti were swarming over the giant ship, opening containers, peering through windows, and playing with tools and equipment. She could only hope they didn't cause any serious damage.

She'd started down the ramp, moving against the tide of curious *efaryti,* when she almost bumped into Raeesha. The girl looked pale and listless. She was being supported at the shoulders by Rajik and a man Lamya didn't recognize.

"Is this the Witch you keep talking about?" the stranger said.

"That's her," said Rajik. "Lamya, this is Iyad. He will be coming with us."

"Welcome," she said without looking at him. She was examining Raeesha, who stared blankly at her surroundings. Her eyes were dilated; the pulse was quick and shallow.

"The demon is sapping her energy," said Lamya. "We need to move fast. Tell the *efaryti* to leave the ship. I'll take Raeesha to the control room and operate there."

While Iyad tried to get the attention of the disorderly *efaryti,* Lamya and Rajik carried their patient to the control room. As she reached for the door, she remembered something. "There's a demon in the control room. It looks dangerous, but it won't hurt you. Just try to ignore it."

She rapped on the door and yelled, "Open up!"

Despite her warning, Rajik gasped when he saw Talkypus. "That's one ugly demon!" he said and, looking at the frozen form of Sky Lord, "Who's that?"

"That is Sky Lord, the designer of this ship. It won't be coming with us." She added, "You should apologize to Talkypus. It understands everything we say."

The big, ropy tentacles were waving around as Talkypus moved to get a closer look at the newcomers. Its sad, fishy eyes stared at Rajik reproachfully.

"Sorry . . . I really meant . . . ," stammered Rajik. "You aren't ugly . . . for an octopus . . . I mean . . . "

Meanwhile, Lamya had laid Raeesha on the floor and was feeling her abdomen for a telltale lump.

Found it!

To Rajik she said, "There are some blankets and a medical kit in the compartment above the door. Get them down."

Then, while Rajik was occupied, she said to Raeesha, "I must apologize for this. I had planned a safer and less painful procedure, but we've run out of time."

"What?" said Raeesha, staring at her vacantly.

Lamya punched her hard in the stomach. Raeesha screamed. A spot of blood appeared on her skirt. It was spreading quickly.

Let's hope this doesn't hemorrhage!

"WHAT ARE YOU DOING?" yelled Rajik, clutching a blanket.

"Extracting the demon. Open the medical kit if you want to help."

Probing Raeesha's abdomen, she didn't find the suspicious lump she'd noticed before. On the other hand, there was no sign it had exited the body. Perhaps it was stuck in the uterus? She applied pressure. Raeesha gasped as something popped out. It looked like a round turtle egg or a big, translucent pearl.

That's it!

She returned her attention to the patient, who was staring at the ceiling, her eyes out of focus. Her pulse was weak and breathing shallow, and her lips were starting to turn blue.

She's going into shock!

Lamya searched through the medical kit for anything that might help. There was a row of neatly-labeled bottles, but nothing she could identify. She opened them one by one and sniffed at the contents. The fourth one she tried smelled like camphor.

If this is all I've got, I'll use this!

She wiped away the blood, then rubbed Raeesha's abdomen with the camphor solution, before wrapping her in blankets and resting her legs on the medical kit. While she was doing this, a tentacle tapped on her shoulder.

"Must leave now!" said Talkypus. With another tentacle, it was pointing to a window where a spectacular volcanic eruption was in progress. Large boulders were flying through the air. Apparently, the demon didn't like being extracted and was objecting in the most violent possible way.

"Yes, yes! Just a second!" She found the cyst where it had rolled into a corner and shoved it down Sky Lord's throat, which was still open in gleeful celebration.

Maybe that will keep it quiet long enough to get out of here!

Give me a hand," she told Rajik, and together they carried Sky

Lord out the door. She saw at once the crew cabin was packed with *efaryti* and with human slaves.

Pushing her way through the crowd, she found Iyad. "I told you to get rid of the *efaryti!*"

"I tried, but the Ghost Feet won't leave their matriarch."

"Where is she?"

"Dead. I think they mean Raeesha."

"Raeesha?"

Iyad shrugged helplessly. "Ask him about it," he said, pointing to one of the Ghost Feet who was carrying a big stick.

"Where's your matriarch?" she asked in Efaryti.

The little *efaryt* swung its stick around, before bringing it down with a *bang* against a workbench. "It is the hairy demon Raeesha who leads us now. She has a magic eye that makes the arrows fly straight. She drew the Gut Eaters into a trap with a mighty spell. She fell in battle and arose from the dead. She commanded the gates of the Wind Bag fortress to open, and they opened. She scattered our enemies with her winds and thunder, and brought down their mighty airships. The earth trembles before her, and the mountains give forth their fire."

The Ghost Feet greeted this speech with loud cheering.

I guess that settles that!

"We'll just have to take them with us," she told Iyad. "I can send them back later. Tell them to raise the anchors." She pointed to the windlasses in the corners of the room.

The cargo bay was just as crowded as the crew cabin. Together, she and Rajik dragged the immobile form of Sky Lord to the rear and tumbled it down the ramp into darkness. In the flickering light of the volcano, she could see everything was now covered with a thin layer of ash and cinders. Sulfurous fumes made her cough.

If we don't get out soon, we're going to die!

"Raise the ramp!" she cried. "We're leaving!"

Back in the control room, Talkypus was wrestling with the controls. "Won't go," it said. "Overloaded."

"Dump the ballast."

Talkypus turned some valves, and a great flood of water fell from the bottom of the airship. It began to rise slowly, provoking a chorus of gasps and squeals from the crew cabin. Lamya spared a moment to inspect her patient, who was still in a daze, but her breathing was regular, and the pulse was stronger. When she looked up, she saw the water level was dangerously low.

"That's enough! Leave some for the boiler."

Even without the ballast, the airship was still close to the ground because of its many passengers and obviously wouldn't be able get over the hills. Looking out the window, she could see the eruption had gotten worse. A yellow, glowing river of lava was approaching their position.

"Pull up the nose! The engines will carry us over."

There was more yelling and squealing from the crew cabin as the giant airship tilted toward the sky. Lamya felt a slight bump as the tail grazed the surface. Then, Talkypus gave full power to the engines, and the ship began climbing.

Looking out the window, she caught a last glimpse of the Wind Bag town, now ruined, abandoned and covered with ash. Then the airship cleared the hills, and the light from the volcano receded into the distance. The storm, she saw, had passed over. Patches of stars were appearing in the cloud cover above them.

"Where are we going?" said Rajik, awestruck by the spectacle.

"Somewhere far from here."

An hour later, the ship was hanging in a starry sky above a landscape of eerie blue clouds in moonlight. Lamya wasn't sure where they were, but the compass said north, and there was a range of mountains poking out of the cloud layer ahead of them.

At least we managed to avoid the ocean.

It didn't matter where they were, she reminded herself. The important thing was where they were going. She'd distributed the summoning stones around the ship, according to a pattern she hoped would include the whole structure and its contents. The hard part would be finding a destination point. Whatever she did, she'd have to do it fast; the remaining fuel and water wouldn't last long.

Looks like I'll have to cut some corners.

Poking through the medical kit, she found a jar of gooey white paste. For burns? It didn't really matter what it was for, she just needed enough of it for the projection circle that she drew in a corner of the cabin. Taking a lamp from its ceiling hook, she set it in the circle. Then she undid her long braid and plucked a single hair, which she lowered into the flame.

"What are you doing?" asked Rajik.

"Making a beacon. It's a form of pyromancy."

"What's that?"

I'm trying to get us home, so shut up!

The only way to shut him up was to answer the question, so she gave him the shortest explanation she could think of: "We still have no fixed destination. The easiest way is to find the *lacuna* that remained when I was suddenly projected. There's a gap where I used to be. People remember me, think about me, wonder where I went. When that happens, I will see it in the flame, and then we will have a fix we can use for navigation. Now be quiet so I can concentrate."

Half an hour later, there was a growing bald spot on the back of her head. She kept plucking hairs and burning them, but she could see nothing in the lamp flame.

I must be doing something wrong.

"This just can't be right," she muttered. "No one in the whole world loves me? No one misses me when I'm gone?"

"I guess that means no one hates you, either," said Rajik.

"Don't count too much on that," said Raeesha, who was just sitting up. She plucked a hair from her own head. "Here, try one of these."

31: Singer

He found Littleton near the camp, gazing wistfully at his uncompleted causeway. As they stood watching, a boulder landed near the tower, bounced and knocked a few stones from the parapet. The pirates were improving their aim.

"Sorry, sir," Littleton said. "I don't think we can save the tower."

"Never mind that. It's just a pile of fieldstones. Tell your men to get some rest, then wake them after dark and move the onagers down to the beach."

Littleton turned to squint at the trebuchet, which was barely visible across the bay, on the other side of Mirajil. "Very well, sir, but I don't think we can silence their siege engine. We don't have the range."

"The trebuchet is aimed at the tower, and there's no way to turn it to fire at anything else. But most of the town is in range. That's your target. I want you to destroy it."

"I can do that sir, but I don't see how it will help us with the causeway."

"It won't. Forget about the causeway for now and concentrate on destroying Mirajil. I want it reduced to kindling."

The dreamy look returned to Littleton's face. This time, his mind was occupied with trajectories and fields of fire. "That will be a pleasure, sir."

"Every time you wake me up at dawn, I think this is it, the end," Tanilhan complained.

"Don't worry about that. You're the last person I want to execute."

"Who would the first be?"

"It's up to them," said Singer, pointing to the row of onagers waiting on the beach. "Whoever that lands on."

Tanilhan shook his head. "You had all this artillery and never used it?"

"It wasn't the right moment. A good general keeps something

in reserve. You want to give the signal to fire, or shall I?"

"Enjoy yourself."

"FIRE! FIRE AT WILL!"

There were a series of crashing and rending sounds across the bay, followed by frightened yells and screams. A few shacks near the harbor flew to pieces.

"You really think this will do any good?" said Tanilhan. "Destroying their homes will only make them angry."

"Anything anger and hate can do has already been done."

"That's where you're wrong. Anger and hate are endless."

"Everything has its end, and you are looking at the end of Mirajil."

The crash of collapsing buildings across the bay punctuated his remark.

"Fool! Your onagers can't reach the far side of town. My men will simply retreat beyond your range."

"You keep calling me that even though you've already lost three ships and your town is being destroyed."

"That can all be replaced. You're no closer to taking Mirajil than before. This is your last gasp, a defeated officer's pointless revenge."

"I'm not here to take revenge. I'm here for justice."

"And you think you can get it by bombarding a town?"

"I can't weigh justice so finely, but it seems fair enough: on one side of the scale, a nest of pirates that no one will miss, and on the other, slaughtered sailors and murdered civilians, and good ships sent to the bottom for the sake of a few coins."

"There were more than a few. There's a fortune in gold and silver over there, but you'll never lay hands on it."

"At least, it's certain you never will."

By evening, most of the buildings in Mirajil were damaged. Singer ordered his men to continue firing through the night, swapping out crews when one became tired. Thanks to the work of the *fui* demons, there was no shortage of ammunition.

He sent for Baldwin. "Are your marines ready for some action, Captain?"

"They always are, sir."

"Good. Move the small boats down to the beach. Be ready to

attack tomorrow, at a moment's notice."

Baldwin smiled as if he'd won the lottery. "What are we waiting for, sir?"

"Mostly just for a favorable wind."

"General, you really are a fool," said Tanilhan. "Do you think my men can't see this?"

Singer had to admit the line of boats waiting on the beach was obvious, even in the dim morning light. "I'm sure they can, Captain. What do you think they plan to do about it?"

"Attack them, of course. Your marines will never get ashore."

"Opposed landings are an old game for the marines. They're rather good at it. And this shore is open and defenseless."

He pointed toward Mirajil. There was hardly a wall standing. Stones from the onagers continued to fall among the ruins. Now and then came a distant *crash* as a bouncing stone hit something that wasn't already demolished.

"A few hundred marines can't take Mirajil. You don't even have enough boats for all of them."

"The first ones can hold a beachhead until we ferry the rest over. Your pirates aren't much good fighting on the land."

"What makes you think they intend to fight there?"

"There's no sign of your fleet. No more barricades. No siege engines. The onagers will destroy any defenses they try to throw up."

"General, you're making a terrible mistake, but I won't tell you what it is. You'll just have to find out for yourself."

"I'll look forward to it."

Toward evening, the wind, which had been landward, shifted to seaward. On the other side of Mirajil, lurking outside the harbor, Singer could see the sails of the pirate fleet.

Singer went to Littleton, where he was directing catapult fire into the shattered ruins of Mirajil. "That's enough with the stones. Take the jars of oil from the supplies and start throwing them. Spread them out as far as you can. I want those ruins soaked in oil."

"Planning to start a fire, sir? Vegetable oil doesn't burn very easily . . . "

"Just do it."

Baldwin was sitting in the stern of a boat, staring intently at Mirajil. "Are your men ready, Captain?"

"They're on pins and needles, sir."

"Good. Sound assembly. Load the boats. You can expect to move within the hour."

"Yes sir. About time!" He paused uncertainly. "General, you said we were waiting for a good wind, but this wind is in our faces!"

"So much the better. They won't expect an attack. But if I'm wrong about that, remember, we can always try again. If I sound retreat, you retreat. Don't be a hero."

"No sir, all the heroes I know are dead."

He sent a message to Capt. Fleming. "Have a group of cross-bowmen conceal themselves near the point. Prepare fire arrows, but don't shoot until I give the word. Repeat: Lie low and don't fire until ordered."

Another message went to Lt. Ogleby. "Bring the special ammunition to the beach, but don't open the crates or discuss it with anyone."

Tanilhan watched the flurry of orders with some confusion. "You really mean to go through with this? You think you can take Mirajil with a handful of marines in small boats?"

"That's the plan, but it could change. You want to see the show?"

"I wouldn't miss it."

"Your funeral."

The pirates had apparently noticed the boats being loaded. Someone lit a beacon. Singer could see the sails of the pirate fleet moving toward the harbor mouth.

"Sir, we need to get going," said Baldwin. "Those ships could intercept us."

"That sounds like a difficult maneuver in such narrow waters."

"The waters may be narrow, but the force is overwhelming. That's the Black Ansel!"

"In reserve, I should think. They're leading with the feluccas."

"The feluccas will never stop us, but they have a schooner too."

Singer examined it with the spyglass. "It's unarmed."

"It doesn't need any weapons. It can just run us over."

Singer saw that while they were engaged in conversation, the feluccas were approaching the harbor. "Well, you better launch your boats, then."

Baldwin went to take his position in the lead boat.

"You just sent those men to their deaths," said Tanilhan.

"Not to death, just into danger. It's what we pay them for."

"It will end in death."

"That's how all battles end."

The marines rowed for Mirajil as fast as they could, but the wind slowed them down. The same wind gave wings to the feluccas, which swarmed into the harbor, then spread out to block Baldwin's men. Singer counted eight feluccas.

They must have raided several villages to gather so many.

Archers in the prows of the feluccas took aim. A shower of arrows pattered down among the marines, injuring none of them. Baldwin continued closing the distance.

"Better recall your men," Tanilhan advised. "They're reaching the point of no return."

Singer, observing the fight with his spyglass, didn't bother to reply. Then a second shower of arrows fell. One marine in the lead boat dropped his oar and clutched a wound.

Baldwin gave a signal, and all at once, the marines laid down their oars and picked up crossbows. The archers fell as hundreds of bolts peppered the feluccas. Three of them went adrift, their crews dead or dying. The remaining five withdrew toward Mirajil.

"Still think I should withdraw?"

"No, now it would be too late. The schooner will destroy those little nutshells and drown your marines." Tanilhan's voice held a note of malicious glee. Preoccupied with the battle, Singer hadn't noticed the schooner enter the harbor.

He may be right about that!

"Sound retreat!" Raising his polished bugle, Kyle sent the notes floating across the bay. The boats turned back toward camp, except for the lead boat, which continued in the direction of Mirajil.

What's wrong with Baldwin? Did he not hear?

"Sound it again!"

Once again, Kyle sounded the call, but Baldwin's boat continued to pursue the feluccas. Through his glass, Singer could see a distant figure standing in the prow, shooting down one pirate after the other.

Damn it! I said I didn't want him to play hero!

There was no way to recall Baldwin if he didn't want to come. The schooner now turned toward the shore of Mirajil, racing after this tempting target.

He's luring it away from his men!

"That's one brave officer," said Tanilhan admiringly.

He's going to be killed because I didn't pay attention. It should be me in that boat!

As the schooner closed on him, Baldwin turned suddenly to port, in the direction of the causeway. The schooner turned to follow him but more slowly because it was a much larger vessel and because it was turning into the wind.

The marines rowed like madmen, Baldwin himself dropping his crossbow to replace the wounded crewman. Time seemed to stop, as every man in the army paused to watch the little drama. The other marines, having reached the safety of shallow waters, stood up in their boats for a better look.

"Faster!" said Tanilhan, caught up in the race.

Having completed its maneuver, the schooner's sails again filled with wind. It bore down with dreadful speed on the fleeing rowboat . . . but suddenly, it cut to port. Baldwin had almost reached the causeway, and his pursuer could no longer ram him without going aground.

As the schooner turned, the marines ceased rowing and swept the deck with crossbow fire: one volley, two, three, and then the ship lurched and began drifting downwind, the steersman dead at the wheel.

"BOARD THAT VESSEL AND TAKE IT IN TOW!" Singer yelled to the marines who were standing nearby. But before they could make any move, a great splash of water went up near Baldwin's boat.

The Black Ansel, a lean, dark, four-masted vessel, was approaching the harbor. The splash was apparently a near miss from one of its ballistas. Baldwin's boat took shelter behind the causeway.

"The game's over, Singer," Tanilhan said. "That's my ship, the Black Ansel. It hasn't any equal in this world. It will smash your boats and destroy your catapults. Then, it will bombard your camp until you give up and go home."

Singer called another messenger. Pointing toward the Black

Ansel, he said, "Run as fast as you can to Capt. Fleming. Tell him to set the rigging on fire. He will know what to do. Go!"

To Tanilhan, he said, "Take a good look at your ship, Captain. You won't be seeing it anymore."

As the Black Ansel entered the harbor mouth, Fleming's crossbowmen rose from behind the mantlets, the ruined tower and other hiding places, and loosed a volley of fire arrows. In an instant, the whole ship was blazing. Singer could see small, desperate figures jumping over the railings.

From behind him came a sound of horror and disbelief. "That's what it's all about," he said. "The siege was only a ruse. As you say, one can't attack a navy with an army. I had to trick them into attacking me.

"And your help was invaluable. You told me what the pirates were thinking. You demonstrated, in person, their boastful audacity, their greed in seizing small victories, of doubling down on every bet. And finally, there you were, standing before them on the beach with all your heroic legend egging them on. I couldn't have done it without you."

Tanilhan made a strangled sound as if forcing words out of an unwilling throat. "You would have done better to kill me than to tell me this."

The burning ship had drifted into the causeway, blocking any escape for the last feluccas. Fleming's men were rounding up the shipwrecked pirates. Baldwin rowed back in triumph to join his marines, who were towing the captured schooner. Cries of dismay came over the water from where the surviving pirates had gathered to watch the spectacle.

Singer said, "There's only one thing left to do." Turning to Ogleby, he said, "Break out the special ammunition. Distribute one jug to each onager. Tell them to fire as far upwind as they can manage. Wait for my signal."

Six large ceramic jugs emerged from six packing crates and were loaded onto the onagers. At Singer's order, the catapults fired one last time. Small flames appeared all over Mirajil, which quickly spread and joined each other in the oil-soaked ruins, rising to the sky in a mountain of flame hundreds of feet high. Inside a minute, the benighted harbor was bright as day. The surviving feluccas fled from the flames toward the waiting marines.

"It's called *alfesfewer,*" Singer explained. "I'd been saving it for this opportunity." He studied the conflagration for a minute, but could distinguish very little in the wall of smoke and flames. The by-now familiar landscape of Mirajil had been expunged. The whole town was a vast oven, an inferno. Even from across the harbor, he could feel the heat on his face.

Baldwin came to give his report: "We've secured the schooner and five of the feluccas. We've also taken a number of prisoners. What shall we do with them, sir?"

"Whatever you like, but be quick about it. Justice loves brevity. I'll see you get a commendation for tonight's work."

"The work itself is reward enough."

He turned to Tanilhan and, taking the golden helmet, put it on his own head. Whatever remained of the fearsome, legendary pirate chief had disappeared. In the light of the burning town, he could see tears running down the old man's face.

Now I see what a pitiful, hopeless figure he really is!

"You said you wanted to see the show. How did you like it?"

"Just kill me and get it over with."

"Not I. I like you better as a ragged fugitive than as a martyr to a lost cause." He drew his dagger and cut the ropes. "You're free to go."

"Go where?"

"Wherever you want. The road to Kafra is open though you may find the natives unfriendly. Or, you can cross the desert into Bandeluk territory. I'm told it takes a couple weeks. Or, for all I care, you can swim back to Covenant. But if you're still here at dawn, it will be your last."

"You call me cruel. But you would give me back my life after destroying everything I treasure."

"I give you back the one thing you treasure above all, your freedom."

"Sir, Tanilhan has escaped!"

Singer blinked sleepily at Kyle. "You woke me up to tell me this? He didn't escape, I set him free."

"Yes, but then he stole a felucca."

"I suppose I should have foreseen that. Help me with my armor."

When he emerged from the tent, it was mid-morning. Pulling out the spyglass, he scanned the ocean without seeing anything.

Surely he couldn't have sailed out of sight?

He turned the glass toward Mirajil, which was now a flat, ashy wasteland, still smoking from the night's fire. He noticed at once a felucca beached in the harbor.

"Doesn't look like he got far. Tell Baldwin to prepare a boat."

Thanks to the efforts of the Free State Contingent, Mirajil was a truly hellish place. Not a single building was standing. Only a scattering of chimneys remained as grim memorials. There was nothing left of the pirate's trebuchet except for a ship's anchor, standing forlornly in the waste. The party's boots sank into the ashes with every step, sometimes treading on burning embers.

The marines found no trace of the former population, except for the sickening odor of roast meat. Despite the sea breeze, Mirajil was hot, and it stank. Singer could hardly imagine that anyone had ever lived there.

A lone set of footprints led into the center of town. "Follow the tracks closely," Singer told the marines. "I don't want you falling into a basement."

"What do you suppose he was looking for, sir?" asked Baldwin. "Survivors?"

"Look around. There were no survivors unless they swam for it, and then they probably drowned. If anyone got away, he didn't come back here. There's no sign of them."

The tracks led into the middle of town, where the fire had been hottest. Singer could see some stones there, outlining the foundations of a once-substantial building. "I guess this was his headquarters," he said.

"Too bad for him, he didn't just stay here."

"That was not in his nature. He was too greedy and vainglorious. He couldn't sit still while others were out killing and plundering."

There was a hole in the ruin where the tiled floor had fallen in, and the stink of roast meat was particularly strong. Singer rested one foot on the foundation to look down inside. It didn't take him long to spot the corpse, burnt black, sitting in what he took to be a pool of water. But then the sunlight lit it with a flash, and he saw it was melted silver, studded with objects of precious gold.

The heat was like a furnace. He could feel it on his face, and the silver bracelet on his wrist was uncomfortably warm. He turned away from the dismal scene. "Tanilhan's treasure," he said. "That's what he came back for."

Baldwin peered over the edge, but quickly jerked his head back. "Too hot to handle," he said.

"Yes, we'll just have to let him keep his treasure awhile longer."

"At least, no one will take it from him."

As he picked his way back through the hot, grey ashes, a hollow feeling overwhelmed him. He'd defeated the pirates, but so what? It was just another step in the Akaddian war of conquest. The whole coast was devastated, and what had he really gained? Could it be true what Tanilhan said, that he was working against his own country?

Getting in the boat, he remembered the landing at Massera Bay. Everything was simpler then: He was just a junior lieutenant with hardly any concept of strategy or politics, and he was fighting for naked survival against implacable enemies.

He'd done what he had to in the heat of the moment, without any thought for the consequences. And then he'd first seen Raeesha, having no idea who she was or how important she would be to him. She was just a stranger with a sword . . .

His thoughts were interrupted by a loud whirring sound as if many wheels were turning. The boat was still in the middle of the harbor, and there were no other vessels in sight, but the whirring kept getting louder.

Then, he noticed a shadow on the water and looked up. To his complete surprise, he saw a great ship hanging in the sky above his head. He could do nothing but stare in slack-jawed bewilderment.

The ship was descending on them. "What the hell is that?" said Baldwin.

"I don't know. Just get us out of here!"

The marines rowed furiously as the monster flying ship half fell, half drifted toward their position. They were still a hundred feet from the shore, when it struck the water with great force, spreading waves that threatened to swamp the little boat. As Singer stepped

onto the sand, he looked behind him to see the ship had rolled over onto its side and was floating high in the water. A throng of ragged-looking people were climbing from the cabin and on top of the wreck to get out of the water.

"Shall we fire, sir?" asked Littleton.

"Not yet. Wait for my command."

The giant ship drew closer, pushed by the wind. Singer saw the people clinging to it were a mixed group of Bandeluks and westerners. There were also a number of small, pale creatures that had big, droopy ears and beaks like birds.

Are those demons? What else could they be?

He was tempted to fire, but the demons weren't doing anything hostile, merely clinging to the wreckage alongside the humans. Eventually, it came to rest in the shallows not far from shore, and the castaways began wading toward the beach.

He called to the nearest one, a bearded Bandeluk in a tattered naval uniform, "Who's in charge here?"

The man simply pointed to the forward part of the wreck, where a hatch presently opened, and a woman jumped into the water. He was surprised to recognize Raeesha. Behind her came her brother Rajik and then the Witch. After her, something with many tentacles oozed out the door and fell with a *plop* into the water.

Raeesha came and threw her arms around him. "What's going on?" he said. "You missed the show."

"Pardon, General, I forget myself," she answered, taking a quick step back and saluting. "I was waylaid, mislaid and delayed, but Sgt. Raeesha is present and reporting for duty, sir! I'd like to accept your offer."

My offer?

"I'm sorry, but I've already given the Standard-bearer position to Kyle . . . "

"Not that, the other one. I want to be an officer."

32: Gallites

Dear Son,

I am making the effort to write a few lines while I still can. The doctors say the disease that is consuming my body will also affect my mind. Because of the death of your brother and the weakness of your mother, responsibility for the entire family falls on you. I hope, by now, you have abandoned your reckless ways and realize what a grave charge you are assuming.

You must never forget there are thousands of loyal tenants, clients, tradesmen and servants who depend directly on you. Take their interests to heart. Do not squander the resources that have been entrusted to you. Loyalty goes both ways: Don't fail them, and you can trust they will never fail you.

Above all, protect the good name of our house, which for over a century has never been sullied by profiteering, intrigue, treachery or scandal of any kind. We are one of the pillars of the nation, having supported it through many crises, and our loyalty to the royal house has never been in question.

You are now the 11th Count Langonnes, and whether there is to be a 12th depends on you. Do not delay any further the serious responsibility of marriage. Remember premature deaths through war, disease or accident are not exceptional in this world. I would urge you also to find a suitable match for your sister Camilla. Though some young men may not consider her charming, there are many who would welcome an alliance with our house.

I don't know what the future will bring. It may be you will face difficult times. No life is free from hardship. But the County Langonnes is broad and green, its people prosperous and loyal, and its fame eternal. This legacy I entrust now to your care.

Your loving father,

Pterierus, 10th Count Langonnes

Sitting in his cramped cabin, Gallites sighed. His father's death, though long expected, had come at a very inconvenient time. After all his other duties, and the mysterious errand his sister had given him, he'd now be obliged to tour County Langonnes, to be seen by the numerous tenants and to inspect the books of the stewards who ran his estates. This letter, which he'd already read three times, was drawing him irresistibly home, to the boring rural life he'd always hated.

Marriage lay before him, bringing with it children, and a multitude of petty domestic problems and quarrels. He'd be expected to attend weekly sessions of the magistrate's court, to pronounce death on poachers and sheep thieves, and to judge the best cattle and swine at the local fair. Every farmer in the county would feel entitled to show up unannounced at his door with some complaint against a drunken bailiff or a petition for relief from taxes.

The only possible escape would be if the King called him to military service or to official duties at court. But despite all his efforts, he'd won no reputation as a soldier. And he doubted the doddering King Diecos would even remember his name, much less entrust him with a royal office.

Besides, how was he supposed to show his loyalty and uphold his family's good name in such times? The crown prince himself had left the capital in disgust, while the King's second son disgraced himself through outrageous sexual misconduct, and the third engaged the nation in a potentially ruinous war for his own self-aggrandizement. And as for the fourth . . .

There was a knock at the door. Prince Clenas came in.

Gallites stood up respectfully. "I hope you're happy with your accommodations, your Highness."

"Don't call me that unless you want to be known as Count Langonnes. This boat is too small for formalities. The accommodations are more than adequate. My only worry is if anyone has been alerted to my presence."

"I very much doubt it, sir. The crew speaks no language but Bandeluki. I told them you were an Akaddian officer returning home on leave."

"No one in the Admiralty knows?"

"Not that I'm aware. This is a private vessel, a charter."

"Excellent. What was in that lockbox I gave you?"

"I honestly don't know, sir. My sister told me not to open it."

"Very discreet, to be sure. But I made no promises. Where's the key?"

Gallites removed it from the chain around his neck. The lid swung open, revealing a complicated lock that sealed tempered steel plates half an inch thick.

"No wonder it was so heavy," said Clenas. He took out a small sandalwood box and opened it. "What in the name of all devils is this?"

Shocked, Gallites saw it contained a severed human finger. "I don't know, sir."

"It looks like my brother's. See, it still has the ring. What does your sister plan to do with this?"

"I can't imagine . . . unless it was evidence in a witchcraft case."

"Then she's sticking her nose where it doesn't belong. I think I'd better take charge of this." He slipped the box in his pocket.

What does she want with that? She won't be happy that Clenas took it!

Clenas pulled out another item, a book with a worn leather cover, and began flipping through it. The ancient, brittle pages were written in a language Gallites didn't recognize. Some of them held sorcerous diagrams, and others, pictures of demons. There were scribbled notes in the margins and on pieces of paper stuffed between the pages.

"This looks like a book of magic," said Clenas.

"Perhaps more evidence from the witchcraft case?" Gallites guessed.

"I can't say I like where this is heading," said Clenas, putting the book aside. "Now this I recognize," he said, taking out a wooden box. "This is my brother's box of mirrors."

He flipped through the mirrors inside, selecting one that had a yellowish tinge. It showed a company of troops on the march. Columns of smoke arose in the distance.

"He had one of these for each of his chief officers," Clenas explained. "They reflect whatever the fellow is looking at. It was supposed to be secret, but word gets around."

"There seems to be some kind of action underway."

Clenas frowned. "I think you're right. Let's look at some more of these." He drew out the mirrors one by one and laid them on the bunk. Most showed troops in motion, but some apparently belonged to officers stationed in fortifications. One, tinted red, depicted a bleak shoreline crowded with ragged refugees. Another showed a headless corpse with a seemingly endless cavalcade riding past behind it.

"Are those Bandeluks?" asked Gallites.

"That or some related tribe. It looks like our little war is heating up."

"Shouldn't you get back to your men?"

"No, I'm sure Krion can handle it. Just another opportunity for him to display his military brilliance. He doesn't like to share the glory. Did you know, I wasn't even invited to the parade?"

"You didn't miss much."

"I missed seeing him thrown from his horse. I would have enjoyed that."

"Maybe you'll have another opportunity."

"Yes," said Clenas. "I'm pretty sure something will come up."

Named Persons
(Includes Spoilers)

In Chatmakstan:
Sheikh Mahmud's Family
  Raeesha – the sheikh's rebellious daughter
  Rajik – her younger brother
  Hisaf – an elder brother
  Umar – her slow-witted elder brother, deceased
  Alim – an elder brother, not seen since the Battle of Massera
      Bay and presumed dead
  Kismet – Raeesha's mother
  Davoud – Raeesha's uncle

Other Natives
  Lamya – a sorceress
  Hikmet – a cloth merchant, in the service of Prince Clenas
  Leyla – his wife
  Anahita – a prostitute
  Omin – a spy
  Evrim – a spy
  Toygar – a goldsmith
  Surume – a street vendor; also the name of a doorkeeper
  Amir Qilij – the Bandeluk governor of Kafra, deceased

Akaddians
  Prince Krion – commander of the allied forces, third son of King
      Diecos
  Prince Clenas – his younger brother, commander of the Royal
      Light Cavalry
  Basilius – a rebel commander, deceased
  Grennadius – commander of the Royal Household Guards

Eubulus – Krion's adjutant
Mopsus – an aide to Prince Krion
Gallites – a supply officer, the son of Pterierus, Count Langonnes
Epidarus – an officer

Free Staters
Singer (Halland) – commander of the Free State Contingent; also called Demonslayer
Erika (Halland) – his former fiancée
Gwyneth (Westenhausen) – her aunt
Ogleby (Halland) – Singer's adjutant
Kyle (Halland) – an aide
Murdoch (Halland) – a doctor
Littleton (Halland) – an engineer
Moffit (Halland) – his assistant
Fleming (Halland) – commander of the Halland Company
Stewart (Kindleton) – commander of the Thunder Slingers
Baron Hardy (Dammerheim) – a mercenary commander
Duvil (Rosa) – commander of the Invincible Legion
Sir Gladwood (Tremmark) – a knight of Tremmark
Twenty Three (Westenhausen) – spokesman of the *fui* demons
Baldwin (Spindrift Islands) – commander of the Spindrift Marines
Finley (Spindrift Islands) – a marine; also the name of a dead pirate captain
Humbert (Spindrift Islands) – a marine
Westcott (Spindrift Islands) – a marine

Citzens of Covenant
Bardhof – an aide to Prince Krion
Grimald – a soldier of the Heavy Assault Group
Murdoon – a soldier of the Heavy Assault Group
Hingaft – a merchant
Lessig – Krion's chief engineer
Radburn – his aide

In Akaddia:
King Diecos – the aging king of Akaddia

Prince Vettius – his eldest son, retired from politics and devoted
    to his family
Prince Chryspos – his second son, a notorious boy lover
Duchess Thea – their sister
Duke Claudio – her husband
Philocratus – her eldest son
Amphitus – her younger son
Camilla – her secretary, the sister of Gallites
Lukas – her butler
Megabastus – a High Court justice
Scolinus – the captain of the palace guard
Herminius – a merchant
Kratos – a judge, imprisoned
Diomedos – a sorcerer, imprisoned
Tissander – a general, imprisoned
Pterierus, Count Langonnes – father of Gallites
Leucos – an admiral

In Kosizar:
Ahmed – Emperor of the Bandeluks
Hervika – the Favorite, mistress of the harem
Prince Murad – their son
Ufuk – his tutor
Prince Beyazid – a half-brother of Prince Murad, deceased
Yasin – the Vizier
Nergui Pasha – the *mushir,* commander-in-chief of the army
Enkhtuya – his daughter, one of Ahmed's concubines
Haluk – the chief admiral
Sardar – the chief of intelligence
Hulegu Khan – the leader of the Seserils, a subject people

In Saramaia:
Tutku Wali – the provincial governor
Dundar – Nergui's chief of staff
Azuzub – an astrologer

In Berbat:
Bogra – Bandeluk commander of the fortress Gedij
Mangasar – his slave

Dalir – a soldier of the Gedij garrison
Tanilhan – a notorious pirate chief, formerly of Covenant
Hovannes – the Hierophant, leader of the Melliki people
Guner – a fisherman

Elsewhere:

Thorndike – Singer's childhood choirmaster
The Old Woman – a sorceress, the legendary Witch of Barbosa
Extinctor – an ancient and terrible demon
Dariea – an ancient sorceress
Long Ear – an *efaryt* of the Ghost Feet tribe
Big Stick – an *efaryt* of the Ghost Feet tribe
Whip Hand – an *efaryt* of the Wind Bag tribe
Sky Lord – an *efaryt* of the Wind Bag tribe
Talkypus – a demon of unknown origin
Iyad – a fisherman
Ferhad – a historian
Lindus – a cryptographer
Amyleus – a dead king

Sailing Glossary
(Usage may vary)

Athwart – at right angles
Beating – sailing as closely as possible upwind
Broach – when a downwind-running ship skews to one
    side, so it is in danger of tipping over
Capsize – when the boat rolls completely over
Capstan – a rotating machine for lifting heavy objects
Centerplate – a retractable keel which fits in a slot in the
    hull
Dead – directly, as in "dead ahead"
Heel – when the boat leans to one side
Jib – a triangular sail at the front of a ship, sometimes
    used to identify its nationality
Jibe – a change in course made downwind
Lateen – a large triangular sail set on a long yard, running
    fore and aft
Leeward – downwind
Port – left
Running – sailing downwind
Scudding – sailing fast directly downwind
Sculling – propelling a boat by moving an oar or rudder
    from side to side
Sheet – sail
Starboard – right
Tack – a change of course made upwind
Trim – adjust the sails
Yard – a horizontal or diagonal pole supporting a sail

CPSIA information can be obtained
at www.ICGtesting.com
Printed in the USA
LVOW13s1458110417
530417LV00012B/1003/P

9 780692 784280